PRAISE FOR TIDAL ANCESTRY

"Blue Reflections had left me on a cliffhanger so I was excited to read Tidal Ancestry right after I finished. It had me captivated from the start and had me turning the pages to know more. The world building was incredible!" –ARC review

"She did it again... left me wanting more! Tidal Ancestry digs more into Selia's past, as well as Damien's lineage. So much of the past comes to light. A little spice and a lot of overcoming. I absolutely adore this series, and yet again, I can't wait to read more!" –Amazon review

"The second book in the Ocean Apothecary series does not disappoint. It had me hooked from the beginning to the last page. Mystery, intrigue, and multifaceted travels through time keep the story moving. The characters are complex and I love their history...so much deeper than first realized." –Goodreads review

"So many questions that I had from Blue Reflections were answered and so many new questions in my mind now. A bit of spice, a little betrayal, and some time travel. Good reading for helping with a book hangover." –Amazon review

"Tidal Ancestry answers all the questions left in the cliffhanger of Blue Reflections. I can totally see why Henrietta is jealous of Peppercorn. I think she may have stolen the show for sure in Tidal Ancestry. She is an amazing fae character. I recommend this book to anyone that loves Celtic mythology and Egyptian gods and goddesses." –Goodreads review

"This book answers a lot of the questions that you're left with in the first book. I love the fae bat peppercorn!" –Amazon review

"This story bounced between Amy and Selia, and it answered so many questions that were left over from book 1. I loved learning more about Selia's past as well as about Damien's ancestors." –Amazon review

"I thought I was in love after book 1, and now here we are... wow I rode the waves of this book all the way to the end. I loved every minute of it." –ARC review

"I was absolutely hooked with this book, I had to force myself to take breaks and sleep. The world building was exceptional and the developments of the story and characters were top notch. Also, who could not fall for Peppercorn." –Amazon review

"This is the perfect book to snuggle up with. Fans of history, myth, and romance will love this next installment in the Ocean Apothecary series. Here is our world with a twist of Celtic magic, sea-born mystery, and romance that's simple, pure, and epic all at once." –ARC review

ALSO BY AMANDA CASEY

Ocean Apothecary Series
Blue Mermaid Memories
Blue Reflections
Tidal Ancestry

Join Amanda's newsletter to receive a free novella!
amandacaseybooks.com

Tidal Ancestry

Book Two of the Ocean Apothecary Series

Written & Illustrated by
Amanda Casey

For our ancestors.
We are here because of you.

CONTENT WARNING

This book contains situations and themes that include blood and violence, language, explicit sexual intimacy, death of animals, ptsd, and hallucinations.

CONTENTS

Present
Scotland
Bat Blitz
Coffee Shop
Masika's
Tidal Cavern

Temple of Salt,
Storms & Starlight
Winter
Forest
Temple of
Isis
Past

PROLOGUE

Summoning Storms

Amy's toes gripped the sharp rocks as wind and rain assaulted her body. With her arms outstretched, she braced herself for the wave preparing to flood the cavern.

Masika's black hair whipped out from her head below where she stood at the cavern's mouth. Like Amy, her arms were also held out to her sides as the surf surged around her. The two sea nymphs came here for one reason. They were summoning the Abyss, hoping to find answers as to why blue minca was disappearing.

Amy climbed down the jagged rocks, her feet catching against barnacles as she descended to where Masika stood. A wave caught her ankles, nearly sweeping her into the sea. She staggered, gathering her footing next to the tide pool where Masika had buried her feet. Her legs and ankles were scraped, having spent the night fighting with the elements.

"You should rest," Amy said, feeling like the salt-crusted wind whipping into the cavern would steal her breath.

"I'm not leaving this cave until we get an answer," Masika barked. She dropped her arms to her sides, her skin red and swollen from the night spent chanting to the violent ocean.

Amy fought the urge to grab her friend and pull her away from the sea. Summoning the ancestral mother of the ocean was not easy. Amy and Masika both knew this when they left the Temple of Isis in Egypt. They'd traveled north together, searching for the cooler waters to give them what they needed. According to the ancient texts, the Abyss was healthier—and her most fertile—in the cooler seas.

The gentle hum of minca moth wings cut through the salt water that rained down in sheets. They, too, needed shelter from this storm. The fae creatures were also curious about the summoning she and Masika were performing.

Masika turned to her, blinking away the tears from the wind and salt. "Chant the fertility mantra with me?"

Amy took her hand. "Gladly."

They faced the cavern's entrance. Amy waited for Masika to close her eyes and initiate their salt trance. She closed her eyes, focusing on Masika's shallow breathing. Her fight with the tide all night left her weak.

They both inhaled. Amy exhaled first, leaving Masika to remember the rest.

Masika's pulse was powerful, a force that Amy looked forward to syncing her own with. Masika's voice filled her mind, the rhythmic mantra flowing through her like waves from the sea.

"Great Abyss, breathe with me. We remember the salt that originates from your womb of the sea. Dragons of old, for which we long. Our ancestors

have kept your ancient songs. Salt, storms, and starlight, of which we sing. Your light we find in the crown of a king."

Masika's mantra evaporated, leaving the cavern thick with silence. Next, they waited, hoping the Abyss would respond to their summoning.

Amy opened one of her eyes. The blurry outline of damp stone and overcast skies clouded her vision. It was difficult to see with the salt crystals coating her eyelashes. "I don't think she's coming."

"Do you see that?" Masika asked, releasing Amy's hand.

Amy looked down at the pool of water the minca moths were hovering over. Other creatures swam within the depths, creatures more adapted to the violent ocean storms.

"There are so many of them!" Amy stammered, marveling at the tiny snouts and wriggling dorsal fins of the tritons swimming at her feet. Their color was greyish-blue. Their nubs for tails and little spiraling fins that made them appear a little less menacing.

Masika reached down, grabbing for the foreign object the tritons were busy guarding.

Amy grabbed her hand. "Careful, they might bite."

Masika's lips curled. "Like you?" She broke free of Amy's grip, dipping her hand into the pool. The tritons darted away from the item the moment her fingers submerged.

Masika grabbed the foreign object, bringing it up for them to see. An item no bigger than her palm wedged between her dripping fingers.

"Is it a triton scale?" Amy asked.

"I think so." Her eyes drifted up, a glint of fear in them.

Amy stood, her hair standing up on the back of her neck. The ominous rumble of thunder echoed in the cavern. The scale matched the shape and color of the scales on the tritons, however, it was ten times the size.

What if something much bigger and dangerous was swimming the cavern?

A full-grown triton had a different name—a storm dragon.

"Throw it back," Amy said, grabbing for the scale.

Masika tore her hand away. The fear in her eyes flickered with the curious fire of adventure. "No. I'm going to make him show himself."

Amy threw her hands down. While she loved Masika's rebellious streak, she didn't like how it often got the better of her.

Masika stood next to Amy, facing the mouth of the cavern. She grabbed one of Amy's trembling hands, threading her fingers through hers. "I'm going to call his name."

Amy shuddered. While storm dragons were massive, their movements through the water made no sound.

A deep reverberation filled Amy's chest. "Do you feel that?" she whispered.

"Brace yourself," Masika whispered back.

The water from the pool lashed out at Masika's ankle.

"No!" Amy said, jerking Masika's arm back.

Minca moths dove in front of Amy's face, their razor sharp wings brushing past her skin. She held her arms in front of her as the torso of a man appeared.

Tendrils of mist rose from the pool like ash from a fire. Hands appeared, but no legs. Glistening black and silver scales shimmered upon his chin and neck. Storm dragons were shapeshifters, allowing them to manifest as either a man or dragon in form. Right now, he appeared to be something of both.

No garment clothed his body. His lower half was concealed by coiling black markings that tapered down his muscular torso. His hair was black and motionless, draping down his front in thick mats.

Liquid pits of ebony filled his eyes. There were no pupils, only swirling ocean storms. Light seemed to disappear into their mysterious depths.

"He's absolutely gorgeous..." Masika whispered as the water coiling around her leg released her.

Jealousy knotted in Amy's gut. How much she wished Masika would gaze at her like she did at the dark, dangerous sea creatures she loved. "Will he eat us?"

"Worse," Masika whispered. "He will take you to the Abyss."

Amy swallowed. The Abyss was the ancestral womb of the sea. Storm dragons had seven territories within the Abyss, all of which guarded her fertility.

She backed away from the pool, trembling. These beasts swam at great depths, rarely surfacing to breathe.

Movement beneath the water caught her eye. What should be long, membranous fins that lined his tail were lifeless. "Is he ill?"

"Why do you say that?"

"His tail, look," Amy said, pointing at the black water where the dragon scale had fallen. Darkness shimmered on the surface, preventing light from penetrating.

Fffffwwwwwwooooommmmmmnnnnnnnn.

Amy took a step back from the dragon as he sent another reverberation through the cavern.

"Apparently he doesn't like you discussing his health," Masika said, taking a step toward the half-man half-dragon beast. "Let's see which of the seven maternal salt pods his territory encompasses." She clapped her hands together. "*Alcyone!*" she cried.

The cavern shook as Masika cried out the name of one of the seven maternal salt mothers.

A wave of water crashed into the pool, knocking Amy backward.

Masika kept her footing as the wave passed over her. "No? Okay. How about *Electra*!"

Lightning zapped through the air as the storm dragon's eyes flashed and his nostrils flared.

Amy ducked as one of the bolts jolted overhead.

"What about *Merope*!" Masika cried.

The water began to spiral, forming a cyclone.

"How many more?" Amy asked, having lost count. At this rate, she might need to name all seven of the maternal salt mothers.

Masika clapped her hands together, the fire in her eyes igniting. "Celaeno!"

The dragon's eyes darkened, becoming bottomless pits. His tail thrashed, and a massive wall of water erupted up from the tidal pool.

Ceeeeeelllaaaaaeeeeeennnnnnooooooooo!

Amy clapped her hands over her ears, sheltering her salt nodes from the storm dragon's thunderous voice. Water came crashing down, soaking them both.

"He's *Celaeno's* storm dragon. Why is he this far north?" Amy asked, wiping her hair away from her face.

"This is concerning," Masika said, worry ringing in her voice.

Amy stared into the dragon's eyes. Great secrets swam in their deep, abyssal depths. What connection did he have with minca's disappearance?

Masika threw the scale back into the tidal pool. "I release you."

Amy took a step back as Masika released the storm dragon back to the sea. His long coiling body flooded out of the cavern, leaving the two sea nymphs gasping. The dragon sank into the water, submerging himself into the darkness.

"I know minca grows far out in the sea, that's what they are teaching us in Egypt. *Where* it grows is what I hope to answer," Masika said, her voice rising as the waves came thundering in.

She crouched down to the tidal pool. Something floated there, something dark and sickly. She trailed her fingers through the water, bringing the substance to the surface. "Minca is sick. It's dying. Unless we act now, I don't know if we can save it."

Amy crouched beside Masika, dipping her fingers into the pool. She touched the substance Masika assumed was minca. The texture was greasy and hot, despite it being submerged in cold water.

A dark, oily film coated the water's surface. Something very dark and ill swam in the water, and it wasn't dissolving.

While the Abyss hadn't shown herself, she had sent them a warning. The ancestral mother of the sea's health was suffering. Whatever this substance was, Amy's heart told her that it was tied to Celaeno's storm dragon. This dark, wicked substance was killing blue minca.

PART I
SALT WOMB

I

THE BAT BLITZ COFFEE SHOP

Amy

Storm clouds brewed on the horizon where Amy stood overlooking the North Sea. Her memory flooded with visions of the day, three thousand years ago, when a mighty storm dragon visited her and Masika. She remembered his vibrant shimmering scales. His dark, handsome features turned sickly by an unknown illness. She didn't often reflect on that fateful afternoon, but when the memories swam up from the depths of her subconscious, they flooded her mind for days in fits of salt and sea spray.

A secret she and Masika kept, summoning not the Abyss like they wanted, but Celaeno's storm dragon.

Masika's memory began to manifest behind the darkening horizon. Her features blurred behind the mist that lingered in her periphery. Remembering her long, wild dark hair, strands of it rebelling against the wind as the beast returned to sea. Masika had been devoted to protecting the flora fae species of kelp known as blue minca.

Fauna fae, however, didn't show their world to just anyone, including sea nymphs. Humans lacked the patience for their magic to emerge, quickly dismissing their existence to mere myth and legend.

Amy had three thousand years of waiting for what she was about to do with the magic associated with a fae minca moth queen—magic only witnessed on the winter solstice.

Fae beings didn't waste their time attempting to prove their existence to humanity. In fact, they preferred if humans left them alone. Their spirits existed in between rocks, within holes in the earth, and even atop the windy, snow-capped mountains. They coexisted with other life, merely existing as beings of shadow and light.

Speaking of light…

A perpetual glow had emitted from Amy's bosom since that morning.

"Finally, you're awake," Amy whispered.

Two glistening blue eyes appeared as the minca moth shimmied her way up from Amy's breasts. The queen's first set of wings had withered away, leaving her with a pair of lumpy, dull, brownish-grey nubs. Like many things in the natural world, what was considered ugly was a sign of beauty yet to come. The queen was in the process of metamorphosing into something that made most fairy tales come to life.

Deep in those dazzling eyes, there was a spark of adventure. The queen's maternal instincts were unfolding, delicately, like a flower's petals during the spring. An *icy* bloom she was. Minca moth queens chose winter to bring their offspring into the world. They were only a few days away from when that winter magic would strike.

The queen shimmied back down into Amy's bosom, her wing nubs the last to disappear.

"Oh, all right," Amy said, stifling her own anticipation. The queen would open a vast window of salt trancing opportunity for her, but only when the time was right.

She turned on her heel and started the ascent from the beach up into the city of Montrose. Not a moment to waste.

The maternal instinct was by far, the most powerful instinct in the sea. When the queen decided to embark on her maternal flight, Amy would follow.

Christmas cheer flooded the streets of the cozy little Scottish seaside town of Montrose. Bright red ribbons clung to window shops and wound around lamp posts. While winter was not Amy's favorite season, the crisp air did give her an excuse to dress rather exuberantly. She wore a long flowing green dress made of thick cozy fabric, complete with the hip new fashion trend of sporting pockets. The tattered ends grazed the tips of her toes as she walked down the street. Wrapped snuggly around her neck and shoulders was a silky silver shawl, which she could easily hike up to cover her face or nose.

The one thing winter did not allow her to do was explore her surroundings barefoot, which of course, even on the sunniest of days, could leave her toes frozen this far north. She'd settled on wearing a pair of lace-up boots, which were a little too snug against her feet. They gave off a witchy vibe, something she'd always been fond of, being that humans had long called her a sea sorceress. Footwear always seemed to give her blisters after little to no time. She had yet to concoct a salt extract that could remedy the painful sores her feet endured.

A wooden sign dangling above the walkway beckoned her. The sign displayed an adorable bat perched atop a stack of books, all of which barely supported outstretched wings that caught the chilly wind blowing up the street.

The Bat Blitz Books, Brews, and Coffee Shop sounded like a *marvelous* excuse to escape the cold.

Amy grabbed the bronze door handle and tugged. She was nearly knocked off her feet as the wind picked up, swinging the wooden door open.

"Don't let the cold in!" someone cried from behind the bar.

She bustled in, the door nearly slamming her on the rear as she was swept inside. The scent of cinnamon and cloves filled the air, mixing with the musky scent of old books and university students. The shop had the charm of a pub with its dingy windows and dim, yellow-tinted light.

A barista behind the counter tossed her hand up, waving. She had mossy bangs, rosy cheeks, and a silver nose ring. "Ma'am, your color is off. Can I offer you a spot of tea?"

The girl was being honest. Amy's complexion had definitely seen better days. The cold made her freckles—especially her sea star-shaped ones—dull and lifeless. "What is Peppercorn's Latte?"

"Oh, that's my new house special! Would you like to give it a try? It has just the right blend of sugar and spice."

Amy eyed the menu again. "I'll have your Bat-Tastic Moon Magic tea."

"You got it. My front room is very full. How about the reading nook this way?"

"Perfect," Amy replied, slipping past the crowd of rowdy university students.

Amy took a seat next to a bookshelf, propping her elbows on the table. She tipped her head sideways, scanning the titles. Books about environmental science, local Scottish flora and fauna, and quite the collection on fairy tales crowded the shelves. One book in particular caught her attention: *The Selkie's Revenge*. Amy couldn't help but giggle at Scottish people's interpretation of a sea nymph.

The barista bustled over to her with a mug of piping-hot tea. A tooth-pick with a bat and a moon charm dangling off its wing clinked against the porcelain. She set the mug down on the table in front of Amy.

"Pixie's my name. My boyfriend Peter and I run the shop. Let me know if you need anything. How about sugar and cream?"

Amy picked up the bat-shaped salt shaker. "I take salt with my tea."

Pixie's brows disappeared into her bangs. "*Salt*?"

Amy grinned. "I have a ravenous taste for the ocean in everything I drink."

Pixie's eyes traveled down to where Amy's own pixie was sleeping away. Amy shoved her finger down her cleavage, hoping the fae queen wouldn't try and emerge. She tugged up her dress and folded her hands on the table. "Your shop is absolutely charming. I feel that you cater to unique individuals such as myself."

Pixie flushed. "You think?"

"Absolutely. I have connections with many others who are looking for this kind of local attraction."

"What kind of connections?"

Amy danced her fingers together. "The magical kind." She straightened, locking her gaze with the hopeful youth. "Well, Miss Pixie. You can call me Amy. I'm only passing through. My hotel arrangement fell short, and I'm in need of a place to stay. Can you help me?"

Pixie's nose scrunched. "I think I can whip something up for you if you're willing to check out my greenhouse."

Amy took a sip of her tea and tipped Pixie generously. "Show me this lovely place you call a greenhouse."

Pixie led the way through the back of the shop, taking Amy outside. Wind whipped through Amy's cloak, stripping away any sensation of feeling warm and cozy.

She clapped her hands to her ears, covering them as the wind ripped through the back alley. "With this cold snap, we've barely been able to thaw the coffee beans! I ordered new stock just last week, and they're just now starting to warm up back here."

A few paces and a cobble-stone alleyway later, a patch of open space that overlooked the beach emerged. A shack constructed of windows appeared. The glass was murky green with hints of brown and yellow.

Amy approached the shack to break the wind tunneling through the alley. "What a perfect place for fairies to live!"

Pixie grabbed the handle on the door and opened it. "Wait until you see what's inside!"

Amy ducked in behind Pixie, who closed the door behind them. The heavy aroma of earth enveloped her. Such a charming little space. Pots lined the entryway, along with shelves with burlap bags stacked to the glass ceiling. The bags housed dozens of different coffee beans.

Stones lined the ground, along with lichen-covered crystals. Were those gnomes with *mushrooms* for hats?

As Pixie began shifting through her supply of coffee beans, Amy became more enthralled with the *fairy hut*. This would be the ideal environment to help the fae queen metamorphose.

"It's not as warm as I'd like it to be. But my coffee plants do love it so far," Pixie said.

"Oh, this is absolutely perfect!" Amy squealed, clasping her hands together.

"Would you like to stay?"

Amy propped her hands on her hips. "You think a hippie like me needs anything more marvelous than a fairy hut?"

The fae queen shimmied between her breasts. She definitely agreed with the temporary living arrangement—at least until her magic emerged on the winter solstice.

Pixie smiled. "I'll see what I can do about getting you some blankets." She left the greenhouse, leaving Amy with a solution to the problem the cold snap thrown at her. Too much cold too quickly would rush the queen's metamorphosis.

One of the sacks of coffee beans above her read *Egyptian Delight*.

Amy sucked in a breath, relishing in the robust aroma. The scent was full of earth and spice. Did that scent ever transcend time? Three thousand years ago, she had been naive and young, and very in love with Masika.

Ever since the fae queen had emerged from the vault, Amy's heartbeat thundered a little more, and paused a little less. Remembering Masika's goal to save blue minca would involve refreshing her memories of when the Blind Moon was born—a time that dated back to ancient Egypt.

2

SEVEN STORMS

Selia

Selia made her way across the street to the park where her boyfriend Damien was busy painting. Being five months pregnant created frequent trips to the restroom, a trip she'd made already three times that morning. The town of Montrose, by far, had been Selia's favorite of Scotland's many sleepy seaside towns. Christmas was well on its way. The month of December had transformed the buildings, giving them a magical appearance. She imagined this cozy town would be the perfect little place for her and Damien to settle down in.

She spotted Damien in the center of the park, sitting on a wooden bench under a giant oak tree. The leaves were vibrant hues of orange and red, which made his chestnut hair look even darker. He had propped up a small wooden easel, facing the sea.

"Purple water?" Selia asked, stopping beside him.

Damien looked up at her, the greens in his eyes contrasting against the autumn colors from the tree. "Who said water can't be a color other than blue?"

Selia laughed. Damien's artistic sense of humor was as colorful as his painting pallet. Ever since he had started seeing colors other than blue again, he had done nothing but paint with them. "With the rate you're painting, we're going to need to find a home with enough wall space just to display everything."

Damien flicked his wrist, sending purple splatter across his paper. "We'll find a place. Just be patient."

Selia sighed. If only her bladder could be as patient with their home search.

"I think we'll find something before Christmas," he said, dolloping more purple onto the sea's surface. He looked up at her, his hazel eyes so green. She wondered if Damien's color too, changed with the magical transition of the seasons.

"Couldn't we rent?" she asked.

Damien shook his head. "No. You don't rent unless you have to. I'm certain our forever home is somewhere here, right under our noses."

Selia set her hand on her stomach. She, too, wanted a place to go home to that wasn't burdened by his Aunt's constant nagging about the vixen sprites invading her garden. She and Damien had been taking day trips, stopping into various art galleries along Scotland's coast to try and find a place that might put them up for the night.

The mysterious art of salt trance wasn't far from her mind. She thought of the three bottles Amy had given to her a few months ago. She'd never really figured out what their purpose was, other than to confuse her.

She set her hands on Damien's broad shoulders, loving his solid warmth. "You are awfully tense. Maybe you shouldn't hunch so much when you paint?"

Damien rolled his shoulders. "I need to work when I can. I don't want my girlfriend to rely on a starving artist to support her."

Selia dug her hands into the knots in his shoulders. He was obviously stressed about money. He wanted to provide for her and buy her gifts and normal boyfriend offerings. With her not working, and him making a little cash here or there by selling his paintings, they were making it, but barely. Even with the small inheritance he'd received from his parents when they passed, she was wondering how purchasing a home was possible.

Sooner or later, she was going to need to find another job.

"What are you painting, anyway?" she asked.

"I'm trying to capture the clouds rolling in," Damien said, holding his paint brush up to the light. "What does it look like to you?"

"An incredibly colorful weather front is blowing in."

Selia counted the other paintings he'd stacked on the bench. "Why did you paint seven?"

"Seven is a lucky number for the fae. Seems like a fitting number, since as of today, it's been seven whole months that we've been together."

Selia flushed at his sweet statement. "Wasn't it June when you came to meet me in Paris?"

"Yeah, well. Technically, we first met at the Celtic Sea in May, remember?"

"Oh, I see. You're going to give Henrietta credit for introducing on the beach," she teased.

Damien scrunched his nose. "No, I'm not giving her credit. I had my eye on you long before that annoying hermit crab ever got involved." He turned back to his painting, holding his paintbrush out in front of him. "What should I name this one?"

"How about *Storm*?"

Damien grabbed her around the waist. "I like it." He set his paintbrush down next to the others on the bench. "Well? What have *you* been working on?"

The downswing in Selia's mood wasn't due to the gloomy weather, nor from the fact that she was dealing with an onslaught of pregnancy hormones. Her mood swing was due to her severe missing of a certain fae hermit crab.

She tugged a sketchbook out of her purse and handed it to him. "Have a look for yourself." She glanced down at her sad excuse of a fingerprint she'd turned into a lumpy stick figure of Henrietta. "I never thought I would say this, but I miss her so much."

"Did you read what I wrote in there?" he asked.

"I did. I spent all morning both laughing and crying."

She caught the swift side-eye from Damien every time she poured over his comical sketches of the sassy little fae hermit crab who'd brought them together.

Selia scanned over some of the recent dialogue he'd written that morning for her.

Look at me! I'm Henrietta the little fae thief!

I'm really a bloody little terror in disguise!

Selia's favorite was of Henrietta wielding a pirate sword, complete with a pirate hat. **I'll pinch your arse and make off with yer treasure!**

A sob escaped her.

Damien looked up. "Love, are you doing all right?"

"I'm fine," she lied. "I never thought I would miss her as much as I do."

"I miss her, too, but I sure don't miss her running off with my art supplies."

Selia laughed at Damien's attempt to lighten her spirits. But she was at a loss. No longer having that spunky little crab around felt like a giant hole had carved itself into her life. "At least she can't steal your artistic talent."

"Speaking of talent." Damien held out his hand. "Ready to try what we've been practicing?"

Selia remembered his statement in the car over a month ago. They'd pulled over to the side of the road not far from where Maria and Sophie, Damien's late wife and daughter, were buried during their drive to Edinburgh.

"Water acts differently around you. Even the water in the air seems to react to your pulse." Damien's words sent a shiver up her spine every time she remembered them.

Selia took his hand into hers, loving his warmth.

His cheeks dimpled. "Work your magic, love."

For the past month, they had practiced this magical routine daily. The more blustery the weather, the easier the water behaved. Selia discovered she didn't need a paintbrush or moonlight to manipulate the water—she could do so with her own pulse.

She closed her eyes, whispering the three salt trancing principles through her mind.

Breath. Memory. Salt.

With the salt trancing mantra floating in her mind, she could feel the water vapor in the air. Damien described his personal painting technique as *letting go.* The sooner she did, the water would take control.

The sensation that washed over her was smooth, then jagged. Warm, then cold. The temperature fluctuated around her as the salt trance took a hold of her heart.

Selia opened her eyes. The three principles pulsed, distending and evaporating, then condensing again. The water on Damien's painting began to dance.

"What do you think?" she asked, taking in her new creation. The painting had transformed into a brilliant purple ocean framed by an orange horizon. The pigments blended together, offsetting each other. How the salt trancing mantra did this, she still didn't understand. But water had a funny way of erasing explanations.

Damien ran his hand through his hair. "I think you've graduated from stick figures. At this rate, I think you're going to put me out of a job," he teased. "I've never seen texture this magical in *any* of my watercolor paintings."

"I've had a great teacher to help me."

He pulled her down into his lap and wrapped his arms around her.

"I still can't explain how it works," Selia said, falling into him.

"The best things in life are unexplainable," Damien said, resting his head on Selia's chest. "You are going to be an absolutely wonderful mom."

Selia looked at their collaborative painting. She never imagined she would be creating artwork like this, let alone having a baby with an artist.

"Now, if only we could find a place to display my paintings and show-case your talents. We could make some quick cash," Damien said.

She raked her fingers through his thick tousled hair. What a mess it was, painting out here all morning in the elements.

Something was pressing against her bladder again. She stood from his lap. "I need to pee."

"Didn't you just go?"

"I feel like this is going to be normal for the next few months."

Damien took her hand and kissed the top. "Go warm up, love. I'll meet you at the Bat Blitz in a few."

Selia made her way across the park to the local coffee shop. She slipped inside, finding the restroom near the front. Pregnancy wasn't the most accommodating situation for a sea nymph's bladder, nor her own temperature regulation. As soon as she got inside the shop, another hot flash bustled through her body, forcing her to shed two layers of clothing.

She did her business and freshened up, stopping to look at herself in the mirror. Her face had more color than she'd ever had. She was displaying that special *glow* most pregnant women experienced. Her hair was thicker and wilder, something Damien always complimented. Her hair wasn't the only thing that had grown—so had her waist. Three sizes later, she'd given up on wearing jeans and settled for over-sized sweatshirts and leggings. Autumn proved to be the perfect season for her pregnancy to occur, as her choice of clothing was currently in style.

She slipped out of the restroom and back into the crowd of university students, and her hip bumped into the twenty-something year old shop owner.

"Well, if it isn't my favorite customer!" Pixie exclaimed, coffee in both of her hands. Pixie's hair was thick and reddish brown—her bangs in a big mossy heap that came down over her eyebrows. Her nose ring had a different charm hanging from it today. Not her usual moon, but a bat hung from the metal ring.

She set the drinks on a table for her customers, then turned to face Selia. "What can I offer you today?"

"Actually, I'm looking for a job."

Pixie's brows drew up. "You want to work in my coffee shop?"

"I do. Can I please fill out an application?"

The corners of Pixie's mouth curled down. "I'm sorry, but I'm fully staffed for the holiday season. Every kid attending university in Montrose is looking for some quick cash to buy Christmas presents."

"I'll do anything. Damien and I are looking for a place to stay." She liked Pixie a whole lot and would love to have her as a boss rather than the cantankerous old crackpot who smoked cigars at the Louvre. "I'll bus tables and mop your floors."

Pixie waved Selia over to the bar where her staff was busy mopping up a spilled drink. Once behind the bar, Pixie pulled out a piece of paper and set it on the counter. "I can't make any promises, but here. Give it a shot."

Selia's heart leapt. It was better than nothing.

She sat on one of the bar stools and grabbed one of the pens sticking out of a cup with coffee beans spilling out of the top. A bat charm dangled from the end as she scanned over the application.

What experience do you have working in a coffee shop?

Are you afraid of bats?

Do you believe in familiars, AKA fae or fairies?

Selia looked up. "I have a question about number three. Figuratively, or for real?"

Pixie smiled. "You can be as real as you want. I like to keep things imaginative around here. Keeps my customers entertained."

Selia wrote her answer, thinking about Damien's fae obsessed Auntie. **I absolutely believe in fairies, especially the ones called vixen sprites.**

She scanned the titles from the stack of books that sat beside her on the bar. Next to *Darwin's Origin of Species*, Pixie had a stack of rather interesting titles. Two read *How Fae Species Differentiate from Current Day Flora and Fauna Species We Know Today*, and *The Common Quirks of the Fae Who Live Along the British Isles*.

"Studying the fae, now, are we?" Selia asked.

Pixie's brows drew up into her mossy bangs as she began hand drying coffee mugs with a rag. "Don't tell my professor that I'm preparing to write my midterm paper on a fae species and not one of the normal ones native to Scotland that he wants us to research."

"Which fae species are you currently researching?" Selia asked, instantly thinking *hermit crab*.

Pixie's eyes darted up to the shelf next to her. "Can you guess?"

Selia glanced up at the decorations resting on top of her shelf. An assortment of every kind of fuzzy-headed, tiny-eared, beady-eyed creature was strung up across the coffee mugs. "Bats?"

Pixie's rosy cheeks darkened. "Exactly!"

"What actually makes fae species different from normal ones?"

"I find that most fae creatures have strange behavioral quirks. Fae are known to blend in with other plants and animals most humans are already aware of."

"What about stealing? Would that be considered a behavioral quirk?"

"Why? Do you have a familiar of your own?"

Henrietta's bobbing shell flashed in her mind. "I've met some rather sassy creatures in my time."

Pixie smiled. "Let's just say that Darwin would have been knocked off his rocker if he was studying the fae kingdom."

"Do you see the fae often?"

"It depends. I think they are intelligent beyond reason, preferring to stay invisible to most individuals."

"Do you think that's because they are shy?"

"Oh, not at all. You must realize, the fae don't open up to just anyone. Even their biggest fans often won't see them at all. They won't show you their magic, unless you are truthful about your intentions with them."

Selia could agree. Henrietta was the most extroverted, adventurous, and opinionated hermit crab she had ever met. Her personality absolutely matched what Pixie was describing, minus her stealing habit.

Selia took a photo of the books and texted it off to Deidra. She hadn't heard a peep from the dryad since their discussion about the ill salt trancing talismans. It wasn't like her extroverted friend to stay so silent, especially when it came to her knowledge about the fae. Selia was starting to wonder if she had somehow pissed the dryad off. Deidra was the only woodland nymph she knew, and there were many possible reasons that she hadn't replied to any of her text messages.

Pixie set a cup of Selia's usual decaf lavender latte in front of her. "Speaking of fae. I hear Sika the selkie is making her rounds again."

Selia grabbed her tea, nearly dropping it. "A selkie?"

"If you and your boyfriend are preparing to make Montrose your home, you'd better acquaint yourself with the urban myth around this selkie."

Selia rubbed her fingers past her salt nodes. The only other selkie she'd met was Amy. The last time they talked, Amy had been trying to remember a friend of hers.

Did Amy know this selkie Pixie called Sika?

Selia finished the application just as the door opened. Damien walked inside, bringing a cold blast of wind and colorful oak leaves.

Pixie swiped the application from the bar and scanned it over. "Any special talents that I should be aware of? Can you juggle?"

"Oh, my girlfriend has talents," Damien said, brushing up behind her. "Love, remember? The appointment?"

Selia flushed. "Pixie, this is my boyfriend, Damien."

Pixie beamed. "The two of you are absolutely *adorable* together."

Damien kissed Selia on the cheek. "I'll bring the car up." He turned and left, leaving Selia to blush by herself.

"Oh, he's lovely. What does he do?"

"He's a watercolor artist."

Pixie glanced at the bare wall next to the bookshelf. "I've got some ideas for the both of you." She slipped the application behind the counter. "I'll have my answer by the time you get back from your appointment."

3

MIDWIFE OF THE SEA

Amy

Amy rummaged through the greenhouse and found the perfect empty pot to set the fae queen inside. She had to warm the moth up quickly if she was to slow the metamorphosis long enough to refresh her memories of Selia's birth.

She reached into her bosom and tugged out the small bottle she'd put Damien's blue memory salt crystal inside. How lucky she was to find it on the beach only a few months ago—a necessary ingredient for her quest ahead.

She shook the bottle, making the crystal clink against the glass. The fae queen climbed out of the pot, perching atop the rim. Her giant eyes shimmered with hunger. Amy uncorked the bottle and tilted the opening toward her hand.

The salt crystal fell into her palm, which she held out to the fae queen. The queen's mouth unfolded, touching the crystal. Within moments, the crystal began to shrink, until nothing was left. The queen's body, while still wingless, began to glow. Her metamorphosis was essential for opening Yule's magical window to the past.

After tipping her salt extract to her wrist, Amy rubbed the liquid behind her ears, dousing both of her salt nodes. She set the bottle on the shelf supporting the *Egyptian Delight* coffee beans and closed her eyes.

Taking a deep breath, she internalized the three principles in her mind.

Breath. Memory. Salt.

Amy's pulse thundered through her salt nodes, submerging her consciousness into a salt trance. Here, she could tap into her blue memories, each swimming next to her as silver spirits.

Remembering Selia's unique birth, and how her emergence into the world resulted in a plague, was the beginning of a very long and troublesome story most fairy tales would have a difficult time retelling.

This tale, she wasn't learning about for the first time. She would be reliving every salty detail of it. First, she had to pay the midwife of the sea a visit.

Amy's feet sifted through fine grains of sand. Not cold like the ones on the beaches of the North Sea, but warm enough to burn her toes if she stood in one place for too long. The Nile was Naunet's vessel for fostering sea nymph fertility.

Naunet's role as midwife to the sea was simple: help facilitate the collection and care of maternal salts into the arms of hopeful sea nymph mothers. Naunet would be curious to know how Masika's research on the disappearance of blue minca was affecting the maternal salt pods in the open waters of the ocean.

Amy walked along the banks of the Nile toward a temple. Once in the shade, she set her hand on the alabaster stone warming in the sun. Trash and pools of human waste floated in the water below. Sections of the riverbank were so packed with this residual sludge that the earth had been stained brownish-black.

Seeing Naunet's domain laden with this filth made Amy tremble. A sea nymph's health—especially when it came to her own reproduction—was *vastly* influenced by the waters she associated with.

Amy entered the temple, the scent of incense making her drowsy. Perspiration formed on her neck and chest. Her pulse quickened as her salt nodes swelled with heat. The fertile scent of the sea's midwife was *impossible* for a sea nymph to ignore. A mixture of earth, spice and salt—Naunet's aroma was simply *intoxicating*. Any sea nymph who consulted with the sea's midwife was bound to absorb that scent, a pheromone from which her own fertility would benefit.

Amy made her way down the banks of the Nile, following the footprints of other sea nymphs. She rounded the hill, finding the air hazy with the pulsing movement of thousands of tiny blue wings. The wings belonged to a fae creature who always flocked to this special scene. Male minca moths migrated inland every summer. They made this journey for one reason only, to find and mate with what the maternal salt pods had hopefully given birth to—a fae queen.

Amy squinted into the sun. No sign of Naunet yet. Other sea nymphs stood around the water, tucked into the reeds of papyrus. Their hair was tied back, the strands cascading down their shoulders. Some were clothed, others were not. You could tell who had visited the fertility bank before, and who was experiencing the maternal salts for the first time.

The sea nymphs who were salt virgins were nude, while second time mothers stood behind them, chanting the word *minca*. Minca was the Atlantean word for *mother*. The blue kelp was a gift from the fae kingdom, something all sea nymph mothers relied on to create and foster healthy fertility. Minca could be turned into quite anything—from incense, to tinctures, to extracts, to aids for creating breast milk. Minca was the go-to ingredient for any Ocean Apothecary. Amy's mother had taught her these things when she was only a child—knowledge she appreciated more just by visiting the Nile.

No men, not even the pharaoh, were allowed to visit the Nile, or maternal salt bank for as long as the maternal salts washed up the river from the sea. This was a *sacred* time that occurred once a year for a few weeks when the Nile flooded. The salts traveled against the current, which in the eyes of the pharaoh, was not something to be trifled with. For the most part, sea nymphs were given the respect and space they needed to collect the salts, as they were seen as minor fertility goddesses that had fled from Atlantis to Egypt.

Amy tilted her hand up to the sun, shielding her eyes as the hum of a trillion little wingbeats impregnated the air. Humidity filled her lungs. Whenever she visited the Nile, a great wave of emotion came crashing over her—how much she missed her mother.

Maybe it was because the salt bank in Atlantis was the last place she remembered seeing her. Her mother had crouched down to the water, just like Naunet did, to gather the maternal salts as they flooded in from the sea. Her mother would spend hours sifting through the maternal salt crystals, gathering the perfect samples for her Ocean Apothecary.

"Amy?"

Amy shook her head, focusing on Naunet's deep, silky voice. Masika's older sister emerged from the papyrus. Naunet stood out among the other sea nymphs. For one, her skin was darker than the others. Her hair did not cascade down her back and shoulders in long rebellious tangles as the case with the salt virgins. Her hip-length hair was tied back into three twisting braids that wove in and out of each other—three phases of the moon.

A midwife of the sea must embody the three stages of a woman's life. Maiden, mother, and crone. Naunet was a matriarch of her kind. She was the very embodiment of the moon goddess, Isis.

Amy's knees felt weak at her sound and her sight. Naunet's voice had taken on that deep, rich tone the moment she stepped into the role as the midwife of the sea. Because her maternal salts originated from Celaeno, she had the *same* stunning dark beauty as her sister. However, she had a much more seductive flair to her nature. Had Naunet not been tied to her responsibilities in Egypt, Amy had considered being romantically involved with both Masika and her older sister.

Naunet ascended the bank, stopping a few paces in front of Amy. "Coming to collect some maternal salts for one of your Ocean Apothecary experiments?"

Amy shook her head. "Not today."

Naunet's dark eyes narrowed. "Then what brings you back to Egypt if not to experience a salt pregnancy?"

Amy shook her head. "You know that pregnancy has never been an objective of mine."

A smirk crept up Naunet's face. "Are you sure? I have a few salt samples from Alcyone. I have a feeling you would be a *wonderful* mother."

Amy caught the slyness in Naunet's sarcasm. Even if she was visiting the maternal salt bank to initiate a salt pregnancy of her own, she highly doubted the salt crystals from her own salt pod—Alcyone—were still fertile. The last time Alcyone's maternal salt pod cycled had been during the sinking of Atlantis, and that was over a century ago.

Amy eyed the salt bank behind Naunet, where trillions of perfectly sculpted salt crystals lay glistening in the sun. Judging by the blisters on Naunet's hands, she had spent the morning raking them in and separating them into seven separate terracotta jars. Part of creating a successful salt pregnancy had to deal with collecting the maternal salts. These salts provided a sea nymph's womb with all the nutrients her body needed to create a daughter. While there were seven maternal salt pods in total, only one salt pod at a time produced a minca moth queen—a sign that the pod was fertile.

Maternal salt crystals weren't the only thing floating in the water. Sea nymphs loved collecting storm dragon scales, which were left over from Poseidon's deluge that sank the great city. A century later, the scales were still washing up in waterways. In Atlantis, Amy's ancestors made jewelry out of them. Both her and Naunet's mothers had adorned themselves in dragon scales gifted by the storm dragon Poseidon.

One of the salt virgins ascended the bank, stopping beside Naunet. She held out her hand, revealing three shimmering salt crystals in the center of her palm. "Naunet, can you please help me identify which salt pod these maternal salt crystals originate from?" she asked, her eyes bright and hopeful.

"Oh, I know!" Amy said, jumping in at the opportunity for some salt identification. "Hold one of the crystals to your salt node. If they are feeling chatty, they will whisper to you."

The salt virgin gave Amy a wary glance.

Naunet merely rolled her eyes. "Amphitrite has a special talent for reading the maternal salts."

The salt virgin did as told.

"Sometimes you have to close your eyes," Amy whispered, eager to see if the salt crystal would reveal its pod of origin. Celaeno's salt crystals were by far the most difficult to identify, as their structure was jagged and abnormally oblong. Their color, too, was darker than the other maternal salts. Celeano's name meant *the dark one*.

Only sea nymphs who were matched with the maternal salt pod they originated from could become pregnant with them. Right now, Celaeno was cycling, meaning that sea nymphs whose ancestry originated from that pod had the opportunity to form a successful salt pregnancy.

Sea nymph ancestry was matriarchal. There was no male equivalent for a nymph. Sexual intercourse with a human male was not required to make baby sea nymphs. Unless, of course, she chose to mate with a man out of pure convenience.

Some sea nymphs chose to mate with men, not wanting to wait for their maternal salt pod to cycle. Since the sinking of Atlantis, the timely cycling of the pods had begun to diminish.

The salt virgin opened her eyes. "I think this salt crystal originates from...Celaeno?"

"You got it!" Amy piped. She'd heard the crystal whisper its identity the moment the salt virgin revealed it in her palm.

The salt virgin jumped, tears brimming in the corners of her eyes. "I must thank Isis for this gift tonight." She gave both Amy and Naunet a small bow, then returned to where the other salt virgins were mingling. Smiles and embraces followed in celebration for their friend who would likely experience a salt pregnancy.

"Naunet?"

Another sea nymph was fast approaching them. Her bare feet shifted in the sand on the dune she climbed up. She wore clothes—not a virgin to these waters. This sea nymph was already a salt mother. In her arms, she clutched a bundle of cloth.

Waaaaaahhhh!

An infant's cries didn't pierce Amy's heart like it did Naunet's. Her maternal instincts were so well honed, they synced with every female's pulse—like ripples in the water. A single disturbance in that pulse, and she knew something was wrong.

Naunet darted over to the sea nymph before she'd summited the dune, her arms outstretched toward the bundle. She took the infant into her arms and tugged the cloth away. An infant's face appeared—not a human infant—but a sea nymph. Amy could tell this because her eyes had no pupils. The first year of a sea nymph's life, her eyes were like little moons. Giant orbs of blue sapphire shone in the sunlight as the child blinked. A white film coated the child's eyes. Something was *definitely* wrong.

"She's not drinking," the mother said, worry clouding her voice.

Naunet's gaze dipped to Amy. "What do you believe this child is suffering from?"

Amy took one look at the infant's salt nodes, and her heart shuddered. "Her salt nodes are deformed."

"They're what?" the mother asked, her face contorting in terror.

"She is still young; her symptoms can easily be treated." Amy dipped her hand into the bag Masika had given her. "Take this back to your dwelling."

The mother took the bottle, her eyes widening. "Is this blue minca? But I thought minca was disappearing."

"Steep the minca in fresh water this afternoon. Set it under the moon for three days in a cool dry place. Drain the minca from the water and set a single drop on both of her salt nodes. The salt will extract any remaining toxins from her body."

"What on earth would cause my daughter to be deformed like this?" the mother asked. "I thought the salt pods were healthy."

Naunet's eyes had the same questions flickering in them. "Isis has shown me otherwise."

The mother nodded, taking her newborn back into her arms. "May Isis bless the both of you."

As the sea nymph left the dune, Naunet turned to Amy, her brows drawing up. "My sister would be impressed."

"Your *sister* is the one who gave me that sample. But neither of us know how long it will last."

Thunder ripped in the sky overhead, and Amy's mind traveled back to the storm dragon they had summoned into the tidal cavern. That day, he'd brought with him a sickening oily substance that made her salt nodes burn.

Naunet turned on her heel, beckoning for Amy to follow. "Come. I must share with you new information on the health of the maternal salt pods."

4

ULTRASOUND

Selia

The hot flash that erupted through Selia's body wasn't like any of the others she'd experienced that week. Today, she was getting an ultrasound—her first real glimpse of her baby. She was both excited and terrified. Would she have a boy, or a girl? She knew so little about pregnancy, let alone sea nymph pregnancy. All it took was one night with a Scotsman to land her in this entirely new life situation.

Damien pulled the car up to the hospital and parked. He opened the passenger door and helped Selia out. Between the cold, the sugary scents in Pixie's coffee shop, and the nerves, Selia felt like she might have a nervous breakdown.

A woman with a baby carrier looped on one arm came bustling up the walkway. Damien approached the door first and held it open for her. Selia caught a glimpse of a button-red nose, pudgy cheeks, and startling blue eyes.

Her heart ached at the sight. A feeling unlike any love she'd experienced. Babies were exceedingly adorable and terrifying at the same time.

They moved into the waiting room, where Selia was overcome by a warm comforting scent. It was a mixture of clean cotton and what she assumed was breast milk. Damien didn't seem fazed by the sudden scent of motherhood that grabbed Selia's attention.

Selia approached the check-in desk, where a woman looked up from her computer. "Name?"

"Selia Fontaine. I'm here for an ultrasound."

The woman handed her a clip-board with paperwork on it. "Have a seat and fill this out. The nurse will be with you shortly."

Selia took the paperwork and sat down next to Damien, who sat next to an aquarium. The fish gathered near the glass, crowding to inspect her.

"Want to see if you can get them to jump?" Damien asked cheekily.

"Don't even think about it," Selia replied. The last thing she wanted was to get everyone in the waiting room staring at her over a talent she still had no idea how to control.

Damien busied himself with thumbing over a watercolor magazine, while Selia surveyed the room. She was undoubtedly the only pregnant sea nymph sitting among other human women. How was she supposed to navigate the seas of motherhood?

She scanned over the medical paperwork that rattled on and on. She still had no idea about her maternal or paternal history. Cancers? Biopsies? Abnormalities of the heart? Who her mother and father were? Siblings? There were none that she was aware of.

She scribbled down the social security number and birth date Deidra had provided her with years ago. She'd never been to a real doctor before, only herbalists and homeopathic practices to help with her memory condition. Her stomach turned over. What would happen when they sent her a bill, realizing she didn't have medical insurance?

Damien glanced up from his watercolor magazine. "Are you nervous?"

"*So* nervous," she said, looking at other women who seemed at ease with what was going on. She didn't even know her own mother, and here she was becoming one?

Another mother finished checking in and sat down across from them. Her child, nestled beneath a blanket in its carrier, began to cry. "There there, we'll have you fed as soon as I warm up the bottle. This cold snap is absolutely horrible!"

Selia held out her hand, not thinking before her intentions spoke. Like a magnet, a bottle went flying out of the woman's diaper back and into her hand.

"That's funny, I swore I had it in here," the woman said as her gaze drifted up to meet Selia.

"Sorry," Selia said, returning the bottle to the mother.

"How on earth? It's so warm!"

Selia shrugged. "I guess I have unusually warm hands?"

Damien chuckled. "Show off."

Even the fish in the aquarium were curious about the sea nymph who had mysteriously summoned the milk bottle into her hand. They crowded around the glass, their mouths opening and closing as though offering her some kind of encouragement.

A door to the waiting room opened, and a nurse appeared. "Sarah!"

The mother tucked her bottle back into her diaper bag. "That's me," She grabbed her baby carrier and diaper bag and stood. "Good luck."

Selia's stomach knotted. She couldn't sit here so patiently. Either she needed to read something, or she would make an excuse to get up again to pee.

She grabbed her phone and shot off a text to Deidra, who hadn't replied to anything she'd sent over the past few months.

Hey, U alive?

Not even an emoji of a tree came through from the snarky dryad.

She pocketed her phone. While Damien was busy dissecting his watercolor magazine, she found a book on breastfeeding. She flipped through the pages, finding a rather interesting description:

`How to shove your breast into your baby's mouth correctly. Use the hamburger technique!`

Moments passed, and after she'd saturated her mind with enough breastfeeding tips to last a century, she set the book down and grabbed the local newspaper. Her stomach hollowed at the headline:

`Selkie Sightings Near the Bay`

`Sightings of Montrose's local selkie, Sika, has been confirmed by the bay near the harbour. The local fishing community isn't thrilled as it could attract more people near the water during prime fishing season.`

The door opened, and a short, plump woman that reminded Selia of Damien's aunt, only a decade younger, emerged with a clipboard in hand. "Selia?"

Selia dropped the newspaper and stood, almost forgetting where she was.

The nurse held the door open. "Right this way."

Selia followed her down the hall with Damien, where she was ushered into a small room with a giant beeping machine. There was a cot and a lone chair in the corner, where Selia set her purse.

"I suspect you are the father?" the nurse asked, turning to Damien.

Damien's cheeks dimpled. "I am."

She smiled, turning back to Selia. "Well then, off with your clothing and put on the gown. Opens in the front. You can keep your undergarments on."

"Right."

The nurse left the room, leaving Selia alone with Damien.

Damien's hands came to her shoulders. "Can I help?"

Selia didn't answer. Even if he wanted to be sweet and flirt, her mind was going a mile-a-minute. She tugged off her sweater and removed her leggings, which Damien took.

He stepped behind her and looped his arms around her waist, crossing his hands at her belly. His stubble grazed past her ear. "Don't be nervous. I'm right here."

Selia wished she could relinquish her thoughts to Damien's calm. What if the fetus wasn't healthy? What if it wasn't the size it should be by now?

She tugged on the gown, the fabric chilly against her skin. But she welcomed it, having sweat so much. Today's hot flashes were enough to make her queasy. Her belly was barely showing anything. What if something was wrong with her pregnancy?

She sat down on the stiff cot. "I really hope they see something." Selia lay back on the table and draped the blankets over her legs and lower torso.

Damien stood next to her, running his hands through her hair. Even with his sweet affection, Selia could tell the need to do something with his hands was due to nerves.

The nurse emerged. She sat next to Selia in the chair and held up a tube. "This is the worst part." She opened the tube and lathered a blob of transparent jelly onto her stomach.

"That is defiantly cold," Selia said, shivering.

The nurse grabbed a grey wand attached to a cord and held it over her stomach. "Are you ready?"

Selia's bladder suddenly went numb. "Yes, I'm ready."

The nurse set the wand on her belly and began circling it. A low *whooosh whooosh whooosh* sound filled the room as the lining of her uterus appeared on the monitor. Everything looked so dark and empty.

Her pulse raced. Where was her baby?

"Oh, there we are," the nurse said, stopping on a little bump that was much too tiny to be anything alive.

Celaaaaeeeeennnoooooo…

"Did you say something?" Selia asked.

"No," the nurse replied. "Sometimes the wand makes some spooky noises."

Selia shifted on the cot. Maybe her salt nodes were stuffy. Either that, or it was the heart monitor. What was the strange mournful song she was hearing?

"Your baby is very healthy. How many weeks are we at?"

"Eighteen," Selia replied, a lump moving in her throat.

"Very good, dear. You have nothing to worry about. This child is going to be very healthy, indeed."

"Then why am I not showing?" Selia asked, feeling like she might throw up.

"Every woman is different. Some mothers don't show anything until they're nearing their third trimester." She removed the wand from her belly and locked eyes with her. "This is when you tell me if you want to know the gender."

Selia glanced up at Damien. "What should we do?"

Damien smiled down at her as he took her hand into his. "Only if you want, love, the decision is yours."

Selia looked over at the screen. The bump was no longer a bump, but a tiny beautiful being—a being that had its own heartbeat.

"I want to know," Selia said, and Damien squeezed her hand.

The nurse smiled. "*She's* very healthy."

Damien's mouth dropped open. "Did you hear that? We're having a girl!"

5

DRAGON TERRITORIES

Amy

Amy followed Naunet down the bank to the boat, which would take them both to the Temple of Isis. The temple sat on an island that shrank this time of year with the annual flooding. Once on the boat, an oarsman worked to steer them across the river. The temple wasn't far. Four vertical, rectangular columns jutted up from the island, each painted with vibrant colors.

Debris floated next to them as they picked up speed. So much filth. This was not the Nile Amy remembered from her youth. She remembered she and Masika playing along the banks, catching male minca moths, and teasing each other about when they would start salt trancing.

The oarsman pulled the boat to a stop on the far bank.

Amy didn't like the look he gave Naunet, who appeared just as disgruntled as they both disembarked.

Crack!

Lightning ripped overhead. Rain began to dollop from the sky.

"I can't trust my scribes not to allow the storm scrolls to become ruined," Naunet said.

Naunet and Amy took off, darting up the bank toward the temple. Carved into the front wall were two massive images of Isis. The fertility goddess's hands were held at different angles, possibly to aid in capturing moonlight.

Amy followed Naunet into Isis's temple. Long rectangular columns separated the temple into sections. Cylinder columns were spread throughout, lining the hallway. The hieroglyphics were painted in blues, oranges, yellows, and reds, with dashes of white thrown in between. The main hall, minus its ceiling, lay open to the sky. This vast open room provided the perfect circumstances for salt trancing in the moonlight.

Standing on the altar was Isis's gorgeous granite statue. Her arms were held up, spreading two massive feathered wings that cast long, crescent-moon-shaped shadows into her temple. Perched atop her head was her magnificent lunar crown. Amy could get lost in those mysterious liquid eyes, which her ancestors claimed witnessed the day the ocean became pregnant with salt.

The shuffling sound of hurried feet echoed around her. A few humans were inside, servants to the pharaoh. They tended to vases that lined the base of the columns near the main hall. The vases were full of water, and the thrashing tails of tritons.

Naunet spoke to one of the servants in an Egyptian dialect Amy didn't understand. There were so many languages mixing here that, she wondered how long their Atlantean language would last. Even the meaning for minca was becoming lost in translation. Who knew how long it would be before the mother kelp was overlooked, its maternal powers forgotten.

The servant gave a bow, then motioned to the others to leave. As soon as they left, the vases began to glow.

"Collecting tritons?" Amy asked.

Naunet eyed one of the vases. "I have a feeling this thunderstorm is going to produce quite a few of them." Her gaze dropped to the table below Isis's statue. "Good thing I came. It looks like my scribes already left for the day," she said, her voice ringing with annoyance. "So much for the pharaoh's son doing his job."

Amy helped to gather the storm scrolls before the rain poured inside. She recognized the inscriptions written on them, an ancient form of pictographic writing that illustrated storm bonds. The inscriptions were painted with Egyptian blue pigment, most of which was in danger of washing away if the sky opened.

Gaia's Order, the governing force that held oversight over the proper practice of Gaia's artforms, had designated the Temple of Isis as a place for studying and practicing the art of salt trance. The storm scrolls Naunet created were mere fragments of a much larger document called Gaia's Codex. Part of Naunet's tedious task as designated by the Order was to perform record-keeping within the Codex. Like her mother Pherusa had done in Atlantis when she reigned as midwife of the sea, Naunet spent hours inscribing everything from salt births, storm bonds, and her observations of the maternal salt pods cycling.

Gaia's Codex was heavily monitored by the Order. It was a living, breathing, changing record of all life. Gaia's soul was housed within the fae life kingdom, and it was through the fae she shared the many fragments of her being. When Amy was a child, she had asked the Order who created the document that goddesses like Isis were so heavily invested in. The only answer she received was that the Codex was created by an ancient cosmic being, who Gaia tasked with creating. Gaia made this request so the fae kingdom could share her many artforms with her daughters.

The art of salt trance was the art gifted specifically to her sea nymph daughters.

Lightning zapped between the vases as tritons poured inside. Egyptians were quickly catching on to the concept of electricity. What was seen as new technology was old power in the old city.

They finished gathering the storm scrolls, stacking them in a wooden shelf meant for storage. Naunet's work as midwife of the sea had become much more tedious since Atlantis sank. After the great deluge, the Order had placed new regulations on the salt trancing, as there were rumors the art had caused the death of the great storm dragon, Poseidon. Naunet was dealing with the aftermath and the tedious documentation for the Codex the Order now required regarding storm bonds.

As Amy piled the scrolls on top of one another, a hieroglyphic on the wall caught her eye—a mural depicting Isis and her brother, Osiris. "Looks like the Egyptians took some of our history from Atlantis."

"The creation stories of sea nymph kind have fascinated humanity for eons. Egyptians have interpreted our story differently." Naunet pointed to the stars glistening above Isis. "Set, the god of chaos and storms, murdered his brother Osiris. He cut his body into fourteen pieces, which were then tossed into the sky. Isis was the one who reassembled her brother's body."

Amy knew the tales from Atlantis. The Abyss was formed when the moon cried, and her seven salt daughters fell into the sea. They became salt mothers, forming the maternal salt pods that housed a sea nymph's fertility. She also knew that Naunet couldn't share everything about her work in the Codex. Storm scrolls were just the tip of the iceberg when it came to what the Codex documented. There were even rumors that Naunet could use the Codex to observe conversations between the fertility goddess, Isis, and her sister goddess of death, Nephthys, as they discussed the timely cycling of the maternal salt pods that occurred within the Abyss.

"How does Egyptian mythology relate to ours?" Amy asked.

"The Abyss is the womb of the sea, the ancestral salt mother from which Gaia's sea nymph daughters were born. She is also the resting place our souls return to when we die. The Abyss is both a womb, and an afterlife." Naunet pointed at each of the seven stars. "According to the Codex, our ancestors stated that practicing the art of salt trance helped to regulate the proper cycling of the maternal salt pods. There are seven cycles total. Do you remember the song of our ancestors as Isis taught it?"

Amy cleared her throat. "Seven maternal salt pods. Seven dragons who guard them. Seven storm bonds formed by our ancestors, who with the tides can find them?"

Naunet smiled. "Exactly. There are twenty-one storm bonds total. Fourteen are visible as constellations in the night sky." Her eyes dipped. "While only seven are reflected in the sea below. These seven storm bonds house the unique power a sea nymph can develop while practicing the art of salt trance."

Amy gazed at the bottom of the mural. Naunet was right. Only seven stars were depicted below Isis's feet in the dark area that represented the ocean. The Abyss housed all seven *wombs* of the sea—the seven maternal salt pods.

The powers formed were all very unique. The more storm bonds present, the better. Salt trancing kept the maternal salt pods healthy, as storm bonds influenced the weather. Blue minca grew in vast groves that encompassed the salt pods, protecting them from the violent ocean storms that threatened their composition. Only a century ago, Poseidon, a great and powerful storm dragon, created a storm so powerful, it caused his death and the sinking of Atlantis.

Thousands of sea nymphs went missing after the great deluge sank the great city. One of the sea nymphs who went missing was Amy's mother. With her mother's disappearance came Amy's inheritance of her Ocean Apothecary. While her responsibilities were nowhere near as tedious as Naunet's, the Order still expected her to perform certain tasks, such as tending to and creating various salt extracts. While her talents with manipulating salt crystals weren't lackluster, she was still nowhere near as experienced as her mother.

Amy's stomach pitted as she recognized the symbol for her mother on the mural—a porpoise. Her mother had a whole pod of dolphins who aided in transporting her to and from Alcyone's maternal salt pod, where she would perform most of her Ocean Apothecary experiments. Amy could still feel the sea spray in her face when her mother brought her out to ride the dolphins—a chariot of incredible power and play. She remembered the rubbery texture of their skin, the enthusiasm in their movements, and the playful noises they made when...

"Amy? Are you all right?"

Naunet's voice broke Amy's focus, the memory evaporating as quickly as it came. Only a century had passed, and she still longed for those days from her childhood.

Thunder rumbled as sheets of rain fell from the sky.

Naunet grabbed a vase from the shelf and two wooden goblets. "We can't go anywhere with this rain. What do you say we enjoy a drink?"

Amy flushed. Drinking wine and flirting over Egyptian mythology? Seemed like a lovely way to pass the time.

Naunet poured Amy a generous amount and handed her a goblet. She then held hers up. "Please, indulge me on your adventures overseas with my sister. Are you still mingling with the sons of Atlantean kings?"

"We are," Amy lied. Masika didn't want anything to do with men. She simply tolerated their presence.

Naunet tilted her goblet, swirling the wine from side-to-side. "They will be angry with us for some time. I would be wary of keeping their company for too long."

Amy knew immediately who Naunet was speaking of. All, but one member of the Sgàthan clan, the lead huntsman who fancied Amy, lived up north. He didn't blame her for the fall of his kingdom. In fact, he wanted her confined to his bed chamber, tossing and turning in ecstasy until the wee hours of the morning.

"The great city fell a little over a century ago. I know the fallen kings of Atlantis have been fighting to recover the wisdom of their ancestors. I hear the Sgàthan clan, is what they call themselves now?" Naunet asked.

"They do. What are you getting at with this?"

One of Naunet's eyebrows arched. "Are you and my sister busy flirting with them, or was this quest to answer why minca was disappearing really an excuse to run away with each other?"

Amy's grip tightened on her goblet. Naunet knew that she and Masika were in a romantic relationship. Amy, however, like Naunet, dabbled from time-to-time in the art of sexual intercourse with human men. Naunet was like her younger sister in many ways. She was rebellious at heart, and not one to follow the current sea nymph marital norms.

"How many students do you have attending your writing lessons?" Amy asked, hoping to change the subject.

"You mean how many men?"

"I don't understand. Are female women not allowed to learn how to read and write?"

"Unless she's the daughter of a pharaoh, only men are allowed to study as scribes."

Amy shook her head. "Sounds like Egypt is already falling into what our mothers said Atlantis was beginning to become."

"Scribes in training come to me for reasons other than to learn how to read and write." Naunet danced her fingers along the wooden handle of her goblet. "Come to the Nile, nobody will know. Add a little salt water, and watch it grow."

Amy looked away from the rather seductive gestures Naunet was making with her goblet. The huntsman she knew didn't need a sea nymph's magical touch to offer him natural male enhancement.

Naunet sighed. "I feel sorry for human women. Their men are so infatuated with the size and shape of their man parts." She giggled and downed the remainder of her wine. "Men have such little knowledge when it comes to the art of pleasing a woman, let alone a sea nymph."

Amy smirked. Naunet was right. A sea nymph's salt nodes were her primary source for experiencing erotic pleasure.

Naunet grabbed the vase and poured herself more wine. "Isis only found thirteen of the fourteen parts of Osiris's body. Can you guess what valuable male part went missing?"

Amy almost dropped her goblet. "His phallus?"

Naunet smirked. "Exactly. She never found it, so she created a new one with magic."

Laughter erupted between them. Amy's arm bumped into one of the storm scrolls protruding from the shelf.

Naunet caught the end of the scroll and swung it open on the table.

"How does this one read?" Amy asked, unraveling the rest of the scroll. Her hair stood on end. The storm bonds reminded her of the coiling black markings on the body of the storm dragon she and Masika had summoned.

Naunet set her goblet down. "The death of the great storm dragon Poseidon brought the great city of Atlantis to an end. After Atlantis sank, Poseidon's son became Celaeno's storm dragon." Her finger trailed off the parchment. "Somewhere along the line, he became ill, abandoning his territory protecting Celaeno's salt pod."

Amy's hair stood on end. An ill ex-guardian of Celaeno? That sounded incredibly similar to the summoning she and Masika experienced. "Does this son of Poseidon have a name?"

Naunet shook her head as she rolled the storm scroll up and placed it back on the shelf. "If he does, I am not aware of it. Storm dragons only reveal their name to the sea nymphs they attempt to bond with."

Amy's hands had gone cold. Her goblet shook, splashing what little wine she had left over the edge.

"Are you feeling all right?" Naunet asked.

"What did Celaeno's storm dragon become ill with?"

A musky haze filled the temple.

Naunet set her goblet down on the table. "We need to leave. They've started burning the incense."

"Why are you rushing out of here like this?"

"I forgot. The Order is teaching a salt trancing lesson this afternoon."

"And what, they just kick you out of the temple?" Amy protested.

Before Naunet could answer, another nymph appeared in the hallway. Long, blond hair tapered down her shoulders. She had porcelain white skin, high cheek bones, and pointed ears. Her cold grey eyes had the slightest bit of color glinting in them. This nymph was one Amy wasn't particularly fond of.

Alexandra walked toward them but stopped in Isis's wing shadow. While her facial features fell into darkness, the colors in her eyes became brighter. "Hello, Amphitrite. It's so good to see that you're back in Egypt."

Amy crossed her arms. "I take it you are the one teaching a salt trancing lesson?"

Alexandra snapped her fingers as servants flooded in, lighting incense behind her. A scent Amy hated—a root that suppressed a sea nymph's heartbeat when she was practicing. "I am. And I can tell you that anyone teaching the art should know the current health status of the sea's storm dragons." She glanced at Naunet. "The storm dragon Naunet was discussing has become ill with something your Ocean Apothecary has no cure for."

Amy bit her lip. Alexandra always had a snide way with words, especially when it came to spreading rumors about her Ocean Apothecary.

"Amphitrite and I were just leaving," Naunet said, grabbing a couple of storm scrolls from the shelf and tucked them under her arm.

Alexandra muttered something that sounded like *contaminated Apothecary* under her breath.

Amy dug her heels into the stone floor, rounding on the smug Iridescent. "What does the Order have to say about my Ocean Apothecary?"

Alexandra's lips curled into a smile. "There might be a rumor going around that you and Masika are wasting your time attempting to solve minca's disappearance."

Heat rippled up Amy's spine. She took a step toward Alexandra. "Our research is not—"

Naunet grabbed Amy's arm. "Enough," she hissed.

Amy tore her arm away. She didn't need this harassment, anyway.

"Don't worry, Naunet. You'll be tempted by the substance soon enough," Alexandra said, her smugness returning as she turned to Naunet again.

"We're leaving, now," Naunet said, turning on her heel toward the exit.

"What did she say about temptation?" Amy asked, hurrying to keep up with Naunet's furious pace.

Naunet remained silent as she exited the temple.

6

PEPPERCORN

Selia

Selia's body was rattling with excitement. A baby *girl*?

She tapped on Damien's arm as he turned the steering wheel. "We need to stop by Pixie's coffee shop."

"Why, do you have to pee again?"

"I do, but I also wanted to see what she had to say about my job application."

Damien glanced sideways at her as he turned the car down the street. "You applied to *work* there?"

"Just this morning. I didn't want you to stress with money as much."

He grabbed her hand. "Sweetheart, I'm not stressing."

"Yes you are."

He squeezed her hand. "That's because I only want the best for you and our baby girl."

Selia squeezed his hand harder. "Can you believe this? We're actually having a baby together?"

"How do you feel about it?"

"I feel like everything is going so fast." She bit her tongue. "I want to tell someone."

Damien took her hand in his. "As do I. I'm contemplating telling Auntie, or my sister. I'll leave the choice up to you who you want to share the news with first."

Suddenly, their baby seemed like such a huge weight on their shoulders. Between them, she was a treasure. But what would other people think when their pregnancy was out in the open?

Technically, she and Damien weren't really family. They were pregnant together, but not married.

She squeezed his hand again. "Can I have a rain check on that?"

Damien chuckled. "You don't have to rush anything. But come our annual Christmas gathering, I'll be sharing with everyone just how lucky I am to be engaged to you."

Selia swallowed. "Let's focus on our living arrangements first. What would your ideal home look like?"

Damien tapped his fingers on the steering wheel. "I know this sounds crazy, but I've really been wanting to open my own art gallery."

"Why couldn't you? You've spent all of this time painting for the past few months." She glanced at the back of the car, where Damien's art supplies and rolls of parchment jumbled together. "We could do a traveling exhibit, where you go from town to town and set up your art shop?"

He shook his head. "No, I want to find a place to settle down. Besides, frames are heavy and expensive, and then you need a space for display. Watercolors need to be framed with glass, or you risk having moisture ruin your painting."

He pulled the car to a stop outside of Pixie's coffee shop and parked. They walked inside. The lunch crowd had thinned, leaving the space more inviting.

Selia walked up to the bar. "Where is Pixie?"

The barista motioned with her hand to the hallway. "She's out back in the fairy hut."

Selia's ears perked. *Fairy hut?*

She and Damien walked through the shop until they found a door that led out back. A small shed-sized building sat in an open space that overlooked the bay. The structure was almost entirely made of windows, except for the occasional metal support beam. The glass was fogged with splotches of brown and green. A wooden sign stuck out of the ground by the entrance, reading: **The Fairy Hut**

Pixie stood by the open door with a pitchfork in one hand and a bucket in the other. She turned, beaming the moment she spotted Selia. "I have *just* the project for you. How do you feel about tending to my plants?"

Selia's heart leapt. "As long as your fairy hut isn't inhabited by vixen sprites."

Pixie shook her pitchfork. "You are hired! Quick, come inside and see what I've got in store for you."

Selia and Damien followed Pixie into the greenhouse. The moment she stepped inside, she was overcome by the scent of musky earth and coffee. Pots lined the floor, and the shelves, all with labels on them. Descriptions on the labels listed the names of the coffee blends.

Cluttered near the far wall of windows were pots full of herbs, dirt, and mulch. The pots were labeled as well, only they had real coffee bean plants sprouting out of them. One of the plants looked more like a palm tree than a coffee plant. A wooden sign stuck out of the soil.

Magical Coffee Beans: Pollinators Welcome

"What kind of experience do you have with gardening?" Pixie asked.

Selia thought about Auntie. "I've had a bit over the past few months."

"It's like my Auntie's garden has come back to haunt me," Damien said as he ducked under the large drooping leaves of the giant palm.

Pixie pointed to the plants that weren't green, but turning an dull shade of brown. "This little corner is where all of the magic happens. Well, it *was* happening, until I discovered the soil was parched. There's a problem with my irrigation. I'm not getting the water out here like I thought."

"What would you have me do?" Selia asked, eyeing the hose looped around the base of one of the pots.

Pixie grinned. "How does being the water fairy in charge of my greenhouse sound?"

Selia clapped her hands together. "I would absolutely *love* to be in charge of watering!"

"As long as there isn't any heavy lifting involved," Damien said.

Selia elbowed him in the side as Pixie's eyes swept between them.

"Nothing heavy to lift at all. Plants are potted and rooted where they need to be. It wouldn't be an ongoing thing. I'll expect you to water once or twice a week. Over-watering can be bad, especially when plants are entering their winter season. If you can spend an hour or so getting everything hydrated today, I'll give you a week's pay."

"I can't accept that," Selia protested.

"You don't understand. This greenhouse is the source of my shop's *magic*. My business won't run if I don't have the herbs and spices to mix with my coffee blends. The Bat Blitz is known to have that special kick in our coffee. Besides, the hippie I'm renting this space to pays me quite generously."

"And you're trusting *me* with it?" Selia asked, looking to Damien for reassurance.

Pixie beamed. "I get the feeling you are *just* the woman to bring the magic back into my greenhouse."

Damien grabbed the hose. "Where do we start?"

"I said *woman!*" Pixie boasted. "Damien, I have another idea for you. What do you think about hanging your artwork up along the empty wall in my shop?"

Damien's face paled. "I'm sorry, did I hear you correctly?"

"The shop used to be an old frame shop owned by my boyfriend's father. We only converted it into a coffee shop within the past year. I have a load of spare frames just hanging on the wall with nothing inside of them. You could use those for your watercolors could you not?"

Damien dropped the hose. "Absolutely!" He kissed Selia on the cheek. "Thank you, Pixie. I'll get right to work!" Damien left the greenhouse, leaving Selia with a smitten Pixie.

"You just made his day," Selia said, rubbing her cheek where his stubble grazed her skin.

Pixie beamed. "I will do everything I can to convince the two of you to stay in town!"

Selia spent an hour familiarizing herself with the spigot where the water came from, as well as the average amount of water each of her spice plants needed. She grabbed the handle for the spigot and turned it on. Lots of air escaped but, only a dribble of water. Now she understood why her watering duties would take an hour. The time tending to plants would do her good. She still needed to process the fact that within a few months, she and Damien would be having a little girl. This could also be an opportunity to test out her new ability. Maybe she could find the location of the kink in the hose.

Selia walked from pot to pot with the dribbling hose. Plants were so easy to take care of. All they needed was sunlight, carbon dioxide, and water, and they created their own food. Soon, she would have a baby to feed and diapers to change, something she had never done before.

Life was such a dormant, fragile thing, merely existing beneath the soil. Water was so simple. Every living thing, no matter how small, needed water to survive. Maybe she could find a purpose for this new emerging talent that too, felt like it had long been dormant.

As she dribbled water over the pots, her thoughts traveled to Alex and Balfour. Both had evaporated out of her life as quickly as Amy had, abandoning her with a mind full of confusion. What had been the point of finding the vault and releasing the fae queen? And was this strange new ability of hers somehow related to the art of salt trance?

Amy had mentioned a friend whose memory was tied to the fae queen. When Selia had asked what happened to her friend, who still remained nameless, Amy's eyes glassed over. She stated that her friend's memory made her heart ache in a way that she could not continue to endure

She would love to find a friend who was pregnant, someone she could talk to. Deidra had ghosted her, leaving her with three very different women to get to know. There was Pixie, who didn't seem the type to talk about babies at all. Auntie, who she still didn't know if she liked her, and Gwen, Damien's younger sister, who had two kids of her own.

Images from her sonogram earlier that day flashed before her. Her daughter was so tiny. The womb was such a deep place, similar to the sea. An abyss of darkness, a mother's body was.

The hose gave an airy *hisssssss*, spitting more oxygen than water. It was time to find that kink and be rid of it.

She set the hose down, closed her eyes and recited the three principles in her mind.

Breath. Memory. Salt.

She held her breath for three seconds, then six, then nine. She'd learned to count until the ache in her lungs subsided. She could sense the blockage in the hose if she focused on her breathing, and where she felt any tightness in her chest. Keep breathing through the tightness, and the water would show her the rest.

Whether she was dipping into a salt trance or not, she didn't really care. All she knew was the water in the air became an extension of her. The sensation felt like at any moment, she could step out of her own skin, and explore the world as seen through the eyes of the water around her body. Water had its own pulse, and she was simply becoming part of it.

A section of the hose pulsed back at her, one not far from where she stood. She opened her eyes. She found the source of the clog all right—it was something that had fallen out of the pot, forming a kink in the hose.

A pot full of peppercorns was located where the water stopped. The plant had long draping vines with dozens of little green peppercorn seeds hanging off it.

Selia shifted the pot sideways, relieving the water pressure and allowing the hose to work again. She peeked inside the pot, which was glowing blue. The dirt seemed to be disturbed, like something had been digging in it.

She poked her finger into the soil, retrieving a tiny fleck of the mystery substance that was putting off the glow. Why did it remind her of the scales from the male minca moth wings in the cavern a few months ago?

She flicked her finger, sending the mystery dust flying. One of the pots full of coffee beans shuffled above her. Something else was living inside the fairy hut.

A fuzzy brown head emerged from the peppercorn vine. The fuzzy head had two rounded ears, and two ink-drop eyes. The creature's nose scrunched as a high-pitched chirp escaped it. Pin-point teeth poked out of its opening mouth.

Selia stumbled backward. A *bat*?

Pixie had asked on her application if she was afraid of them.

Scrrreeeeeech!

The little bat began thumbing its way down the peppercorn vine, its wings acting more like legs as it fumbled onto the pot. Perching there, its little brown face swiveled back and forth as the creature seemed perplexed at its own sudden exposure.

Fwip!

Before Selia could step back again, the bat launched itself from the pot and landed on her shoulder.

"Hello there," she said, holding out her hands. What if this bat didn't like her?

Membranous wings jostled up her arm, until the fuzzy brown face was inches from her ear.

The door to the greenhouse opened, and Pixie appeared. "Oh, my. It looks like you made a friend!"

Selia turned slowly, afraid she might spook her new acquaintance. "What do I do?"

"Don't worry. She's harmless. Feisty, but harmless." Pixie reached out, scooping the little bat into her hand. "Peppercorn, where are your manners? I name my house latte after you, and all you want to do is hide out in the greenhouse?"

Shreeeeek!

"Yes, I know. You've been ignoring our customers!" Pixie tickled Peppercorn's chin with her finger. "Looks like you're getting a little chubsy ubsy, too. If I didn't know any better, I'd say you were eating for three, or four. I have no clue how many pups your species has."

"Now I know where you got the inspiration for the name of your shop."

Peppercorn began making the most adorable little squeaking noises. Like Henrietta, this little creature seemed to love being the center of attention.

Pixie continued scratching her chin. "Bats are mammals like us. They have live young and nurse them. They have the most species in their family next to rodents—over thirteen-hundred, in fact. Quite the diverse little devils."

"Why did you name her Peppercorn?"

"I found her roosting behind my peppercorn spice one day. But lately, she's been acting strange. She wants to hide in my fairy hut and sleep the day away."

Peppercorn jumped from Pixie's hand and landed once again on Selia's shoulder. This time, she scurried up quickly and tucked herself away under Selia's hair.

"Oh, my. She's taken a severe liking to you. I haven't seen her this excited in weeks. Ever since the weather took a dip, she's been a fuzzy little grump."

Selia tried to reach in and grab the little bat before she became tangled in her hair, but she'd already tucked herself tight against her scalp. Just in time, as Damien came darting into the greenhouse.

"Selia, you won't believe this. While I was hanging my artwork, a gentleman came into the shop. He said one of my paintings looked like the view from the house he's just about to list on the market. Let's go have a gander and see if we like it?"

Selia's heart leapt. "I'll be right there!"

Damien turned on his heel and disappeared.

Pixie's eyebrows disappeared further up into her mossy bangs. "Go, now!"

"What about her?" Selia asked, failing to grab Peppercorn's fuzzy body.

"Why don't you take her with you? I promise she won't be any trouble. When night comes, she'll be gone."

Peppercorn nuzzled Selia's ear. She wasn't Henrietta, but something about this quirky little bat told her she was also a fae in disguise.

7
SALT VENOM

Amy

Amy followed Naunet down the sandy banks of the Nile toward her dwelling. The air on the island was thick with drizzle and the hum of minca moth wings, but not as thick as the anger she felt for Alexandra. How dare that petty Iridescent spread rumors about her Ocean Apothecary?

She focused on the swaying motion of Naunet's long braided hair as she walked along the water's edge. A couple of storm scrolls were tucked under her arm, preventing them from becoming wet.

Raindrops settled on Amy's arms as her feet shifted in the sand. Tucked behind a grove of papyrus, a small dwelling appeared. The structure was built from mud brick. A staircase led up to a flat roof, with a wooden overhanging perched atop. Two small windows faced the Nile. The doorway had no door, only a simple linen cloth.

Naunet stopped outside of her dwelling. Amy stopped behind her. Pheromones in the air thickened—pheromones Naunet's body was creating.

Naunet repositioned the storm scrolls under her arm, turning to Amy. A glint of embarrassment shone in her eyes. "You'll have to excuse the mess. I haven't had time to tidy up."

Amy followed Naunet into her dwelling. While her space was small, Naunet had maximized it. The main room served as her kitchen and dining area. A table sat beneath the windows. Only one stool sat next to the table. Shelves lined the space between the windows. Her kitchen was a collection of baskets, a few metal pots, and a mud brick wall separated the main room from another. The wall had a stack of papyrus scrolls on it similar to the shelf in the Temple of Isis.

Amy walked around Naunet's room. While her dwelling might be considered crude on the outside, it had the flair of an Egyptian sorceress on the inside. Amy adored how Naunet decorated. She had created an altar for Isis, adorning the base of the statue with her dried minca bouquet—a gift her mother Pherusa gave her when she came of salt trancing age.

Placed around the bouquet were a few jars full of water. These were canopic jars—ones that humans used during the embalming process for mummifying their dead. Naunet frequently used discarded canopic jars to propagate minca.

"Aren't they cute?" Naunet asked.

"Your minca samples are far healthier than anything I can grow," Amy replied.

"Looks can be deceiving. Touch one and tell me what you think."

Amy dipped her hand into one of the jars, propping the little minca propagation into her palm. The sample was light, but the base was hardy and firm. A bundle of nodules made this propagation healthy enough to split from.

The texture wasn't slimy, but silky. And the aroma was fresh, not fishy. Minca's scent was more similar to soil than most kelps or seaweeds. The mother kelp was believed to grow in great forests in the open sea. Naunet's samples had the gaseous bulb that formed when the minca decided to float, exposing itself to the moonlight it needed to grow.

"My mom would be so proud of you," Amy said.

Naunet shrugged. "She expects this of me."

Amy's stomach knotted. While Naunet didn't have the best relationship with her mom, at least she had one. Amy's mother had disappeared during the great deluge that sank Atlantis, leaving Pherusa, Naunet and Masika's mother, to adopt her as her own daughter.

She returned the minca propagation back into the vase, wishing the mother kelp didn't stir such emotional turmoil about her *own* mother. After the deluge, Amy had taken her minca bouquet and infused it into her salt extracts. She saw the act as a way to pay respect for the knowledge of minca that she'd never inherited from her mother.

Naunet walked to the table and set down the storm scrolls. She withdrew a small canopic jar resting beneath a statue of Isis. This jar didn't have one of the heads of Horus's sons decorating the lid. It wasn't meant for the stomach, intestines, lungs, or liver—all organs the Egyptians believed a human needed in the afterlife.

The lid of this jar was shaped as a heart with a serpent coiling around it.

Naunet held the vase out in front of her. "This is the substance Alexandra was speaking about."

Amy's pulse quickened as Naunet grabbed the heart, tipping open the lid. The air thickened, as did the pheromones Naunet was creating. Heat coiled at the base of Amy's spine, branching up her back. When the heat reached her heart, something wickedly arousing began to swathe over her chest.

The liquid was caressing her skin, searching for a way to reach beneath her flesh. If only she would let it in. The substance was calling to her, *demanding* her attention. Something dark was swirling on the water's surface—something thick like the oily substance she'd seen in the cavern with Masika.

She didn't remember the substance having this effect on her, warming her from the inside in an impossible way. She hadn't even touched the water. All she'd done was breathe.

Naunet's eyes dipped seductively to the jar in her hands. Her pupils had turned to slits, snake-like. "Savor it. Surrender to it," she whispered, the heat on her breath carrying through her—seducing her. "All salt daughters of Celaeno will be tempted by it."

Amy's body quivered as Naunet's words seduced her into a salt trance. Naunet's pheromones mixed with whatever substance was fast evaporating into the air.

Amy dipped her pinky finger into the liquid, which was surprisingly cold. Her body, however, was beginning to warm as the liquid aroused her senses. The bitter taste of salt welled up on the back of her tongue as blackness cloaked her periphery.

Naunet's dwelling went dark. White-blue light flooded Amy's periphery. Waves thundered before her, the surf surging in a fit of white caps.

The white caps split, dissolving back into the depths of her consciousness. However, those dangerous, dagger-like salt crystals were still threatening her—*tempting* her.

Pain and pleasure juxtaposed as the substance surged through her. The rush that exploded through her body was orgasmic.

Amy opened her eyes, finding Naunet's blurry face dancing in front of her. "What is this seductive substance?" she breathed, trembling.

Naunet set the lid back onto the jar, smiling wickedly. "Salt venom."

"*Venomous* salt?" Amy asked. Suddenly, the serpent coiling around the heart on the lid made more sense.

"The venom inside the salt is what causes this pleasurable reaction. It remains dormant, only awakening as the wave of euphoria washes through a sea nymph."

"What awakens it?"

Naunet's eyes darkened. "The rhythm of one's pulse awakes the venom from dormancy. Like many thing born from fae beings, it possesses both powers of life, and death."

"Salt venom originates from the *fae*?"

"You need to see the big picture to understand where it originates." Naunet unraveled one of her storm scrolls. A lunar chart appeared. A full moon sat at the center, with waxing and waning crescents on either side. Isis was drawn above the moon, her wings framing a massive space below. The space depicted the ancestral womb of the sea—the Abyss—which took up the entire scroll.

Inside the Abyss were seven separate spirals, each depicting one of the seven maternal salt pods. Each was painted in vibrant Egyptian blue pigment. All but one had a clockwise-shaped spiral. Amy knew what these spirals symbolized. Clockwise spirals symbolized a salt pod that was sterile—its mass in the sea wasn't producing maternal salts.

The one salt pod with a counterclockwise spiral had the symbol for Celaeno written beneath it.

Naunet set her finger on pod labeled Celaeno. "Every ten years, one of the seven maternal salt pods cycles. This is when the salt pod produces a minca moth queen. When the queen emerges from her pod, so does the production of fertile maternal salts. We are currently in Celaeno's fertility cycle." Her eyes lifted, finding Amy. "Celaeno's fae queen, however, is where this problem with salt venom has resulted."

"I don't understand. Is salt venom related to a minca moth queen?"

"Salt venom is born from her blood. She is the one who introduced the toxin into the ocean. The salt has the power to preserve one's spirit, while the venom corrodes the flesh. Salt venom is an elixir of both life, and death."

Amy straightened. "Well? What are we waiting for? Why not find her and get her out of the sea?"

"I have Celaeno's fae queen in my possession. But removing her from the water has not stopped what she has introduced into the ocean."

Amy's throat seemed to have closed. Her heart was pounding so hard, she could hear it echoing in her salt nodes. "Where?"

Naunet's eyes traveled to the jar with the salt venom. "She is sleeping inside. The salt venom prevents her from awakening."

"What about a healthy fae queen? Have the other salt pods produced one?"

Naunet shook her head. "The last healthy queen I collected was from Alcyone almost two decades ago. The maternal salt pods have since cycled to Celaeno. The cycle seems stuck. I believe the salt venom has sterilized the salt pods temporarily. If the maternal salt pods are not cycling, they are not producing queen minca moths, who need vast groves of blue minca to lay their eggs in."

Amy looked from the lunar chart, back to the jar. She was starting to see the big picture; one she didn't like at all. "Will our ability to produce a salt pregnancy be effected by this?"

Naunet's eyes darkened. "No cycling could result in the salt pods dissolving, resulting in the complete sterilization of the maternal salt pods."

Silence fell between them. That silence was pregnant with fear.

"Sooner or later, the maternal salts will not swim up the Nile. When that day comes, a plague will be upon us," Naunet said, emotion clouding her voice.

"What kind of plague will this be?"

"This plague will not attack humanity. A plague born of fae blood will strike Gaia's nymph daughters. It will strike the hearts of sea nymphs."

Amy looked at the small figurine of Isis propped above the jar of salt venom. She and Masika's quest to answer why minca was disappearing from the ocean became ever more pressing. "Minca's disappearance isn't helping this situation at all, is it?"

"Minca is not only the protective barrier that encircles the maternal salt pods, it is also where the minca moth queen lays her eggs. Minca is her *home*. The fae moths gifted us the art of salt trance so we could make their home at sea healthy. If we do not salt trance properly, not only will their home suffer, but so will our fertility."

"What about the storm dragons? What about the bonds that influence the weather the dragons create?"

"The sons of Poseidon are few and far between. The last group of sea nymphs who embarked on their salt stash returned to Egypt empty-handed. None bonded, because no storm dragons presented themselves. They've all seemed to disappear into the sea."

"Where have Poseidon's sons gone?"

"The Order believes that after Atlantis sank, Poseidon's sons retreated into the Abyss. If this is the case, who knows how long they will be sleeping there. Storm dragons have long had an umbilical connection with the Abyss. They have been known to sleep for centuries, even thousands of years, before they awaken and attempt to establish a new territory."

"Are there any storm dragons who remain awake? Or have they all retreated into the Abyss to sleep?"

"The Order has reported sightings of one of Poseidon's sons." She pointed once again to Celaeno's salt pod. "Celaeno's storm dragon."

Amy's body went cold. She knew this storm dragon—it was the beast she and Masika had summoned into the cavern not long ago.

Naunet glanced up at her, concern glinting in her eyes. "I'm sorry, Amy. I know how bringing up the Abyss makes you think of your mother."

Amy blinked away what could have been tears forming. "You mentioned that Celeano's storm dragon was ill, correct? Why hasn't he retreated into the Abyss like his brothers?"

"I can't say. But I do know one thing." Naunet's eyes flashed. "When storm dragons began to disappear from the ocean, so did blue minca."

Amy's mouth dropped open. "Do you believe that storm dragons and blue minca are related?"

"I do. But I have no way to prove it. My assumptions are just that, assumptions. Only our ancestors hold this knowledge. Not even my mother knows, and she was the last midwife of the sea before Atlantis fell. That's why I need you and my sister to help me prove to the Order that the relationship between storm dragons and minca is not only an assumption." She glanced over at the jar with the fae queen sleeping inside. "I can't help but wonder if minca's absence is what caused the fae queen to produce salt venom. She is a *minca* moth, after all."

Amy bit her bottom lip. The tang of iron filled her mouth. "Is there no way to neutralize this toxin?"

"According to the Codex, any toxin born of fae queen blood can be neutralized in one of two ways. One would be to bond a sea nymph with the storm dragon who encompasses the territory of the salt pod from which the fae queen was born."

"What's the second way?"

Naunet's eyes darkened. "Spilling the blood of a fae king."

Amy's mind worked its way back to Winter Forest. The only fae king she knew of was the one Ewan tracked into the highlands every winter. When the king drank from a pool atop the sacred mountain, he would lift his clan's prayers up to his ancestors—the fallen kings of Atlantis.

Amy tipped her head sideways. "If one were to spill the blood of a fae king, how would one go about using his blood to heal a victim infected by salt venom?"

"Apply the blood of the fae king to the victim's wound, and the salt venom will return to dormancy," Naunet replied as she returned her gaze to the scroll. "There should not be any need for bloodshed, as long as Celaeno's storm dragon is willing to cooperate." Naunet kept gazing at the scroll, an invisible weight settling on her shoulders. "Just as every storm is not born from the sky, not every dragon has wings. The most powerful storms known by our ancestors were created by the sea." Her eyes lifted, worry filling them. "If you and Masika don't find the reasoning behind minca's disappearance, our fertility will suffer. Salt births could become a thing of the past."

Amy swallowed. "Meaning that if a sea nymph wants to bear a daughter, she will be required to mate with a man?"

Naunet's eyes darkened. "Sexual intercourse with men rarely produces children. If pregnancy does result, the health of both the mother and child will suffer."

"*Wahhhhhhh!*"

Amy jumped. Speaking of children. Was there an infant in her dwelling?

Naunet left the room. She returned moments later with a bundle of cloth in her arms. The bundle shifted as two pudgy legs kicked out. Pudgier arms grabbed Naunet's breast as she pressed the infant to her chest.

"Shhhhh..." she cooed to the crying infant as she tucked her face into her dress to nurse. The child had swirls of dark hair on her head. Her salt nodes also appeared healthy.

"You didn't tell me you were expecting," Amy said, her voice breaking.

Naunet shot her a disapproving look. "You know the midwife of the sea becomes sterile while she is serving. This child is not my daughter, although I have taken her in as my own."

"Then whose daughter is she?"

Naunet jolted as the infant latched to her breast. "She is a salt daughter of Celaeno."

Amy's mouth had gone dry. "A *moon* child?"

Naunet smiled. "Shortly after I discovered Celaeno's toxic fae queen, I discovered her in the Nile."

Amy's bewilderment intensified as she watched Naunet nurse the tiny daughter born from the womb of the sea. As rare as they were, the Abyss did produce moon daughters after so many moon cycles.

"I have named her Selia," Naunet said.

"Why Selia?"

"Selia means blind moon. A moon child is blind to her own mother's existence, as she is born from the womb of the sea, not the womb of a sea nymph."

Amy looked into Selia's eyes. Such depth and mystery was hidden in them. Selia's eyes mirrored the meaning for Celaeno's name—*the dark one*. So much darkness shone back from their depths.

Naunet cradled Selia in one arm and grabbed the lid off the jar of salt venom with the other.

"What are you doing?" Amy asked, startled.

Naunet tipped the jar over a vase, dropping in a single drop of salt venom. She held Selia's body over the surface of the vase with the oily film of salt venom swirling in it.

8

THE LIGHTHOUSE

Selia

Selia's body trembled with excitement as she hopped into the passenger seat of their car, nearly spilling the contents of Pixie's decaf latte all over herself. "Who is the guy who told you about this property?" Selia asked as Damien floored the gas to keep up with the little orange truck puttering up the hill.

"He goes by McGill. He says that if he finds the right buyer, he's willing to strike us a Christmas deal."

Screeeeech!

"What was that?"

"Nothing..." Selia tucked her hand behind her ear, finding Peppercorn was crawling out to expose herself.

Damien's mouth opened. "What in the world? Is that a *bat*?"

Selia nodded, not knowing what to say. Peppercorn nibbled her ear, piping out an adorable little *squeak!*

"Why do I get the feeling that is not a normal bat?"

"Her name is Peppercorn, and she's coming with us. According to Pixie, she is definitely not a normal bat."

"Where did you get her?"

"The fairy hut."

Damien groaned. "Another fae? I thought I had it rough with hermit crabs..." He shot Peppercorn the stink eye. "What do you like to steal?"

Squeeeeech!

"She doesn't like your sense of humor."

Damien sighed. "Don't tell the landlord, okay? I don't want him thinking that we're setting his property up with an infestation of bats."

Peppercorn tucked herself back under Selia's hair and was once again nuzzling her ear.

It didn't take long before they summited the hill.

An elderly man Selia assumed was McGill was already standing outside of his truck. His hair was will-o'-the-wisp white, and he had the weathered face of a fisherman. Damien parked next to him and turned off the car. He got out and opened Selia's door.

Selia's boots crunched as she stepped onto soggy gravel. A thick fog had blown in, casting the field that surrounded them in mist. A few spruce trees swayed in the distance, their pointy outlines making them look like dancing Christmas trees.

McGill gave a throaty huff. "Malloch, is it?"

Damien threw out his hand and shook McGill's callused one. "Yes. This is my girlfriend, Selia."

McGill's watery blue eyes landed on Selia. She wondered if he'd spotted Peppercorn. She tucked her hair behind her ear, finding Peppercorn's fuzzy brown body huddled in a ball. The bat was at least cooperating, for now. "Miss Selia, ye be afraid of selkies?"

Selia glanced at Damien, whose expression was just as confused. "No, why?"

A row of yellow teeth flashed as McGill cracked a wiry smile. "We have a local myth around one I'm sure ye both will become well acquainted with if ye purchase my property."

He turned on his heel and took off up the hill. Damien grabbed Selia's hand, and the two followed. A few paces in, and Selia's foot sank into a frozen hoofprint. It did not appear to belong to a horse, as the hoof was cloven.

"What made this track?" Selia asked.

"Red deer," McGill confirmed as they walked alongside the animal tracks. "Ones that live now are tiny compared to the ones who lived here thousands of years ago—the great Irish elk."

"Wow, *elk* used to live here?" Selia said, hurrying along as the wind picked up.

"Aye. Some say their spirits still roam these parts, drifting in and out with the fog."

The scent of seaweed and salt drifted in the air. Seagulls cried in the distance, invisible due to the thickening atmosphere. The blurry outline of a structure much too tall to be a home appeared in the fog.

Selia dug her feet into the ground, stopping. This wasn't just a house. "A *lighthouse*?"

Damien stopped, too, squeezing her hand. "I had a feeling you would like it."

The main building was attached to the beacon tower. Both were painted white. There were so many windows attached to both structures, Selia couldn't count them all.

The three walked up to a giant red door. McGill pressed a key to the lock and propped it open. The smell of wood, plaster, and dust filled Selia's nose as they walked into the home.

She let go of Damien's hand, spreading her arms wide. Wooden beams lined the ceiling. She did a circle in place, her hair trailing behind her as she spiraled. "This space is absolutely massive!"

Damien chuckled. "I'm glad you like it so far."

Selia walked into the kitchen. Although it wasn't modern, it still had the major appliances—even a double oven. A pantry wasn't needed, given all of the cabinets.

Damien seemed to be overwhelmed by the space in an entirely different way. He walked into the main room that sported a stone fireplace. He propped his hands on his hips and looked toward the wall of windows facing the North Sea. His shoulders rolled backward as he blew out his cheeks. "Wow, just look at that ocean view."

Selia walked to the fireplace. The hallway was lit up by the daylight flooding through the windows. "An ocean view, *and* a place to display your paintings?"

"You read my mind," Damien said, grinning.

McGill clapped his hands together. "Glad to see ye both are lovin' it so far. This home has updated amenities, including central air."

Selia walked over to McGill, eager to see the rest of the space she and Damien were both in love with. "How many bedrooms?"

"There are three rooms total. There is a master over here. All ground level, with easy access to the main room—a perfect space for entertaining your guests."

"And for kids," Damien said, grabbing Selia's hand. "Show us the rooms?"

"I'll show ye the master first."

They followed McGill down the hallway. Peppercorn let out a tiny *squeak.*

"Can we see this room first?" Selia asked, and Peppercorn began nuzzling her ear again, realizing that was the bat's way of agreeing with her.

Selia's heart leapt. A crib sat in the corner by the window.

McGill poked his wrinkly face into the room. "If you like this little room, then wait until you see the master."

Selia followed Damien into the bedroom at the end of the hall. There were two large windows facing the ocean. Centered between the windows was another stone fireplace. Even the bedroom had a king-sized bed, complete with a love seat at the foot, facing the fireplace.

"Why is there so much furniture?" Selia asked.

"The last folks who lived here were military. They didn't stay as long as they wanted and ended up breaking their lease. I'm done renting the space out. I want this property to be for people who want to turn it into a forever home." His eyes dropped to Selia's belly, then back up to meet her gaze. "Well, what do you think?"

"I thought you said there were *three* rooms. You've only shown us two," Selia said.

McGill chuckled. "That's because you haven't seen the tower yet." He waved his hand and took off down the hallway. "I think I know why the previous renters broke their lease—it had to do with Sika."

"Sika the selkie?" Selia asked, trying to keep up with McGill.

"Aye."

"A friend in town told me about this urban myth. What do you know about it?"

"The myth around her goes back longer than Scotland has been a country. Sika was cursed when the tides stole a song from her ancestors."

"A song? What did it sound like?"

"It sounds different to everyone. Some hear it. Some *feel* it. I believe the song speaks of what the individual's heart is searching for."

McGill stopped at a door at the end of the hall and opened it. "Go on, you two. You can't make a proper decision without giving the lantern room a view."

Damien brushed up behind Selia. "Ladies first."

A spiral staircase swirled above Selia's head. She set her hand on one of the black metal guardrails and took her first step. Each of hers and Damien's steps echoed in the tower.

Ceeeelaaaaaaeeeeeenooooooooooo...

Selia stopped. She blinked a few times, hoping the ominous sound would dissipate. "Damien, did you hear that?"

"Hear what?" he asked, stopping behind her.

Selia looked up into the tower, her vision blurry.

"Are you feeling all right?" Damien asked.

"I'm a bit dizzy is all." She continued her ascent, wondering if what she heard was just the wind or not. Had she heard the song the urban myth about Sika McGill warned about?

"Maybe it was Peppercorn dropping a hint we should buy this place," Damien mumbled, his tone half-enthused-half-annoyed.

Selia's breath began to puff out in front of her as the cold worsened with each creaky step. Her boots clanked along the metal stairs, until she reached the top.

The entire lantern room was encased in glass, which made a rattling noise as the fog blew in from the sea. She counted six windows total in the hexagonal tower. The scent of rust and salt filled the air, as this place had at least a century's worth of weathering created by violent storm fronts.

At the center of the room was a space Selia expected there to be a light of some kind. Instead, there was an empty spot where a light could have been at one time.

Damien raked his hand through his hair. "That was one little quirk he did mention to me—there is no actual lens to light it up, no beacon."

"A lighthouse that doesn't light up? That can't be right."

Damien nudged her. "Go on—let's go out on the balcony."

Selia walked out of the lantern room, the chilly breeze catching her scarf and nearly taking off with it. Her hair blew out, and a fuzzy brown bat went flitting past her. Suddenly, she and Damien were alone together, enjoying the wide open space. If there was ever a more romantic place to gaze out over the North Sea, this would be it.

"Wow, would you look at that view," Selia said, her breath catching. Nothing but the steel grey color of the North Sea and horizon lay before them. The surf crashed along the rocky shore below as patches of fog drifted across the ocean. Fishing boats drifted out as far as the fog would allow her sight to go.

Damien came up behind her, pressing himself to her back. His hands wound around her and clasped over her belly. "Your bat seems to like the view, too."

Peppercorn flitted above them, seeming to agree.

Damien rounded his shoulders. "Well, I'm basically sold on this place. How about you?"

Selia bit her bottom lip. "You'd have to paint a whole lot to pay for this. And I don't think watering plants is going to pay the bills."

Damien unraveled his arms and spun her to face him. "With your permission, I say we buy this place. He's willing to sell it to us on the spot. We could make this a dream home, love."

Selia's heart welled. It seemed too good to be true.

Damien pressed his lips to her forehead and kissed her. "I want nothing more than to take this next step in creating a family with you."

Selia's belly warmed at Damien's sweet words.

Peppercorn darted overhead, catching a clump of Selia's hair with her wing.

Damien laughed. "See? She wants you to go through with it. What do you say?"

Selia glanced from Peppercorn back to Damien's hopeful gaze. "I'm in love with you, then this place, in that order."

Damien pulled her into his arms, embracing her. Selia relaxed, the adrenaline from the moment washing through her.

She pulled away and clapped her hands together. "Let's go tell McGill we want to buy his property!" She turned and started walking toward the lantern room.

She jerked back as Damien's gravity held her in place.

Damien's face paled. "Before we seal the deal, there is something else I need to ask you."

"You look like you've seen a ghost," Selia said, startled at how white his face had become.

A lump moved in Damien's throat. He dropped to his knee. A ray of sunlight shone through the clouds, catching the ambers and greens in his eyes. "Selia...will you..." A box fell out of his pocket, landing with a clatter on the metal. He grabbed it and opened it, revealing a shiny stone perched atop a silver ring. "Selia, will you be my wife?"

9
SELIA'S IMMUNITY
Amy

Amy's salt nodes were screaming. Naunet submerged Selia's tiny fragile body in the salt venom. Her eyes were closed, blissfully unaware of what was floating on the water's surface.

She curled in on herself, facing down. Her salt nodes opened, allowing her to breathe while her nose and mouth were submerged in the water. She floated in the vase, bobbing up and down. Infant sea nymphs often slept in water in this pose, as it offered a memory of the womb.

"Do you feel that?" Naunet asked, her eyes leveling with Amy.

"I do," Amy replied, setting her fingers on her chest. Her own heartbeat seemed to be responding to the ripples Selia's pulse was creating in the water.

Naunet held out her hand. "Close your eyes, and salt trance with me."

Amy closed her eyes, taking Naunet's hand into her own. Naunet's slender hand was so similar to her sister's. Her grip was sensual and warm. Caring and compassionate.

Beyond anything, Naunet's hand was strong.

Amy took a deep breath, sucking in extra oxygen for Naunet. The pulse that filled her salt nodes was so powerful, her own heart struggled to keep up with it.

The melody from Selia's pulse echoed creation and destruction. A feeling of great euphoria filled her body. The melody blended with the sounds of a baby crying. The last breath of a dying loved one. A song that mixed the beginning and end of life, all wrapped up into one.

Amy opened her eyes, finding that Naunet's eyes were damp. Maternal instinct was flooding her. Naunet wanted this moon daughter of Celaeno as her own.

Naunet wiped her eyes with the back of her hand. "It's beautiful, isn't it?"

Amy squeezed her other hand, which she still hadn't let go. While beautiful, she had not become so emotionally invested in it. "Her pulse is unlike anything I've heard before."

"Selia's pulse protects her from the salt venom." Naunet released Amy's hand, dipped her hands into the vase, and pulled Selia out. She bundled her in a linen blanket and began rocking her. "Taste the water."

Amy grabbed a wooden goblet and dipped it into the vase Selia had been sleeping in. She tipped the goblet to her lips. The water that entered her mouth was cool and refreshing, fresher than anything she had tasted from the Nile. "Does Selia's pulse purify water?"

Naunet nodded. "Moon children have unique heartbeats. The rhythm of their pulse syncs with the tides, which cleanses the water. Imagine what her heart could accomplish if she were to bond with Celaeno's storm dragon."

Amy's body went cold as memory of the storm dragon she and Masika summoned flashed before her. Poseidon had taken her mother to the Abyss. Was she brave enough to face Poseidon's son in an attempt to bond him with Selia?

Naunet tucked Selia inside her dress, encouraging her to nurse. "I will raise her until she is mature enough to bond, but I am afraid by the time she has matured, the Order will have changed the ancestral teachings of the art."

"What do you mean by change the teachings?"

"The Order suspects the fourth principle had something to do with Poseidon's violent storms that sank the great city. They have implemented a regulation on who can perform a salt stash. All adolescent sea nymphs preparing for their first salt stash will report to the temples for a pulse test. If her pulse shows any sign of abnormality, she will be subject to practicing without the fourth salt trancing principle."

Amy's mouth dropped open. She threw her hands in the air, her body shaking. "This is ridiculous! A pulse test? What are they going to do, say that your heart isn't beating fast enough, so you can't perform a salt stash?"

"I'm afraid salt stashing might become a thing of the past," Naunet said.

"Oh no, no, no, no. Salt stashing is a coming of age ritual that dates back *prior* to Atlantis. How do they think salt trancing talismans are *made*? The Order can't just shove their noses into a sea nymph's salt trancing development."

Amy paced the room, unable to comprehend such blasphemy. "Alexandra wasn't teasing me in the temple earlier, was she? She was speaking the truth, wasn't she?" Her blood was boiling. How could the Order get away with such regulations on the art without properly understanding the way pulse operated?

Naunet's gaze leveled with her. "I have a very big favor to ask of you. The Order has been harassing me about the toxic creature for a month now. Would you dispose of the fae queen for me?"

Amy's breath caught. "Dispose of her? What a waste of such a beautiful being." Amy tilted the chrysalis. Her wings had the oily substance on their surface. "Why can't you dispose of the queen?"

"My maternal salts originate from Celaeno. I would be disgracing Isis in disposing a sacred lunar fae being who was born from my maternal salts." Her dark eyes lit up, luminous pools of hope. "But your maternal salts originate from Alcyone. You could do so without any repercussions from our ancestors."

Amy knew how superstitious Naunet was when it came to her knowledge of the maternal salt pods. Besides, leaving Egypt wasn't an option for her. She had her hands tied caring for a Celaeno's moon child.

Amy's pulse quickened. She wanted to help Naunet. But she also wanted to help Masika. Could she not find a way to make both sisters who cared about minca happy? "Only if you don't tell the Order that I'm really doing them a favor."

Gratitude flickered in Naunet's eyes. "Do not share with anyone the meaning for Selia's name, not even my sister. Nobody but I know who her mother is. The pharaohs believe she is mine."

"Why must you hide her?"

"Humans do not understand the origin of our ancestor's womb at sea. They are becoming quite fearful of it. But I cannot overlook their fear. I've foreseen great darkness, far greater than any plague that has, or will ever, sweep over Egypt."

Amy eyed the infant clutched against Naunet's breast. Would Selia be forced to suppress her ability to salt trance? Would she be fated to live a life among humans, afraid of her talents?

"Amphitrite, did you hear me?" Naunet asked, repositioning Selia against her other breast.

Alexandra's words clouded Amy's thoughts. "*The storm dragon Naunet was discussing has become ill with something your Ocean Apothecary has no cure for.*"

"I heard you," Amy said, turning to face Naunet. "I will dispose of the fae queen. When Selia is grown, I will return to Egypt."

PART 2
FERTILE WATERS

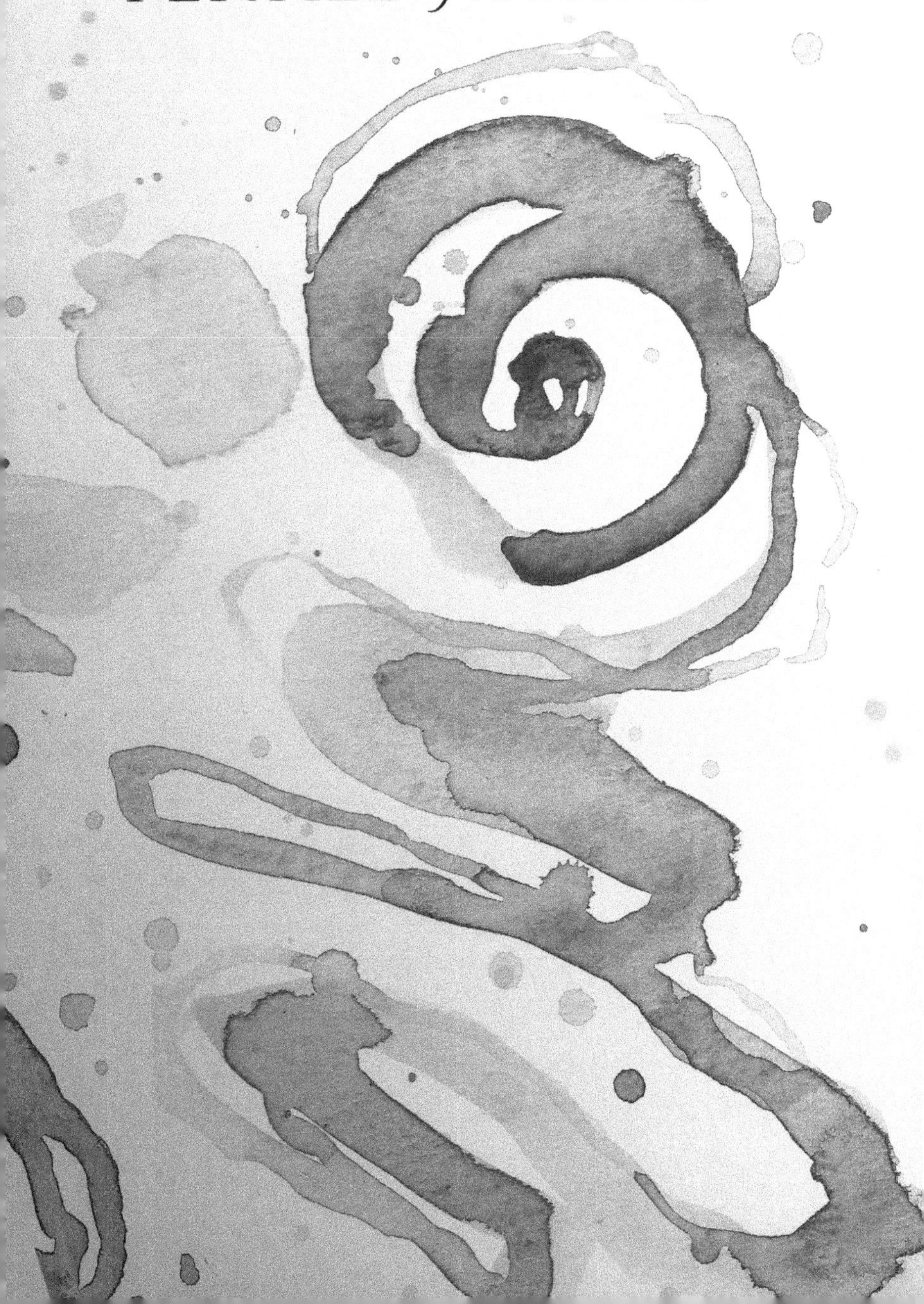

10

THE JOURNAL

Selia

Selia's entire body was tingling not from the cold, but from adrenaline. She couldn't take her eyes off the silver ring sitting in the box on Damien's palm.

"Well?" Damien asked, his voice shaking.

Selia looked up at her teary-eyed boyfriend. "Of course I will marry you!"

Before Damien could fully stand, she flung her arms around his neck, hugging him.

"I love you so much," he whispered in her ear. The blur of the ocean and Damien's chestnut hair whirled together. His warmth washed over her.

She pulled away, taking his face into her hands. "I love you, too."

"Can I put it on your finger?"

Selia had completely forgotten the ring. She only wanted to look into Damien's hazel eyes and get lost in them. She released his face and held out a trembling left hand.

Damien removed the shiny silver ring from the box and slipped it onto her finger. "Look at that, a perfect fit!"

She tilted her hand to the side. The silver band caught the overcast daylight, transforming it into something magical. "What is this lovely design?"

"The Celtic knotwork dates back to the origin of my clan, long before we were called Clan Malloch. Back then, we were Clan Sgàthan." He brushed his hand through his hair. "I know this might sound cheesy, but it was a ring that belonged to our ancestors."

"Wow, and here you are, giving it to me?" she said, her voice trembling. "What does the knot symbolize?" Selia asked, looking from the ring to her new fiancé.

"The knot symbolizes the Sgàthan clan's unique spiritual belief, that memories and the spirits of our ancestors mirror one another." He took her hands in his and tipped his forehead to hers. "The ring has been in my family for generations. Gwen gave it to me after I lost Maria. I never thought I would marry again." His eyes locked with her. "Selia, you've brought so much light back into my world. I want to share the rest of my days with you."

Selia grabbed his face and forced her lips to his, claiming him as hers.

Damien pulled her into his arms. He picked her up, spinning her in place, then set her back down.

Selia soaked him in. His creativity. His strength. His *warmth*.

She pulled away, locking eyes with her new fiancé.

Damien's eyes were glassy with tears. "Selia, I love you more than anything. I can't wait to start a family with you." He pressed his lips to hers. He kissed her slowly, the heat from his mouth blending with her lips. She wanted to savor this moment for as long as she possibly could.

He pulled his lips away from hers. "What are you thinking?"

Her hand trembled. "I have never been engaged before. I don't even know *what* to think." She grabbed his face and kissed him again. "But my heart is full. I want to tell everyone I'm marrying the man I adore."

Giddy with their moment, Selia and Damien stumbled back inside the lantern room and began their descent down the spiral stairwell, laughing and stopping to kiss each other every few stairs. Once they reached the bottom, Selia grabbed the door handle and bustled with Damien back into their new home, a dream come true. She glanced over at McGill, who was beaming at them.

"Well done, well done!" he said with a hefty clap of his hands. "I can see from the ring on your finger that this fairy tale turned out the way it was meant to."

Selia shot Damien a look. "Wait a minute—you planned this, didn't you?"

"I did," he said with a chuckle. "I knew this lighthouse was going up for sale. The McGill's have been family friends for a long time. The moment he told me the owner was selling the property, I knew it was the perfect place to propose to you."

Selia gazed at the massive gemstone glistening on her ring finger. It would take a while for the adrenaline to settle, allowing her to appreciate the details.

"How do we make this lighthouse our home?" Damien asked.

"Sign a few papers, and you can move in tomorrow," McGill said. "I'm so glad to have this property in the hands of a new family before the holidays."

After they signed the paperwork, Selia climbed into the passenger seat as Damien folded into the driver side.

Selia grabbed his hand. "Getting engaged and buying a lighthouse in one day? Damien, you're spoiling me."

"Honey, of course I am. I want what's best for you and our family." He pulled the car onto the street.

"Where are we going?"

"I want to introduce you to my sister, Gwen. She works not far from here. She'll be thrilled to meet you."

Nerves flooded Selia's body. She'd just gotten engaged, and still hadn't met anyone else from Damien's family other than his aunt. Supposedly, he had thirty-nine aunts, uncles, and cousins scattered across Scotland, with a majority of them living not far from Montrose.

Selia jabbed her fingers to her phone, shooting off a text to Pixie.

> **Good news? Well, Damien and I will be regulars at your shop, moving forward. We are purchasing a lighthouse!**

> **OMG!!!**

> **Damien proposed to me! Bad news, I don't know where your bat went.**

> **Forget my silly bat, I want to see the ring!**

> **I'll show it to you in person when I see you next!**

Damien parked the car outside of a cozy-looking shop with a wooden sign hanging in front: **The Dragon's Lair Used Bookstore**

"What a lovely name for a bookstore!" Selia said as she left the car and walked with Damien up to the window.

"If you thought I was quirky when I came to folktales, wait until you meet my sister. If there is anything you'll quickly learn about Gwen, it's that she's in love with books and fairy tales, especially those about dragons."

Damien grabbed the door and swung it open.

The melodic sound of chimes filled the chilly air as Selia walked inside. The entryway had a giant painting of a dragon hanging from the wall, framed by other hanging windchimes and other trinkets, most of which were fairies, mushrooms, and musical notes.

The scent of old parchment, leather, and incense filled the shop.

Damien's hand came to her waist. "Gwen must be in the back. Have a look around and I'll bring her out, okay?"

"Don't mind me. I'm already in love with this place."

Damien walked toward the desk, leaving Selia to stare at a handwritten label stuck to the bookshelf in front of her: **Women Rule**

She tugged out one of the books with an outline of a busty female torso accentuating the spine. *How a Pair of Breasts Dominated the First Male Clans of Scotland*

Selia continued thumbing through the titles that all seemed to revolve around female empowerment. Tucked beneath *Why Women Prefer to Tame the Dragon and not Slay Him*, she found a label that read: *Selkies and Storms—The Ancient Bond Between the Womb of the Sea & Dragons*

Celaaaeeeennnoooooooo.

Selia clutched her chest. Her heart was racing. That thunderous sound she'd heard in the lighthouse echoed in her ears. Why was she hearing it again?

She found a dragon sculpture perched atop a bookshelf. His massive wooden wings created a shadow over the shelf. Other than collecting dust, Selia guessed the dragon's purpose was to guard a hidden collection of books below. A label below the shelf read: *Selkies and Fertility Secrets of the Sea.*

Selia grabbed one of the books that had thicker paper. The jagged edges reminded her of Damien's watercolor paper. Perhaps it was a journal meant to paint in?

She flipped open the leather cover, finding the paper was yellow and splotchy. She ran her fingers over the surface. The rough texture reminded her of the rare artifacts she dealt with at the Louvre—Egyptian artifacts.

Was the paper papyrus?

Damien's voice broke the thunderous rhythm that had pulsed through her again. Selia peered around the corner, finding him talking with a woman that appeared too old to be his younger sister.

She turned her attention back to the journal in her hands. The paper didn't lay flat. It rebelled against the other pages. Had the weight of the leather not held it in place, she was certain it would have unraveled. She flipped through the pages, captivated by how blank the journal appeared. A few imperfections dotted the surface, mostly where someone would have touched the corners to flip through them. A dark stain appeared at the center.

Selia touched the parchment. The texture was oily. Spirals bled through the stain on the opposite side. The coiling spirals reminded her of the designs on her salt trancing talisman. A coincidence? Maybe. Or was there some historic context behind the design? Amy had shown her that the salt chrysalises of male minca moths created the talismans over time.

Words began forming on the paper.

Selia blinked as the spirals became readable.

Tides of our Ancestors

Selia's breath caught. Did this symbol have something to do with the *tides*?

She blinked, and the words faded, reabsorbed by the dark stain at the center. Her salt nodes began to pulse, then ring. Were the strange images in the journal, *singing*? A deep reverberating voice filled Selia's ears. Not a yell, nor a whisper. The windblown sound was that of liquid mixing with air.

"Savor it. Surrender to it. All salt daughters of Celaeno will be tempted by it."

"Selia—"

Selia snapped the journal closed.

Damien peeked over the bookshelf, his brow furrowing. "What are you doing back here in the dragon's nest?"

"Nothing. Where is your sister?" Selia asked, shoving the journal into her jacket. Who was this Celaeno? And what was the *it* her daughters were tempted by?

"Gwen isn't here. The lady up front said she went home for the evening." He blew out his cheeks. "She never leaves this place unless there is an emergency. I tried calling her, and she wouldn't pick up. I guess we're headed to see her."

"I'll meet you up front."

Damien set his hand on the bookshelf, leaning toward her. "Are you keeping secrets from your fiancé?"

"No, I'm just having fun Christmas shopping." She dipped under his arm and walked to the counter. "I'd like to purchase this."

The cashier took the book and rang it up. "Gwen will be pleased that someone is taking advantage of the books her dragon guards."

Selia left the bookstore and slipped into the passenger seat of the car.

Damien sat in the driver seat, taking two seconds to find the journal she tried to hide from him. "What did you buy?" he asked, grabbing the journal and flipping it open.

Selia flushed with heat. An image that had *defiantly* not been there before appeared on the parchment. A naked woman who appeared to be in the midst of pleasure was wrapped in the body of a coiling serpent.

Or was it a dragon?

"Oh, this looks like something naughty. What is this? Some kind of kinky sex book?"

Selia stared at the seductive image, wondering if she'd simply skimmed past it. She'd flipped through the entire book in the bookstore, only finding a few pages with oily stains on them.

Damien handed the book back to her, slipping his hand onto her thigh. "How did I get so lucky to have you agree to marry me?"

"You painted my portrait, then made violently passionate love to me."

"You can expect more of that. I can't wait to give that book a look over with you when we move in to our new place." He turned on the car and steered them out onto the road.

"Is Gwen like your aunt?" Selia asked, hoping to change the subject.

"Like Auntie, she has a slight obsession with the fae. Although she doesn't obsess over fae pests like vixen sprites."

"Are there any fae she's particularly obsessed with?"

Damien shook his head. "Don't tell my sister you bought something from her dragon shelf. She'll think you have some infatuation with the mythical creature she's obsessed with."

"Are you saying Gwen is obsessed with dragons?"

"She named that bookstore after them. She's loved dragons ever since we were wee kids. We would build a fort out of pots and garden tools and old wooden planks of wood Auntie used for the garden bed. She would be the queen of the fort, then she would leave her older brother—the dragon she enslaved—for dead."

Selia laughed. "So, Gwen was the younger sister who put her older brother in his place?"

"Exactly."

"Why do I get the feeling you're slightly intimidated by your little sister?"

"Hey, a brother can only play the big dumb dragon for so long."

Selia giggled, trying to imagine Damien playing the role of a dragon. Sure, he was protective and a bit goofy. She grabbed his hand. "I want to make sure I make a good first impression."

Damien brought her hand to his lips and kissed the top. "Talk about dragons, and Gwen will warm right up to you."

II

MASIKA

Amy

Amy sat outside of the greenhouse as the sun began to set. She didn't remember walking there, but with the memories from her past flooding her, she was surprised she hadn't ended up in the ocean.

She'd spent many a lonely evening like this perched atop a rocky hill, wondering when Naunet's sister would return from her adventures at sea. Three thousand years later, she was still wondering if Masika's spirit would return to her. Her memory had been suppressed for so long that, remembering those moments with Naunet left her stomach queasy.

Amy had learned from Naunet that neutralizing salt venom could occur in one of two ways. Either she could spill the blood of a fae king, or she could bond Selia with Celaeno's storm dragon. She'd never been very keen on killing anything, so jumping at the opportunity to help the young sea nymph bond with the dragon when she came of age seemed like a golden opportunity that she couldn't pass up.

She remembered how Naunet's pupils had turned into vertical slits as the salt venom seemed to possess her. *"Savor it. Surrender to it. All salt daughters of Celaeno will be tempted by it."*

Her salt nodes tingled just at the memory of that wickedly additive substance. Over three thousand years ago, Naunet had given her a *tool*. That tool had drifted in the ocean until Selia helped her to recover it only a few months ago in the vault.

Amy had failed once before in her attempt to neutralize the salt venom. This time, she would turn the tides in her favor. She had since changed the name of the salt venom Naunet had given her. She'd kept the substance a secret for so long because so much darkness was tied to it. The story of renaming salt venom to something else had pain behind it—pain she didn't know if she was ready to remember.

Starlight flickered in an inky black sky above where Amy stood at the edge of the cliff. Waves crashed below her, striking the rocky shore. The cold stung her nose as she inhaled a deep breath. While she had been to Egypt, Masika, too, had been on a journey, as she would often spend weeks exploring tidal caverns and rocky outcroppings in search of any minca that had washed in from the sea.

She tugged her robe around her shoulders, fighting with the cold that was now threading through the land. Dirt caked under her fingernails. Her hands were numb from the earth she'd spent digging through that morning. She had buried the canopic jar Naunet had given her. She was still deciding on what she should do with the fae queen.

Should she dispose of her, or give her to Masika? How would Masika react when she shared the knowledge about the maternal salt pods she'd gained from her older sister?

She withdrew her hands into her robe, wrapping her arms around herself. She would need to decide about the queen soon. By giving Masika the queen and not disposing of her as Naunet had requested, she would be betraying a salt sister. But killing a fae being because she was toxic? She couldn't justify acting so harshly.

Amy's breath caught as a familiar silhouette rose against the horizon.

Masika approached her, stopping at the crest of the hill where Amy stood. Her black hair threaded with strands of moonlight. Her clothing was made of animal furs and hides, much thicker than Naunet's linen garments. Her footwear was minimal; like many sea nymphs, she preferred to go barefoot when exploring the land around the sea. All that protected her feet from the cold earth were a pair of sandals with leather wrappings that coiled up her legs. Darkness from the sky and earth clung to her like a cloak. A true salt daughter of Celeano—the dark one—Masika was.

"Well? Are you going to stand there and gaze at the stars all evening?" Masika asked, stopping a few paces away from Amy. She propped her hands on her hips, her dark eyes glinting.

Amy closed the distance between them, wrapped her arms around Masika's neck, and pulled her into an embrace. "I can't bear having you leave me for this long."

Masika returned her embrace, pressing her cold face to Amy's ear. "I wish I could take you with me."

Amy closed her eyes, relishing Masika's affectionate words. She buried her face into Masika's hair, inhaling her scent. Her dark hair coiled around her, blocking out the light—making her think back to the storm scroll Naunet had shared with her in Egypt. Her jealousy of Masika's infatuation with the sea evaporated for a moment she wished would last forever.

Masika was the first to release her grip, pulling away. When their eyes met, Amy could see the questions already swimming in them. "You've been to Egypt to see my sister, haven't you?"

"How did you know?"

Masika reached up, trailing her finger past one of Amy's salt nodes. "I can smell her pheromones on you."

Amy leaned into Masika's affectionate touch. She wondered if Masika could pick up traces of Celaeno's moon daughter on her.

Masika lowered her hand. "My sister's scent is difficult to cover. She has served as midwife of the sea for so long, I wonder if she will ever retire and become a mother."

Amy bit her tongue. As far as she was concerned, Naunet was absolutely a mother. She was fostering Celaeno's beautiful baby moon daughter. "Naunet is concerned about your obsession with minca's disappearance."

One of Masika's eyebrows arched. "That's nothing new."

"She wants to know why you would rather spend all of your time exploring tidal caverns than beside the sea nymph who loves you?"

"I think it is *you* who is concerned about my obsession with minca, not my sister," Masika replied. She leaned forward, grazing her lips past Amy's earlobe. "Have you grown jealous of the *sea*?"

"How can I *not* be jealous? You are dealing with powers that sank the kingdom of Atlantis!"

Masika laughed. "Luckily, we have the luxury of meeting the sons of that kingdom here. I'm sure that a certain huntsman from the Sgàthan clan has kept you warm this winter."

Amy flustered. She had long wondered if Masika's obsession with minca's disappearance was slowly replacing her. "You know *men* are not who I treasure," she replied, thinking of the warm hazel eyes of the huntsman who pursued her.

12

GWEN

Selia

Selia and Damien walked together up the drive toward Gwen's home. The vague outline of a cottage came into view as Selia huddled next to Damien to avoid the cold breeze ripping across the sea. The last rays of sunlight dipped below the horizon as their adventurous day came to an end.

Her ears were still ringing with the strange song she'd heard in both the lantern tower and Gwen's bookstore. The ringing wasn't high-pitched, but instead, low and slightly eerie. The sound was a mixture of both liquid and air. If evaporation had a sound, the liquid voice captured it.

Selia stepped onto the front porch, finally sheltered from the bitter wind. A light next to the door lit up. The angular head of a cast iron dragon with a long coiling tail gripped the glowing orange light bulb.

Selia held her breath. Before Damien could knock on the door, it swung open. A whirlwind of curly reddish-brown hair launched through the air. "Damien!"

Damien caught his sister as she flung her arms around his neck. "Hi, Gwen."

Gwen pulled away from him and gave his shoulder a slap. "Well? Introduce me to this lovely woman!"

Selia found herself facing Damien's younger sister. Spunky was an understatement. She wore a form-fitting red sweater over black leggings and a pair of black leather riding boots. Her hair was auburn in color—a little darker than Damien's chestnut color. The glowing orange light gave her hair a fiery-red glow. Her eyes were a gorgeous hazel, nearly identical to her brother's.

Damien placed his hand on Selia's lower back. "Gwen, this is my fiancé, Selia."

Gwen's face drained of all color. "*Fiancé*?"

Damien squinted at his sister. "You got my message, right?"

Gwen's eyes darted from Selia to her brother. "I want details! This is *wonderful* news! Have you told Auntie yet?"

"Gwen, it all happened today. We're both still waiting for it to sink in," Damien said as he looped his arm around Selia's waist.

Gwen scowled. "Leave it to my artist of a brother not to keep his family in the loop. Come inside—we have a wedding to plan for!"

Selia's heart could have turned inside out with joy. For the first time in her life, she was being welcomed into the warmth of a family she could see herself learning to love.

The aroma of cloves, cinnamon, and citrus filled Selia's nose as she entered Gwen's charming, Scottish, sea-side cottage. Heat instantly broke over her, warming her to the bone. Gwen bustled about the foyer, ushering them inside. She was the complete opposite of her brother's calm demeanor. Gwen's charisma and energy were as contagious and flamboyant as the dragon artwork sitting atop her mantelpiece.

Two Irish setters came bounding into the room, tongues lolling out of their mouths. One of them attempted to jump and lick Selia's hand.

Gwen snapped her fingers, and the dog sat on its haunches, fluffy tail wagging. "Tales has a way with the ladies. Scales is an old curmudgeon who would make a better lap dog than a hunter's hound. Can you guess what they're named after?" Gwen asked, her sharp look narrowing on Selia again.

"Dragons?" Selia said, thinking back to the bookstore where she worked.

Gwen smiled. "Dragons will always keep a special place in my heart."

Tales was wagging his tail lazily, his large droopy red eyes sagging as he nuzzled Damien's hand. "Where are the kids and Sean?" Damien asked as he gave the dog a friendly head pat.

Gwen's gaze dipped to Scales. "The kids are off at camp. Good thing Gemma and Bram went, because I have so much work to catch up on at the house. They'll be back on Sunday."

"And Sean? What about him?" Damien asked.

Gwen's lips pursed. "He's working late at the fishing yard again."

"Does the guy ever stop fishing?"

Gwen's expression became a fierce one. "Not when the guy prioritizes his boats over his wife."

Selia caught Damien's wary glance.

Gwen snapped her fingers, and off Tales and Scales went. "Come grab a plate while it's still hot. I have leftovers. I hope the two of you don't mind eating in the living room. It's closer to the liquor cabinet."

Damien shook his head, following his sister toward the kitchen, which looked like a bomb had gone off. Cabinets were missing doors. Some of the counters had plywood planks draped over them in place of countertops.

Damien set his hands on his hips. "Wow, sis. For some reason, I imagined your kitchen renovation would be finished by now."

Gwen sighed. "It didn't help that we left for holiday in the middle of this. One thing I learned. A kitchen renovation won't finish itself." She walked over to the stove, where two pots were bubbling. The sink had dishes stacked all around it. The second half was so full, Selia wondered how it hadn't caved in.

"Help yourself. It's nothing special."

"You seem to be a bit out of it," Damien teased, nudging his sister's arm.

"I came home from holiday to an inventory disaster at the bookstore, the renovation, and on top of everything, Sean's boat broke down again," she huffed. "I swear, that man spends more time flirting with that stupid old engine every winter."

Another passive aggressive jab aimed at her husband made Selia wonder—were they having marital issues?

Gwen and Damien piled beef, potatoes, carrots, and what appeared to be spinach onto their plates. The aroma made Selia nauseous, so she helped herself to a few items, hoping her stomach would settle. They ventured into the living room by the fireplace.

Selia sat in the loveseat, Damien next to her. Gwen sat across from them after setting a pot of coffee on a warmer on the coffee table.

"*Don't eat me!*"

Gwen jumped in her seat, nearly sending her plat of food flying.

Scales came running over and dug his nose into Gwen's side. He nudged her leg, sending what looked like an orange beanbag onto the ground.

Gwen reached down, grabbing the screaming ornament. "These blasted little things. The kids dug them out early for Christmas." She tossed it across the room, and Scales went flying after it.

Gwen set her plate of food on the coffee table and walked to the liquor cabinet, where she took down three teacups that all had differently colored dragons on them.

Selia's stomach churned. What would her excuse be not to drink alcohol?

Gwen lugged down a massive bottle of *Dragon's Blood* whiskey.

"How was your holiday anyway?" Damien asked before shoving a fork-full of potatoes into his mouth.

"The Caribbean was good, but also not so good," Gwen said.

"How so?" Damien asked.

"It didn't help that Sean and I had a big fight right before we left. We've been arguing about leaving in the middle of the kitchen renovation." She lined up the three teacups and poured a dash of coffee into each. "When we got home, I had a voice message on the answering machine. I'd applied for a full-time position at the library in the genealogy department. I didn't get it."

"I didn't know you were searching for full time work again," Damien said.

"I love the bookstore, but part-time work just isn't paying the bills. Sean has been pulling double shifts down at the harbor. What I wouldn't do to have him home for the holidays with the kids instead of working in that stupid boatyard."

Gwen set the coffee pot down and grabbed the bottle of *Dragon's Blood*. "Do you like whiskey in your coffee?"

Selia looked from the coffee pot to Damien. "Actually, I—"

"—Ah, you're like me then. You like drinking the dragon's blood right out of the bottle!" She tipped the bottle to Selia's teacup, nearly filling it to the top. Selia's nose burned at the fiery tinge of the alcohol.

Damien reached out, grabbing the cup. "What Selia is trying to say, is that we are both going sober this evening."

Selia sighed, grateful he had moved the teacup sloshing with whiskey.

Gwen's eyes swiveled between them, a quizzical look spreading across her face. "You two are *no* fun at all. If you don't learn to hold your whiskey early on, good luck when it comes to the winter solstice gathering. I was supposed to host this year, but I don't think that's happening." She grabbed the bottle of *Dragon's Blood*, poured herself a triple shot, and downed the fiery liquid.

"Gwen, what's going on? Why are you drinking so much?" Damien asked.

Selia's pocket was vibrating. Her phone was going off. "Will you please tell me where your restroom is?"

Gwen held up her teacup. "Down the hall, first right."

Selia excused herself from the living room, eager to find out who was calling her this late in the evening. She grabbed her phone out of her purse and rounded the corner.

Her phone stopped buzzing. Drat. She'd missed the call. Hopefully whoever it was had left a voice message.

Ching!

The voice message icon lit up, making her stomach hollow. Why on earth was the doctor's office trying to reach her at this hour?

She pressed the speaker to her ear, her heart thundering as the voice of someone began speaking.

"*This message is for Selia Fontaine. We are calling regarding your recent sonogram. Please contact the doctor's office immediately, or—Beep!*"

Something about her sonogram? What did that mean?

She redialed the number. A voice message rattled back through the speaker. "*Our office is closed. Office hours are Monday through Friday, eight AM to seven PM.*"

Selia nearly dropped her phone. Panic surged through her as she walked back to the living room, hearing Gwen laughing hysterically. Damien was standing next to her, a concerned look on his face.

He approached her.

"Damien, something is wrong," Selia said.

"What's wrong?"

She grabbed his arms. "Something with my baby."

His hazel eyes searched hers, his expression stormy. "What? Did someone call you?"

"The doctor's office called. They mentioned something about my sonogram."

"But tomorrow is Saturday. You won't have any luck reaching them until Monday rolls around."

Selia peered into the living room, and found Gwen tipping the bottle to her dragon teacup once again.

Damien grabbed her coat and handed it to her. "I think it's best we get going. Gwen is having some issues, too."

"With what?"

Damien grabbed his coat. "It's best I tell you in the car." He walked over to his sister and pulled her into a hug. Whatever he said to her was muffled beneath Gwen's sobs.

Gwen walked them over to the door, her eyes bloodshot with tears.

Damien blew out his cheeks. "Gwen, get some rest. I'll call you tomorrow. We're moving into our new home, and we would love for you to come by and see it."

Gwen nodded as she withdrew from them.

Selia's heart ached for her. What was going on that she and Damien had to rush out of her home so soon?

She and Damien hopped inside the car.

Damien started the engine and steered the rickety vehicle onto the road. "Well, that was fun. So sorry about that. She's usually better about drinking, especially when meeting people for the first time. It's not like her to get wasted like that. She was drinking before we arrived."

She grabbed his hand. "It's okay. It sounds like she's going through a lot of stress right now."

"Stress is an understatement." His shoulders squared and his voice dipped. "Gwen thinks Sean is having an affair."

Selia's body tensed. "What? Why would she think that?"

Damien shook his head. "She said she discovered a text message on his phone about seeing another woman down at the boatyard."

"Another woman?" Selia asked, thinking about the myth around Sika.

"Doesn't make any sense to me. Sean has always been a stand-up guy. I can't see him doing this to Gwen and the kids," he ground out, his voice dipping. "She's tough as nails. She doesn't crumble like that unless she really thinks something is wrong."

Selia tugged out her phone. The phone number from the doctor's office still shone on her screen.

His hand came to hers. "It's just a reminder that no matter how perfect things seem, marriage is never easy. Let's focus on moving into our new place this weekend, all right?"

She put her phone away. Why wasn't Damien taking the scare with their baby more seriously?

"I think it's best we keep the baby a secret," she said.

"Why?"

"I don't want to add any more stress onto an already stressful situation."

He squeezed her hand. "I'll do whatever makes you feel comfortable, love."

She squeezed his hand back, but his words didn't quite sink in. Things were moving so fast that she barely had time to feel what was right and what was wrong.

The song she'd been hearing—now she was worried it wasn't only a song. What if there was something wrong with her baby's pulse?

13

MASIKA'S TREASURE

Amy

Amy walked with Masika down the hill and into the moonlit trees. As far as they knew, they were the only sea nymphs inhabiting Winter Forest. They were not alone, however. A clan of huntsmen lived here, too. The sons of Atlantean kings used the island as a hunting ground during the winter months.

She kept pace with Masika, not wanting to mix company with the group of meat-hungry men. The Sgàthan clan had set up a temporary base camp at the mouth of the river then made the long journey to the sacred meadow in the highlands. Orange firelight flickered off the trunks of the giant red trees along the path. The scent of wood smoke stung her nose as they ventured past the outskirts of their camp.

That time was coming when Ewan would approach her about journeying with him through the frozen terrain. He and his fellow huntsmen followed the herd of fae elk, who, every winter, migrated to the top of the sacred mountain. His bribes were always the same. He promised he would feed her, please her, and keep her incredibly warm. Every year, Amy rejected him.

While it was no secret that Ewan had a healthy appetite for women, She was his one and only selkie. And with his sexual appetite, he had likely already sired many children of his own. For one reason or another, he wanted her to bear him children. Little did he know about the necessity of salt when it came time for a sea nymph to reproduce.

Her foot caught on something woody, sending her step sideways. The uneven earth was caused by the roots growing out of the red giants. The trees grew in great red rings, their roots binding them together underground. This tree, in particular, had been hollowed out by fire. With the center gone, it made a perfect home for the two sea nymphs while sheltering from winter storms.

"Finally, home," Masika said, walking inside the hollow.

Amy followed. She adored the smell of the earth inside, too—nothing like the scorched, dusty air she'd breathed in Naunet's dwelling along the Nile. She preferred the cold air over the sweltering heat from Egypt any day.

The fire she'd prepared earlier was still alive, and she quickly tossed more kindling upon it. While their dwelling wasn't anything spectacular, it kept them both sheltered and warm.

She gathered the skewers hanging from the wall, each strung up with fresh game Ewan had prepared for her earlier. It had taken every ounce of her being to convince him not to stay and enjoy it with her.

Masika sat down on a wooden stump, her dark eyes flickering with orange firelight as she scanned the hollow. Her gaze landed on the bundle of foliage Ewan had made for Amy the week before. "I see there have been special offerings since I was last home?"

Amy set the skewers atop the stones circling the fire pit. Masika knew about Ewan's pursuit. Why she didn't become jealous frustrated her the most.

"It's a shame men don't understand the fertility cycles of sea nymphs," Amy said, sarcasm ringing heavily in her voice. She took a place across the fire pit opposite Masika, crossing her arms.

Masika grabbed a stick and stoked the fire. "Ewan is a son of Atlantean kings. He wants to rebuild his clan. In his eyes, you are the fertile vessel who will make that happen."

Masika's words drifted into Amy's ear and out the other. She was focused on the orange firelight dancing across Masika's breasts. How beautiful she was, glowing like a liquid ember. Cinders and ash drifted past her face, catching in her hair like stars clung to darkness.

"When did you visit Egypt?" Masika asked, sending another plume of embers into the air. She arranged a few logs atop the licking flames.

"A few weeks ago."

"Why did you go?"

"Naunet requested that I visit her," Amy lied, clenching her arms tighter in front of her. She'd gone to Egypt out of pure curiosity regarding the new developments in teaching the salt trancing art.

"Did she give you a lecture on her storm scrolls, or was she too busy bragging about her duties as midwife of the sea?"

"You have such a lovely appreciation for your sister's work," Amy teased.

Masika stood and arranged the skewers across the fire. The meat spit and sizzled as it began to cook. "Naunet and I have never seen eye-to-eye on everything, especially when it comes to the teachings of our ancestors." She sat back down and gazed into the growing flames. "I must keep searching for an answer. What relationship the fae moth might have with minca is still unclear to me. Until I discover it, I won't understand what is causing minca's disappearance."

Amy couldn't deny that Masika had taken on an enormous task most sea nymphs wouldn't dream of accepting. Her pursuit of that knowledge was what made Amy fall in love with her. She cared about the ocean's mysterious nature. The more mysterious, the more infatuated she became with understanding its dangerous secrets.

Masika continued to stoke the fire. "Do you remember when we summoned Celaeno's storm dragon into the cavern?"

"How could I forget that day?"

"Do you remember what was left in the tidal pools?"

Amy remembered the black, oily substance that clung to the water's surface.

"*Minca* was left in the water. I know it was. Even though it was dark and sickly looking, deep in my heart, I know the storm dragons have something to do with its diminishing health." Masika held out her hand, clenching her fingers into a fist. "Minca is the fabric that holds the ancestral mother salt pods together." She unraveled her fingers, curling them back and forth. "Without minca, the maternal salt pods will dissolve back into the Abyss."

"You know, I've always seen those moths as pests," Amy protested. "Only you obsessed with them. I remember when we were just starting to salt trance, and you sent the minca moths swarming by the thousands in the temples where Alexandra was busy sucking up to the Order."

"It was just a prank," Masika replied, rolling her eyes.

"The Order has started rumors about my Ocean Apothecary again," Amy said, her fists balling. She dropped her arms to her sides, wishing she could strike out at something.

"Your Ocean Apothecary has had rumors around it since you inherited it from your mother. I remember you experimenting with concocting your first salt extracts when we were children. You thought they needed some color, so you gathered a bunch of papyrus reeds and dried them in the sun and mixed the result with salt water. The entire Temple of Isis had to evacuate that afternoon."

"Hey, how was I supposed to know that papyrus reeds would smell like a dead rat in the middle of the summer?"

Masika laughed. She grabbed for the spit that sat atop the fire. Fat dripped into the flame, where it hissed and popped. "Speaking of dead rats. What creature is this meat from?"

"Ewan called it an elk?"

Masika returned the spit to its place on the fire. "You know I don't eat meat, let alone fae beasts."

"No, but the meat would do your boobs well to perk up a bit."

Masika laughed. "Maybe one day my boobs will be as big as yours."

Amy flushed. "I wish you would spend time enjoying my boobs as much as you enjoy flirting with the ocean."

Masika pointed her fire stick at the wall. "What's that over there?"

Amy walked over to the garment hanging from the wall and tugged it down. Long wooden drapings rattled against each other that hung from the animal hide shoulder straps. "Another gift from Ewan. It's a dress made of driftwood. I haven't tried it on yet."

"Is Ewan kinky?" Masika asked, her tone curious.

Amy flushed. Kinky was an understatement. "You could say he is adventurous."

Masika's eyes narrowed onto the garment. "A driftwood dress? Why would a man want to gift a woman that?"

Amy shrugged. "He's running out of creative ways to impress me."

Masika eyed the dress. "Nipple splinters, anyone?"

Amy snorted. "That's why I've refused to try it on."

While Masika burst out laughing, Amy's stomach seemed to cave in on itself. There was a gift she'd brought all the way from Egypt, a small jar Naunet wanted her to dispose of.

She walked to the pile of blankets that made up her bed bundle and crouched to the ground. She reached beneath the blankets and dipped her hand into the hole she'd dug in the ground. She withdrew the jar and stood, turning to face Masika. "I brought something back from Egypt to share with you."

"A canopic jar?" Masika asked.

"Yes."

"What's inside? Some dead guy's guts?"

Amy walked to Masika's side and handed her the jar. "Open it."

Masika tilted the lid open. "Is this what I think it is? A minca moth *queen*?"

Amy nodded.

"Where did you *find* this?"

"Naunet discovered her in the Nile when she was tending to the maternal salt bank. This fae queen emerged from Celaeno." Amy swallowed. "Her blood is toxic. She has introduced a substance into the ocean called salt venom."

Masika's expression darkened. "*Venomous* salt?"

"Try dipping into a salt trance and see for yourself."

Amy took the jar from Masika and dropped a single drop of salt venom into Masika's palm. Her pupils turned to vertical slits, snake-like. Amy braced herself for Masika's reaction. All she wanted was for that lustful desire Masika felt for the ocean to be shared with her.

Wind siphoned through the tree hollow, tearing through the fire pit. Amy backed away as the embers coiled up Masika's body, siphoning away the oxygen in the air. She coughed, choking on the lack of oxygen as Masika's heart reacted to the venom.

Masika's skin began to shimmer with an oily sheen. She held out her hands, observing her body's reaction. "This substance is wickedly powerful, far more potent than any of the maternal salts." The shimmer on her skin dulled, but the possessed glint in her eyes remained.

"Naunet said that all salt daughters of Celaeno would be tempted by it."

"And you? Do you not feel the intense desire to merge my soul with the world beneath the sea like I just experienced?"

Amy remembered the orgasmic rush of the venom. If her reaction was that, she couldn't imagine what Masika must be experiencing. "No. Apparently, the salt venom does not have the same effect on me, as it does daughters of Celaeno."

Amy remembered the lust swimming in Naunet's dark eyes, how wickedly they flickered in the dim light of her dwelling. She remembered the orgasmic rush flooding her body. "Naunet said this substance would eventually bring a plague upon Egypt. She wanted me to dispose of her."

Masika's face contorted. "In other words, she wanted you to *kill* her?"

Amy's pulse jumped into her throat. What would Masika do with the queen?

Masika set the jar down, taking Amy's hands into her own. "Amy, this queen could help give me answers as to why minca is disappearing. She is a *minca* moth queen, and she is such a treasure. How can I repay you for this?"

Amy locked her eyes with Masika's dilating ones. "By spending less time with the ocean, and more with me."

Masika's eyes became luminous pools of desire. Aroused by the salt venom or not, the substance had absolutely changed her attraction toward her.

She grabbed the strap of Amy's robe, tugging at it. With her other hand, she traced her fingers past her cheek. "You are my ocean, Amphitrite."

14

SALT MOTHER

Selia

Saturday morning came too early. Selia and Damien spent their last night before move-in day at a local bed and breakfast. Even with Damien's warm, husky body pressed up against her through the night, cold still crept into Selia's bones. It didn't help that she had a nightmare about the sonogram.

In the nightmare, the image on the monitor wasn't her baby, but a storm. A monstrous black sky danced with the violent white caps of waves. The waves synced with each other, dancing and fighting until they formed the coiling black tail of a dragon. Selia's baby was somewhere in those waves, fighting to swim through the storm. The dragon's tail rose into the sky, scales catching the yellow lightning before it came thundering down into the ocean.

Cold beads of sweat clung to Selia's chest and arms. She sat up in bed, ready to put distance between her and that stormy nightmare. Damien had already left the bedroom, probably to grab them breakfast. His watercolor set sat open on the nightstand. The glass of water sitting next to it began to ripple.

Selia's salt nodes flushed. There were secrets inside the journal that she needed to know.

She grabbed the dragon journal and propped it open. The seductive image of the woman and the dragon coiling around her body was gone.

The last time she'd seen liquid writing like this in a journal was when Amy was communicating with her. She'd lost that journal in Auntie's cottage.

Were there other books like the journal Amy had given her?

The voice created by water and air whispered past her salt nodes. *"Savor it. Surrender to it. All salt daughters of Celaeno will be tempted by it."*

Who was Celaeno? And what was this *it* that her daughters would be tempted by?

More than that, who was behind the images and writing inside the journal?

She grabbed one of Damien's paint brushes and dipped it into a glass of water on her nightstand, then lathered the bristles across a vibrant blue Damien had been using a lot lately, Egyptian blue pigment.

She ran the brush across an empty page. The parchment drank up the pigment like a thirsty animal would water.

Another sign this journal might very well be a magical artifact. Like her salt trancing talisman, it had a chalky, almost weathered appearance. Held in the right light, the oily stain at the center of the pages had a blue sheen to it.

She ran the brush across the paper, writing the question that had eaten away at her for the past day. **Who is Celaeno?**

The oil stain began to darken, and Selia's blue question was absorbed. Liquid spirals began to uncoil from the stain, singing like the voice had before. **She is your ancestor.**

Selia almost dropped the paintbrush.

"What ancestor is she of mine?" Selia said aloud as she dipped the paintbrush back into the blue pigment and wrote out her question.

The oil stain began to pulse on the paper, absorbing her words. Three times, the stain pulsed, before another liquid voice whispered past her salt nodes. **Celaeno is your salt mother.**

Selia's mouth dropped open.

Celaeno—her *salt* mother?

Knock, knock, knock!

Selia jumped as Damien came bolting into the room. "I got a call from McGill. We're good to move into our new place!"

Selia's mind blurred with questions as Damien drove the car to the lighthouse. Celaeno? Her *salt* mother? What did that mean? Did all sea nymphs have salt mothers, or were they something different from a normal mother?

She set her hands on her belly, wondering if she should tell Damien about the strange singing voice she'd been hearing. For all she knew, she was having a hormonal reaction to all the firsts over the past few days. She was becoming a first-time mother. She'd gotten engaged, and they were purchasing their first home. Perhaps it was best that she ignored the journal until she and Damien had settled in.

They made a quick stop by the grocery store, grabbing essentials for the next few days. Damien parked the car outside the lighthouse, and excitement took over. They both abandoned their groceries, taking off in a jog for the front door.

Damien grabbed her around the waist. "Wait up, my lass."

"Let me go!" Selia said, giggling as Damien's gravity won her over.

"I was trying to give you these!" he said, holding the keys out for her to take.

Selia grabbed the keys from his hand, steadying herself. She pressed the key to the lock and swung the giant red door open.

"Wait a second," Damien said, grabbing her hand and pulling her back. "It's bad luck for the wife to walk over the threshold by herself."

"But we aren't even married yet."

Damien chuckled. "Who cares? We will be soon enough." He slung his arm behind her knees, picked her up, and carried her through the doorway. Once inside, he spun her around and set her down.

"I can't believe this is ours," she said, walking over to the sofa, where she plopped down.

Damien plopped down next to her. He propped his chin on her belly, his hazel eyes meeting hers. "How did I get so lucky as to have both a fiancé *and* a baby on the way?"

Selia ran her fingers through his tousled hair. "Here I was thinking that I was the lucky one." Her stomach gave a grouchy rumble.

"Yeah, I'm there, too. What do you say we cook up some brunch?"

They got to work unpacking the groceries. Selia picked strawberries and pickles. For some strange reason, she imagined them tasting marvelous combined in a salad together.

Damien opened one of the kitchen drawers, finding a few forks, a spoon, and a very large spatula shoved in there. "Ready for a breakfast of champions?"

"I'm ready to eat anything," Selia agreed, patting her belly as another grouchy rumble erupted.

Once inside the kitchen, Damien reached into the grocery bag, and tugged out a tinfoil cylinder of cinnamon rolls. "It's nothing like Auntie's cooking, but it's better than nothing. Pre-made cinnamon rolls, here I come."

Selia preheated the oven while Damien got to work forking out the lumps of cinnamon roll onto a baking sheet.

She opened one of the cabinets, then jumped as something shiny flashed in front of her face. The item was made of brass, and it had the head of a dragon jutting from it. She reached into the cabinet, grabbing the metal item that was much heavier than it appeared. Even though it was the size of a small cantaloupe, she struggled to walk it over to the counter where Damien was unpacking the remaining groceries.

"What is that?" Damien asked, setting a bag of potatoes next to the apples on the counter.

"Did McGill say anything about the previous owners having any strange hobbies?" Selia asked as she set the strange metallic device down. She reached for the globe-like sphere at the top, touching the brass circle that intersected with another. Seven spheres total began to dance around each other. The two larger spheres on the outside had a design on them that resembled dragon scales.

"Oh, I know what this is," Damien said, grabbing the two metal spheres and spinning them. "This is some kind of nautical navigational device. Maybe it's an astrolabe?"

"It's really pretty," Selia said, setting the mysterious device on the counter. As the brass rings danced and swerved, the scales shimmered in the light.

"Some believed they didn't merely chart, but even predicted weather patterns." Damien turned on the radio. "*Batten down the hatches and get yer Christmas shopping done early! A blustery snap of a winter storm is heading our way!*"

"Speaking of weather, sounds like we're in for a big one," Damien said.

Soon, the cinnamon rolls were filling their home with the scent of Christmas. Selia took in the atmosphere. She'd spent the holidays alone in Paris where most romances blossomed. She'd never imagined that one day she would leave the Louvre, falling in love with a Scottish watercolor artist.

"Ladies get the first bite," Damien said, dropping an ooey-gooey cinnamon roll onto Selia's plate.

She bit into her breakfast. The sugar, cinnamon, and pastry erupted over her tongue.

He dropped a second cinnamon roll onto her plate.

"I'm haff-way dwwun!" she said, laughing through her second bite.

"You're eating for two now," he said, downing his in three bites. "How do you like your cinnamon rolls?"

Warm and buttery like you, she wanted to say. Instead, she shoved the second roll into her mouth.

They shared a glass of decaf coffee, which Selia was starting to get used to. Since she'd discovered her pregnancy in early September, she'd started weaning herself off caffeine, which Damien had given up with her.

He grabbed her hand and brought her fingers to his lips. "Let me help you with that," he said, licking the frosting off her.

"You are such a tease," she said, pulling her finger out of his mouth.

"Oh, I'm just getting warmed up. Now that we have our own place, you can expect a lot more of that to come."

Selia flushed. She was going to have to get used to this new 'nesting' phase in her relationship with Damien. His sexual appetite was something she was only now getting used to.

Damien waggled his eyebrows at her. "What ever happened to that kinky journal you bought?"

Selia reached into her purse and tugged it out.

Damien grabbed it. "Let's see where we left off." He flipped through the pages, brows drawing up. "Did you go and rip that naughty image out?"

Selia bit her tongue. Should she tell him about the strange *Ceee-laaaaaeeeenooooooo* sound she'd been experiencing? Or the writing? "I did not. There's something magical about this journal."

Damien closed the journal. "Didn't Amy give you something like this before? The one with all the salt trancing lessons that randomly showed up in it?"

"She did. However, I misplaced it."

Damien set his hands on the counter. "We came all the way to Scotland to track down that fae treasure, and she just abandons you with her salt trancing lessons? Didn't she promise to teach you about the purpose and everything behind the fourth principle?"

Selia shrugged. "Maybe she up and forgot her promise. Apparently, Amy has just as bad of a memory as my own."

"But why would she jump ship with the fae queen and completely stop talking to you?"

Selia thought back to when she and Damien had discovered the shady activity going on at the Rusty Selkie. Alex's henchman, Balfour, brought Alex the vault with the fae queen locked inside. Alex had said something that still stuck in her mind, *"Minca's disappearance has made this treasure even more dangerous."*

She turned the radio volume down. "I have no idea. I honestly feel a little put out by it."

"What was the last thing you remember discussing with Amy before she left?"

"She mentioned a friend." Selia set her hand on her chest. "Amy said that she could feel her friend's *pulse* when she was near me."

Her phone chimed. Pixie had texted her.

> My plants are already responding to your magical watering! I can't thank you enough!

"Looks like Pixie is happy with my watering services," Selia said, setting her phone back down.

"I'm glad you have another girlfriend in town. My sister can get a bit pushy. Don't be afraid to establish boundaries with her early on, or she's sure to take advantage of you."

"Advantage of… as in?"

"Gwen's always wanted a sister. Don't get me wrong. We are very close, being the only siblings. But she's very… female… if that makes any sense."

Selia laughed. "What, did you think you wouldn't be protective of her when she told you about her marital issues?"

"Believe me, I've been running through my head how I'm going to approach Sean."

Selia grabbed their plates and walked over to the sink. "I've wanted another woman to talk to about my pregnancy. Last night, I was going to tell her, then with the phone call and her own personal life, I decided maybe I should hold off on telling her about our little one."

Damien came up behind her, looping his arms through hers. He pressed his face to her neck, planting a kiss behind her ear. "Why are we keeping our baby a secret from her anyway? Who cares? It's not like she has any say on how quickly we start our family." His hands dipped lower. "I say we head back to our bedroom and christen this place before we do any more unpacking…"

A horn beeped twice outside.

"Oh, lookie who decided to show up ahead of schedule," Damien growled.

A bright red truck sat parked outside. Gwen emerged from the passenger side, and a man wearing a plaid shirt, jeans, and boots hopped out of the driver's seat.

Damien didn't unravel his arms from Selia's belly, gripping her tighter instead. "Looks like cheater boy decided to come, too," he said, his chest hardening against Selia's back.

"Let's not get too huffy now. If they are together, it's a good sign," Selia said, assuming the best. She unraveled herself from Damien's embrace and made her way to the front door.

She opened it, finding that Gwen was already standing there, smiling over a huge cardboard box bulging full of tinsel and Christmas ornaments.

"Surprise! I brought you some house-warming gifts. I hope you don't mind."

"Not at all!" Selia said, stepping aside to let her soon-to-be sister-in-law inside.

Sean was making his way toward the door with the item he'd unloaded from the truck. Something large was wrapped in a blanket, which he drug by a rope across the ground. In his other arm he held what appeared to be a wooden log.

Thunk!

Damien bent down, and picked up a log with the head of a dragon carved out of the end. "What's this beastly thing?"

"Gwen insisted you have one of her special dragon Yule logs. Spits fire in every direction when you toss a match on it." Sean's piercing blue eyes moved from Selia to Damien. "King D., where do you want it?"

Damien's chest puffed. He positioned himself between his sister and Sean. "Right here is fine," he grumbled, setting the log on the counter.

"King D., huh?" Selia said.

Damien shrugged. "Ignore it."

"Oh, there is quite the story behind how my brother got that nickname."

"I guess it's better than Captain Rusty Dicks," Selia teased.

"Captain *what*?" Gwen boasted.

"*Oi*, help me with the tree, would you, love?" Sean said as he wrestled a tree out from beneath the blanket.

"I love it!" Selia squealed. Even with all the needles shedding on the floor, she'd never had a real Christmas tree before.

Gwen grabbed her husband's arm and turned him to face her. "Selia? This is my husband, Sean."

Sean nodded, raking his hand past his short dark hair. "Lovely to meet you. You're becoming family just in time for the holidays."

Gwen rolled up her sleeves, revealing two coiling black dragon tattoos interwoven with Celtic knot patterns on each of her arms.

"My sister and I are opposite when it comes to artistic expression," Damien said.

"Oh, hush. Try majoring in Celtic literature and folklore studies without having a cool tattoo. You wouldn't survive." Gwen grabbed the cardboard box bulging with clothes. "Will you show me where I can put this extra clothing?"

Selia led the way down the hall. Once out of earshot, Gwen was quick to open her mouth. "I absolutely adore this new place! I can tell you are going to turn it into a real home. As long as you don't have bats, I'm sold."

Selia slowed her pace. Speaking of bats. She'd not seen Peppercorn for almost twenty-four hours.

She dipped into the hallway. "How are you and Sean doing?"

Gwen stopped in front of her, repositioning the box. "Better. He and I had a heart-to-heart about what's been really bothering us. We bickered the entire drive over here. The annual Malloch winter solstice gathering is in a few days. There is absolutely no way the two of us can get our kitchen prepped by then to host it."

"A winter solstice gathering?" Selia asked.

"Yes, it's a huge Malloch clan tradition when all thirty-nine aunts, uncles, and cousins get together and have a banger of a time." One of her finely-sculpted eyebrows arched into her hair. "Damien didn't tell you about it?"

Before Selia could reply, Gwen darted into the small bedroom. "Oh my, this room will make a lovely nursery!"

"You read my mind," Selia said, forcing herself not to set her hands on her belly. Her center seemed to be the place her hands wanted to go, even when she wasn't thinking about it.

Gwen set the box on the dresser and undid the flap. "I have some sweaters in here you can have. Wool is my go-to once the Scottish winters blow in."

"Thank you. This is so incredibly kind," Selia said.

Gwen gave her a wary glance. "Look, I know I gave off a bad first impression last night, but I promise our family isn't all crazy. I've just had a hoot of a time this holiday season."

Selia's heart warmed. "It's all right. I know you are stressed, and I'd love to find a way to help." She led the way back to the living room, where Damien and Sean were each sharing a glass of *Dragon's Blood*.

Gwen bustled up to her brother, holding her arms out wide. "I don't know. With all this space? You could easily get a hundred people in here. This would be an absolutely magical place to have a solstice gathering."

"Whoa, whoa, whoa. Before you go volunteering our home for the gathering, you need to speak with the queen of the castle." His eyes dipped to Selia.

Selia clapped her hands together. "I have a great idea. Why don't Damien and I host for the winter solstice gathering?"

Gwen grabbed her shoulders. "You read my mind!"

One look at Gwen's face told Selia she'd made the right decision, even if it meant not having the slightest idea what to expect.

15

SELIA'S SALT STASH

Amy

Amy shifted in her bed bundle, suddenly stirred from her slumber. The sun hadn't come up the hill, and yet, someone was rummaging through the greenhouse. One of Pixie's shop workers was busy shuffling a bag of coffee beans down from the shelf, and a couple of pre-packaged scones fell.

Amy grabbed one of the pastries and ripped open the package. While she'd rather not stay inside a greenhouse all day stuffing her face full of prepackaged sweets, she still had more memories of her own to refresh.

Masika had taken the fae queen. What she would do next with her was still a mystery. Memories of Selia, however, were beginning to flow out of her subconscious.

Gulping down the pastry, she shimmied her way back to her hiding spot where the fae moth slept. She peered over the pot where the queen was still resting—her metamorphosis for her maternal flight delayed for hopefully another day.

"Please show me more of that blue memory," Amy said, whispering to the fae queen, and the boundaries of time crystallized for her once again.

Amy made her way up the Nile River toward the Temple of Isis, where Naunet was sure to be sorting through her storm scrolls. It had been well over a decade since Amy last visited Masika's sister. During their last encounter, Amy had lied to Naunet, telling her that she'd disposed of the fae queen. Instead, Masika had taken the canopic jar and had attempted to rehabilitate her.

The queen remained in a deep sleep, similar to hibernation. Masika had yet to awaken her. When she did, Masika planned to work with the queen, attempting to gather information from her about minca. The fae queen was a minca moth, after all. Masika was sure that she was the key to understanding the dwindling health with the maternal salt pods.

Sand spread through Amy's toes as she ascended the bank. She had come to Egypt to find Selia—the Blind Moon—a sea nymph who had an immunity to this illness born out of the maternal salt pods, which, if not treated, would eventually sterilize the ocean. Selia was the antidote to the wicked substance the fae queen had created.

Amy had promised Naunet that she would return to Egypt when Selia had reached the age where she could begin salt trancing. She'd volunteered to assist Selia with her coming-of-age ritual known as salt stashing. The ancient ritual involved a sea nymph bonding with a storm dragon.

In Amy and Masika's youth, Poseidon had been the only storm dragon to bond with. With his death, and the sinking of the great city of Atlantis, other storm dragons were slowly regaining their territories protecting the maternal salt pods. But their names—along with their powers over the weather—were still very much a mystery. Amy didn't know if the same seven storm bonds formed like they had for their ancestors. Naunet had even mentioned that storm bonds might become a thing of the past, if the problem with minca was not remedied.

Movement down by the water caught Amy's eye. A young sea nymph was crouched on the maternal salt bank, running her hand across the water's surface. She wore a linen dress while her long dark hair caught rays of the sunlight. Like Amy, she was also barefoot.

The sea nymph stood, turning her gaze against the warm haze brought inland with the annual swarm of the male minca moths. She walked toward Amy, a smile dimpling on her youthful face. A basket was tucked under her arm, one that had papyrus reeds in it. By the look of her salt nodes, she was well into puberty. Salt trancing would allow her to sync her own fertility cycles with the cycles of the sea.

She stopped a few paces away from Amy, squinting into the sun. "Hello, my name is Selia. Can I help you?"

Amy's breath caught. The maternal salts glistening behind her seemed to brighten at her voice. She glanced in the basket tucked under Selia's arm. *Another* sign of maturity. Selia was gathering her first samples of minca moth salt chrysalises deposited along the riverbank. "I see you have quite the collection," Amy said.

Selia grinned. "I've just started collecting for my first salt stash. I'm sorry, what is your name?"

Amy flushed. If only this moon daughter of Celaeno knew how much she already knew about her. "My name is Amphitrite."

"Oh, you must be the friend Mother mentioned, who has her own Ocean Apothecary!"

Amy's breath caught. "*Mother?*"

"You know my mother, Naunet, right?"

Amy bit her tongue. What else had Naunet not told Selia about her unique birth circumstance? Did she know that she was, in fact, Celaeno's *moon* child? "Yes, I do know your mother. And yes, it is true about me having an Ocean Apothecary. Where is Naunet, anyway?"

Selia sighed. "She has been working late at the Temple of Isis. I rarely see her."

Amy tucked herself beneath the papyrus, shading herself from the sun. "I'm sure you've heard all of the rumors the Order is spreading about my Apothecary being contaminated?"

Selia gave her a shy smile as she readjusted the basket under her arm. "I don't believe the Order. They've started spreading all kinds of nonsense across Egypt."

Amy smiled. She liked this moon child. She propped her hands on her hips, kneading the hot sand with her heels. "I'll tell you more secrets if you share what the Order is currently teaching you about the art. Deal?"

Selia looked away.

"You *are* practicing the art of salt trancing, right?"

"No, I am not."

"But you are clearly of the right age. Why are you not practicing?"

"I've asked Mother, and she wants me to wait another year."

"That's ridiculous!"

"I agree with her."

Amy threw out her hands. "I don't understand."

Selia set her hand on her chest. "Sea nymphs with maternal salts originating from Celaeno are treated differently than others."

"How different?"

Selia's eyes dipped again. "Considering I'm the only one in my class who is one of Celaeno's salt daughters." She set her hand on her heart. "My pulse is different from the others."

Amy remembered Naunet mentioning the *pulse test* sea nymphs would need to undergo when they first reported to the temples. But how was holding Selia back another year preventing her from encountering the inevitable? That she was *brilliantly* different from other sea nymphs her age?

"Selia, your ancestors never would have treated you this way. Regardless of where your maternal salts originate, every sea nymph is born with the right to learn and practice the art properly."

"What good are my ancestors' opinions of me? They're dead!"

Amy hiked her head back and laughed. "Do not mock them!" She set her hand on Selia's shoulder. "Let's have a little talk about the maternal salts, shall we?"

Selia smiled, one that warmed Amy's heart.

Amy led the way back to Naunet's dwelling. When she and Selia walked inside, she found the space empty. Naunet's storm scrolls must all be at the temple, for none were present on the shelf in the corner.

Selia set her basket of sodden salt chrysalises down next to Naunet's minca propagations. Even her samples of minca appeared to be dwindling. They no longer had the robust, earthy aroma, nor the vibrant blue color.

Amy clapped her hands together. "Well then, what would you like to know about first? How storm bonds are formed, or should we discuss the maternal salts?"

Selia rounded on her, eyes widening. Her mouth opened and closed a few times before a weak string of words came pouring out. "Can I ask you a personal question first?"

Amy lowered her hands to her sides. "Sure?"

"Which storm dragon did you bond with?"

"The only mature storm dragon around in my youth was Poseidon, so all sea nymphs your age at that time bonded with him."

"Does bonding hurt?"

"No. Think of the event as a celebration of your connection with the sea. Every bond is unique." Amy remembered how Naunet's mother, Pherusa, often hosted lavish parties in Atlantis, where Poseidon was considered a guest of honor. His storm bonds were so abundant, he often handed them out like candy. Amy, along with Masika, had both received dresses made out of scales from his tail. Shortly after they had adorned themselves with his offerings, their storm bonds developed. At the time, nobody knew the issues that he and Isis were having, let alone, the problems their powerful bond would create for the city.

"What is your storm bond?" Selia asked.

"My talents have always been crystalline in nature."

"A *crystal* bond?"

Amy flexed her fingers. "Manipulating salt crystals to create salt extracts will always be my specialty."

Selia beamed. "At least I know one of the seven bonds now."

"Do you not know the names of the seven storm bonds?"

"The Order won't share them with us. They say it best to have the storm dragon we bond with reveal our bonds individually."

Amy scoffed. "Wow, that's incredibly inconsiderate of the Order keeping you and your peers in the dark. In my youth, we would always tease one another about which bond we—"

"—That's not the only personal question I wanted to ask," Selia said, cutting her off. Her eyes dipped, then found her gaze again. She grabbed one of the minca propagations and began to fiddle with it. "Have you mated with a man before?"

Amy's body flushed. Had Naunet not given her the *fertility* talk yet? "Why do you ask?"

"In the temples, they are saying that if we don't practice the art of salt trance by a certain age, we will be forced to mate with a man if we want to bear a daughter one day, regardless of what fertility cycle we are in."

Amy shook her head. "The Order is lying to you. Your fertility cycle is your own to regulate, which salt trancing is used for. You have a choice in how you wish to become pregnant. I know that mating with men rarely produces children. He would need to be a king among his people to bear a sea nymph offspring."

Selia's eyes widened. "A king, huh? Do you know any kings?"

Heat ripped up Amy's neck as Ewan's muscular torso glinting in the firelight came thundering into her mind. "Last I heard, most of the good kings sank with Atlantis. However—I have known a few kings in my time."

Selia grinned, a new appreciation glinting in her eyes.

"The maternal salts are our best option for producing offspring. Their health, and the production of minca moth queens, is vital to our reproductive success. Regardless of what fertility cycle we are in, it is your *choice* whether you want to bear a daughter. Salt trancing will help you regulate your cycle."

Selia sighed. "Good, because I don't see myself mating with a man any time soon. If you did want a daughter, what would your choice be? To rely on the maternal salts, or mate with a king?"

Amy shrugged. "That would depend on what mood I was in."

Selia nodded, seeming to sense Amy had given her enough of a fertility talk for the day.

Amy clasped her hands together. "I must ask you a personal question. Has your mother ever mentioned the health of Celaeno's salt pod? That during her last salt cycle, she gave birth to something out of the ordinary?"

Selia searched her face. "No, mother has not mentioned anything like this at all."

Amy scanned Naunet's lunar altar. She did not see any canopic jars that resembled the one she'd given to Masika. Maybe the presence of salt venom was not as common now. Or maybe she'd stopped collecting it.

One of Naunet's storm scrolls that lay open on her table. The hair on the back of Amy's neck stood on end. The symbols on the scroll were indicating something she'd not seen in Naunet's inscriptions before.

"She marked this the other night. I don't know what it means," Selia said. "The two descriptions I can make from the symbols are *dragon* and *land*."

Amy knew what Naunet had written on the papyrus. Celaeno's storm dragon would be arriving on land within the next moon cycle.

"I must go. I will return. When I do, I want you to be ready to show me where this nest of male minca moths is in the temple. We are going to make sure you are prepared for your first salt stash when the time comes."

Selia nodded, hope and fire in her blue eyes. The same fire Masika had when she discussed minca's disappearance.

16

FERTILITY FOLKTALES

Selia

As soon as Selia unpacked the kitchen supplies Gwen had gifted them, her phone chimed. Gwen's icon of a flaming red dragon appeared on the screen.

> Ladies Night! The men can drink while the women play. Come over for dinner. I want to thank you for hosting the solstice gathering and share my special folktale collection with you!

Selia looked up from her phone, spotting Damien wrestling with one of the droopy branches on their Christmas tree. "Gwen texted me. She wants to thank me for agreeing to host the winter solstice gathering by having us over for dinner."

Damien shook his head. "I still can't believe she came barging in here and volunteered our new home for the gathering. My sister has no tact!"

You got a lumpy poooootatooooo in your stocking!

Selia jumped as Damien removed his foot from one of the screaming ornaments.

He walked over to her, and placed both of his arms around her waist. "I was hoping we could retire early tonight. What do you say we light that Yule log and shack up for the night?"

Selia grabbed her fiancé's wandering hand. "I'm sure we will light the hearth before long." She gave their barren cabinets a glance. "Besides, I wouldn't mind eating something more substantial than cereal for dinner."

A grunt escaped him. "All right. But we aren't staying for long."

Selia unraveled herself from Damien's arms, spinning to face him. She pressed her lips to his. "I need to freshen up first."

Damien waggled his eyebrows at her. "Sounds like a shower date."

Selia left the kitchen, heading into their bedroom. The one thing she didn't get a good look at was the ensuite. The shower was massive, definitely updated from the rest of the building. A large sliding glass door framed the space, which could easily accompany two adults.

The images and sounds from her nightmare flashed before her. She wanted to withdraw. Worry crept in, crippling her thoughts to the worst-case scenario.

What if her baby wasn't healthy? What if something was wrong with her pulse?

She turned on the tap, shed her clothing, then jumped in. Her hair and body were soon soaked.

The door opened. Damien had already shed his clothing and walked in. He brushed up behind her, the lower part of his body hardening. "Screw the fireplace. My sister can wait."

"How did I know you would follow me?" Selia teased. She spun around and wrapped her arms around his neck.

"Hey, look at me," he said as his hands clasped around her back. "I can tell you're worried about the baby."

"Worried is an understatement."

"Then let me take it from you," Damien whispered. He pressed his lips to hers as he moved under the tap, kissing her tenderly. Water poured over them soaking them both.

His taste, a mixture of tea and cinnamon, washed over her.

"Is the water cold for you?" he asked, pulling away.

"I can fix that." Selia said, suddenly breathless from his kiss. She eyed him, taking in his dripping body—the beautiful father of her daughter. All it took was indulging in him to make her heart beat fast enough to warm the water to the perfect temperature.

Selia sat on the tile ledge in the shower as Damien draped his watery kisses across her shoulders. He kissed her breasts, then her navel, lowering himself to the ground. He worked his mouth between her legs, both the water and his tongue pleasing her as he explored.

She grabbed a handful of his thick curling hair, guiding him where she wanted his tongue to go. He circled his tongue around her clit, licking and sucking until she was swollen. As a wave of pleasure nearly peaked, Damien pulled away.

He looped his arm around her waist and helped her to her feet. His hands dropped to her hips, and he turned her away from him. He lowered his mouth to the back of her neck, brushing his stubble past the cusp of her ear. "Put your hands on the wall, love."

Selia shivered from the desire in his voice. She set her hands on the steaming tile, bracing herself for his entry. For one reason or another, they'd discovered intercourse in the shower proved the most comfortable. She had a feeling they would both be spending a lot more time beneath the steaming tap together.

A little past seven, the two got into the car and drove up the road. Gwen's house was ten minutes, at most, away from the lighthouse.

Damien pulled the car into Gwen's driveway, parking behind the red pickup truck. He opened the door, setting his arm on the frame, preventing her from escaping. "Why are we here and not ruining the bed sheets in our new home?"

"We just ruined the shower," Selia said.

"I was only warming up," he said, pressing his body against her. "I want you to know I'm here for you, no matter what." He took her hands into his. "Selia, you and our baby have my whole heart."

"I just want to know she's healthy. I'm so scared."

"It's okay to be afraid. You have every right to be. But I can tell you something. It's not worth being afraid alone. I spent ten years doing that."

His eyes caught the orange glow of Gwen's front porch light. He had so much faith, even after what he had lost.

She wrapped her arms around him, tugging him close. The gemstone on her ring reflected the light of the first stars peeking out from above. She breathed in his clean scent. "I'm so glad I'm not alone in this."

The front door flung open. Gwen's flamboyant silhouette sprung out onto the front porch. "There are my guests! I was wondering when you might arrive!"

Damien released Selia, turning around to face his sister. "I have a feeling we're in for an exciting evening of entertainment."

They walked up to the front porch and stopped before Gwen.

"Welcome to an evening full of folktales and festivities!" Gwen cried, holding her arms out to her side. She spun in a circle, displaying her exuberant costume. A wreath of twigs sat atop her head, each shimmering with silver and gold tinsel. She wore a loose-fitting red garment, more a robe than a dress. The silky fabric had the pattern of a tree with long, Celtic knot patterns weaving up the back.

"Well, now, don't I feel under-dressed for the occasion," Damien said, shooting his sister a wary glance.

Gwen waved her hand. "Just because you're hosting the winter solstice gathering doesn't mean I'm not going to go all out and decorate for it." She draped her arm behind her, sending her silk robe swaying. "Come and join in on the pre-solstice festivities!"

They both walked into Gwen's home. Selia stopped in the foyer, where Gwen took hers and Damien's jackets. The entire vibe of Gwen's home had changed. The scent of cloves and pine filled the air. Peering into the living room convinced Selia that Gwen's version of going all out was an understatement. Framing the windows were long strings of red and gold garland that glinted in the dim yellow light. Spruce branches draped over one another with candles centered in the middle.

Gwen came up behind them, clapping her hands on their shoulders. "Don't be shy, come in!" She pushed them forward.

Selia walked into the living room. A Yule log burned in the fireplace, spitting and crackling just like Sean said it would.

Sean came into the room, rolling his eyes. "Gwen has a flair for the dramatic when it comes to the ancient Celts." He hiked his head to the left. "Come on, King D. Let's have a drink while the ladies share their sisterly stories with one another."

Damien grazed Selia's cheek with a kiss. "Good luck." He took off toward the kitchen after Sean, leaving Selia face-to-face with his spitfire of a sister.

Gwen handed Selia one of the robes she was wearing. She tugged it over her shoulders, loving the silky texture of the fabric.

"You will be lady blue, and I will be lady red. How does that sound?"

"Absolutely lovely," Selia said, already loving the festive vibe Gwen was putting off. Gwen's fiery charisma reminded her of Amy in so many ways. And just like Amy, Gwen was an enthusiastic drama queen.

Gwen coiled her fingers. "Welcome to the dragon's lair, where a coven of women share the secrets of their kin with one another."

"I love the dragon theme you have going on," Selia said, noting the rather large overhanging tapestry hanging behind their Christmas tree. Their tree, too, was a Scotch pine, which was so decked out in decorations, the branches appeared deformed. Tinsel and ornaments wrapped around the tree, which Selia assumed was supposed to mimic the coiling body of a dragon. Perched at the top wasn't a star, but a vibrant set of wings arched behind a snarling dragon head.

Gwen threw her hand out, coiling her fingers toward an assortment of bags on the table. "Have a seat and pick your tea."

Selia sat down on the loveseat by the fire. A stack of dragon teacups sat next to a tea kettle on the coffee table. She heaved a sigh of relief. Thankfully, there were only tea options. No alcohol.

She grabbed a bag of sensual orange zest and set it in her dragon teacup, which had a more Asian flair to the design. The dragons on these teacups were all serpentine in shape, their bodies long and slender.

Gwen sat next to her and divvied up the hot water, pouring the steaming liquid into both of their cups. Her setup reminded Selia of Amy's love of all things worth celebrating.

Speaking of Amy.

"Whatever happened with the woman down by the boatyard you were worried about?" Selia asked as she tugged on her tea bag, allowing the tea to steep.

"Who mentioned her to you?" Gwen asked, her expression darkening.

"Damien did. Do you know if she had flaming red hair and dazzling green eyes?"

"I have not seen her in person. But as far as I know, she's disappeared for now." Gwen tossed up her hand. "I'm not about to allow rumors of this mystery woman to take over what I have to share with you this evening."

"What did you want to share with me, anyway?"

Gwen's hazel eyes lit up. "Stories of our kin. Our clan. Our *ancestry*."

Selia froze. She didn't have stories about her family, siblings. Nothing of the like. She only had a memory of the past decade of her life.

"Now that you are marrying into Clan Malloch, I wanted to share a special tale with you. A family tree is at the center of this tale, one that spans back long ago to Clan Malloch's ancestors—the Sgàthan Clan."

Sean dipped his head into the room. "Oh no, she's sharing *those* folk-tale with you. The baby-making ones."

"Be gone!" Gwen cried, tossing her hands at her husband as he disappeared back into the kitchen. "These folktales are only meant for the eyes of women." She bounded up from the sofa, leaving Selia to gaze into the crackling fire. The dragon Yule log crackled, casting the cozy little room in a warm orange light. Selia squinted at the flames, swearing she saw a little dragon scurry across the log.

Gwen returned to the room carrying a wooden box. She sat next to Selia, placing the box on the table in front of them. A gorgeous Celtic knot pattern of a gold-leafed stag was engraved in the wood. A title was written across the box, as equally golden and framed by the stag's mighty antlers.

Reflections: A Tale of Salt, Storms, & Starlight

Selia was familiar with the *Reflection* folktales Damien had shared with her a few months prior. The one titled *Strands of Moonlight* had illustrated the story between a man and a selkie—both of whom were lost in one way or another. In the end, it was that folktale that had brought them both together.

Gwen tipped the lid of the box open. There was no book like Selia expected. Tucked inside of the box was a collection of rolled parchment.

"Scrolls?" Selia asked.

Gwen's face flickered with firelight. "Go on. Open one."

Selia reached into the box and grabbed one of the scrolls with a blue smudge at the base. She worked her fingers over the parchment, which seemed too rough to be normal parchment. The fibers were thick and woven, almost too dense. The texture reminded her of the strange journal she'd discovered in Gwen's bookstore.

"Who made these scrolls?" Selia asked, perplexed by the inscriptions on them. The symbols seemed ancient, a cross between Celtic and Egyptian.

"That, I do not know. However, someone attempted to translate the language into this." Gwen reached into the box, tugging out a piece of paper. She cleared her throat and read aloud. "Two selkies set out to restore fertility to the ocean long ago. They chanted an ancient mantra, praying to the ancient womb that would grant their wish." Gwen set the paper down and took one of the scrolls from Selia. She unraveled it on the coffee table, held her hands out wide, and said. "Great Abyss, breathe with me. We remember the salt that originates from your womb of the sea. Dragons of old, for which we long. Our ancestor have kept your ancient songs. Salt, storms, and starlight, of which we sing. Your light we find in the crown of a king."

"Did they summon the Abyss?"

Gwen shook her head, a look of whimsy glinting in her eyes. "No. Instead, it was a dragon they summoned." She splayed her fingers, maneuvering her hands from side-to-side. "This dragon was sick with something, a warning for a great illness that would befall the sea if they did not mend the illness. He was a dragon like none other. This dragon did not spit fire, nor did he have wings. His tail alone was known to create the violent storms that reined the seas."

Gwen's lips moved slowly as the words, "*He spoke the language of storms,*" rolled off her tongue.

The Yule log in the hearth spit and crackled, sending embers onto the rug. Selia jumped, standing as a long thundering song bellowed through her salt nodes.

Ceeeelaaaaaeeeeennooooooooo...

Gwen's hand came to Selia's arm. "Dear, are you all right?"

"I'm fine," Selia lied. "Will you excuse me? I need some fresh air."

"Sure."

Selia left the living room and found the back door. She walked out of it, spotting Gwen's two Irish setters playing outside. The one she remembered as Scales looked up at her, questions in his dark, playful eyes.

She walked into the yard and rested her hand on one of the pine trees as a wave of nausea washed over her. She dug her fingers into the scaly bark, wondering if she had lost her sanity.

The folktale Gwen shared with her depicted *two* selkies. The story had an uncanny resemblance to what Amy had shared with her about her friend. Together, they'd set out to restore the fertility of the sea. What if the other selkie was in fact, Sika?

17

EWAN

Amy

Amy's feet gripped moss-covered stones as she walked farther into the trees. Her feet always needed time to adjust to the rocky terrain when she traveled back to Winter Forest. A painful blister had formed on her heel, preventing her from darting up and down the path like she enjoyed. The earth was solid and sturdy, nothing like the sandy banks along the Nile.

Amy had traveled back to Winter Forest, still needing to put a piece of her plan into action for Selia's salt stashing ritual. The only storm dragon she was aware of was rumored to be the ex-guardian of Celaeno. She and Masika had summoned a storm dragon only a few years ago.

If she could confirm the storm dragon living on this island was the same beast that she and Masika had summoned, she might be able to introduce Selia to him. Their bond could be the cure for this wicked substance called salt venom.

She made her way down the hill, stopping at her hollow. Masika was still gone, probably working to rehabilitate the fae queen. Since she'd given her the creature, Masika had spent many days and nights away from their home. So many, that Amy wondered, at times, if she would return.

Her mouth was parched. She also wanted to tend to the blister on her foot. She grabbed her water gourd hanging from a tree branch and made her way down to the stream. She found a fork in the path, paralleling the stream as it flowed downhill. Leaves drifted in the water. Most of the foliage had turned yellow and red. The red giants, however, kept their deep green needles year-round. Winter would soon be upon them, covering their branches in snow.

She reached a clearing where the stream emptied into a large flowing river. The sound of thundering water echoed between the trees, along with the voices of men. Two huntsmen were resting on the rocks by the river, filling their water gourds. Both were dressed in animal hide tunics with white fur jutting from the arms. Each had a quiver of arrows slung across his back, along with a bow.

Amy dipped behind a tree to eavesdrop on them.

"The two selkies have lived here a while. What are they here for?" one of the men asked.

"No idea. They keep to themselves. I'm pretty sure they are lovers," his buddy replied.

"Are you sure they don't want something to do with him?"

Amy's ears perked. Who was this *him* they were discussing?

"He's Poseidon's son, isn't he? Who is to say he won't try and destroy what we rebuild on this island one day?"

Amy's body went cold. Poseidon's son was living in Winter Forest?

The men slung their water gourds onto their backs, each tied off with a cord. "Winter is fast approaching. Who knows if he will survive another here with us." They left the river, taking off up the trail toward their base camp. It wouldn't be long before they were heading up into the highlands, tracking the fae beasts who migrated through every winter.

Amy almost forgot how thirsty she was. Her heartbeat was racing. Celaeno's storm dragon *was* living on this island, displaced just like Naunet said, according to her storm scroll readings. According to the huntsmen, he didn't live far from this stream.

She dipped down to the river. The water was high for this time of year. Even with late autumn, there was still plenty of snow melt flowing in the river from the prior winter. Not wanting to get her robe wet, she tugged it off, exposing her leg above the knee. That annoying blister on her foot was beginning to swell, and she desperately wanted to wash it.

The second her foot hit the icy water, the blister began to numb. She dug out one of her salt extracts and tipped the bottle to the water. The river hissed and bubbled as the salt worked its magic.

She tugged her foot out of the water, finding the blister was gone.

"Well, look who the tide brought in."

Amy turned, finding a man standing behind her.

He was dressed like the others that had stopped before, although this man appeared much older. His tunic, too, was made of animal hide. A quiver was strung upon his back. His hair was long and wiry and reddish-brown with grey streaking behind his ears. It was braided and tied up on the back of his scalp.

He tilted his head to the side. "A selkie sitting by the river all alone, bathing her skin?"

"I was just leaving," she said, straightening and reaching for her robe.

"Wait a while. I wasn't trying to rush you," he said, closing the space between them.

His hand fell to his side, withdrawing something sharp from his belt. Amy gulped. Being at the end of a flint dagger was not how she wanted to be welcomed back north.

"I hear selkies have some of the most beautiful skin around," he said, tipping the blade to her cloak. "Why don't you stay a while and give me a show?"

"Fergus, she said she was leaving."

Amy shivered in the huskiness of the male voice descending upon them.

Fergus turned, his head whipping around.

Nobody stood behind them. Trees shifted and water trickled over river stones.

Thud!

Something heavy muffled against the earth behind her.

Amy turned, finding no man. Only two hazel eyes peeking out from the trees—eyes with greens that were dangerously deep.

The huntsman pocketed his flint and straightened himself. "Ewan, I was only having some fu—"

Fwip!

Fergus jerked to the side as a stone flew for his head. He landed on the ground, cowering. "I didn't mean any harm!"

The trees moved as Ewan emerged. With every step he took down to the riverbank, Amy felt a little smaller. He moved with stealth-like grace, not making a sound.

A hand bigger than Amy's head gripped the neck of Fergus's cloak. He brought him to his face, grimacing. "Touch a single hair on her head, and I'll have you skinned like the beast I'm bringing back to camp."

With a flick of his wrist, Ewan sent Fergus tumbling back to the ground. Fergus gathered himself, panting. Not saying a word, he turned on his heel and retreated back into the forest, leaving Amy face-to-face with the incredibly large and handsome lead huntsman of the Sgàthan clan.

Ewan's thick locks of auburn hair tapered down his muscular shoulders. His musk was that of pine, earth, and wood. His deep-set hazel eyes with dangerous shades of viridian dancing within them—darker greens only found in the deepest places of the forest.

"It is not wise for a woman to expose her skin to men who have not had the company of a woman for almost half of the year," Ewan said, his tone cautious, yet his broad cheeks were dimpling.

Amy was out of breath, still. She didn't want to admit that part of her breathlessness was due to Ewan rescuing her.

He held out his wide hand, which Amy took. Her fingers barely slipped past his palm as he helped her to her feet.

"Why do you men call us selkies, anyway?" Amy asked, trying to remember the word Masika also used to describe a sea nymph.

Ewan chuckled. "Seal women. Time spent in isolation this far north make men not only lonely, but they begin to hallucinate. They see the seals sunning themselves on the rocks as beautiful women. Seals are thus, not a beast that we hunt."

"Speaking of hunts, I've been toying with the idea of accompanying you on one of your winter adventures into the forest."

Ewan's thick brows lifted. His beard stretched as a grin dimpled his cheeks. He slapped her on the butt. "My goddess, Amphitrite, how I thought you would never ask! I would adore having my prized selkie at my side when we embark on our trek to the sacred mountain."

Amy adored Ewan's flirtatious, over-the-top nature. While he was incredibly full of himself, his intentions were always to please those around him. Kingly in his might, he was absolutely the son of Atlantean kings in his birthright.

His hand splayed against her back as he embraced her. He cocked his head to the side, the viridian in his eyes becoming greener by the second. "Yule is upon us. Will you join me in my dwelling tonight? I promise to keep you warm."

His voice dipped as his eyelids hooded.

Amy's body heated. While she had dabbled in the art of sexual intercourse with this gallant huntsman, she wasn't a huge fan. She'd told Selia the truth when she'd asked her about her fertility cycle preference. There was also the fact that Ewan was massive, which made the sexual act much more interesting. Son of Atlantean kings or not, it shouldn't be allowed for a man be that well-endowed.

Amy unraveled his muscular arm from her waist, turning her attention to the crimson blood stain on his neck. "I will see about tonight. What have you done to yourself?"

He wiped his hand past his neck, bringing the blood to his palm. His gaze dropped to the body of a creature laying on the ground. "I have brought you a gift, dearest."

She walked over to his kill. The beast's neck was arched back at an awkward angle. Its dark eyes gazed out into the forest, its soul long gone. Branching from its head were two large antlers. "An elk?"

"Yes. You will be eating well tonight, as will I," he replied, his voice ringing with pride. His gaze fell hungrily on her—a kingly fire glinting in his eyes.

Her heart ached for the creature. She would rather stuff her face full of the dry blades of minca that Masika had gifted her than feast upon this sad sight. "I see."

"I'll have this buck skinned and a cloak prepared for you by the time you arrive back at my dwelling this evening."

Amy blinked as a few white snowflakes fell into her eyes.

Flurries settled upon his thick flowing locks of chestnut brown hair. "Winter is upon us. This season is my favorite time of year. When the hearths of our clan are warm, the meat is plenty, and our women are near."

He tugged her cloak around her. "It is definitely becoming colder."

He reached for her again, this time finding a strand of her curling red hair. He brought her hair to his nose and inhaled her scent.

She tugged her hair away from his thick fingers. As much as he wanted to rebuild his kingdom, she couldn't help him. She'd not shared one very important detail about sea nymph reproduction. Sea nymphs only gave birth to daughters. No sons were born of the womb of a sea nymph, nor the womb of the sea. As much as Ewan wanted her to produce a new lineage of men to rebuild his fallen kingdom, she wouldn't be the one to provide him with a son to help pass on his lineage.

But that didn't mean she couldn't have fun with him.

A rhythm vibrated through the ground, sending her hair on end. Gooseflesh rippled up her spine.

Ewan frowned, darkening the green in his eyes. "We have a storm dragon living among us."

Amy's mouth dropped open. The sound was near identical to the sound she'd heard from baby Selia in Egypt.

Amy heard the rhythm all the way up the path, feeling the pulses of the earth sync with her own heartbeat. She spotted a hollow in the trees. Fear gripped her body. If this was the storm dragon she and Masika had summoned, would he remember her?

If so, would he threaten to take her to the Abyss?

When she met the entrance of his dwelling, the rhythm stopped. The rhythm of her heart, however, was spiking into her throat.

She stared at the flap of animal hide hanging across the doorway, trying to get her heart to slow. According to Naunet, the only way to neutralize salt venom was to bond Selia with Celaeno's storm dragon, or spill the blood of a fae king.

She was not a murderer. But she also didn't want to have what happened to her mother happen to her.

Digging her feet into the frozen earth, she held her breath. There was only one way to know if the storm dragon living in this forest was in fact Celaeno's.

She shifted the animal hide sideways and walked into the hollow, treading lightly as the earth shifted from damp to something spongier. The dwelling was beyond crowded, but there was some strange organization to its flow. Most of the items scattered about the tree trunk were wooden. Animal skin hides were also strung up in the corner.

A man sat opposite of her, his body folded over in an almost unnatural way. While his build was large, he was much skinnier in frame than Ewan. He wasn't the same rippling chords of muscle and scales of a dragon she remembered. Storm dragons could be deceiving. They were shapeshifters, able to blend their appearances with the surroundings that best favored them. In this case, his bones—ribs—showed under his skin. He seemed as weathered and worn as his wooden dwelling.

Amy took a step forward, her toes crinkling into the damp earth. "What is your name?"

The dragon held up his hand, and a horrible rattling sound escaped his mouth. His chin dipped to his chest. With shoulders rolling forward, his head arched back

Celaaaaeeeeeennnnooooooooo!

Amy jumped back as a ghastly cough blew out of his mouth, sending wood fragments and leaves flying. The burst of wind that erupted from his mouth was sickly. This dragon was nothing of calm—not with that blast of sickly wind blowing from his chest.

Judging by the sound of his cough, he was absolutely Celaeno's storm dragon—the son of Poseidon who had not retreated into the Abyss to sleep. Clumps of his hair was missing. His skin stretched over his cheek bones, making his face look sunken. The skin on his arms and hands was splotchy, like great sores had only just healed over.

"Do you remember me at all?" Amy asked.

She locked eyes with the dragon's sickly gaze. A drop of cold sweat trickled down her rib cage. A sigh of relief escaped her. There was no way that in his current health situation, he would be able to take her to the Abyss.

This was her chance to neutralize salt venom in the ocean for good.

She took a step forward, closing the space between them. "I know you are ill, but I need you to help me. How would you feel about meeting a moon child?"

18

STORM SCROLLS

Selia

Sunday morning rolled in with fog and a severe temperature drop. So much, Selia wished she would have slept with her sweater on. She and Damien had passed out as soon as they arrived home from Gwen's house, too exhausted from everything to light the Yule log.

He lay next to her, still sleeping soundly. Even with his body heat warming the bed, cold crept into their home. A loneliness drifted in with the fog, loneliness wrapped around the folktale Gwen had shared with her about two selkies summoning a storm dragon.

What if the friend Amy mentioned was really this Sika from the local myth around Montrose?

Selia sat up in bed and grabbed the journal from her nightstand. She flipped through the journal until she found the pages with the oil stain. She grabbed a pen and wrote out the question that had haunted as the coldness of winter crept into her home. **What is a storm dragon?**

The oil stain morphed on the pages, forming a reply. **An ancient beast who protects the maternal salt pods.**

Selia's breath caught. *Maternal salt pods?*

She wrote out another question. **What are the maternal salt pods?**

They house the fertility of the ocean, as well as your salt ancestry.

Selia's fingers had gone numb. She forced the pen to the paper, writing out another question. **What relationship do storm dragons have with the maternal salt pods?**

Storm dragons protect the maternal salt pods by forming storm bonds with sea nymphs.

Selia's body was vibrating. *Storm bonds?*

Celaaaaaeeeenooooo.

That was the sound she had been hearing for the past few days. Was a storm dragon responsible for creating that sound?

She wrote another question. **You said Celaeno was my salt mother. How can I find her?**

The oil stain began to fade.

"No, no, no! Don't disappear!"

The stain formed a reply. **Obtain the storm scrolls. You will find answers inside the one that looks like a moon.**

Damien's arm looped around her center. "Morning, love."

Selia closed the journal as her fiancé's grip won her over. She fell back onto her pillow, staring up at the ceiling.

He pressed his face to her ear. "Why don't we spend the morning warming up our bed?" He worked his face down her chest, kissing as he went, finally laying his ear atop her belly. "Oh, she's talking. What a rumbly wee one we have."

"She has been rumbling all night," Selia said, suddenly queasy.

Damien continued kissing her down her belly.

Celaaaaaaeeeenooooooo...

Selia grabbed a fistful of Damien's thick hair, stopping him before he ventured any lower. "You don't hear that?"

"Am I hearing that my fiancé isn't in the mood this morning?"

"Damien, please. I'm worried. Just listen for a moment."

Damien set his ear onto her belly again. "Nope. Just the same grumbly sound." He propped his chin on her belly, his eyes meeting hers. Concern flickered in them. "Did something happen last night at my sister's place?"

Selia looked away from his hazel gaze. Damien had the same eyes as his sister, but they were deeper. "She shared a folktale with me about selkies. For some strange reason, it has me thinking about Amy."

Damien blinked. "I wouldn't give too much thought to it."

"Why not? The Strands of Moonlight tale you shared with me had a lot of history tied to the art of salt trance behind it."

Damien took her hand. "Look, I know you're under a lot of stress with the baby. Don't worry, we—"

"Don't worry?" she bit out. "That's easy for you to say. You're not the one carrying a child who has an abnormal pulse."

"We don't know if anything is wrong. The doctor will tell us, okay?"

"I'm not waiting for the doctor to tell me anything. This is my baby's life!" She sat up and threw the covers off her body. She jumped to her feet. "I can't take this anymore."

Damien stood, blocking her from leaving the room. He took her hands in his. "Selia, we are a family. *We* are going to have a baby together. Your worries are my worries. We are going to make a healthy family together like I promised you we would."

Selia looked away from him, scared to face the emotion in his eyes. He'd always worn his emotions on his sleeves for her. Right now, the emotions were too much.

He squeezed her hands. "What would make you feel better? I will do anything."

Her pulse pounded in her ears. *Obtain the storm scrolls. You will find answers inside the one that look like a moon.* "I need to see for myself if the folktales your sister had are related to Amy. I can't be in the dark any longer. The only truth I've discovered about my past has come through the folktales both you and your sister have shared with me."

Damien sat back down on the bed, not letting go of her hand. He gazed up at her, his expression hopeful. "I have an idea. Gwen is going Christmas shopping for the kids this afternoon. Why don't I take her out for lunch? If the folktales really mean that much to you, I'll drop you off at their place and you can have a look around."

Selia's heart leapt. "You would do that?"

"If it would make you feel better, then I will. But don't get too occupied, okay? And make sure you put everything back *exactly* how you left it. My sister guards those folktales like a mother hen does her chicks."

Selia leaned in, kissing her fiancé. "What would I do without you?"

Damien smiled. He grabbed her around the waist, tugging her sideways until her belly was flush with his. "As long as I get more of that when I get home, we have a deal."

An hour later, Damien pulled his car up to Gwen's home. His sister was down at the boatyard with Sean, leaving their home wide open for Selia to explore. He handed Selia a key. "This should get you in the back door. I told Gwen I'd head to the boatyard soon to pick her up, so you will need to act quick."

"Right." Selia took the key, pecked him on the cheek, then jumped out of the car. She walked up to the back door and pressed the key to the lock. The door opened.

She stopped in the kitchen, listening for the car engine as Damien drove away. The space was eerily quiet. There were no Irish setters bounding up to meet her. Tails and Scales must have been with Sean down at the boatyard.

She walked through the living room, then back to the space where Gwen had gone to retrieve the box full of storm scrolls. A wooden bookshelf at the end of the hall displayed a gorgeous Celtic knot with a stag engraved on it. Its antlers were inlaid with gold leaf, making its crown stand out. The antlers towered over a collection of beautiful book spines on the bookshelf below.

Tires crunched in the gravel outside.

Selia walked to the window, finding a school bus was driving away. She walked back to the bookshelf, and reached behind the king's golden crown. Her fingers scraped against the wooden box she remembered Gwen handling.

Ceeelaaaeeeennnoooooooo…

She brought the box down and tipped the lid open. She'd not seen the artwork beneath the lid the night before, as Gwen had set it aside and dove right into the fertility selkie folklore. Selia set the lid on the bookshelf, focusing on the storm scrolls inside. They were stuffed neatly together and could have passed as faded paper cigars. She searched the box, and found the piece of paper Gwen had read off the night before. A note was there, scribbled between the last phrases. **`Inscriber: Midwife of the Sea`**

Selia traced her fingers over one of the scrolls, finding an image on the edge that resembled lightning. She needed to find the scroll with a moon on it if she wanted to learn more about this storm dragon.

She counted one, three, six. Where was the seventh one?

Frantic, she tilted the box from side-to-side, hoping it would show. There had to be another scroll. She'd counted seven total the night before, right?

The back door opened.

Selia grabbed the lid and secured it back onto the box and set it back onto the bookshelf.

The pitter-patter of feet darted into the house, then stopped at the end of the hallway.

A little girl stood on the rug, red pigtails flapping on either side of her face. She had Gwen's eyes and the adorable dimples that reminded Selia of her fiancé. Even though she was scowling, not smiling, those dimples made her face look much rounder.

Selia had completely forgotten—Gwen had mentioned that her kids were getting back from a week at camp on Sunday.

The girl squinted at her, grabbing the shoulder straps of her backpack as she slung it to the ground. "Mom didn't say I would have a babysitter after school," she said, hopping up to her, pigtails flopping at her sides. "Who are you?"

"I'm Selia."

"Uncle Damien's *wife*?"

Selia laughed. "We're not married yet."

Gwen's daughter slung her backpack forward, from which a paper fish tail waved at her feet. "I'm Gemma. Look what we made at camp!"

Selia eyed the fish tail that undoubtedly belonged to a mermaid. The fins had been painted with pink, purple, and orange dots, along with a few sequins that were glued on to mimic scales. "That's cute!"

"It's my mermaid tail. I want one of my own, don't you?" Gemma asked.

Gwen hadn't been joking about her daughter's imagination. This little girl had seen right through her.

"I can't wait to show Uncle Damien! I want to be an artist like him when I grow up."

"Where is your brother?"

"Bram? He's with dad at the boatyard. But I took the bus home because Mom said Uncle Damien was visiting. And, well, I thought he might be here and not you."

Selia's heart warmed. This little girl obviously favored Damien as her favorite uncle.

Gemma darted for her. Selia moved out of the way in time to realize why Gemma had been standing there so patiently. The wooden antlers on the bookshelf served as a place to hang her backpack.

"You weren't looking at the adult fairy tales, were you?"

Selia locked eyes with Gwen's curious daughter. "No."

"Well, in case you were. Mom keeps the key on the mantelpiece behind the dragon where Bram and I can't reach. She thinks it's a secret, but we both know that key is for wherever she keeps the forbidden folktales she doesn't want us to see."

"Where are these forbidden folktales, do you know?"

Gemma shrugged. "We're pretty sure she keeps the naughty ones at the bookstore."

Her phone lit up. Damien texted her.

> Gwen is with Sean. I will be there soon.

Selia grabbed her phone and thumbed out a message.

> Gemma is here...

> Ok. Show her this message and slip out the back. Gemma, love. Your uncle wants you to visit this evening to decorate for the winter fairy, but your mom needs you to do your homework first.

Selia went to Gemma, holding out her phone. Gemma scanned the message, her eyes got huge.

Damien knew his niece well. In a matter of seconds, she'd grabbed her backpack and darted back into her room. She tore out a text book and began scribbling in it.

> **Change of plans. The whole lot is coming over to decorate.**

Selia walked into the living room, finding the wooden dragon on the mantelpiece. She reached beneath the dragon's tail, finding the cool surface of glass.

It wasn't the seventh scroll or a key. She discovered a small, murky bluish-green bottle. She tilted the bottle back and forth, observing a dark, murky liquid inside. The color seemed identical to the oil stain in the dragon journal. Did the two go together?

Her gaze dropped to the label on the bottle.

Salt venom?

19

SALT SUMMONING

Selia

Amy peered into the pot where the fae queen was dozing. Her blue light had faded, but Amy still had many memories of her own to keep remembering.

She poked her finger against the queen's stiff body. No use trying to wake her. She was conserving all her power to metamorphose in time for the winter solstice.

Amy gathered her cloak around her. She had a quick errand to run, one that required her to leave the greenhouse. She scurried down the hill, spotting a dock jutting out from the beach. Boats were humming about, their puttering engines traveling across the water.

She walked along the beach, finding herself under the dock to shelter from the cold wind blowing in. A pair of boots dangled above her head. That was peculiar.

She peered over the dock. One of the fishermen was sitting on the dock, preparing his boat for a day's catch. His net appeared to be tangled. A string of curse words sailed out of his mouth, followed by a swift kick to the net that was now strangling his boot.

He jumped into his boat, and with a rev of the engine, veered out into the River Esk toward the North Sea, leaving Amy the opportunity to swoop in and pay her salt stash a visit.

Flop!

She jumped from the boardwalk, landing on the rocky shore with oodles of exposed rock faces. She just had to trust one tiny little pebble. The sea would do the rest when it came time to extract what she was after.

She reached into the bank, spreading her fingers wide through the sand and stone. Closing her eyes, she whispered the three salt trancing principles with her mind.

Breath. Memory. Salt.

Sand and stone shifted beneath her fingers, and out popped a salt trancing talisman. Her pulse quickened as she curled her fingers around the damp piece of limestone. More of them emerged from the sand, which she gathered into her cloak. The salt inside of one talisman was all that she needed. It had preserved a memory, one that desperately wanted to share its own creation locked inside of it.

Selia's hurried footsteps echoed off the dusty walls of the temple. Since Amy had arrived back in Egypt, the young sea nymph couldn't wait to show her the male minca moth nest. According to her, it had been a location other adolescent sea nymphs had discovered and had fought over.

Amy's bare feet scuffed along sandy stones as Selia came to a halt, causing Amy to nearly bump into her.

"There," Selia said, pointing up at the corner of the temple.

Amy squinted as sunlight caught her eye.

The gentle hum of the moth's wings filled the temple. The fae creatures were drowsy with daytime. The blue haze was caused by the wing scales sloughing off as they prepared themselves for their nightly molt and flight. They conserved their energy by sheltering from the heat of the sun. At night, the males would molt and leave behind their salt chrysalises. Amy knew why the fae creatures preferred Isis's temple. It provided shelter from the sun during the day, and the perfect window for moonlight at night.

Replenished every night with the minca moth's molting routine, these salt chrysalises were in pristine condition, perfect samples for a sea nymph looking to embark on her salt stashing ritual. The moths created their nests out of something they gathered in the waterways—storm dragon scales, which Poseidon had provided plenty of.

Another nymph approached them, one wearing a white robe. Her long blond hair was braided behind her, swinging back and forth. The brooch she wore on her robe indicated this nymph was working for the Order.

Alexandra was teaching today. Oh, how *marvelous* this day had become. Amy wanted to hear all the nasty rumors the Order was spreading about her Ocean Apothecary.

"Who have you brought with you today?" Alexandra asked, her grey eyes dipping to Selia.

"Amphitrite," Selia replied.

Alexandra didn't even look her in the eye.

Two other nymphs with long blond hair wearing white robes began to walk toward them—each with wooden staffs with light blades illuminated at their ends. Apparently, Gaia's Order deemed it necessary to have other Iridescents guarding the temple.

Alexandra held up her hand, and the guards lowered their arms and returned to their posts. "No. I want to see what business she has here."

Selia's eyes drifted up to Amy. "You know each other?"

"Oh, Alexandra and I go back a *long* time," Amy replied, unable to hide the laugh in her voice.

Selia's gaze became a frightened one.

Alexandra sneered at Amy. "I'm happy to see you've decided to interrupt our lesson."

"I'm only here to observe," Amy said, not attempting to suppress the laughter in her voice.

"Naunet has done nothing to train Selia in how the art should be practiced," Alexandra said as she faced Selia, light flickering in her grey eyes.

Amy crossed her legs, tilting her head toward the pettiness that was Alexandra's existence. "Maybe because you're teaching it *wrong*?"

Alexandra's face flushed as she folded her arms in front of her chest. "There is nothing wrong about what I am teaching."

"Selia tells me that you've given the other pupils preference of the minca moth nest. Is that true?" Amy asked.

"Don't," Selia said, her face flushing.

Alexandra smirked, turning on her heel. "Students? Let's show Amphitrite what we've been studying. Today, we will be practicing our technique in salt summoning."

Selia's expression became horrified. "I'm going to be in so much trouble. This is the technique that I barely practice!"

"You will be fine," Amy said, grabbing Selia's hand and walking with her after Alexandra. "Who said you can't have a little fun when collecting for your first salt stash?"

Alexandra lined her pupils in front of Isis's statue, facing the moon goddess. She left no place for Selia. How it made Amy's blood boil watching this kind of favoritism taking place.

Amy took Selia's hand and tugged her forward. She stayed beside her, holding space for Selia so she wasn't shunned by the others.

Alexandra stood before the group, aligning herself with Isis's statue. She faced her pupils, the blond spikes of her hair falling into her face as she centered herself. "Today, you will perform a basic summoning practice where you will summon the salt of your ancestral origin. No matter the maternal salt pod cycling, you will summon the salt your ancestors originate from."

Selia's feet shifted.

"Why are you so nervous?" Amy asked, nudging her with her arm.

"This is the one exercise that I'm terrified of practicing."

"For those of you who are listening," Alexandra cut in. "This exercise is essential when it comes time to bond with a storm dragon. There are seven storm bonds total. Only one of them will present to you, if of course, he chooses to bond with you. He will look to see if the maternal salt pod his territory encompasses aligns with your own."

"And from the depths of the sea, the Abyss will find you," Selia said.

Alexandra's gaze fell onto Selia. "The Abyss will feel your heart—she will know when one of her salt daughters is practicing the salt trancing art."

Amy bit her bottom lip. She didn't like how Alexandra talked down to Selia. Selia was obviously well versed in the lessons provided by the Codex, where using one's pulse was specifically stated.

She pulled Selia aside. "Before you start, what does it feel like when you practice this technique?"

Selia pressed her hands together as beads of moisture formed on her forehead. "It's difficult to describe."

"Does your heart race, like it's about to explode?"

Selia shook her head from side-to-side. "No. That's why I know there is something wrong with my pulse."

Amy remembered what Naunet had told her about Selia's unique pulse. Not only was she immune to the toxic salt venom born from Celaeno's fae queen, but apparently, something else happened that was enough to terrify her.

"Well? Are we practicing? Or are we backing out?" Alexandra asked, her voice dipping.

Selia turned to face Isis's statue, her knees trembling. "No. I'm here to practice."

The gentle hum created by the minca moths' wings became agitated. They weren't dumb creatures. The moths could sense the change in the atmosphere before it even happened—especially when it came to salt.

"All you need to do is focus on your pulse, okay?" Amy whispered down to Selia's trembling body.

"I'm so nervous," she whispered. "What if I mess up?"

Amy set her hand on Selia's shoulder. "All it takes is for you to trust in your heart, and your pulse will make it so. Now, summon the salt from your ancestral salt mother, Celaeno."

Selia nodded, determination brimming in her eyes.

Alexandra held her hand out, pointing at Isis. "Begin."

The pupils clasped their hands together, holding them to their hearts.

Selia closed her eyes, and her hands dropped to her sides. With her palms facing up, she sucked in a breath, exhaling through her nose.

The light drifting down between Isis's statue seemed to thicken.

Selia's breathing began to slow. Settling upon her head and shoulders was an ethereal glow. Her salt aura was beginning to show.

Amy's chest caught at the sight. How much *talent* this young sea nymph had. For a sea nymph whose maternal salts originated from the *dark one*—her spirit had so much light.

The hum of the minca moths began to stir, creating a song of her ancestors.

"What is she doing?" Alexandra barked.

Amy smiled. "She's showing your pupils what it means to salt trance with your heart, not your mind."

The minca moths began to dart down from their nest now, swarming between Isis's statue.

One of them dove down to Alexandra, grazing her lip. A thin line of blood began to trickle down her face.

Salt chrysalises rained down from the nest as the frenzied moths dislodged them. Sea nymphs screamed in delight, sprinting to gather the valuable items before they were snatched up.

The bluest of them fell at Selia's feet as the moths swarmed around her. Sea nymphs sprinted about the room, gathering them frantically as the frenzy of moths drove Alexandra out of the temple.

PART 3
TEMPTATION

20

THE VENOM SPEAKS

Selia

The second Selia got into the car, Damien was venting about his afternoon with his sister. Apparently, Gwen had changed plans about Christmas shopping, insisting they decorate their new home for the winter solstice gathering.

Damien shook his head, his brow furrowing. "I'm starting to feel like she's going to be that sibling who is always trying to impede on us. There was a reason I moved to France to set up my art studio." He reached over, grabbing Selia's hand. "Do you feel any better about the baby?"

"I do," Selia lied. All she could think about was what she was going to tell the journal when she didn't have any luck with locating the storm scroll it wanted her to find.

Damien unbuckled his seat belt. "Good, because we have a few minutes before my sister and Sean head over to our house." He reached over, cupping her face in his hand. He worked his lips past hers. "Why must you smell so good all the time?"

Selia sucked in a breath as his hand dropped to the base of her sweater. He reached up, grabbing one of her breasts with an experienced maneuver.

While her fiancé explored her, Selia's thoughts drifted to the bottle of salt venom she discovered on Gwen's fireplace mantle.

Selia grabbed Damien's wandering hand. "Love, you'll make me sore again."

"I can be gentler," he whispered, his hand returning to her breast.

Selia's phone chimed.

She grabbed her phone out of her purse, finding a bat icon from Pixie flashing on the screen.

> Can U do me a huge favor? Come water this afternoon? For some reason, half of my plants are dying... :(

"Looks like Pixie needs me to go water her greenhouse. Drop me off, and this evening I promise we'll pick up where we left off?"

To Selia's gratitude, Damien agreed to drop her off at Pixie's shop. She walked out back to the greenhouse. Even through the glass walls, she could see the color of the plants were off. She walked up to the door and opened it, finding her assumptions were true. Plants were wilting, and there was a definite musky odor that replaced the robustness of cinnamon and cloves.

Pixie stood in the corner, her shoulders hunched and her head shaking.

"Did I *over* water?" Selia asked, dipping under the drooping brown leaves of the palm tree near the entrance.

"No, the soil is still fairly dry. But something very strange is going on with the temperature in here. I think it's the cold snap that's gone and changed everything. I hoped to keep my coffee plants alive all winter. But at this rate, they might not survive through Christmas." She locked eyes with Selia. The bat charm hanging off her nose ring reflected in the dim light of the greenhouse. "Have you seen Peppercorn at all?"

"No. Last I saw her was right before Damien proposed to me at the lighthouse."

"That's funny, she'll usually have returned from her hunt by now. I hope she's okay." Her eyes dropped to Selia's left hand. "Your ring is absolutely *gorgeous*. The stone is almost an exact replica of your eye color."

"I'll get to watering right away," Selia said, grabbing the hose and shoving past Pixie.

"Is everything all right? You seem a little flush," Pixie said.

"I'm fine," Selia said, desperately wanting some privacy with the journal.

"I can't thank you enough for coming on such short notice. I would do the watering myself, but we have a mandatory meeting with Peter's father. This meeting will be quick, I promise. I can run you back home as a favor when I'm done. It will give me an excuse to see this home you've purchased!" Pixie left the greenhouse, leaving Selia alone with the wilting plants.

Selia turned the tap on low and set the hose into one of the pots. Her fingers were shaking.

She collapsed to the ground, tugging out the journal. She flipped the cover open, finding the pages had dampened with a message bleeding through the parchment. **`Where did you find the salt venom?`**

Selia swallowed. How did the journal know she'd obtained it? Maybe this would be the time to set some boundaries with the journal. She still had no idea who she was talking to, or what it wanted with her.

She grabbed a pen and wrote out a question. **`Who am I speaking with?`**

The stain morphed, quickly forming an answer. **I am the selkie the locals know as Sika.**

Selia dropped her pen. This whole time, she was talking with a spirit? She grabbed the pen and wrote out another question. **How did you know that I had the bottle?**

The stain morphed, quickly forming an answer. **I can taste the salt in the air and on your skin. I can taste the venom's desire for your flesh…**

Selia shivered. *The venom's desire for her flesh*? She wrote out her reply. **I discovered the bottle at Gwen's house.**

Gwen, the sister of your fiancé, Damien?

Another cold shiver ran up her spine. She wrote a hesitant **yes**, wondering how much more about herself the journal knew. **Do you know what salt venom is?**

I know the history behind its creation. Amphitrite only bottled so many samples of it before her Ocean Apothecary became contaminated with its wickedness.

Selia's breath caught. The journal knew Amy?

The paper coiled again as another liquid reply bled through the parchment. **Let me taste it.**

Selia reached into her pocket, retrieving the bottle. The glass was no longer cold, but warm. Should she trust it?

I'm sensing hesitation. You want to know your ancestry, don't you? A single drop to the paper is all that is needed for the salt to show your past to you.

Selia held the bottle over the paper. Her heartbeat pulsed through her fingers. She tipped her thumb to the cork stopper, removing it.

Fwwwisssshhhhhhhh.

Out came a breath of something that exuded wickedness. Selia's throat constricted. Her vision darkened. The thundering voice of *Celaaaaeeeeenooooooo* exploded through her salt nodes.

The journal began to blur as the oil stain darkened, erasing the message. She tipped the bottle forward. A single drop of the salt venom fell toward the parchment.

Blinding blue light flashed in Selia's periphery. The violent crash of waves filled her ears as her senses were flooded with water. Her body was at the mercy of the water, threatening to rip her away from a sandy bank of earth.

The force of the water was overcome by two hands that came to her rescue. She was thrust forward, and her lungs filled with oxygen for the first time.

The warm, caring hands of a woman came to her, cradling her to her breast. *"Blind Moon, welcome to Egypt,"* were the words that echoed through her.

The vision of the motherly woman faded, washed out again by the darkness clouding her periphery.

The plants in the greenhouse were no longer wilting, they were alive, and gripping for her.

Selia kicked away, struggling to find the ground. It felt like the earth had fallen out beneath her. The vision of the woman, how much she wanted to return to that moment again. Her fingers met damp earth. The pot she'd set the hose into was overflowing.

She crawled toward the journal, finding another message there.

The salt venom preserved the story of your birth. It was born from Celaeno's womb shortly after she gave birth to you.

"Hey!"

Selia jumped, closing the journal.

Pixie came rushing into the greenhouse and turned off the spigot.

"Sorry. That was my fault," Selia said. The hose had a giant hole in it from where the water had gotten so hot, it must have exploded.

"Not to worry, I have another hose to spare," Pixie said as she tossed the shredded hose aside. "Is everything all right? You seem a little flush."

"Everything is fine," Selia lied. Her talent, whatever caused it, had reared its ugly head again. Had the hose exploded due to her interaction with the salt venom?

"Turns out they canceled the meeting." Pixie said as she straightened herself. "Damien texted me, saying that his sister wants to meet me about catering for some big winter solstice gathering?"

While Selia drove with Pixie up the road toward home, her mind was a blur with the interaction she'd had with the salt venom. What she'd experienced was not a hallucination—it was real. From the single drop of the wicked substance, a memory of her own had emerged, a memory of her *birth*.

She'd felt the warmth of a mother's arms cradling her, tucking her to her breast, and whispering to her ear. "*Blind Moon, welcome to Egypt.*"

She kept the bottle of salt venom in a pocket away from the journal in case another memory decided to flood through her.

"Oh, I see it!" Pixie exclaimed, pressing on the gas and accelerating up the road. "Look at that lighthouse!"

After Pixie parked, they both left her car and walked toward the front door. Gwen came bounding onto the porch, her hands springing to her side. "There you are!"

"Is that Damien's sister?" Pixie asked as she grabbed a platter of pastries out of her car.

"Yes, that's Gwen."

"Wow, she has a ton of energy."

"You have no idea."

Selia wanted to turn around and head back to the greenhouse. She wanted to feel the warmth and love from the woman who'd pulled her into her arms.

"Ah, you must be Pixie!" Gwen said as she descended the stairs.

Pixie thrust her arms forward. "I brought a few samples of the bakery items I cater. I hope you like pumpkin and cherry, because those are my most requested."

Selia's stomach turned over. The entire drive over from the coffee shop, those scones had made her feel nauseous.

Gwen clapped her hands together. "Absolutely! Anything to help with the winter solstice party."

Selia followed Gwen and Pixie into her home. Her eyes ached just looking at all the bright red and green colors. In only an hour, Gwen had completely overturned their home, transforming the space into a Christmas wonderland.

"I hope you don't mind; I went a bit overboard with the decorations."

"It looks fantastic," Selia said, her voice weaker than she wanted it to sound.

"There you are, love."

The warm male voice didn't register. It was hard and distant, masked behind confusion.

"Selia?"

The man cupped her face in his big warm hands, but only coldness met her skin.

"Selia, dear. You look like you've seen a ghost," Gwen said.

Selia looked from the man to the woman named Gwen. Where was she? She didn't belong here, not with this family.

She belonged to the story behind the salt venom—the story from Egypt.

"I think I'm going to be sick," she said, retreating down the hall. She needed to be alone in her bedroom with the voices ringing in her salt nodes.

Once inside, she closed the door behind her and sat on the bed. Reaching into her bag, she tugged out the journal again. She flipped it open to the center, finding another message.

Your mother is not the woman who pulled you out of the Nile river. Your mother is Celaeno. She is part of the Abyss.

"Who is the Abyss?" she asked aloud.

The stain on the parchment began to form an answer. **The Abyss is the womb of the sea, the ancestral salt mother of all maternal salt pods.**

Selia's mind thundered with questions, too many for her to form a response.

You stole something from our ancestors that I want. It is connected to the storm scroll with the moon on it.

Selia shook her head. Had she heard her right? What *she* stole from their ancestors?

While your heart is immune to the salt venom, the heart of your daughter is not. Do as I say, or your past will come back to haunt you in ways that will harm your daughter.

Selia's vision began to blur. "How do I protect my daughter's heart?" she asked.

Another liquid message appeared, much darker than the others. **You must remember everything you can about your ancestry.**

"Selia?"

Selia closed the journal.

A man entered the bedroom. She remembered him now, the man with the warm hazel eyes. He was the father of her child—Damien.

Damien snatched the journal from her. "We need to talk." He closed the door and turned to face her. "Pixie just told me that you were on the ground in her greenhouse." He crouched down, leveling his gaze with her. "Selia, what's going on?"

Selia's salt nodes flushed with heat. She wanted to strike him, to take back what was hers—what the salt venom had promised her.

The story behind her ancestry and her birth.

Damien tossed the journal across the bedroom, where it landed with a heavy *thud*.

Selia bent over, setting her head between her knees as the nausea returned.

Damien set his hand on her back and began rubbing in circles. "All of this stress with the baby is making you sick. Enough with the folktales. We need to get you feeling better."

Selia's vision was blurry. Her mouth was parched with the bitter taste of salt. She wanted to run back to Sika's messages. She needed to remember everything she could about her ancestry if she was to protect her daughter.

21

MASIKA'S CURSE

Amy

Amy sat inside Naunet's dwelling, watching the moon rise over the Nile. Such a sight was her silver body, pregnant and glistening over the water. Minca moths were on their way out of the temple, freshly molted and their wings sharp enough to cut through the wind without a sound.

Seeing what Selia had accomplished in the temple was enough to make Amy's heart sing. Those razor-sharp wing tips had found Alexandra's face, slicing into her upper lip. Let it be a lesson to the Order for allowing such a cocky nymph attempt to keep Selia out of the temples all because she refused to participate in the Order's manipulation of the art.

Selia slept on the bed in Naunet's dwelling, moonlight coursing in through the window. The salt chrysalises she'd collected from the temple sat in a woven basket next to the bed. She clutched one in her left hand. The salt was glowing, casting her features in a blue light only the fae could create.

Selia had shown every other student in Alexandra's class what it meant to salt trance with your heart, not the mind. The Blind Moon was an absolute *master* at pulse, and she'd only started learning about the art. Naunet had given her a fitting name. Celeno's moon daughter was sure to illuminate what others were quickly becoming blind to.

"All salt daughters of Celeno will be tempted by it."

Amy looked up. Someone was fast approaching Naunet's dwelling. Even in the pale moonlight, Amy could make out their dark hair.

"Naunet?" she asked.

The sea nymph who entered was not Naunet. Her face was sickly looking, and her dark eyes were glassy with fear.

She turned, facing her. "Amphitrite, where is my sister?"

Amy staggered to her feet. "Masika? What's wrong? What are you doing here?"

Masika walked into the dwelling, stopping near the table. "I came to speak with my sister. I wanted to share my discovery about minca's disappearance with her."

Amy grabbed her arm, which was hot to the touch. An oily substance shimmered on her skin. "What happened to your skin?"

Masika pulled away from her, ignoring her question. Her gaze dropped to the young sea nymph sleeping beneath the window. "Who is this child sleeping in my sister's home?"

Amy's mouth refused to move. Her throat had gone dry.

Masika's brow furrowed. "Why didn't you tell me my sister produced a child?"

"Everyone in Egypt believes Selia is Naunet's child, but she is not. Naunet swore me to secrecy about who her true mother is."

Masika's eyes darkened. She walked to one of Naunet's storm scrolls open on the table, and scanned its moonlit inscriptions. "So Celaeno gave birth to something else besides the contaminated fae queen?" She walked over to Selia and looked behind her ear. Her salt nodes now formed, took the shape of crescents.

Masika gasped. "A *moon* child?"

Amy reached for Masika. Her hand passed through her arm. The places where moonlight hit her body became transparent. Bones and flesh and something else shone there—an oily film coated what was left of her.

Amy staggered backward, overcome with sickness. Masika's body had become a festering wound, her skin decayed and hanging from her bones. Salt crystals protruded from her flesh, each with the dark, oily liquid dripping from them. "What's happened to you?"

Masika glared at her. There was no beautiful luster of desire in her dark eyes. Her gaze was full of anger—betrayal, even. "The fae queen has infected me with salt venom."

As Masika stepped into the moonlight, the remains of her body withered. Her heart was visible behind her ribs, blackened and charred-looking. The salt crystals were the thickest and sharpest around her heart, many protruding from the blackness. "The venom will continue to corrode my body. However, the salt will preserve my spirit. I will live on, unable to die."

Amy swallowed. *This* was the darkness Naunet had foreseen overtaking Celaeno's salt daughters. She struggled to take in the gruesome sight of her friend. Masika's cheekbones were sunken behind the oily salt venom coating her skin. Her hair was torn and mangled, slimy in texture.

Masika retreated from the moonlight, dipping back into the shadows.

"Masika!" Amy cried, chasing after her. "Masika! Please! I want to help you!"

Amy's feet shifted in the sand as moonlight consumed her. She collapsed onto the ground, her heartbeat thundering. Where had Masika gone? What would she do? How could she save her from this curse she had put her through?

Her fingers scraped against something cold in the sand.

All that remained of her friend was a single black crystal of salt venom.

22

DESIRE

Selia

The journal Damien threw across the bedroom danced in Selia's periphery. Her mouth was parched. The taste of salt on her tongue was driving her crazy.

Damien's hand continued making small circles on the small of her back as the nausea worked its way through her body. The nausea was too overwhelming to endure right now. She needed to listen to Damien and give herself time to recover.

Her heart ached in a way it hadn't ever before. The memory of that woman pulling her out of the water, her scent of earth and spice still filled her senses. That woman, whoever she was, had cared for her like she was her daughter.

Laughter sounded from outside the bedroom.

Damien stood, grabbing Selia's hand. "Come on. You can't let Gwen make all the decisions when it comes to the winter solstice gathering."

Selia stood, her legs both weak. She forgot that Pixie and Gwen were both in the kitchen discussing catering.

Damien picked up the journal from the ground and tucked it under his arm. As he left the bedroom, a ripple of anger uncoiled up Selia's spine. She reached into her pocket, finding the smooth cold glass warming beneath her fingers. She still had the bottle of salt venom.

Bits of Gwen and Pixie's discussion sounded as Selia entered the kitchen. Gwen was standing with her arms crossed in front of her chest, while Pixie was holding up a cookie shaped like a bat.

"I hate those creatures. They are filthy," Gwen said, tossing her hands into the air.

"Bats are *not* filthy! In fact, you wouldn't have coffee if they didn't exist! Everybody thinks bees are the only pollinators out there," Pixie replied, her voice much higher in pitch.

Damien walked into the kitchen, holding his arms out at his sides. "All right, ladies. We've had a long day. Selia isn't feeling good, so I'm going to ask that everyone leave for the evening."

Pixie shifted the pastries off her platter and onto a plate. "Go ahead and nibble on these and tell me what you think?"

Gwen smirked. "I'll take the one without the bat on it."

Pixie gave Gwen an eyeroll as she walked over to Selia. "Don't worry about coming to the greenhouse to water. Get well before the gathering! I'll text you, okay?"

Selia nodded as Pixie gave her a big hug.

"You can call me anytime if you want to talk, okay?" Pixie whispered.

Selia squeezed her back, but not with the force she wanted to. "Thank you for everything."

Gwen bustled over. "Selia, before I leave. I need to show you the decorations I put on the—"

"Enough," Damien said, shoving himself between Selia and his sister.

"Oh, all right," Gwen huffed as she gave Selia a hug. "Let my brother take care of you. He's been a nervous wreck without you here today."

Damien saw both Pixie and Gwen to the door. Once they were gone, he made his way back to the kitchen. Selia hadn't gotten a good look at him with all of the adrenaline burning through her system.

He stopped in the hallway, halfway between her and the kitchen table. He looked like he'd been run over by a truck. His hair stuck out in places it shouldn't, and he had dark bags under his eyes.

"Gwen was right. You've had me spooked all day. I need to know exactly what happened at the greenhouse. Did you pass out?" he asked, his voice no longer soft. His tone rang with annoyance and was unusually hard.

"I had a dizzy spell," Selia lied, thinking back to how the plants in the greenhouse had become monsters.

"Well, you aren't going back to that greenhouse alone, or to my sister's again. I'm not letting you out of my sight."

A mixture of fear and anger welled in Selia's stomach. "You can't tell me what to do," she spat.

The greens in Damien's eyes flashed. "You bet I can, especially if this concerns the health of my fiancé and our baby." He closed the space between them, setting his hands on her shoulders.

"Where did you put the journal?" Selia asked.

"I'm not telling you."

That anger that flooded through her body went from uncomfortable to painful. "You can't keep it from me!"

"Hey!" He grabbed her arm. "What has gotten into you?"

Selia blinked, unable to lock eyes with him.

Damien held her in place. "When I asked you to marry me, I vowed to give you my better judgment, for better or for worse. Right now, the health of you and our baby is my priority, got it?" He pulled her into a hug, embracing her. "We can endure one more day together before the doctor's office opens back up, all right?"

Selia didn't reach her arms around him. As he worked his hands down her back, emotions blurred through her. Confusion. Resentment. Even betrayal, were all blending as one. What would she do if she couldn't speak with the journal about the salt venom?

She still had the bottle. She could feel the contents just as Sika had described. *"I can taste the salt in the air and on your skin. I can taste the venom's desire for your flesh..."*

Damien relaxed his grip on her, but not enough to release her. "Let's get you something to eat and drink. What do you want? I'll get you anything."

"I don't want anything."

"You need to. You're probably dehydrated. Being pregnant means you need to stay hydrated, no matter how much it makes you have to pee, got it?"

Selia sat down on the chair behind her.

Damien shifted one of the pastries toward her. "I'm not eating anything until I see you take the first bite."

Selia grabbed the pastry and shoved it into her mouth. The sugar did little to take the edge off the bitter taste on the back of her tongue. She grabbed a glass of water and drank. While the taste of salt was diluted, the voice she was hearing did little to soften.

Damien took her glass and refilled it, returning it to the table. "Better?"

Selia stared at the ripples on the surface of the water. Her salt nodes were filling with that voice again.

Damien shoved one of the pastries into his mouth and gulped half of it down. "I wish you would have been here when Gemma was here, too. She put a lot of effort into decorating."

After Selia had eaten her fill of pastries, she followed Damien into the hallway.

Damien looped his arm around her, nudging her ahead of him. He stopped behind her, setting his arm on the door frame. "Have a look."

Selia walked into the nursery. The room was full of Damien's art supplies. Paint brushes and pans of watercolor paints were scattered on the ground. The wall next to the baby crib had been painted in a rainbow of colors. "Who painted that?" Selia said, noting the name Sophie next to a mermaid painting that had been made by a child.

Damien walked in behind her, wrapping his arms around her center. "Gemma did. She was never able to meet Sophie, so she often paints her as a mermaid." His body hardened as his voice dropped. "Sophie was only seven when the accident occurred—seven years of bliss of having her in my life."

Selia's body warmed. She could feel Damien's pulse thundering against her back. Her foot brushed past one of the painting palettes, spilling water onto the floor.

Damien lowered himself to the ground and grabbed a towel. He sat on the floor and began blotting up the water. A few drops of liquid fell to the ground, mixing with the paint.

As Damien's salty tears mixed with the water and pigments, the numbness and confusion Selia experienced over the past few hours was replaced with a new sensation. It felt like her heart might explode right now. Between the care and love and devotion this man had—all were exemplified by what he'd lost.

She glanced around the remainder of the room, emotion gripping her as Damien and Gemma's mural collaboration washed over her. He'd painted a patch of blue kelp, and a very mischievous looking hermit crab with a paintbrush between her claws. "You did this for our baby?"

"I did this for the both of you." He glanced up at her with glassy eyes. "Having a daughter is one of the most magical experiences, something you will never forget." He reached out, grabbing her hand. "Selia, you're giving me a real gift having me experience that love again."

Selia's body flushed with heat. Something was awakening inside of her, a new kind of arousal born from a rush of desire.

She lowered herself onto his lap. "No, you have given me a gift, Damien Malloch." She grabbed his hand, bringing it to her chest. Pressing her lips to his, she began kissing him.

The corners of Damien's mouth turned up. "What's gotten into you?"

"You," she whispered, kissing his parting lips. She needed to taste the salt on his skin. She grabbed his lower lip with her teeth and tugged.

Damien's body tensed beneath her. His hands reached under her sweater. "I need to know that you are okay," he whispered. "I…"

"Shhh…" She stroked her fingers down his torso toward his lap, finding him hardening.

"I knew I was marrying a goddess," Damien rasped into her ear. He slid his other hand up into her sweater and lifted it over her head, her bra coming with it.

He buried his face in her breasts, kissing her chest. He took her nipple into his mouth and sucked.

Selia moaned as he grabbed her other breast and sucked harder. A powerful euphoric rush was building inside of her. She grabbed his thick hair and tugged his face away from her chest.

"Bed. Now," she said, climbing to her feet and grabbing his hand.

Damien launched himself up from the ground. Selia led the way to the bedroom, slowing as she approached the door. He made a motion like he was preparing to sweep her off her feet before they walked inside.

She set her arm on his shoulder, stopping him. "No, I want to be in control of *your* pleasure, love."

His nostrils flared as she reached for his pants and pulled off his belt. His pants fell to his feet, revealing the hard bulge beneath his boxers.

"You need to wear your kilt for me soon again," she teased. "It's so much easier to access the part of you I crave." She slid her fingers into the top of his boxers and tugged them down, releasing his enlarging cock.

"I've never seen this side of you," he whispered, setting his hand on the doorframe. He leaned toward her, his stubble grazing past her cheek.

Selia tracked her fingers down his torso, tracing circles above the base of his cock. "Do you like it?"

"Like it?" he growled, pinning her against the doorframe. "I *love* it."

She stroked the head of his cock with her fingers, making it jerk as she teased him. She lowered herself to the ground, kneeling between his legs. She grabbed his cock, holding him in place. Just the sight of him made her clit ache.

She licked the salty head, loving how she could make him harden. Slowly, she took him into her mouth.

"That's nice," Damien growled as his hips thrust forward. He placed his other hand on the doorframe, bracing himself. A groan erupted from his chest, followed by another thrust from his hips.

Selia quickened her movements with her mouth, pulsing over him as his pleasure heightened. She withdrew him from her mouth, and slid up beside him. "What position do you want?"

He wiped her hair out of her eyes, his breathing heavy. "Whatever is most comfortable for you and the baby."

Selia pushed him backward until he met the edge of the bed. "Lay down."

He grabbed for her, but she pulled away before he could reach his arms around her. She slipped her leggings and panties off, and tossed them away. She climbed on top of him, straddling his center. She teased her entry with his head, sliding down on top of him. Damien's thick penetration was exactly the painful pleasure she needed. She gyrated her hips as she worked to accept every glorious inch of him.

His mouth came to her breast, which he sucked as his hips began to thrust upward.

Selia jolted as the friction became too much. The sucking and thrusting stopped as Damien slid out of her. She pushed Damien back onto the bed and reversed herself atop him.

"Get back here, I'm not done," he grunted, grabbing her hips and pulling her toward his face.

She pushed her hips back, and his tongue dove deep inside of her. Lapping and sucking with his mouth, he pressed his fingers into her. She grabbed his cock and began working her hand over him.

Selia fell to his side, not taking her hand away from his purpling cock. "I need you inside of me. I need every inch of you."

Damien rolled to his side and stood. He grabbed her legs, tugging her to the side of the bed. He grabbed her hips, and flipped her over. He entered her again. He was so thick inside of her, the pressure blurring between pain and pleasure.

Selia forced herself back against him, her body aching for release. With each thrust, he penetrated deeper.

His body shuddered as his orgasm combined with hers.

Selia collapsed onto the bed as Damien fell beside her.

"What has gotten into you?" he breathed, his chest heaving.

Selia flipped over, pinning him against the bed. "I'm only warming up."

23
HENRIETTA'S REVENGE
Amy

Amy fell to the ground and retched. As the innards of her stomach sloshed onto the damp, sandy beach, the memory of Masika's sickly body purged from her system. The nightmare was back, an oily nightmare that tried to suffocate her. She couldn't get the scent of Masika's decomposing skin out of her nose. The scent of burned flesh clung to her mouth and throat.

Another wave of nausea rolled through her stomach, and she retched again. A sickly, rattling breath, that memory had become. The venom had made quick work of Masika's body, corroding it.

"I'm so sorry…" Amy whispered as tears began to streak from her eyes. She gazed out at the open water of the North Sea, hoping the crashing sound of the waves would soothe her thoughts. She hadn't seen Masika since that day. Masika had become cursed by the salt venom.

The salt venom had done something to Masika, something Naunet gave Amy no warning of. While the venom corroded her flesh, the salt preserved her spirit.

All that Amy kept of Masika from that day was a single black salt venom crystal. She had buried it in the past, along with many painful memories she had suppressed. But the memory of what salt venom did to Masika's body still remained. The selkie salt skin was the name she gave to the substance that cursed her friend.

Amy stood, centering herself. Soon, she would dig up what she buried in the past, and she would right what she had made wrong. She had the queen in her possession again. This time, she wouldn't mess up.

Amy focused on the crunching gravel beneath her bare feet. She had a lot of little steps to take in so little time before the winter solstice. Something darting across the beach caught her eye. It wasn't a bird, or a piece of litter blowing in the wind.

It was a seashell, with two ink-drop eyes poking out of the top.

Panic erupted in Amy's chest. Ever since she'd released Henrietta back into the wild, she'd become even more of a fae pest.

She patted her breasts and her sides, finding one of her pockets felt different. She dipped her fingers into her pocket, and discovered a hole in the fabric.

"No! That blasted little thief!" Amy cried with no use. Her voice was stolen by the bitter wind blowing across the water. She'd let her guard down for *one* moment, and a jealous fae hermit crab took off with not only one, but all of the salt trancing talismans she'd extracted from the beach.

Of *course* the tides would turn against her, leaving her to deal with the vengeance of the sea's most annoyingly opinionated fae creature. Now the fate of her plan sat in the claws of a jealous crustacean.

Her plan could not unfold without one of the talismans. She would need one when it came time for her to track down Celaeno's storm dragon.

Amy made her way down to the beach, following Henrietta's trail. Why did fae creatures have to be absolute pests? She sifted through blue bottle caps and plastic wrappers. No salt trancing talisman in sight. Sea nymphs had been known to return to their salt stashes years after they'd created them, only to discover a marine fae creature had made off with them.

Snow flurries swirled around Amy's face and hair as she ventured farther down the beach. She tugged up her robe, but the fabric did little to stop the cold air from biting her neck.

Stepping onto the beach without proper footwear was a mistake. Her toes froze within seconds. Her nose burned with cold air. She didn't want to give in to the weather so soon. A fleet of fishing boats bobbed along the dock. Nets became spider webs of icicles. Their fibers held taut by the wind, frozen like ghosts. Soon her hair began to freeze, stiffening on her shoulders.

She squinted at the dock where the boats were quickly becoming locked in by the ice.

No way—were a pair of *boots* sitting there on one of the frozen posts?

She scampered up to the boots, and swiped them from the wooden post where they'd been hung. She worked her fingers through the icy laces, unraveled the knot, and slipped them on. They were perfectly sized, and her toes thanked her the moment the soft, warm interior wrapped around them.

"*Oi!*"

Amy froze as a waving hand appeared from one of the boats. A woman hopped out and landed in front of her. "Have you seen a pair of boots?" The woman asked as her hazel eyes dipped to Amy's feet.

"I'm sorry, I have not," Amy lied as she tucked her feet under her robe.

The woman sighed. "Ah, they must have fallen into the water. I guess that's what I get for trying to swap them out for another pair on the boat." She swung one of her legs out, showing off a pair of rubber ones. The corners of the woman's eyes were red.

"What is wrong, my dear? You appear to be distressed."

"It's my husband's boat. With the recent cold snap, he can't get it started. The last thing I want is for him to spend the holiday's down here with this stupid boat fishing and not home with his family."

Something about her freckles reminded Amy of Ewan.

"The *Mad Malloch*, huh?" Amy said, noting the name painted in bright red paint on the side of the boat.

"The boat belonged to my father. My brother didn't want it. He's never been a sportsman. He's more of an artist."

Amy's heart leapt. "Is your brother's name Damien Malloch?"

She nodded. "Yes, why do you ask?"

Amy's mouth dropped open. Damien had a *sister?* "My name is Amy. So very nice to meet you."

Gwen smiled, but it was weak. "I'm Gwen."

"What's wrong with the *Mad Malloch*?"

"Mice have been chewing through the electrical cords that help to jumpstart the engine."

A familiar seashell went scurrying behind her.

Amy bit her lip. Of course, Henrietta would hide her shiny little crab arse aboard a fishing boat. "There might be something other than mice that are snipping through your electrical cords. Would you and your husband allow me to have a peek inside the boat?"

Gwen's hazel eyes narrowed on hers. "He told me there have been sightings of a mysterious woman about the port with red hair and green eyes."

"Gwen!" A male voice called from inside the boat.

Gwen ducked back inside.

Amy stepped onto the boat and followed her toward the string of curse words flying into the air. The scent of burning rubber filled the little room where Gwen went darting over to a man who was cursing up a storm.

A little shell darted into the corner. Amy spotted the stowaway who'd almost started a fire inside of the stuffy little boat! She walked over to where the little thief had attempted to burrow deeper into the corner.

"Oh, no you don't!" She swooped in and grabbed the little thief before she could get into any more trouble. "Did you really think you could outsmart me?"

Henrietta snapped her claw at her. She grabbed one of Amy's curls and sliced through it.

"Where did you put it?"

But Amy spotted the corner where she'd tried to dart and quickly discovered who had been causing the *Mad Malloch* engine trouble. Henrietta had shoved blue bottle caps and even a handful of blue tootsie rolls into the corner. The entire flap of the engine was stuffed full of her blue treasure hoard.

Stuck beneath a blue candy wrapper was her salt trancing talisman.

Amy walked to the spot, and retrieved her talisman from Henrietta's stolen items. She pocketed the talisman, then set Henrietta back onto the ground.

The crab circled around her boot, then launched herself down into a crack in the floorboards.

"Good riddance. I hope I don't ever have to deal with your horrible behavior again," Amy huffed.

"Something real mad got in here and jumbled it all up," Sean said, waving his hand through the smoke. He turned back to the motor, as did Gwen.

With their backs turned against her, Amy reached into her bosom, and tugged out a purple bottle. The fuzzing *hiss* and *pop* of the salt inside complimented the gurgling putter of the struggling motor.

She walked over to where a plume of steam was issuing out from the steering wheel and uncorked the stopper. She tipped the bottle forward, releasing a single drop into the engine.

Vrrirrmmmmmm!!!

The engine sprang to life. Its gears ground out an angry putter, then settled back to a steady hum.

"Fixed it!" Sean yelled, staggering up to a standing position.

"Oh, thank goodness!" Gwen piped, wiping the back of her hand across her brow. "And to think I was stressing about Damien's engagement!"

Amy's mouth dropped open. Not only was there a party full of whiskey and the celebration of Yule to be had, but Selia was *engaged*?

Gwen clapped her hands together, turning to face Amy. "I'm hoping he announces the engagement to everyone at the winter solstice gathering tonight at the lighthouse."

Amy chewed her cheek, biting back the question she wanted to ask. The furious look Gwen gave her was enough to imply that she was not invited to the solstice gathering.

Gwen turned on her heel, setting distance between them. "If you will excuse my husband and I, we need to get prepared for the evening."

Amy scurried off the dock, elated with the new information she had obtained. Gwen had given her everything she needed to put the final details into place for an evening full of Yule's magic.

Oh, how much she adored a good gathering of Scottish people, especially when too much alcohol and kilts were involved. One thing was for certain. She couldn't celebrate the winter solstice without first finding a proper outfit—one that was sure to send everyone who gazed upon her into a spell they wouldn't forget.

24

THE SGÀTHAN CLAN

Selia

Moonlight filtered through Selia's bedroom window, illuminating the aftermath of her and Damien's lovemaking. A night spent in ravenous sheet-ripping passion left her quite pleased with herself. She loved this man more than air, the sweet, protective, sexy father of her daughter.

Something long dormant had awakened inside of her. Her salt nodes were swollen with residual heat. Maybe the heat was left over from the euphoric rush of each orgasm she'd experienced. By the time she'd hit her seventh one, that heat surged through her like an electrical jolt, evaporating as quickly as it came.

Selia traced her finger over Damien's chest, loving that he was still sleeping so soundly. She didn't consider their sex life lackluster, although the night before was explosive to the point she'd not ever known. Something in her gut told her that the possessive wave of whatever it was, had been caused by the salt venom.

While Damien dozed, Selia's thoughts drifted back to the journal. It was *calling* to her, much easier now to decipher with the energy *hussshhhhhed* through her salt nodes.

A hollow sound was coming from the fireplace, a sound that made the hair on her neck stand up. She left the bed and walked over to the hearth, finding the voice wasn't the wind, but it was coming from beneath the dragon Yule log. The voice was eerie and liquid, full of space, yet constricting.

Damien had hidden the journal in the hearth beneath the log. Maybe he'd planned on burning it, who knew. Sika's words were tempting her as she spoke through it.

Selia took the journal and the salt venom and walked into the nursery. She sat down, propping the journal open in front of Damien's gorgeous painting. "I must know about my past. I want to know about my ancestry," she said aloud.

The oil stain rippled on the parchment, but no words formed. The *hushhhhhhhh* filling Selia's salt nodes soon became a voice. "It is not me who will show you. The salt preserves what the venom has corroded of your ancestry. To understand your past, you must first understand the bond between you and Celaeno's storm dragon."

Selia looked down at her engagement ring, then up at the mural Damien had painted for their baby. "Show me the bond between me and Celaeno's storm dragon."

Damien's mural went blurry. Fluffy white clouds became storms, and the moon a monster. The moon's rays of light began to ripple on the dark surface of the water.

The gentle *hussshhhhhhhh* flowing through her salt nodes became thunderous as the electrical energy pulsed through her.

Selia's hands were chapped from the cold wind and salt water. Her fingers ached. Judging by how violently the cold surface she was laying on shuddered, she and Amy were still somewhere in the open sea.

"Selia! Come up and see this!" Amy cried from the opening where sea water was sloshing into the boat.

Selia glanced out of the small peephole window that led out into the sea. A long sinuous tail slashed against the water, propelling their vessel across the deepest, darkest ocean she'd ever seen. The farther north they traveled, the colder the water became. The waves were capped with hard white edges and were unforgiving.

While the coiling motion of the waves could be mistaken for a dragon, Selia knew this was not the case. Amy had a knack for navigating triton currents—massive forces of turbulent water created by storm dragons. She'd maneuvered their boat into the powerful tail of one of these long, coiling currents to bring them back to the land where Celaeno's storm dragon was living. Waves rolled and pitched, cascading down the window opening.

Selia held her hands out, her fingers gripping splintered wood as the current thrashed against the boat. She feared the water was becoming too violent, threatening to flip them both overboard. Her stomach clenched with hunger, gripping tighter. They'd been riding this current for over three days now, with nothing to eat or drink other than some bread and a little bit of wine. The only water they drank came from collected rainwater.

She was homesick for Naunet, but not the Egyptian temples where Alexandra was busy corrupting the art of salt trance. Today, she would meet with Celaeno's storm dragon, hopefully forming a bond with him.

Amy appeared in the entryway that led up to the upper deck of the boat. Her red hair curled against the violent gales of wind, whipping past her trembling shoulders. "Get up here and watch the waves with me!"

Selia fought the urge to retch as she hiked her way up from the lower deck, saltwater sloshing between her toes. Clouds drifted across a steel grey horizon, one that seemed as endless as the violent ocean before them.

"There!" Amy pointed, running for the front of the boat.

Selia squinted at the horizon. The scent of woodsmoke met her nose. A tiny orange light flickered in the distance.

"That's Winter Forest!" Amy squealed, her face breaking into a grin. How she had this much enthusiasm after three days at sea was beyond Selia, who could hardly keep what little food they had aboard their boat down. Amy's freckles looked so much darker as nightfall descended upon them. Her emerald eyes stood out against the darkening horizon.

Amy withdrew a robe from a trunk resting on the dock. She swung it around Selia's trembling shoulders. "We'll have food and a warm bed to sleep in tonight. The Sgàthan clan never fails to disappoint."

Selia swallowed down a burp that threatened to become vomit. "I can't wait to be on land again."

Amy's eyes were glinting with glee. Selia would finally meet the clan of huntsmen she'd raved about since they'd journeyed from Egypt. The Sgàthan clan—a nomadic group of huntsmen who were the sons of Atlantean kings.

Amy turned toward the front of the boat, clapping her hands together. "I release you back to the sea!"

The crashing, coiling tail of the triton current released the boat, submerging itself back into the ocean. The boat vibrated beneath Selia's feet as the wooden hull scraped against land. The scent of damp, cold soil met Selia's nose—so different from the hot, parched sands in Egypt.

Amy hopped from the boat, prancing up the shore like a child waiting to dart into the unknown. Selia stepped onto the earth, grateful it didn't give beneath her soles. The soil was so different here. It didn't shift through her toes—it clumped. For being winter, there was still so much green. What were they called? Mosses? Ferns? Lichens? There were so many flora species Amy had told her about that grew on the island. Many of them were flora fae species full of medicinal powers like blue minca.

She inhaled the cold, nose-burning air, trying to imagine just how green this foreign land was during the day. While starlight flickered above, the sky seemed shallower, cut off by pointed, black silhouettes. *Trees*, that was one floral species she could identify. Trees were silent giants whose roots held the soil in place, preventing it from eroding into a river or a sea. The ancient ones were immovable, unlike the grassy reeds enveloping the Nile that were harvested for papyrus.

Amy scanned the shoreline, searching for something along the rocks. With it being so dark, Selia could hardly see the landscape before them. There was a hill, and a hill beyond that. Her body ached with cold and hunger. Who knew how long it would be before she could get her famished body to start walking again.

Amy made her way back to her, holding what appeared to be a garment in her petite hands. "It's been a long voyage, time to dress up for our arrival." She handed Selia one of the garments—the oddly-shaped one, that clattered when it fell into her hands.

"What is this?" Selia asked.

"It's an offering from the clan," Amy said, her eyes glinting dangerously.

Selia held up the frumpy garment that appeared to be constructed out of driftwood. "I think this is nipple splinters waiting to happen."

Amy hiked her head back and laughed. "My friend said the same thing when she saw it."

"Where is your friend? Is she still here?" Selia asked, hearing the emotion in Amy's voice.

Amy didn't look her in the eye, instead, she busied herself with her own nipple-splintery garment. "Not to bother. We have so much to do and little time to introduce you to Celaeno's storm dragon." She shimmied her body into her garment.

Selia's stomach churned with something other than hunger. What if Celaeno's storm dragon didn't like her? She did what she could with the frumpy dress of drift wood, giving up half-way with the bizarre strap that she assumed was meant to fasten over her shoulders. She fastened her pouch full of salt chrysalises to her side. It was the only real possession she'd brought with her from Egypt.

If everything played out right, the storm dragon would turn the chrysalises into salt trancing talismans. With them, she would be able to practice salt trancing like her ancestors did, and summon some of the most powerful storms known in existence.

The stout silhouette of a giant someone appeared up the path. "How is my favorite selkie in all of the seas?" the silhouette asked, a plume of condensation billowing when he spoke. His voice was deep and earthy like the forest.

Amy launched herself into the arms of the giant silhouette, her body dwarfed by his size. He walked with her clung to his side, the muscles of his arms catching the orange torchlight.

"Oh, Ewan. I've missed you," Amy said as Ewan lowered her to his side. He was almost twice as tall as she, and a good arm's length as wide.

What Selia could make out of the huntsman in the dim light was exactly as Amy had described. His face was strong and square. His cheeks and half of his neck were concealed behind a thick mass of reddish-brown facial hair. Long, unruly locks fell to his shoulders. Ewan's eye color was that of wood—both brown and green. Not the sea green that Amy's eyes often turned when she was curious about something. Ewan's green was deep and layered, capturing a place where woody plants thrived.

His forest-green eyes landed on Selia. "Is this who you've brought to meet the storm dragon?"

"Selia is a spectacular fit for him," Amy said, her voice high and breathy.

"The sooner she meets him, the quicker he leaves my hunting ground," he said, his gaze intensifying.

Selia gave a small nod toward Ewan as the knot in her stomach tightened. "I am eager to meet this storm dragon. I'm so glad to finally meet you."

His eyes softened. "Likewise, daughter of the Nile." He held out his hand, rippling his thick fingers in a come-hither motion. "Please join us by the fire, Selia. As of tonight, you are part of our clan. There is much feasting and enjoyment to be had."

The crisp winter air became flavorful as Selia walked with Amy and Ewan up the hill. The sizzling scent of animal fat and something floral filled her nose. She didn't usually eat meat, but given the circumstances, she would devour almost anything.

More firepits appeared along the trail. A clearing emerged, where the subtle sound of laughter quieted. Seated along the length of a long wooden table were at least a dozen huntsmen. The members of Ewan's clan were dressed similarly to the lead huntsman. They wore kilts and cloaks made of animal hide. Their hair was thick and similar in texture and coloration. Some had tattoos on their arms and necks, each a bold, interwoven knot pattern.

"Men, let us welcome our guests!" Ewan bellowed, swinging his massive arms out to his sides.

Selia kept walking, not catching the cue to pause in her step.

Ewan stood before his fellow huntsmen, his cloak catching the yellow firelight from the hearth. Embers licked at his kilt as he squared his hips, turning toward the other eager male faces gazing up from the table. "My fellow huntsmen. I introduce to you, Amphitrite, goddess of the sea. And the Daughter of the Nile, Selia!"

The sound of teeth grinding against bone and flesh cutting through the crisp night air stopped. The feast had only paused for this moment of introduction. Laughter erupted from a few of the men, combining with the sizzling *pop* of meat from a roasted animal upon a wooden platter.

"You can't entertain guests with that beast. Yer kill is weak. I have a better trophy than that!" one of the huntsmen said, pointing up at the large stone hearth behind Ewan. A set of antlers hung from the trunk of a tree, illuminated by the orange flames.

"The hunt has only started," Ewan boasted, his shoulders squaring. His voice rang mighty and warm. "You know Errindoor is the only king worth following."

The men laughed, raising the legs of their feast in the air.

"Who is Errindoor?" Selia asked, amazed at just how large the antlers were. If Ewan would hold his arms out to his sides, she was convinced the antlers from this beast would still be wider than the massive huntsman.

"The fae king who migrates to the high meadow atop the sacred mountain every winter," Amy whispered. "Ewan and his men track Errindoor's movements every year, hoping to communicate with their ancestors."

Ewan walked to the head of the table beneath the antlers and tugged out two stumps on either side.

Amy flopped down on the stump to his left, while Selia took the one to his right.

"Is the dragon joining us tonight?" one of the men asked.

"We will see," Ewan replied, his gaze dropping to Selia as he took his seat at the head of the table. "We have a guest of honor he would be wise not to ignore."

Soon, wooden plates of meat and sloshing goblets of frothy beverage were flying toward Selia and Amy. The table was cluttered with sizzling meat, some kind of greens, and a few ripe berries.

Amy glanced up at Ewan, her brows drawing up. "Why aren't you feasting like the rest of your men?"

His hand dipped beneath the table. "I'm saving my appetite for something extra sweet tonight."

Amy flushed bright red as Ewan's hand worked up her leg. She grabbed one of the roasted legs of a foreign beast and brought it to her lips. Her canines dug into the meat, spraying droplets of fat.

Selia stared at the sizzling leg with bone protruding from the crackling flesh. She couldn't eat. Her nerves had turned her stomach into a knot. She wanted to meet Celaeno's storm dragon first.

"Well? Where is he?" Amy asked.

A lump in Ewan's throat shifted up and down as he gulped down his beverage. He set his goblet down on the table, rattling his plate.

Ewan glanced over his shoulder. "Speak of the devil, here he is now."

Selia's stomach knotted tighter than a freshly picked reed of papyrus.

A tall, sickly-looking man appeared to Ewan's left. Mats of dark hair clumped on his shoulders. He wore a robe that was the same gray color as Selia's driftwood dress, while it appeared to have much less texture. His eyes were as dark as the Temple of Isis on a moonless night. Not even starlight escaped their abyssal depths.

Cupped in his hands was a creature. It had feathers sticking out of its side at odd angles. Something dark and greasy coated its wings.

Was it *oil*?

Ewan held out his arm, grabbing the dragon's cloak. "Apologize to Selia. She has come a long way and does not deserve your lack of respect."

Selia's stomach turned over. Did Celaeno's storm dragon just sneer at her?

He sat across from Selia, next to Amy. While the huntsmen busied themselves with passing platters of meat and goblets of mead toward him, he refused to eat.

Selia felt like she was see-through. This dragon would rather stare out into the forest than interact with her. The dragon Amy wanted her to meet wouldn't even *look* at her. Was this really the storm dragon Amy wanted her to *bond* with?

Ewan dipped his chin, and a vein in his temple twitched. "Another victim of our recent storm, I take it?" he asked, his eyes dipping to the creature in his hands.

The dragon didn't say anything, his gaze shifting instead to Selia's. His eyes were anything but calm—they had deep brooding black storms swirling in them. He stood from his seat and turned, not looking back as he exited toward the forest.

As the evening wore on, Selia found herself feeling more frozen and alone. Her meeting with Celaeno's storm dragon hadn't gone as expected. He absolutely *hated* her.

With their plates cleared, and bellies full, Ewan's men retreated from the feast into their dwellings. A dusting of snow flurries began to fall upon the now cleaned table. The plates and goblets and bones were evidence of a night full of celebration, yet Selia felt like she'd already failed.

She didn't *like* this place. It was cold and wet and smelled of sweaty men and meat. She wanted to go home to Egypt. She wanted to curl up into a ball and cry. She was exhausted, and the food didn't sit well with her.

Amy's arm came to hers. "It's all right. Just give him time, and he is sure to warm up to you."

Selia tore her arm away from Amy and darted into the frozen forest.

25
MEMORIES

Selia

Selia's fingers scraped against the fabric rug beneath her. She lay on her back, gazing up at Damien's watercolor painting on the nursery wall. Her heart was pounding in her throat.

"Well? What did the salt venom share with you?" Sika's voice hissed.

Selia jolted to her side. The journal was lying on the ground, wide open.

She sat up and grabbed the journal. The pages were damp, and the oil stain darker than before. "Amy brought me to Winter Forest to form a coming-of-age ritual called salt stashing. Celaeno's storm dragon is who she wanted me to bond with." She remembered the dragon's sickly body and his severe dislike of her. He didn't want her there. She remembered his dark eyes catching the orange firelight. His eyes were so dark, even starlight was swallowed by them.

"You met Celaeno's storm dragon?"

"I did, but I was upset." She swallowed down a hard, parched knot in her throat. "I felt like he didn't want me there."

"Do you know *why* Amy brought you to meet with him?"

"He was sick. Amy brought me there to help make him better."

The voice went quiet, retreating like smoke. The quiet made Selia's mouth dry and parched. "Who else was there?"

"Men from the Sgàthan clan."

"Was Amy fond of any particular one of them?"

"She was, well, *he* was rather fond of her," Selia said, remembering how Ewan had placed his hand on Amy's leg. Even across from the table, she could feel the sexual tension building between them.

"Ewan knew if I bonded with Celaeno's storm dragon, that he would leave the island. But when the dragon ignored me, I got scared, so I ran into the forest." The coldness from that dark, hopeless moment enveloped her. "I want to know what happened. Where did I go from there?"

The sound of someone humming filled the hallway.

Selia snapped the journal closed. She shoved it under the rug as Damien peered into the nursery. The only article of clothing he was wearing was his boxers. The moment he spotted her, the bulge at his front hardened. "Good morning, my sexy goddess."

Selia's mouth dropped open. Her fiancé was like a miniature replica of the giant huntsman. While Damien was nearly half his size, his build was nearly identical. Even the dimpling cheeks were present. Everything from his eye color, facial structure, to his hair reminded her of Ewan.

He sauntered into the room, maneuvering in a funny way until he stopped at her side. His hand dropped to her cheek, where he brushed his fingers past her face. "I have never seen a side of you quite like what we had last night."

Selia locked her gaze with Damien's hazel eyes, the greens in them like little flecks of fire against the browns.

She climbed to her feet, stepping in front of the rug hiding the rectangular outline of the journal.

Damien cupped her face, holding her gaze level with his. "Whatever came over you last night, I want more of it." He pressed his lips to hers, kissing her tenderly. He pulled away, locking his gaze with her. "I want to marry you *now*. What do you say we make it official on the winter solstice?"

"How would we get married on such short notice?"

"My cousin is a minister. And I'd love to make it happen sooner than later. We wouldn't have to set a date or invite everyone. All of my family will be there."

Selia looked into his eyes, overcome with his sweetness.

He worked his hands down her neck. "We can spend our honeymoon as a babymoon together. We can make it simple. I was thinking we could go back to my art studio at the Celtic Sea where we first met." He pressed her against the wall. Why don't we head back to bed? You always taste the best in the morni—"

Screeech!

Selia looked past Damien's face, finding a fuzzy brown dart flitting in the room. "Peppercorn?"

"Oh, no. I'm not about to get blue balled by another fae pest," Damien said, repositioning himself in front of Selia.

Peppercorn swooped in, and landed somewhere near his foot.

"Ouch!" He stepped back, fumbling over the spot where the journal was.

"She *bit* me!" he cried, hobbling back.

"You probably stepped on her."

Selia's cell phone chimed.

"Go grab my phone, will you? I'll contend with her."

Damien left the nursery, grumbling something about *bloody little fae pests always ruining everything.*

"Hey, what are you doing?" Selia asked, lowering herself to the rug.

Peppercorn was perched atop the rectangular square of the journal under the rug. Her ears were pinned back against her furry head. The sounds she was making were not friendly at all. No longer high-pitched squeaks, she was creating a sound that could be mistaken for a growl.

Selia reached for the rug.

Peppercorn lunged at her, too, flitting over to her hand and nipping at her finger, drawing a tiny bit of blood.

Selia pulled her hand back. "Wow, what's gotten into you?"

"It went to voice message," Damien said, tossing the phone to Selia.

She grabbed it, and pressed Pixie's bat icon to call her back.

"Damien sold a painting!" Pixie exclaimed through the speaker.

"Wow, really?" Selia said, watching Peppercorn give Damien the death stare as he tried to inch closer to the rug. "Who is the buyer?"

"An older gentleman. I've had a lot of strange folks visit my shop, but this guy was really bizarre. The second he walked inside, my espresso machine froze up and refused to pull shots. That has never happened in all my time working here."

"That's wonderful news! I know Damien will be pleased."

Damien looked up, as Peppercorn took another dive for his foot. "Got ya, you little pest," he stammered, but Peppercorn outsmarted him, aiming for his face. "Ouch!"

Two little red pinpricks appeared on the tip of his nose.

"Are you *kidding* me?" He pinched his nose with his fingers and staggered out of the room cursing.

"Would you both like to stop in for breakfast?" Pixie asked. "It will be my treat. There is news about a winter storm blowing in. The sooner you get over here, the better. You know it's gonna be bad when they've gone and docked the fishing fleet for the day."

"I have some decorations to tend to," Selia lied.

"Well, send Damien over instead. I'll have some more of those scones I left with you last night and hot coffee waiting."

"He's preoccupied at the moment. With your bat, actually."

"I knew she'd show up eventually."

"How many paintings did he sell?"

"The bloke wants to buy *all* of them."

"That's lovely! I'll let him know right away and send him over!" Selia ended the call, and pocketed her phone.

Damien returned into the nursery, a bloody tissue in hand. "That's it. The nose-biter is out. No more fae creatures are welcome in this house!"

"Damien, you sold a painting!"

Damien's brows rose. "I did?"

"Pixie wants you to go over as soon as possible to meet with him before the winter storm blows in." She glanced outside at the thickening snow falling from the sky. "Why don't you leave Peppercorn with me, and you go meet up with the man who wants to purchase your artwork?"

"Are you trying to get rid of me?"

"No!" She grabbed his face, and kissed the red tip of his nose. "I don't think this is an opportunity my sexy stud of an artist fiancé would want to pass up."

Damien's cheeks dimpled. "Only if I get to come back to more of that before lunch." He gave Peppercorn a snide look before turning toward the hallway.

She left the room to see Damien off. He changed into a pair of jeans and a flannel shirt, while Selia pulled on a pair of leggings and the over-sized sweater Gwen had given her.

Once his shoes were on, he grabbed the car keys and made his way to the door. He left their home, bounding down the stairs and into the car. He peeled backward in reverse, then disappeared up the drive.

Selia let out a sigh of relief. At last, she was alone. The snow was already falling heavily, bringing a blanket of silence around their home. She could finally get back to the journal and see what other memories the salt venom had to share with her.

She walked toward the nursery, tugging out the bottle of salt venom from her pocket. The salt crystal inside was still rock hard with no sign of becoming liquid. Perhaps it was frozen? Either way, she didn't care. She wanted the salt venom to share more with her about her memories with Amy, Ewan, and Celaeno's storm dragon in Winter Forest.

When she re-entered the nursery, the rug had been turned over, and the room was full of shredded paper.

"No!" Selia cried, dropping to the floor and gathering what papers from the journal she could. Peppercorn had ripped out everything, leaving the journal's leather binding open.

Peppercorn was flying through the air, shrieking. She dove back and forth, turning her fuzzy little face until a series of high-pitched squeaking sounds escaped her little crinkling mouth.

"Why did you do that?" Selia scolded the bat.

With a quick flit of her wings, she drifted out of the room, leaving Selia alone with the remains of the journal.

She gathered what she could of the shredded pages and stuffed them back into the leather binding.

A massive *hsussususushshshshsh* filled the room. Selia's salt nodes were on fire. She reached into her pocket, tugging out the bottle of salt venom. The crystal had shattered, filling the bottle with a shimmering silver mist that swirled behind the glass. She had to release whatever the force was before it ripped through her.

She uncorked the stopper, releasing what appeared to be water vapor.

Windows clattered. Darkness enveloped her periphery. A darkness she remembered seeing in the eyes of Celaeno's storm dragon.

26

ALEXANDRA

Amy

Snow flurries swirled around Amy's face as she made her way up from the dock into town. She took off with the salt trancing talisman in search of its creator—a storm dragon. The talisman had a gravity of its own. It was a compass that she could use to find a storm dragon's location. Right now, it was tugging her straight toward the Bat Blitz Coffee Shop.

Storm dragons were the true masters of understanding the unpredictable nature of the sea. Everything from hurricanes to monsoons to droughts were in some way traced back to a storm dragon. They were very moody beasts, and their irritability was something to look out for. A cold snap was oftentimes a warning sign for greater cold to follow.

A bell on the door rang as Amy walked into Pixie's coffee shop. A familiar-looking man was standing near the window, looking over an exhibit of paintings on the wall.

"Hello, Amphitrite," a cool voice said from the room tucked behind the bookshelf.

Amy rounded the corner, finding the Iridescent Alexandra sitting at a table. She froze, wishing fate hadn't brought them together.

"I knew you were coming," Alex said, her voice hard. "I could feel your pulse."

Amy smirked. She knew Alex was jealous of her achieving her goal in the cavern with the Blind Moon. Releasing the fae queen into her possession was exactly what the Order wanted to prevent from happening. "What do you want?"

Alex folded her fingers together on the table. "Ever since our little bout in the cavern beneath the Rusty Selkie, I've been paying more attention to my own pulse. Then I realized, you went through all this trouble with Selia to redeem yourself for harming someone you loved."

Amy's hands balled into fists. "I don't need you to remind me of my past. I've already had enough of it flooding through me."

Alex dipped her chin. "Celaeno's storm dragon will be the one to remind you, not I."

Amy swallowed. Celaeno's storm dragon had lived alongside Selia for thousands of years, never stepping backinto her life until the salt trancing talisman appeared at the museum. That talisman had been one of many that resulted from Selia's first salt stash, which he assisted in forming.

Alex smiled. "All it takes is a single contaminated salt crystal for the venom to awaken from its dormancy. This was Naunet's last written record that she inscribed into the Codex."

Amy glared at Alex. She knew Naunet's work in the Temple of Isis had been eventually erased. When the plague of salt venom broke out, the Codex was greatly damaged, the venom corroding all but a simple statement.

"Do you remember the saying? What Naunet's last written words were that she had inscribed in the Codex?"

Amy remembered the seductive look Naunet had given her the moment she had her salt trance with the venom.

"Savor it. Surrender to it. All salt daughters of Celaeno will be tempted by it," Amy said, not taking her eyes off Alex.

Alex's eyes darkened. "Disturbing the graves of your ancestors is not wise. Who knows which spirits of your loved ones you might anger in the process."

Amy clenched her fists. "You're just angry that you couldn't stop Selia from opening the vault and releasing the fae queen to me."

Alex's lips curled up into a grin. "Masika will continue to haunt your memory. The voices of your ancestors are sure to turn the tides against one of you before this is all over."

Amy blinked. Alex was gone. As quickly as she'd appeared, the Iridescent had vanished, leaving behind a shimmering mist that slowly began to freeze. Ice crystals formed, reminding Amy why she'd come to the coffee shop. She had a storm dragon to convince in helping her crash Clan Malloch's winter solstice gathering.

27
FLIRTING WITH DRAGONS
Young Selia

Dull grey light illuminated the small dwelling Selia was currently huddled in. Running off like she had the night before left her alone and cold. She had been so exhausted, she didn't remember falling asleep. Nor did she remember finding a large warm blanket to snuggle up under.

She sat up and gazed around her dwelling. She'd stumbled into a hole of some kind—one animals would have used to shelter from the cold. *She* was the scared, frightened animal out here so far away from home. She missed the Nile. She missed the minca moths hovering back and forth between Isis's temple and the water. She'd not seen a single one of the fae creatures since arriving in this foreign winter land that made her body ache with cold.

She ran her fingers past the hair jutting out from the blanket. Was it fur? The blanket had two layers. Long thicker strands she could sift her fingernails under, and a soft fluffy layer was nothing like the scratchy texture of her linen clothing in Egypt.

Was it the hide of an animal? If so, what beautiful creature made this?

She dug the small linen bag of salt chrysalises out from her dress. She'd brought them all this way from Egypt, only to have Celaeno's storm dragon ignore her. Maybe she should just dispose of them. He'd barely made eye contact with her the night before. What made Amy believe that he would want to bond with her?

A pair of green eyes appeared in the hole above her. Amy's face shimmied into the hole, her wild red hair curling in every direction. "Good morning, my rebellious one," she said, her voice as hard as her uncoiling hair.

Selia's breath caught. The frozen forest towered over Amy, the red color of the bark almost matching her hair. She realized the source of the hollow she'd found refuge in from the snow.

Amy withdrew her face from the opening and appeared near the larger entryway. "Here, put this on," Amy said, tossing her another article of clothing.

Selia grabbed the cloak with fur that had the same texture as the garment she'd slept under. She fastened the cloak around her body, tugging it close to her core.

Amy crossed her arms in front of her chest, watching her. Her freckles were much more prominent out here in the cold. The seven starfish-shaped ones were even a little purple. Her brow, too, was furrowed. "Had it not been for Ewan, you would have frozen. What were you thinking running off like that?"

Selia looked away from Amy's penetrating gaze. She'd seen her angry before. She didn't want to be on the other side of Amy's wrath. She was a sea goddess after all. Angering her might result in something far worse than a swarm of angry male minca moths.

"Did Ewan give me these items?" Selia asked, raking her hands through the cloak.

Amy cocked her head to the side, sending a stray curl of her red hair down her shoulder. "He sure did. It didn't take him long to find you passed out in this hollow."

"How?"

Amy laughed. "Ewan is a *huntsman.* It's his job to track the wild beasts who live on this island. In this case, it was a petty little sea nymph who threw a fit and scampered off into Winter Forest!"

Selia tightened the cloak around her shoulders. "Is this from one of the beasts who live here?"

Amy wore a robe with the same color fur as the blanket. "Yes. That hide is from the fae elk who live here."

"What does an elk *look* like?"

Amy held her hands up over her head, splaying her wrists and fingers out wide. "They're quite terrifying. Especially the males—they have the big antlers that can gouge a huntsman in half."

Selia jumped. She glanced over her shoulder, half-expecting one of the beasts to be sneaking up on her. She knew there would be beasts on the island, but fae beasts that could cut you in half with a single swipe of their head?

"Where did you sleep?" she asked, noticing a spot on Amy's neck that seemed redder than most of her freckles.

Amy tugged the fur up to hide it. "None of your business."

Fwwissshhhh!

Selia jumped. The sound of crashing waves exploded in the air.

A couple of Ewan's men went darting up the hill. Both carried wooden bows.

Amy spun on her heels. "Bring the chrysalises. We have some catching up to do with our storm dragon."

Selia tucked the bag of salt chrysalises into her robe and walked with Amy after the men, her breath catching as she summited the hill. Anger rippled through her. She didn't want to meet with the dragon again, not after how he'd treated her the night before.

A pod of seals was jumping in the surf, their shiny, silver-grey bodies catching sunlight. They were so well camouflaged against the water, picking them out was nearly impossible. The only thing that gave them away were the white caps on the waves.

Seals weren't the only ones playing in the waves. Amid them was a group of sea nymphs.

"Selkies are here to play," one of Ewan's men said, propping his bow on the ground and wresting his hands atop it. She felt a little better knowing that Ewan's men didn't hunt sea nymphs.

Selia could see how the men could have mistaken sea nymphs for seals. They swam and dove together, their movements with the waves near identical. Some of the sea nymphs jumped into the water to play with the seals, while others stood on the rock, holding out their hands in a posture that meant they were busy salt trancing.

Selia's stomach clenched. She knew why the sea nymphs were gathered there, standing on the rocky outcroppings. They were here to claim a stash of their own. To do so, they would need to form a bond with a storm dragon.

She clutched the bag of salt chrysalises in her hand. She had competition for this island. A whole lot of it, judging by the others who looked to be right around her age. She clenched the bag harder, throwing out her idea of disposing of them earlier. She wasn't about to let another group of sea nymphs come in and steal what she'd worked so hard for.

Amy squinted at the horizon. "Do you see him yet?"

Selia scanned the water. "No."

Amy's freckles darkened. A mischievous gleam flashed in her eyes. "Look closer."

Fwwwwisshhhhh!

Water erupted once again from the sea. Something else appeared behind the water that *wasn't* a wave, but the coiling tail of water and sea spray.

Storm dragons kept their tails concealed behind fog, water vapor, or flashing veins of lightning. A storm bond was formed when he presented his tail to a sea nymph. He chose what the bond would be, not the sea nymph who presented salt chrysalises she'd collected. That bond served as the magical force that turned the chrysalises into salt trancing talismans.

A ripple of hope spread up Selia's spine. He'd not gone as far as to reveal his tail to any of the sea nymphs screaming in excitement. As far as she knew, he'd not chosen any of them to bond with.

Amy clapped her hands together. "Storm dragons are *complete* show-offs. They're no brains and all tail."

Fwwwwisshhhhh!

The dragon's coiling wave of a tail crashed against the rocks, sending sea spray over the jumping nymphs. Their elated voices carried on the air as their fingers branched for the rainbows created by the spray.

Amy hiked up her robe, perking up her breasts. "Are you ready?"

"Where are we going?"

"Out to demand an apology from him, of course!" Amy grabbed Selia's hand.

Selia dug her feet into the ground. "Absolutely not!"

"Why not?"

"He hates me."

"He does *not* hate you!" Amy cackled. "He's simply trying to *impress* you!"

Selia squinted at the shower of rainbows misting over the elated sea nymphs. Was all of this show really for her?

She started walking down the hill, wondering if Amy's assumptions were true. Maybe she'd misread his silence the evening before.

Selia and Amy descended the rocky slope, stopping at the beach where the surf broke against the shore.

"I don't feel like getting my hair wet, do you?" Amy asked.

Selia shook her head. The water was much too cold for her to even consider submerging herself.

Amy clapped her hands, and the water formed before her, parted for her to walk. Her salt trancing abilities were legendary—all it took was for her to use a single drop of her salt extracts, and with her pulse, she could manipulate saltwater without a second thought.

Selia took one step from the beach onto the path that emerged before her. She was walking along the bottom of the sea, creatures shifting behind the waves as she and Amy approached the rock where the sea nymphs were busy flirting with the dragon.

Sea nymphs in Egypt had taunted and bullied her for not having a salt stash yet of her own. What would the locals do when she decided to show up?

Amy took the first step onto the rock. Selia followed, gripping the slippery greenish-brown surface with her fingers and toes. She came eye level with five young sea nymphs close to her age. They were beautiful, each having long, reddish-brown hair. Their skin color varied. Some were honey tans, while others were bright creamy white. Almost all of them had blue or brown eyes.

"All right, gals, party's over," Amy said, and the other sea nymphs scowled at her. One-by-one, they dove into the waves, abandoning the rock.

The current began to spiral in the opposite direction. A male torso appeared, his greenish-purple flesh shimmering with scales. Two arms unfolded at his sides, palms facing up. Another spray of mist exploded through the air, revealing his face. His appearance was much more pleasant by the water than it had been by the orange firelight. His color appeared healthier—his expression vibrant.

Matted black hair draped past his shoulders. The lower half of his body was concealed by a coiling wave of siphoning ocean water.

Selia's heart leapt. Would he reveal his tail to her?

His eyes drifted to hers, dark pools of water. She recognized their cold depths from the night before. While they weren't any less deep, they were much warmer.

Selia caught the jealous looks on the other sea nymphs watching from the surf as the storm dragon approached her.

Amy took a step toward the storm dragon fast approaching. "I believe you have something to say to Miss Selia for how you treated her last night?"

The dragon thrashed his tail against the rock, sending spray into the air. A rainbow appeared in the sky. The sea nymphs cried out in delight as a rainbow rained down over her.

Selia's foot slipped, and she fell back. With an icy splash, she fell into the sea. The waves coiled around her, drawing her under.

Bubbles exploded from her mouth as she exhaled her breath into the water. Her chest seized as panic set in.

Was he going to drown her?

The bubbles settled, revealing the dragon as he approached.

Selia's fear was soon replaced with calm. How impossibly beautiful he was, shimmering like a blue diamond submerged in the water. Great intelligence shone from eyes that were as liquid as his surroundings. His eyes housed something ancient, great wisdom from times long ago. For a creature that was the son of such a violent storm dragon, Poseidon, there was great gentleness in his soul.

His face was long and angular, complete with a muzzle, with silver whiskers flowing out from either sides of his flaring nostrils. A long, scale-covered neck flowed with the current, curving like a giant blue serpent. His body was longer than it was wide. Storm dragons were sea serpents, their bodies following the ebb and flow of the tides.

Selia reached out, grabbing his jaw. His scales were oddly smooth, not sharp like she imagined them to be. She traced her fingers along his angular jaw, finding the texture roughening the closer to his chin she became.

"Blind Moon..."

His voice, a great thunderous echo, filled her.

He was speaking to her mind.

No, to her *heart*.

Her pulse slowed, matching with the rhythm of the current surrounding them.

"Tell me your name," she said, bubbles erupting from her mouth. Her words were lost to the sea, swallowed by the current.

The dragon shifted away from her, retreating with the current. The kindness in his eyes disappeared behind the bubbles as she was tugged back into the water.

28

SEAN

Selia

The bitter taste of salt filled Selia's mouth. She'd been under water, breathing in the ocean with a storm dragon who was bonding with her. At least she thought he was. The storm dragon's tail remained hidden, concealed by the dark ebony water.

Those deep, liquid eyes—where had she seen them before? They were hauntingly familiar. And why did she think of Alex when she remembered them?

She rested on her hands and knees, recovering what she could of her own breath. She could hear his low, thundering voice in her salt nodes.

"Daughter of Ceeelaaaeeennnoooooo..."

Was the storm dragon the one creating that low, reverberating sound all along? If so, was he still trying to communicate with her?

The bond they had formed, what was it? She had to know. The current had evaporated before she could feel it thundering through her body. The sensation was a mixture of pleasure and pain—a sensation of euphoric drowning.

The bottle of salt venom sat on the ground next to her. There was no crystal inside it. Had it evaporated? Why was her skin burning? Her throat, too, was parched, like she'd drank something incredibly dry and sharp.

The rumbling sound of a car engine purred up the drive.

She tucked the empty bottle into her pocket and climbed to her feet to gaze out the window. While had been immersed in the salt venom's liquid breath, the landscape had transformed from brown and green to white. Both Damien and Gwen were making their way up the drive toward the house. His arm was around his sister, whose face was as white as the snow.

Selia walked into the kitchen in time for Damien to walk with Gwen through the front door.

"Well? What did the buyer say about your artwork?" Selia asked.

Damien's jaw was clenched, his expression hard. "The jerk wasn't even there. But I'm glad I went, because Gwen had something come up that she needs help with sorting out."

Gwen flopped down on one of the kitchen chairs, not looking at Selia at all. Her eyes were glassy, and her lips trembled. "Sean. Gone," were the only words that escaped her mouth.

Selia jolted. "What?"

Damien brushed the snowflakes out of his hair. "We don't know what happened to him."

Gwen was trembling. "I stopped by the boatyard this morning to help him with the *Mad Malloch's* engine. After we got it up and running, I went to grab us some lunch. When I returned to the boatyard, his boat was gone..."

Selia swallowed. "Have you tried calling him?"

"He's not answering his phone either," Gwen replied. "The entire fleet was docked for this storm. You've heard the alerts. They're telling people this could be the storm of the century, and my husband is somewhere lost in it." She reached into her coat pocket, tugging out an item. "This is what I found on the dock where his boat should have been."

Selia's stomach hollowed. The item had a remarkable resemblance to a salt trancing talisman. "May I see that?"

Gwen handed the item to her. The stone was damp and cold, unusually heavy for its size.

Her salt nodes began to fill with the eerie liquid voice again. "*Ceee-laaaeeenoooooo.*"

She pocketed the item.

Another vehicle pulled up outside. Pixie and Peter appeared from the car, both carrying armfuls of what appeared to be baking ingredients.

Selia opened the door, allowing them inside.

"Okay. This went from pretty to maddening in less than an hour," Pixie said as she bound into their home. "I sent everyone at the shop home early. No use having people get hurt out in this mess."

Selia closed the door as soon as Pixie and Peter came in. Pixie's eyes were red, but not red like Gwen's. "What's up with all of the ingredients?"

"My oven is out," Pixie replied. "Did you get my text asking if I could borrow yours at least for the afternoon? If I'm going to cater this feast of yours tomorrow, I'd better get baking."

"That's fine with me."

She and Peter set bags of flour, sugar, and three cartons of eggs on the kitchen counter.

"Sean isn't the only one missing," Pixie said. "Have you seen Peppercorn yet? I'm awfully afraid of her being out in this storm."

"Who is Peppercorn?" Gwen asked.

Damien pinched his nose. "Pixie's pet bat."

Gwen jumped up. "You have a *bat* living in this place?"

"She's been acting strange lately," Pixie said. "Selia, didn't you say that she bit Damien on the nose?"

Selia stifled a giggle as Gwen clasped both of her hands over her face.

"Enough about the bat. We have a man missing and times a-ticking." Damien crossed his arms in front of his chest. "Well? Who is looking for him? We can't just sit here on our arses and let this storm threaten his life."

Gwen let out a sob.

"We've started a search party. The Coastguard is on their way now," Peter said, looking from Damien to Pixie, then back to trembling Gwen. "I'll do everything I can to bring him home."

"Where are Gemma and Bram?" Damien asked.

"They're baking cookies with Sean's parents right now," Gwen said as her eyes began to water. "I'll call them and ask if they can stay the night. I can't let them know their father is missing just yet."

Damien wrapped his arm around Gwen again. "We'll find him, okay? There's still plenty of daylight."

Selia glanced outside at the sleet and snow accumulating. "You can't go out in this."

Damien was already tugging on his coat. He grabbed a hat and stuffed it atop his head. "I have to. You heard the radio. This cold can *kill*. Someone from my family is stuck out in it."

Peter kissed Pixie on the cheek as he stuffed his hat down onto his head.

Selia looped her arms around Damien's neck, pulling him into a hug. "Promise me you'll both come back safe?"

He squeezed her back, brushing his face past her ear. "I promise. I love you."

The afternoon crept by as Selia and Pixie got to work baking for the feast. Gwen locked herself in the guest bathroom, for fear of having a '*wretched bat*' show up, leaving Selia alone with Pixie in the kitchen.

In only an hour, the amount of snow had quadrupled. Gale-force winds battered the windows, making the lighthouse creak and groan.

"Oh, how I hope this is all just a misunderstanding and Sean shows up somewhere safe," Pixie said as she slammed her fist into a wad of dough. "Tell me again how many we're baking for?"

"Thirty-nine aunts, uncles, and cousins according to Damien and Gwen."

Pixie wiped her hand past her face, smudging her nose with flour. "Good thing I came over. I feel just awful for Gwen. Even if she does hate bats, I can't imagine how scared she must be feeling right now."

Selia needed something to do with her hands. She couldn't stand here for hours and do nothing but worry about the three men battling the cold front that seemed to manifest out of nothing.

She stared out at the snow, suddenly overcome by the quiet. The white powder seemed so beautiful and light, yet the cold could easily claim a life. The memory of the sea nymphs jumping up to catch the sea spray rainbow crashing over their heads came to mind.

Gwen appeared in the kitchen, her face still ghostly white. Her hair was sticking out on end, and she had dark bags under her eyes. "I'm so scared. What if they don't find him?"

Selia walked up to her. "I'm so sorry that you are going through this." She reached into her pocket, finding the item Gwen had given her.

Fwip!

Selia jumped as the bag of flour exploded into a white puffy cloud.

Schreeeech!

A tiny white face poked out from behind the bag that was now torn in half.

"Oh, there you are!" Pixie squealed.

Peppercorn shook her fuzzy little head, sending puffs of white into the air.

"Get that little devil away from me!" Gwen cried as she went running out of the room.

Peppercorn fluttered across the table and landed on the item Peter had found by the dock. She clamped her tiny black feet around it, and with a swift flap of her powder-white wings, took off.

"Oh, no you don't!" Selia said, taking off after the bat that now looked like a ghost. She checked both the nursery and the bedroom with no luck. The door to the lantern tower was cracked open. Had she flown up into the tower?

Selia climbed the stairs, cursing with every step she took. "I swear, if I get all the way up here and you're just trying to play a prank..."

The tower moaned as wind and sleet pelted the metal surface. She summited the last step, finding the lantern room was frozen solid. Her breath froze into icy puffs.

The item lay at the center of the lantern room on the platform where the beacon was missing. The second she grabbed it, her salt nodes swelled with heat. The storm swirled around her as the liquid *husssshhhhhhhhhh* filled her mind.

PART 4
WINDOW TO THE PAST

29

DRAGONS & QUEENS

Amy

Amy felt the temperature change on the back of her tongue. The sensation felt as though she'd drank something that couldn't decide if it wanted to be cold, or warm. Now that she had petty Alexandra out of her hair, she had storm dragon to confront. If she was to convince the fae queen to open her window to the past, she would need his assistance. Her magic was as beautiful and icy as a snowflake forming on the winter solstice.

"Marveling at dragons now, are we?" Amy asked, sliding up beside Celaeno's storm dragon. He didn't even as much as grunt at her. The artist's signature she recognized as none other than Selia's fiancé.

Amy swallowed. Damien Malloch had named his paintings on display simply: **Storms of the North Sea**

Why *wouldn't* a storm dragon be flattered? The human imagination was such a beautiful thing, especially when it came to dragons.

"Ahem..." Amy tapped her foot on the ground.

There was no breaking the spell Damien's artwork cast on him.

"Speaking of storms, I need to ask a favor of you." She slipped in front of him, standing between him and Damien's paintings. She shimmied in her spot, however, she wasn't tall enough to block his gaze from the painting behind her. Celaeno's storm dragon was such a moody beast.

"Haven't you heard? Yule is fast upon us, and I know that, like this artist, you have a magical touch when it comes to manipulating the weather."

One of his large bushy brows lifted.

Amy's heart jumped. So far, her bribe was working. She tapped on his shoulder. "Can you sit with me? I have a certain fae creature who emerged from your ancient territory at sea. I think it would be wise if the two of you were, how should I say this, reacquainted?"

He dipped his chin, making his deep-set eyes visible. His movements were so slow and clumsy. He took a step backward, holding his arm out to his side. He pointed toward an empty table in the corner.

Amy led the way through the coffee shop. They sat opposite one another at a table beneath the window. Snowflakes fluttered outside, streaking past the glass and sticking to it in clumps.

One of Pixie's baristas came bustling over to greet them. "Are you the gentleman who was interested in purchasing the paintings? My manager told me to be on the lookout for you before I head home for the afternoon. We're closing the shop early as an arctic front is blowing in."

The dragon kept his gaze on his hands, which were turning blue.

The barista's gaze dropped to him.

Cooouuuuuggghhhhhnnnnnn!

Amy jumped, as did the barista, who cupped her hand over her mouth. "Oh, that doesn't sound good. Why don't I get you something warm to drink? I can spike it with something if you'd like." She whipped out her pen and notepad.

Amy patted his arm as his growl became more threatening. "He'll have tea for now."

The barista nodded and retreated back to the bar.

Amy tucked her hand into her bosom, finding the sharp edges of the fae queen's wings. "I have a wintry gift for you."

She returned her hand to the table, cradling the queen in her palm. The queen fumbled out onto her wrist, her wings not yet fully formed. They were dull and lifeless. No shimmer, but a crusty brown. Coaxing her out into the open when she was not at her most beautiful was a feat. Even fae creatures were insecure when they lacked their beauty.

His dark eyes dipped to the queen as she scurried around Amy's wrist, seeming disoriented and dazed. The light of day was not her favorite, nor was the noise created by the customers at the coffee bar.

He closed his eyes. His shoulders rolled back, and the clutter of voices began to quiet.

Amy's breath caught. Her pulse became the only thing she could hear. Storm dragons could not only control weather patterns, but they could dull sounds by manipulating the water in the atmosphere. He must have sensed the queen's distress. As the blanket of silence descended upon them, magic unfolded between the dragon and the fae queen—ancient magic her ancestors would have seen as medicine.

This was a spectacle worth seeing. It was a reunion of large and small. Male and female. Ancient, and newly formed.

He set his hand on the table. The fae queen seemed to recognize him. She could sense he, too, was an ancient soul—one that at one time, guarded her maternal salt pod of Celaeno.

Amy's ears were stuffy with the silent air. Her fingers cramped with cold.

His breathing became so shallow. She wondered if he had dozed off. Why were his eyelashes turning white? Were there ice crystals forming on them?

Amy set her hand on his beefy arm. "What are you doing?"

"Oh, it's drafty in here!" the barista said, bustling over.

Fwip!

The barista's legs went slipping out from beneath her. Both mugs full of piping hot liquid froze mid-air. "What in the world?" she said, shielding her face from the wave of ice spreading over her head. Both mugs fell to the ground, shattering on impact.

Fsssshhhhhhh!

"What's going on?"

"*Oi!* The pipes are bursting!" someone cried from behind the bar.

The fae queen scurried up his arm, perching herself atop his shoulder.

Amy found her footing and stood. "Stop this at once!" she cried, slamming her fists down on the table. The wood had ice splinters creeping over the surface.

The dragon opened his eyes, both dark pools of ebony storms swimming inside of them. This was an entirely different side to his moodiness, one Amy wished she would have braced herself for better.

Squaring his shoulders, he stood.

"Oh, no you don't!" Amy said, reaching for the fae queen as she scurried further up his beefy shoulder.

He turned on his heel and made way for the nearest exit.

"Hey! Where are you going?" Amy cried, but he'd already stormed toward the hall.

Crash!

One of Damien's paintings fell, the glass shattering on the ground as the dragon's thick shoulder brushed past the frame.

"Wait!" Amy cried, but she was too late. He had already stormed out into the snow.

30

STORM BONDS

Young Selia

Selia spent the remainder of her evening revisiting what Celaeno's storm dragon had shown her beneath the water. She sat in front of the fire, snuggling under her fur cloak as embers whipped past her.

Something had happened beneath the water she hadn't expected—the sea had filled her lungs not with water, but with oxygen. She'd breathed more clearly down there than she ever had walking along the banks of the Nile, where the air was quickly becoming as polluted as the dying river.

From what she remembered from her teachings in the Temple of Isis, there were *seven* storm bonds total. Six of them encompassed weather, while the seventh was so rare, that it was in danger of becoming forgotten. The last sea nymph to form the seventh bond had been Isis. She'd formed the bond with Poseidon.

She gazed around the fire, finding the sons of Atlantean kings had thinned. They were preparing for a hunt, moving about camp sorting their supplies, while Ewan settled next to Amy.

The two had whispered to each other all evening, Ewan sometimes dipping his face behind Amy's ear. Selia wondered what it felt like having a man brush his rough facial whiskers so close to her salt nodes.

Ewan stood from his place by the fire, carrying in his arms another one of the elk hides he'd given to her earlier. "A young lass shouldn't go running out into the wild without someone to protect her," he said, tossing the hide to Selia.

The soft fur landed in her lap, which she tugged around her legs. "Thank you for giving this to me last night. Amy tells me that I wouldn't have survived the night without it."

Ewan's hazel gaze dipped to Amy. "Amy tells me you made quite the impression on the storm dragon this morning?"

Selia shook her head, resentment filling her stomach again.

After the hearths dwindled to smoldering ash, Selia walked with Amy down the path into the forest. As much as she hated to meet with the storm dragon again, something inside of her desperately wanted to know if a bond had formed. The only way she could know, was to meet with him again.

They ventured into the forest, stopping outside one of the hollowed red giants.

Amy grabbed her hand as they stopped outside of his dwelling. "Celaeno's storm dragon is waiting for you."

Selia's stomach pitted. What would happen next? "If for some reason a bond doesn't form, promise me we can return to Egypt?"

Amy squeezed her hand before releasing it. "I promise. If no bond takes place, we will leave for the Nile first thing in the morning." She turned on her heel and walked farther into the forest.

Selia shifted her feet against the cold ground, not wanting to commit to rejection again. She tugged the robe Ewan had given her around her core. Snow had started to fall, this time in thick flakes that stuck to her robe. The flap of animal hide covering the opening to his dwelling shifted in the wind, letting out a blast of warm air.

Selia grabbed the flap, peeled it back, and walked inside.

Steam filled the hollowed space, making it difficult to breathe. She coughed as she entered the warm, damp hollow of the tree. The scent of earth and wood filled her senses. A dull orange glow illuminated the wooden walls.

A firepit sat in the center of the room, which was the source of the steam billowing up into the hollow tree. Rocks had been placed over the dwindling coals. Logs and branches draped over her head, preventing the steam from escaping.

Fwissshhhhhh!

Another burst of steam issued from the fire as the silhouette of a man appeared. He stood behind the hearth. His face remained concealed by the steam billowing into the room. His upper body was not clothed. His chest and torso were visible through the burning water vapor.

The steam parted, revealing his face. His eyes were bloodshot and sickly looking—not the deep, healthy pools of darkness she remembered when he'd been in his dragon form.

Selia's hands balled into fists. "Well? Have you chosen to form a bond with me?"

He pointed at the fire where the steam began to die.

A wooden bowl full of water sat next to it.

"Do you want me to pour water on the hearth?" she asked.

He nodded.

Selia crouched beside the fire and grabbed the bowl, finding the stones at the center weren't normal looking. They were oblong in shape, and each had a slight spiral at the center.

So he *had* salvaged the salt chrysalises after all.

Selia grabbed the bowl sloshing with water and poured it toward the chrysalises, which appeared to have changed into stone.

Abbbbbyyysssssssss.

Another plume of steam erupted from the hearth. Selia set the bowl back on the ground. She looked from the fire, to him. His dark eyes had an apology swimming inside of them.

He crouched down opposite of her across the hearth and reached his hand out through the steam. Water vapor rose up, catching his palm and changing the color of his skin. A shimmering layer of purplish-green scales began to form on his hand. The colors were beautiful, almost hypnotizing.

An image appeared at the center of his palm, an image of the world beneath the sea. She could feel the tug of the current siphoning around her, threatening to pull her under.

Something dark swam there in the water, something long and coiling. His tail, this was it! He was revealing it to her!

Waves crashed and lightning enveloped the image. A storm was brewing deep within the sea. Darkness enveloped the water, swallowing the image.

"I didn't see anything," Selia said, fighting not to cough into the steam.

The salt chrysalises began to explode in the fire, each sending another burst of steam as they popped.

"*Abbbbyyyysssssss,*" erupted from the fire.

Selia's eyes became heavy as the room began to blur. Darkness settled upon her as the steam filled her lungs.

31
ANCESTRY

Selia

A loud *screeeeching* sound filled Selia's ears as the lantern room reappeared. She gripped the metal railing in front of her as her pulse settled. The screeching wasn't Peppercorn, but something else.

Her ears began ringing. No, her *phone* was ringing. She grabbed her phone from her pocket. The doctor's office was calling.

She pressed the answer key and brought the speaker to her mouth. "Let me give you all an earful. Nobody in their right mind calls a pregnant woman about rescheduling a sonogram only to keep her waiting all weekend. Now, unless you're calling me to reschedule, I say you stop harassing me, or someone is going to lose their head!"

The sound of typing followed through the speaker.

"Hello?" Selia stammered, anger rising through her.

"I've made a note on your account. How about we schedule you for nine AM Monday morning?"

"I'll be there."

She ended the call, feeling quite content with herself. She began her descent down the spiral staircase. The tower warmed with each step she took.

She walked through the door, finding Pixie standing there. Her mouth was half-way open, and her brows were arched into her bangs.

"What did you hear?" Selia asked, realizing the tower might have acted like a megaphone, projecting her voice into the house.

"Nothing. Well, something about the health of your baby, and the fact that you were going to rip someone's head off if they didn't reschedule your sonogram."

Selia sucked in a breath.

Pixie's eyes widened. "It's true? You're *pregnant*?"

"Yes, it's true. Damien and I are expecting."

Pixie clapped her flour-coated hands to her cheeks, sending white puffs into the air. "Oh my gosh! No *wonder* you've been avoiding caffeine!" She gave Selia a hug. "You are going to be an absolutely amazing mom."

Selia's heart warmed.

"Does Gwen know?"

"No, she doesn't," Selia said, pulling away from Pixie. "Damien and I haven't told anybody yet. Promise you won't tell?"

"Of course!"

A shriek pierced the air.

Gwen came running through the hall as Peppercorn's fuzzy white body came flitting after her. "She's going to eat me!"

"She's not going to *eat* you," Pixie piped, holding out her hand in the air.

Peppercorn swooped down, landing on Pixie's palm.

"What on *earth* has gotten into you? Biting people's noses? Diving into my flour, then chasing people down the hall? I expected better of you!"

Selia stifled a laugh. She wished that she had the same effect on Henrietta. There was no use trying to knock any sense into that opinionated little hermit crab.

Peppercorn tucked herself behind Pixie's hair and disappeared before Gwen could see where she went. "Come on, you two. There is no way I'm going to make enough meat pies and pastries for thirty-nine guests alone. We need to start cooking now, or this winter solstice feast isn't going to happen!"

After spending a few hours elbow deep in bowls of scone batter and baking sheets full of cookies, nightfall was well on its way. Selia's mind began to drift between her memories with the storm dragon, and what horrible things might happen to her fiancé. Damien and Peter could very well be gone all night looking for Sean. What would happen if they didn't find him before sundown?

The memory of ash and fire and water vapor wasn't helping her thoughts at all. Had the bond between her and the dragon formed? If so, why was it clouding her memory with darkness?

"It's weather like this where Sika is out having her fun," Gwen said as she unloaded another batch of scones from the oven and set them on the table. "She's probably the one creating this storm."

As Selia poured cake batter into another pan, memories of Winter Forest flashed before her. Ewan had been preparing to go on a journey to track the fae king, Errindoor. "The folktale where the two selkies attempted to summon the Abyss, how did the last line go? Didn't it mention something about a *king*?"

Gwen cleared her throat. "Salt, storms, and starlight, of which we sing. Your light we find in the crown of a king."

"I wonder who the king is," Selia said.

Gwen shrugged. "Beats me. That was always the most confusing line for me. The king could be anyone, really. I imagine he could even be some distant relative of ours from Atlantis."

Both Pixie and Selia shared wary glances.

"How do you know that?" Selia asked.

"I've done my fair share of poking and prodding through Clan Malloch's ancestral records over the years. Hasn't Damien shared anything with you about our ancestry?"

"He's mentioned the Sgàthan clan, but nothing about Atlantis," Selia replied.

"After Atlantis sank, a refugee group of huntsmen known as the Sgàthan clan traveled north and repopulated the land where we live today. Clan Malloch originated from these people. The name Malloch has a few meanings. The most popular is *son of Ian of the bushy eyebrows*."

"What's the other?" Pixie asked.

"The clan motto—*S rioghal mo dhream*, which means, *my race is royal*. Sgàthan is the Celtic Gaelic word for *mirror*. Our blood mirrors that of royalty. I like to think that royalty originates from Atlantis."

Selia's stomach hollowed. Ewan—the huntsman who had a striking resemblance to her fiancé. Was Ewan Damien and Gwen's huntsman ancestor?

Peppercorn came flying in, carrying something between her feet. She dropped the item onto the table, sending a white *poof* of flour into the air.

Gwen squinted at the leather binding. "Why did you rip up one of my books?"

"I didn't, Peppercorn did," Selia said as Peppercorn fluttered out of sight.

Pixie went chasing after her, waving a spoon and yelling, "Enough of this harassment!"

Gwen grabbed the shredded remains of the book. "I recognize this binding from the bookstore."

"I bought it when Damien and I stopped in."

"Oh, that's the one that whispers," Gwen said, flipping over the cover.

Selia's mouth went dry. "You've heard it, too?"

"Why do you think I tried to set it away from the others?" Gwen grabbed the journal and held it up to her face. "I had a feeling this thing was bewitched. What did it say to you?"

"I'm more concerned with who the voice belongs to. I think the voice belongs to Sika, and that she has been speaking to me through it."

"Sika, the selkie from the urban myth?"

Thundering footsteps echoed up the hall. Pixie darted into the room, beaming with Peppercorn perched on her shoulder. "They found them!"

Gwen launched herself from her seat and toward the front door. Selia didn't wait to follow suit.

Damien, Peter, and Sean were all inside, each looking like they'd survived the torment of a blizzard.

Gwen jumped at her husband, who nearly toppled to the ground. Pixie, too, dove toward Peter, who caught her in his arms.

Damien's face was red with windburn. His hair stuck out wildly, like someone had yanked it in every direction. Bags shone under his eyes. But his cheeks dimpled, returning hope to Selia.

He grabbed her, burying his face into her neck. His cheeks and nose were freezing still. Even his embrace, which always warmed her, brought cold to her center. "I'm so glad to be home," he whispered.

Selia looped her arms around his neck, taking a handful of his thick hair. "I can't tell you how worried I have been."

With the storm finally cleared, Pixie, Gwen, and Peter all climbed into their vehicles and left. Selia and Damien retreated to the bedroom with a couple of meat pies and a bunch of muffins Selia and Pixie baked.

"Wow, you ladies sure know how to cook," Damien said as he sat on the bed and downed one of the pies.

Selia sat next to him. With the stress from the day finally behind them, she, too, seemed to have recovered her appetite.

Damien wrapped his arm around her, tugging her close. "Tomorrow is the big day when you get to meet everyone. Are you ready to surprise everyone and tie the knot?"

She grabbed his other hand, which was still cold. "I can't believe you went out in the weather like this."

"You do whatever it takes for family," he said, squeezing her. He squinted at the fireplace. "Where is it?"

"Where is what?"

Damien released his grip on her. "The journal."

Selia's stomach hollowed.

He stood, walking over to the fireplace and crouched down to the Yule log. "Selia, did you remove it?"

"Peppercorn found it."

Damien's brows drew up. "Then where the hell is it?"

"Peppercorn ripped it apart. I'll show you." Selia took him into the kitchen, showing him the remains of the book. She sighed. Thank goodness she had Peppercorn to blame for its destruction.

Damien bent down, grabbing a handful of the shredded parchment. "I'll hand it to the nose-biter. She sensed something dark about it, too."

A stone wedged in Selia's stomach. Why was she lying to the man who would risk his life in the middle of a dangerous snowstorm for his family?

He wrapped his arm around her. "Come on. Let's go light that Yule log and make the most of it."

They returned to the bedroom, where Damien tossed the shredded paper onto the hearth. He grabbed a match from the mantle, struck it against the wood, and tossed it toward the Yule log. Within seconds, the dragon-shaped log was spitting fire, filling the fireplace with orange and yellow flames.

"As long as that thing is gone, that's all I care about," Damien said, sitting back down next to Selia and taking her hand into his. "One thing I learned, never let a fairy tale come between you and those you love."

While the room filled with warmth, Selia was still chilled with the cold, liquid voice ringing in her salt nodes. Maybe it was the voice inside the paper that was screaming as the parchment caught fire.

Something dark escaped the shadows, the darkness she remembered in the eyes of Celaeno's ill storm dragon.

32

ICE QUEENS

Amy

Amy spent the past hour scouring the beach, wishing that she could turn back time. She'd shown the storm dragon the fae queen in the coffee shop. The second she did, he blew out of there like the winter storm he was.

But taking off with the precious cargo? That was not what Amy had expected of him.

Amy buckled at the core, setting her hands on her knees and bending over. As her blood pounded in her ears, she tried to visualize her backup plan. She didn't have one. Running up and down the beach screaming his name like a mad woman wasn't going to help do anything other than get the local seagulls laughing at her.

She squinted at the horizon. Whatever was fast approaching the beach was no normal cloud. The air was pregnant with moisture that was quickly freezing over.

Amy held her arms out at her sides, bracing herself for the new front of frozen weather. She closed her eyes and exhaled as the frozen temperatures billowed past her. The icy fog blew past her face, sending her hair out and freezing the ends in place. She reached out, catching one of the ice crystals that seemed to hover before her. The air was so thick with cold, her own breath froze before it could disperse.

Something no bigger than her hand was hovering in front of her.

Amy gasped, choking on the cold air. The glow was created by the rapid beat of a pair of wings that moved so quickly, they were impossible to see. The fae queen fluttered down, her icy body landing on Amy's wrist. She was oddly warm for such a beautiful winter fae being.

"Oh, my. How gorgeous you have become!" Amy said, clasping her free hand to her cheek. The queen, too, seemed to know how beautiful she was. Her belly was swollen with eggs. Ice crystals shimmered on the salty scales that coated her body. She circled in place, shimmying as she displayed her new set of wings.

Amy had seen these markings before—on Naunet's storm scrolls. Fae queens had the spiraling weather patterns created by storm dragons on their wings. They displayed these patterns proudly, as they would rely on these patterns to help them navigate the journey of her maternal flight.

Amy's body trembled with excitement. Yule was upon her. Tonight, the fae queen's icy magic would spread over Scotland, freezing the boundaries of time. Winter Forest didn't seem like such a distant memory any longer. With the help of this remarkable fae treasure, Amy's window to the past would open.

33
WINTER SOLSTICE

Selia

The morning of December twenty-first came in a flurry of ice and snow. As the first rays of daylight streamed through the window, Selia busied herself with decorating the last empty spaces in the kitchen. Through the day, she and Pixie had baked enough meat pies and pastries to feed an army. Gwen and Sean had spent the afternoon helping place the last details into play for their family to arrive. Snow was falling right on time for the evening festivities to start.

Gwen walked into the kitchen and clapped her hands together. "Come on, kids, go put your costumes on! Everyone will be here in a bit!"

Gemma and Bram darted down the hall, each fighting for who would change into their costume first.

"Were we expected to dress up?" Selia asked as she approached Gwen, who was sporting one of her silky red dragon robes.

"I can't be the only dragon queen tonight," Gwen said as she handed Selia one of her silky garments.

"You brought one for Pixie, too?" Selia asked.

"Of course!"

"Did someone call me?" Pixie asked, tending to a baking sheet full of muffins.

Gwen tossed the green robe at Pixie, who dropped the baking sheet on the counter in time to catch it. "Come, my lovelies. Tonight, we will be the solstice sisters!"

Selia tugged on the silky blue robe. Pixie tugged on the green one.

"Where is Damien, anyway?" Selia asked before Gwen whisked her away with the Christmas festivities Clan Malloch seemed to adore.

Gwen pressed her fingers to her lips and blew a whistle.

"*Oi!*" Damien said, popping his head in from the kitchen.

Gwen tugged out a plastic bag and tossed it at her brother. "Let's give 'em a show."

Damien sighed. "I'm only doing this for old-time's sake, got it?" His face was redder than normal, especially his nose.

"You were out all night. Can't you take a nap?" Selia asked.

She set her hand on his forehead. "Oh, you are very warm. I think you're coming down with a fever. And your nose is red!"

"The party is about to start. I can't let a little cold stop me now." Damien grabbed the bag Gwen tossed him and left the living room.

Moments later he re-entered the room, head drooping and shoulders hunched.

"Here comes your uncle," Gwen said.

Damien emerged, dressed in something that made Selia's insides tickle. A furry brown and white onesie, complete with a massive wrack of antlers springing from his head.

"It's the winter solstice king!" Gemma cried, running up to Damien and launching herself into his arms.

Bram, too, darted for his uncle, grabbing him around the center.

Damien fell backward, giving in to the two children who tackled him to the ground.

"Take us to the North Pole!" Gemma cried, casting her fairy wand over her head.

Damien climbed to his hands and knees, crawling on the ground to where Selia stood laughing so hard, she could barely keep from falling over.

He hobbled up to her. "Well, I hope you like your kings with hooves and antlers."

"You look ravishingly kingly. Now I know where you got that nick-name," Selia teased.

"At least now my red nose will fit in with the reindeer theme I have going on."

She ducked under his drooping antlers, kissing him on the nose.

Damien grabbed her waist. "Wait until the lot clears out. This king is going to be wanting more of that tonight."

Ding-dong!

Selia jumped. Their guests had arrived. She walked to the door, sud-denly terrified. On the other side of the door were her new family mem-bers—Damien's clan. What if they didn't like her at all?

She reached for the handle and opened the door wide. Before she could say a word, dozens of people flooded inside. Husbands, wives, children. Aunts, uncles, and cousins. So many Scottish people swarmed their home, it was impossible to keep track of them.

"You must be Selia!" a woman cried as she grabbed her shoulders.

"Everyone, this is Damien's fiancée!" Gwen piped. "She is the owner of this lovely home!"

Selia couldn't have done anything to prepare herself for the flood of heartwarming cheer that came barreling through the front door. Each of Damien's family members gave her hugs, kisses, or friendly pats as they entered her home. Gwen flitted between each and every one of them, dusting flurries out of their reddish-brown hair. Hardy-faced men and rosy-cheeked women were soon everywhere.

Selia's heart warmed. Damien's family was absolutely gorgeous. Their energy was full of cheer and splendor. Gemma and Bram were busy playing with some of the other children over by the *bobbing for bats* game Pixie had set up. They tossed strands of garland onto Damien's antlers, stringing it around and draping it over his shoulders. Sean took up place by the open bar, where a group of younger men all made a circle around him.

"Oi! Nice place you've got here, King D.!" said one of them as he gave Damien a hefty clap on the back.

"Looks like Damien is already dressed like a king!"

The men howled with laughter as Sean worked on passing out drinks. Every one of them was wearing a kilt, so many Selia couldn't keep count. In fact, her fiancé was the odd man out. Too bad, because she loved seeing him wear that sexy Scottish garment.

As Pixie helped with handing out food and Sean manned the bar, the room was soon full of Damien's clan. Children piled Yule logs into the stone fireplace, and Gemma cast a few of her own *fire fairy* spells as they fell into place with the others.

"How do you like it so far?" Damien asked, coming up to her side.

"I love all of them," she replied, grabbing hold of his drooping antlers and straightening them.

"I was sad to hear that Auntie couldn't make it," he said, tilting his antlers sideways.

"Let me guess, she's having another problem with the vixen sprites?"

Damien chuckled, grabbing her around the waist and pulling her into an embrace. He leaned in, kissing her on the cheek. "You're already part of the family. I can't wait to make you mine tonight."

Selia's stomach turned over. She'd completely spaced the *tying the knot* part.

Damien swung his head around. "Ah, here's my cousin now!" He walked toward an older gentleman who was already tipping a drink to his mouth.

"This room is practically breathing testosterone," Gwen said, pointing to the group of men huddled around the bar. "Just wait until they get the Celtic jigs going."

"Did someone say *jig*?"

Two men walked over to Gwen, one holding a fife and the other a fiddle.

"If it isn't my two favorite cousins!" Gwen piped.

Damien maneuvered away from the bar, stopping between Selia and his sister. "Was that who I think it was?"

"The Meddling Mallochs are back!" Gwen replied. "They started a band a few years back. Broke up, then, I guess they're playing again."

Damien walked over to his two musician cousins and whispered something to a third man who held a bagpipe. He then returned to Selia's side. "Before we get this party started, I have an announcement to make." Damien's gaze met Selia's. "Come here, love."

Selia walked with Damien's hand in hers to the center of the room.

He stopped, facing his family. "I would like everyone to meet the reason you're all here tonight."

The fiddles silenced, and the laughter quieted.

Damien turned to face her, his eyes glassy with emotion. "Selia, you've given me something I never thought I would have again. I promise to love and cherish and think of you always as part of my clan."

A few sniffs filled the room. Everyone in this lighthouse *loved* Damien.

He held her hand up. "Selia and I are getting married tonight!"

The room erupted into a fit of hearty laughter, claps, and whistling.

"Tie the knot! Tie the knot!" a few of Damien's cousins bellowed, frothy beverages sloshing down their fronts.

Damien brought her hand to his lips, kissing her fingertips. His eyes met hers, tears and fire burning in them.

Her knees buckled, and she found herself falling into him.

"Cheers to the new king and queen!" a female voice said, followed by a whimsical giggle.

A giggle unlike the other laughs trailed over the others.

The vigorous sound of clapping came from behind the crowd of onlookers, which parted for a petite woman wearing a bedazzling blue dress.

"What a glorious introduction of your new fiancé," she said, walking through the crowd.

Everyone focused on the charismatic female presence who had sauntered into the center of the room. A gleaming smile spread across her freckle-dusted cheeks.

Selia squinted at the woman. She recognized the sea star-shaped freckles that stood out from the others. This woman *couldn't* be Amy. As long as Selia had known her, she'd adorned herself in green. Not this evening, however. Amy wore a long flowing dress of blue velvet. A silver bodice framed her perky little breasts, accentuating her bust with layers of lace. Blue gemstones shimmered like crystals upon her chest and shoulders, giving her an icy look.

"Amy?" Selia whispered, walking over to her. "You look absolutely spectacular."

Amy's emerald eyes leveled with hers, reminding her of the flames of adventures she'd seen flicker so many times from within their whimsical depths. She whirled around, spinning and laughing, until she stopped to face the crowd. "Don't look at me!? It's time to celebrate our newly engaged couple!" She clapped her hands together. Her body shook as her contagious laughter filled the room, sending icy ripples up Selia's spine. "It's time to celebrate the king and queen tonight!"

Bagpipes blared, and fiddles and fifes joined in. Soon, the entire room was full of cheering and dancing Mallochs.

Damien was grabbed by his cousins and lugged off to the bar.

Selia could keep an eye on her fiancé by seeing his antlers bobbing up and down behind the wall of testosterone that was quickly becoming drunk.

Amy seemed to be more preoccupied with the Scotsmen in kilts swarming the room.

Selia grabbed Amy's hand, tugging her away. She was so extroverted, it was hard to get her into a quiet place. So many questions blared through her mind. Questions about her memories of Egypt and the storm dragon.

Stopping in the foyer, Selia released Amy's hand and faced her. "Why are you here?"

Amy tilted her bosom forward. "A few reasons. I'm sure you remember this little beauty?"

Selia's mouth dropped open. "You brought the fae queen?"

"Of course! There is nothing quite like revealing her magic on the winter solstice!" She scanned the room, her emerald eyes glinting with firelight. "What a lively bunch! I absolutely adore Scottish people. In fact, they used to be much larger." She eyed the men wearing the kilts, all laughing in a circle. "The ancestors of these men would make them all appear as dwarfs."

"Who told you about the gathering?" Selia asked, wanting to take the conversation back into her control. She knew how easily distracted Amy could become. Her energy and charisma often got the better of her.

"Damien's lovely sister!" Amy grabbed the drink of dragon's blood and squinted at it. She tipped the glass to her lips, scrunched her nose, then promptly set it back down. Her eyes darted across the room. A ravenous hunger glinted within their emerald depths.

"Who are you looking for?" Selia asked.

Amy's hand withdrew behind her dress.

Selia swore she saw a glass bottle dancing between her fingers. "You aren't playing with your salt extracts, are you?"

Amy gave Damien's cousin a wary glance, who lifted his glass at her.

Selia whipped around. Damien's reindeer antlers were visible from across the crowd.

"Ah, there he is!" Amy waved her other hand in the air, catching his attention.

Damien made his way over. "Amy? What are you doing here?"

A mischievous grin spread across her face. "I've come to enjoy the party!"

Damien looped his arm around Selia's waist. "Apparently, my cousin is already hammered. There's no way he can officiate us." He shot a sour look toward his cousins, who were already beard-deep in their frothing beverages.

His eyes got big as he eyed the sea nymph that had caught both of them by surprise. "Amy, would *you* do the honor of wedding the two of us?"

Amy clapped her hands to her cheeks. "Honored? Why, I would be delighted!" she squealed. That hungry fire glinted in her eyes again. She grabbed Damien's hand and tugged him sideways. "Come and share the details with me."

Amy whisked Damien away, leaving Selia to deal with Gemma, who began sprinting around her with her fairy wand, yelling, "The winter solstice fairy has arrived!"

When Damien returned, he was much redder in the face. "Boy. This costume is itchy," he said, running his hand past his neck.

"I think you're coming down with something," Selia said, worry ringing in her voice.

Damien grabbed her hand, locking his eyes with her. "I gave Amy all of the details. Love, are you ready for this?"

Amy clapped her hands again, quickly gathering the excitement of the moment back in to her control. "Everyone! I must gather your attention at once! We have a very special announcement!"

The cheer died down, and suddenly, everyone in the room was staring at them.

Amy elbowed Selia's side. "Go on and face one another. I'm only doing this once."

"Before we go through with this," Selia said, grabbing Amy's hand. "I need to tell you something."

She tugged her away from the crowd of onlookers, darting through the back door and out into the snow.

"What was that all about?" Amy asked, her voice high and flustered. "Is that man not the most exquisitely beautiful thing that has walked into your life?"

Snow whipped between them. "Your friend, the one you said you could feel her presence around me a few months ago. Was her name Sika?"

Amy's expression nearly matched the same confusion she'd left Damien with. "How did you learn about Sika?"

"I have a journal like the one you once gave to me. She's been speaking to me through it."

Amy glanced over her shoulder as a violent gust caught her dress, whipping the fabric. "You must be imagining things."

"I'm *not* imagining anything. I know about the Abyss. I know about salt venom. I remember how you tried to form a bond between me and Celaeno's storm dragon!"

What was left of Amy's enthusiasm was quickly gone. Her eyes became glassy, her sea star-shaped freckles darkening. "There is no way that

Masika could be healthy enough to speak, not after..." Amy began to shake. She gripped the fabric of her dress with trembling hands, unable to look Selia in the eye. "How could she possibly have shared all of this information with you?"

"*Masika*? Is that Sika's full name?"

Amy's expression had gone blank. Her face paled. She looked like she might retch.

Amy spun on her heel. "I must go. My window to the past has opened."

"Wait, a window to the *past*? Where are you going?" Selia's foot slipped out from beneath her, nearly sending her to the ground. "Amy, wait! Tell me what you are doing!"

Amy was gone as quickly as she appeared, vanishing into the frozen mouth of the winter storm.

Selia backed into the lighthouse as a violent wind whipped over her.

Her breath caught.

Damien was lying on the ground.

Gwen was standing over him, her head whipping back and forth. "All right, who gave King Malloch too much to drink?"

34

YULE'S MAGIC

Amy

Fear pitted in Amy's stomach as she made her way down to the beach, careful not to lose sight of the fae queen taking off into the night. She would soon be salt trancing in uncharted waters. But she would have it no other way, not if she could save Masika's spirit from the darkness that had consumed her over three thousand years ago.

Amy slowed her pace, careful not to slip on a stone or a seashell. She stopped at the water's edge, inhaling an icy breath. Salt trancing became magical during Yule, when everything was coated in ice.

Something on the surface of the North Sea caught her eye. A reflection rippled in the water. Not her own, but someone else's.

A woman gazed up at her, her eyes luminous with ebony. Amy fought the tears forming in her eyes. She sucked in an icy breath, exhaling the emotion welling in her chest. Masika's spirit was there, waiting for her.

"I'm coming for you. I promise, I'll help you," she whispered.

Masika's reflection iced over, leaving Amy's fingers frozen.

Amy crouched and untied her boots. She removed them from her feet, stepping onto the frozen beach. She stood and ripped her bodice from her body, taking with it the velvety blue fabric of her dress. Sharp dagger-like pains branched through her foot as she took her first step into the North Sea.

She kept breathing, slowing her pulse. Her body screamed at her to stop, to turn around and head back to the warmth and celebration back with Clan Malloch. She needed Damien's ancestors to help her. All she needed to do was to slay the mighty fae king Errindoor so she could finally put Masika's spirit to rest.

The fae queen dropped from the sky, falling like a star. The second she dove into the sea and her wings hit the surface, a ripple of light exploded, illuminating the ocean.

Amy sucked in a breath. Her window to the past had opened.

She cycled the three principles through her mind, focusing on her pulse.

Breath. Memory. Salt.

Surrendering her body to the trance, her spirit departed from the present and mingled with memories of the past—a time when huntsmen and fae beasts roamed the ancient realm of Winter Forest.

35

DAMIEN'S SLUMBER

Selia

After Damien's spill, the festive energy at the gathering died away. Damien's cousins hoisted Selia's unconscious fiancé onto the sofa, where he currently lay.

"I told him he needed to rest," Selia said as she sat next to him. "He was out all night looking for Sean."

"He'll sleep it off," Gwen said as she cleaned up the empty whiskey bottles from the bar. "This isn't the first time I've seen my brother get pass-out drunk. It's too bad, because we were all getting ready to have some real fun."

As the last of the guests bustled out of their home, Selia's thoughts drifted back to Amy. Why had she even come to the gathering? What were her plans with the fae queen?

Before she'd stormed out into the night, she had said, "*My window to the past has opened.*"

Gwen and Pixie stayed behind to help clean up as Sean corralled his two sleepy children. Gemma was fading fast, her fairy wings dropping as she slouched with her brother on the sofa opposite Damien. "But Uncle Damien told me we were going to see the winter fairy!"

Gwen grabbed Gemma under her arms and hoisted her to her feet. "Well, your uncle went and had too much fun."

"Damien, wake up," Selia said, grabbing his shoulder and tugging him.

Gwen came to Selia's side. "He's breathing. He'll be fine. Boy, he's going to be embarrassed as hell when he comes to in the morning."

"No, something is wrong," Selia said as she set her hand on his neck. "This isn't alcohol." He'd complained about his costume being itchy. Splotchy red skin appeared behind his ear. "Oh my goodness! Something's bit his neck!"

"It was probably that disgusting bat!" Gwen chided.

"Hey, don't go blaming Peppercorn for this!" Pixie countered.

Selia stood, panic rising in her chest. "We need to get him to the hospital, now."

"We can take my car," Pixie said as she grabbed her coat.

Gwen grabbed her coat too. "Sean? Take the kids home in the truck. But first, help me load Damien into Pixie's car."

Sean nudged both of his children out the door.

"Should we call an ambulance?" Pixie asked.

Selia grabbed Damien's freezing hand. The mark on his neck was worsening by the moment. Had Amy done something to him? Had she put him into a salt trance?

A feint *buzzing* sound filled he ears. Her salt nodes became itchy. Was she experiencing the same symptoms Damien had before he passed out?

The lights began to flicker.

Pixie tugged on her coat. "Better hurry up before this storm gets any worse, or we won't be driving anywhere."

Selia's salt nodes flushed with a heavy *abbbbysssssss...*

Sika's voice filled her ears again.

"*To protect your daughter, you must learn everything you can about your ancestry.*"

The front door flew open as another individual walked into the lighthouse. It wasn't Sean. A woman with short blond hair and cold grey eyes stood in the entryway. Wind whipped through the door, sending ice and snow through her cloak.

"No modern-day medicine will help him," she said.

"And who the heck are you?" Gwen piped, rounding on the nymph Selia recognized.

Alex approached the sofa where Damien lay. She touched his face with her hand, tilting his head sideways. "The fae queen did a great job on him."

"The fae queen did this to him?" Selia asked.

Alex's eyes darkened. "She's injected him with salt venom."

Selia's breath caught. *Injected him?*

Gwen's brow furrowed. "What fae queen? Do you two know each other?"

The scar on Alex's upper lip twitched. "Selia and I go back a long time. But I'm not here to indulge you on our past. I'm here to make sure the past doesn't repeat itself."

Selia began to panic. "Why would the queen do this to him?"

"Don't worry," Alex replied. "To humans, salt venom is far less deadly. By the looks of him, he will likely be sleeping for days."

Alex snapped her fingers. A bolt of white electricity crackled from her fingertips, striking Gwen in the chest.

Pixie too, was stunned by the same electrical bolt as it bounced between them.

Both women slouched over on the sofa next to Damien.

Selia rounded on Alex. "What did you do to them?"

Alex held her arms out, chanting something under her breath. "Keep your voice down. The creatures outside can taste the salt on your breath."

Selia faced the window. The swarming cloud outside thickened like an angry fog, bringing that terrible buzzing sound with it.

Selia backed away from the window, where a dark shadow began to manifest. "What are they?"

Alex curled her fingers in on themselves as she braced herself. "A fae parasite that emerged from Egypt three thousand years ago."

PART 5
SPIRIT MEDICINE

36
MEDICINE BUNDLES

Amy

The steady slow rhythm of Amy's heartbeat pulsed in her salt nodes. That sound had been the only constant since dipping into her salt trance. She was at the mercy of the icy window the fae queen opened for her.

The queen's maternal instincts would bring her back to a time and place that was most suitable to deposit her eggs. A time when blue minca still had a presence in the ocean.

Flashes of blue light darted in and out of her periphery as the darkness released its grip on her. The rhythm of her heart began to throb faster and faster, until the blue lights from the queen's wings illuminated her periphery. Her fingers began to warm, as did her arms and chest. Something cold landed with weight upon her head and shoulders.

Amy's eyes broke open, finding that a blanket of fluffy white powder covered her body from head to toe. She tried to shimmy out of her snow cocoon, but that movement was impossible.

Great! Of course the queen would drop her into the heart of Winter Forest.

"Oh, cold, cold!" Amy huffed, wiggling her toes. Golden rays of daylight branched down above her. Her fingers met a solid wooden surface, answering why she couldn't convince the snow to shift.

She was stuck inside a hollowed-out pine tree.

Panic rippled up her spine. Her toes shifted, and the snow beneath her began to move. Down she went, sliding through the tree's hollow. She landed on a branch, which thankfully broke her fall. Staggering, she stepped out of the hollow, entering a world that was completely frozen.

Her breath caught. Some of these trees were over a hundred feet tall. Their spirits were old and wise. An ache filled her chest. Only a thousand years from this time, these trees would be gone—the spirits of these ancient giants forgotten. The giant red trees would be harvested for their wood, forming mantelpieces and furnishings in cottages all over Scotland.

Coming back here reminded her of how special these trees were to her. Nobody was alone in the midst of winter. This ancient forest had magic breathing in it.

A chill rippled up her spine. She threw her arms around her naked self, shivering. Clothing—that's what she needed first. She couldn't go gallivanting through Winter Forest with the fear of her nipples freezing in a matter of seconds.

She walked a few paces, searching for any sign that a group of huntsmen might be nearby. The tracks she spotted in the snow were only created by the local wildlife.

A few squirrels chattered overhead, sending snow cascading down Amy's head and shoulders once again.

"Off with you!" Amy cried, shivering as she dodged one of the nuts falling from a cluster of angry squirrels now harassing her. She glanced back at the tree she'd fallen through. Apparently, she'd disturbed a nest or two.

The tree behind her shifted.

A pair of hazel eyes appeared through the drooping, snow-covered branches.

"There's my goddess," growled the familiar voice of the huntsman now approaching her.

Amy's body rippled in gooseflesh. With each step that Ewan took, a little piece of herself shrank. This was not the ideal situation for Damien's ancestor to find her in the midst of the forest. Shivering, vulnerable, and *naked*. This was exactly the kind of situation he would be hunting for.

"I've been searching all morning for you," he said, stopping in front of her. His boots crunched in the snow. His cloak was covered in a white layer of freshly fallen powder. Strung across his back was his bow and a quiver stuffed with arrows.

Amy blinked a few times, trying to take him in. He was so much larger than she remembered. And she could feel the heat coming off him. His scent—a lovely mixture of pine and earth—washed over her. Having him look at her again, with desire swimming in his eyes, was almost too much for her to process.

She took a step back, gathering her arms around her shivering body. "I was foraging for..." She glanced over his shoulder, spotting one of the squirrels snacking on something red. "Berries?"

Ewan chuckled, his voice reverberating like earthy thunder. "And you decided to do this without clothing?" He reached his hand beneath his cloak, tugging out a couple of garments. "I told you I would turn my recent kill into a cloak fit for a queen, did I not?"

Amy eyed the garments slung across his massive forearm. Both a tunic, and a cloak. He'd turned the hide of an elk into the warmth that she desperately needed.

He dropped to his knee, reaching his arm around her shivering body. The second the silky warm fur hit her shoulders, her body warmed.

"Does it fit?" he asked.

"It's lovely," Amy said, resisting the urge to wrap her arms around his neck and tug his body close to speed up the warming process.

She grabbed the tunic and slipped it over her head first, then fastened the cloak around her shoulders.

His hand dipped to his belt, where another leather garment was strung. Unraveling two items, he dropped them in the snow.

His hand dipped to his belt, where another leather garment was strung. Unraveling two items, he dropped them in the snow.

"You made me footwear, too?" she asked, amazed by his talent.

"Did you think you could go on a hunt with my men and expect the lead huntsman to not treat you like a queen?"

Amy slipped the boots onto her feet, thankful for how quickly they warmed her freezing toes.

"Now you look like a huntswoman," he teased, standing. He grazed his cheek past hers, his beard frozen with ice crystals.

Ewan held out a hollow gourd Amy assumed had been harvested from a species of tree. A strap of leather was tied around the neck. A stopper made of wood jutted from the opening where one would drink. "Keep this close to your body. It will help prevent the water from freezing. We stop only at night to melt snow by the fire. The farther inland we go, the colder the forest becomes. If it freezes, you will go an entire day with nothing to drink."

Amy nodded, knowing that the heart of Winter Forest was a frozen one. The idea of water being such a precious commodity baffled her. Even in Egypt, the mouth of the Nile was a bounty. But traveling up north in this frozen landscape was about to prove just how precious water was.

She looped the leather strap around her shoulder, tucking the gourd next to her side.

Ewan dipped his hand under his white robe, and withdrew another item. The shiny surface of flint caught the sun—a stone dagger. The sharp flint had been fastened with sinew to a handle made of bone. "I tried to make it small enough your grip would fit."

Amy took the dagger, three of which could have easily fit into Ewan's massive palm. The handle fit snug between her fingers. "This is absolutely lovely," she said.

His cheeks dimpled. "My men don't know you have this."

"Let me guess, they don't want me to?"

"Keep it close to you. You never know when you might need it."

Amy assessed the travel items Ewan had gifted her. She was so very lucky to have his generosity. Even though her spirit was visiting a memory of this time in her life, that didn't mean she could take her own survival any less seriously. If she was to travel with him to the sacred meadow, she would need to mimic the survival tactics he and his men had fine-tuned since they'd fled from the fallen city of Atlantis.

White smoke issued up from the trees behind him.

Ewan turned on his heel. "The hearth is ready. If you are to join us on this hunt, you must attend the white prayer ceremony."

Amy followed Ewan toward the smoke mingling with the wide branching green fingers of spruce and pine arching over their heads. She tried to focus on one of a thousand finely shaped needles branching above her. No matter how hard she tried to focus on the bigger tree, each needle seemed to center her thoughts.

Right now, she was one of those tiny needles, trying to serve a greater purpose in the massive tree. She was a single woman embarking on a journey through a frozen forest with a clan of huntsmen. Her goal was not to track the giant fae beasts, but to slay the king who guarded the mountain. His blood is what she needed to free Masika from the curse the salt venom had put her in.

"Wait here," Ewan said, holding his arm up.

Amy stopped before stepping into the clearing by the hearth. Why didn't he want her to follow?

He walked over to the fire, standing opposite her. He folded his arms together under his robes. "It is time to offer our prayers to our ancestors."

His men appeared from their temporary dwellings made of wood, tree branches, and animal hides. As the men gathered their belongings and packed them into satchels, Ewan piled rocks onto the coals at the center of the fire. He set a bundle of dried herbs on the rocks, turning the smoke white.

Ewan's eyes met hers as he reclaimed his place across the fire. He nodded, signaling for her to walk toward him.

She approached. The blank expressions on the huntsmen's weathered faces told her one thing: none of them wanted her here.

Ewan raised his hand in acknowledgement of her. "This is Amphitrite. She is our medicine woman. If you fall ill, she will be the one to help you regain your health."

Amy swallowed. If poison was medicine, then she would absolutely fit the role Ewan had assigned her. She still needed to develop a plan on how to draw blood from the fae beast who was likely a giant.

A few men jumbled their bows. Some shuffled their feet in the snow. Their silence spoke to the thickness she felt in the air.

He beckoned for Amy to approach. She took her position to his left, facing the hearth like the others. With so many disapproving men in the group, she was thankful that he kept her at his side.

Ewan withdrew his other arm from his robes, holding a white leather pouch in his hand. "Men, offer your prayer items. Remember, once they are sealed in the bundle, nobody must look at them. Gazing upon prayer items before the prayers are offered will cause the items to lose their medicine." He handed the bundle to the man to his right.

The medicine bundle moved between the men, each dropping items inside. Some put in dried herbs, others bones they'd carved into beads or animal figures.

When the bundle reached her, Ewan's gaze dropped to her. "Women are not allowed to partake in making an offering. However, for this journey, I have made an exception."

Amy grabbed the bundle, which bulged with all nine of the men's offerings. What should she put in?

What physical items she possessed Ewan had provided. She'd come to the past completely vulnerable and literally naked. Emotion welled inside of her. How very vulnerable she felt out here, exposed to these men and the elements.

The bundle blurred as her tears formed. Three dolloped down her cheeks, landing on the white leather. "I hope tears can be considered an offering," she whispered, embarrassment heating her chest.

His warm hand met hers as she handed the bundle to him. "Your tears will be accepted. Whoever you are here for, we will be sure to honor them," Ewan said, his voice and affection the encouragement she needed.

He took the bundle and tied it off with a piece of twine.

"Wait, what did you put in?" Amy asked, wiping the back of her hand past her cheek.

"That's between my forefathers and me." He tucked the bundle beneath his robes and motioned to the man on his right. "Proceed."

Fwwwiisssshhhhhhh!

One of the men tipped a gourd of water toward the fire, sending smoke and ash into the air.

Amy focused on the silver tendrils rising out of the hearth, allowing the smoke to take her back to the memories of Selia during this time.

The night Celaeno's storm dragon brought Selia into his dwelling. A sweat lodge, where he would present one of the seven storm bonds with her. Storm bonds created from the same ingredients before her—from fire and ash and water vapor.

With those ingredients, a storm dragon could send a sea nymph into the Abyss, trapping her for as long as he wanted. Something in Amy's gut told her that like her mother, Selia had disappeared into the Abyss, and that Celaeno's storm dragon was responsible for it.

The smoke rising from the hearth thickened. White wisps of ash and water vapor came to life as elk walking through the forest began to spiral around the hearth. Perhaps the magic in this ancient forest was already answering her prayers.

Sgàthan clan legend stated that the white herd migrated to the top of the mountain every winter for one purpose only—to drink from the sacred pool. It was said that when the elk first drank from this pool, time stood still. Time became a frozen blanket of stars that shimmered above the mountain. The stars that fell from the sky during those frozen moments became the white herd that eventually populated the forest.

Why Ewan and his men followed the white herd on their migration was not for their meat, but for the ability to communicate with the stars—the final resting place for the fallen kings from Atlantis. The moment the mighty fae king Errindoor bowed his crowned head and drank from the sacred pool, the prayers from the sons of Atlantean kings would be answered.

Ewan took his bow and quiver and held them over the steam. "Great ancestors, we are the sons of Atlantean kings. I offer my weapon in request for a safe journey to the mountain. May you give us guidance on how to rebuild our kingdom."

He set his weapon on the bundle of herbs. Flames licked up around the rocks, engulfing his bow and quiver. He doused the hearth with more water, sending more steam up into the air. "Everyone, be sure to offer your prayer to our ancestors."

Amy closed her eyes, imagining Masika's face before her, healthy and pure. The fire of adventure in her eyes still flickering, still longing for the answer behind minca's disappearance. Her body was strong and vibrant, not covered in the horrible black salt crystals that penetrated her flesh.

She forced that memory out of her mind and opened her eyes. Ewan's men were passing around a goblet.

Amy took the goblet from the man next to her, which was surprisingly heavy. She tipped it back and forth, sloshing what was left of the liquid. She tilted the goblet forward, spilling the contents into the snow.

"She disgraces the ancestors!" one of the men bellowed.

Ewan held his arm out, preventing him from bustling over to her.

The snow began to hiss, then spit.

Ewan dipped his finger into the melted snow and brought the liquid to his lips. His nose scrunched and he spat it out. "Who prepared this drink?"

Silence followed Ewan's question.

"I will dismiss all of you if someone does not step forward now," Ewan growled, his fists clenching through the smoke.

"Ewan," Amy said, standing up next to him. She set her hand on his massive forearm. "I think I can speak for myself."

She set her foot near the melted snow and closed her eyes.

Breath. Memory. Salt.

As she repeated the three principles in her mind, she exhaled, surrendering to her pulse.

A crackling sound ripped through the air. She opened her eyes, finding the snow began to freeze, creating a thin layer of ice. Like veins would return blood to the heart, the ice forming on the snow would seek out the truth to Ewan's question. The ice formed a jagged line, branching between each huntsman as it rippled to the source.

The ice vein snaked its way around the hearth, stopping at a man catty-corner to her. The ice had shown her the truth.

Ewan threw his arm out to his side, pointing toward camp. "You are dismissed from the hunt."

The man's eyes darted up from the ice snaking its way around his feet. "You trust the magic of a selkie over your fellow men?" he spat.

Ewan's shoulders stiffened. "I trust the ancestors over your lack of respect."

The man stood, grabbing his bow, slinging it over his back. "She will poison you all, just like her ancestors did our kingdom."

As he left the hearth, the others shifted their gazes down to their feet.

Ewan surveyed the group, his brow furrowing. "I will not tolerate this kind of treatment of anyone on our hunt. Man, woman, or selkie, all members of the hunt must be treated as equals. Do you understand?"

In unison, the men chanted something foreign. They slung their belongings and bows over their shoulders, and took off up the hill.

While Ewan had asserted himself over the others, the wary glances of the men became fiercer than before. Amy couldn't blame them. Her ancestors had powers that were responsible for sinking the kingdom of their forefathers—the great kingdom of Atlantis.

37

SISTERS & SALT FLIES

Selia

Alex clapped her hands together. As soon as her palms met, strands of short blond hair rose from her forehead.

The buzzing black cloud of fae parasites outside hummed so loudly, Selia clapped her hands over her ears. The sound was cutting and angry, like a thousand swarming bees had decided to gang up on her.

Alex's grey eyes flashed as a mantra escaped her lips. "I summon the light of Gaia. With the binding threads of the fae kingdom, I illuminate your darkness!"

Light pulsed from her hands as an electrical shock filled the room.

The swarm was quickly replaced with a snowy gust of wind that made the lighthouse quake.

Alex lowered her arms to her sides. "That should hold them for a while."

"What are they?" Selia asked. The itching sensation in her salt nodes vanished.

"Salt flies," Alex replied. She shifted her hand, gathering what remained of the light illuminating the icy window. As she trailed her fingers in front of her, the glass began to glow, creating a barrier. "Unlike the minca moth, which is a lunar light fae, salt flies are shadow fae parasites that feed on toxins born from fae blood."

"What toxin are you talking about?"

Alex turned on her heel, facing Selia. "The bottle of salt venom, where is it?"

Selia went into the bedroom and retrieved the bottle. She returned to the living room, and set the bottle down on the coffee table between her and Alex.

Alex eyed the bottle, a shimmer of fear glinting in her grey eyes. "This is the toxin the fae queen introduced into the ocean three thousand years ago."

Selia stared at the dark crystal resting at the bottom of the bottle. "Salt venom was created by the fae?"

Alex nodded. "Yes. Salt venom was born from the blood of the minca moth queen you released from the vault."

Selia's breath caught. Why hadn't Amy told her anything about the relationship between the fae queen and salt venom?

Alex closed the space between them. "Amy has kept samples of salt venom in her Ocean Apothecary for a long time. Many of her samples have been traded and stolen by humans who believe the toxin to have magical properties. Naunet considered it to be an elixir of life and death." Alex grabbed the bottle and tilted it to the side. "She gave salt venom a new name after what it did to her friend, Masika. What it did to her skin, in particular."

"What did she rename it?"

"Selkies are known to shed their skin in many of the Celtic myths that surround sea nymphs."

Selia's mind drifted. Why did the words *selkie* and *skin* ring a bell? She thought back to the bottles Amy had given her to experiment with while practicing the art of salt trance. "Is the selkie salt skin is salt venom?"

Alex nodded. "Yes. While the venom corroded Masika's body, while the salt preserved her spirit." She set the bottle down onto the table and crossed her arms. "I'm sure Masika has shared some of the seductive properties of salt venom with you."

"How did you know Masika has been talking to me?"

Alex reached into her robe, and tugged out a journal similar to the one Peppercorn had destroyed. "The venom is not shy about who it speaks to. It has shared quite a lot of interactions between you and Masika with me."

"Where did you get the journal?"

"The midwife of the sea created many of them. She also created the storm scrolls Masika has harassed you about."

"Naunet created them?"

"Yes. Naunet's cursed younger sister is free to both speak and listen through the journals."

"Wait, Naunet and Masika are *sisters*?"

"Masika is very protective of Naunet. I wouldn't say anything about Naunet you wouldn't want Masika to hear. Her spirit is always present when the venom is near." She returned the journal beneath her robe. "I have heard every discussion between you and Masika, including the details of your pregnancy. Historically, storm bonds are formed prior to pregnancy, as they allow a sea nymph to control the spontaneous bursts of emotion her pulse displays."

"I can say for certain that I have been experiencing these spontaneous bursts. I had a feeling they weren't hormone related." Selia set her hands on her stomach. "Why are you here telling me all of this?"

Alex straightened herself, clasping her hands gingerly in front of her robes. "The woodland nymph I left in charge of you failed in her assignment, therefore, I have decided to intervene."

Selia squinted at her. "I'm not following."

"The friend who has stopped replying to your texts?"

Selia's mind worked, her thoughts tripping over themselves. "*Deidra?*"

"Deidra works for the Order. She serves under my command. She's training to become an Iridescent like me. I can say for certain she has not passed her test."

"What was her test?"

"To prevent Masika from discovering your whereabouts." Alex sighed as disappointment riddled her expression. "I'm afraid all Deidra has done is left you horribly confused about your past."

Selia sank into the sofa. Her vision had gone blurry. Had Deidra's advice about Gaia's Order all been some kind of cover-up? Had she been working with Alex the entire time she'd known her?

Alex's eyes narrowed onto her. "What is the last childhood memory you have experienced?"

"I was at Winter Forest. I was inside a dwelling with Celaeno's storm dragon, attempting to form a bond."

"What rose up out of the fire?"

Selia closed her eyes, as the heavy *abbbbysssssssss* filled her salt nodes. The dwelling had gone dark. "The word abyss filled my ears, and I blacked out. That's the last thing I remember."

The corners of Alex's mouth curved down. "This is why Masika has been harassing you about your ancestral salt mother. You had been there for the past three thousand years, sleeping."

"Been where?"

"Inside the Abyss. Celaeno's storm dragon brought you to the Abyss after the plague of salt venom broke out in Egypt."

Selia's mind blanked. "This doesn't make any sense. I was at the Louvre. I was—"

"—Have you not ever wondered what filled the void between now and your childhood in Egypt?" Alex cut in.

Selia opened and closed her mouth, but no words escaped. "I know my memory is not the best, but how can this be possible? Me sleeping for three thousand years? When did I wake up?"

"You have been awake for approximately twenty years, ten of which were erased when you came in contact with the salt trancing talisman at the Louvre. Deidra was in charge of integrating you back into society when you awoke from the Abyss."

Selia's mind worked, her thoughts skipping and plundering. Deidra had always been in her life, only until a few months ago. Until she'd discovered the journal in Gwen's bookstore, the furthest back she could remember was when she had discovered the talisman in her office.

Selia shook her head. "This has to be a dream. The memories from my childhood, how do I know they are real? What if I'm just going insane, and all of this is just a hallucination?"

A laugh escaped Alex. "When you meet with Celaeno's storm dragon again, he will be the one to confirm the truth."

Selia's mind traveled back to the fragmented memories she had experienced from her childhood. Those memories told a story about how she journey she made with Amy from Egypt to Winter Forest to bond her with Celaeno's storm dragon.

Instead of the bond forming, had he taken her to the Abyss?

She glanced up at the Iridescent, confusion coursing through her. "I thought the Abyss was a being, not a place."

"The Abyss is both a place, and an entity. Storm dragons have long been her guardian and form territories around the seven maternal salt pods who compose her."

"What does Masika want with me? And why is the Order getting involved?"

"You, Masika, as well as Naunet, all share the same salt ancestry. Your maternal salts originate from Celaeno, from which the toxic fae queen was born. After Masika became infected by the fae queen, she sealed her in a vault and placed an incantation on it only the Blind Moon could open." Alex closed the space between them. "Does this sound familiar at all? Say the name of the fourth principle, and the vault will open. Only the Blind Moon can remember its origin."

Selia's thoughts drifted to a few months ago, when she and Damien were attempting to track down the vault. Those exact words had drifted as light across one of Damien's paintings. "It does sound familiar."

Alex's gaze fell heavily onto her. "I attempted to stop you from opening the vault because the moment it opened, Masika would know where you were. She has been searching for you for as long as she has been cursed."

"I thought *Amy* sealed the queen into the vault. She told me that she did."

Alex shook her head. "Amy lied to you. She used you for one reason—to open the vault, so she could make off with the fae queen and attempt to release Masika from her curse."

Selia's gut hollowed. She felt like she'd been punched. Anger and betrayal surged through her. "Amy never intended to teach me about salt trancing, did she? She was using me? Why did she need the queen to save Masika?"

"The fae queen has allowed Amy a brief window to the past, where she is attempting to free Masika's spirit from the curse salt venom has placed upon her. However, I can say for certain that Masika will try and stop her. Ever since Masika became cursed, she has sought a new way to achieve what she and Amy set out to accomplish with the art of salt trance—to restore the art to the way their ancestors practiced salt trancing in Atlantis."

"By practicing with pulse?"

"That is correct."

Selia's fingers crammed into her palms. "From what I remember in Egypt, it was the Order who decided to forbid the use of the fourth principle."

Alex's shoulders stiffened. "The Order had to take precautions after Celaeno's fae queen introduced salt venom into the sea. If you remember from our salt summoning lesson, pulse could cause all kinds of problems with fae beings."

Suddenly, the white scar on Alex's upper lip looked red. When Selia had salt tranced with her pulse, she'd caused the moths to frenzy into a swarm that had resulted in sending Alex running out of the Temple of Isis.

A sense of satisfaction, even pride, swelled in her chest. Her pulse had power that Amy had encouraged—power that Alex wanted her to suppress.

"Have you noticed any changes in your salt trancing abilities? Have any new talents emerged?"

Selia stood and grabbed one of the bottles of whiskey from the bar. "Why don't I show you what I've been experiencing?"

She closed her eyes and held the image of the bottle in her mind. As she sucked in a breath and exhaled, she imagined the oxygen filling all of those small invisible spaces.

The bottle began to warm.

Selia opened her eyes when she felt the water was ready.

The cork went flying, narrowly missing Alex's face.

Alex grinned. "I see you have been practicing."

Selia set the bottle full of bubbling whisky down on the table. "When I breathe a certain way, I can manipulate water."

"Would you say water acts differently according to your emotions?"

"Yes. Items full of liquid have been attracted to me like I'm a magnet. I can warm liquids very quickly, too. But I can't control it."

Alex's smile became a sly one. "That's what your storm bond will allow you to accomplish."

Selia glanced at the bottle of salt venom sitting next to the whisky. "Can salt venom be destroyed?"

"No. Salt venom can only be returned to its dormant state in one of two ways. Either with the blood of a fae king, or by bonding a sea nymph who possesses the same salt ancestry as the storm dragon who encompasses Celaeno's territory."

Selia's fists clenched. "The memories I have of Amy and I all revolved around her trying to get me to bond with this dragon. Now I know why. What I don't understand is why Masika is coming after me. Does it have something to do with my storm bond not forming?"

"Yes. Masika wants to prevent your bond from happening, because it will neutralize what remains of her power—her ties with salt venom. She has no body to return to, so her spirit is free to do what she wants with it."

"What will happen to her if the bond *does* form?"

Alex's eyes darkened. "Masika's spirit will be forced to return to the ancestral mother of the sea. The Abyss is both a womb, and a final resting place for sea nymphs."

Selia worked her hands over her stomach, emotion suddenly clouding her heart. Naunet's warm dark eyes haunted the corridors of her mind just as much as her sister. "Is Naunet my mother, or is Celaeno my salt mother like Masika said?

Alex's eyes softened. "The Order forbids me from sharing the story of your birth with you. But I am here to help you pick up from where you left off forming the bond three thousand years ago."

Selia sat next to Damien. "Masika isn't going away, is she? She's going to continue harassing me until she gets what she wants from me?"

"Masika will stop at nothing to ensure your storm bond never forms."

The lighthouse groaned as the wind picked up.

Alex tucked her hands beneath her robes. "The salt flies are a warning for what's to come. We need to focus on protecting you from the fae creatures the salt venom attracts, before Masika makes any more attacks on your loved ones."

Selia glanced between Damien, Gwen, and Pixie, all lying unconscious on the sofa. "What protection do I have against her salt flies?"

The scar on Alex's upper lip twitched. "We must pick up where we left off in your salt trancing lessons. It's time you stop suppressing your talents and start using them."

38
WINTER FOREST

Amy

Amy set out with Ewan and his men into the beginnings of Winter Forest. Amy stayed behind them. Ewan did not lead his group. He fell into Amy's footsteps, sandwiching her between his men and him.

It didn't take long for the terrain to transition from rocky hills and meadows to dense timber. The brisk scent of pine bit Amy's nose. Woodlands became shrublands and back again as the highlands transitioned between landscapes. Most of the vegetation had gone brown in dormancy for winter.

At this point in their journey, she could see the snowy peak of the sacred mountain. With each step they took, its beautiful white surface was swallowed by more of the trees as they approached the denser section of the forest.

After an hour of trekking through the snowy landscape, Amy found herself thanking Ewan for the gear he'd provided. While the cloak was hardy, it was light enough she could remove it from her shoulders when her body temperature warmed.

The breath of the wild lived out here. The scent was open and free, not bound by hot scorched sands like she remembered from Egypt. When she feared she might need to strip her cloak from her body to avoid breaking a sweat, Ewan's men slowed their pace. They huddled together, their quivers and packs jostling against one another.

"We approach the threshold," one said as he shot an accusatory gaze toward her.

Amy stopped a few paces from the men, not taking her eyes off them. They could shoot death stares at her all they wanted, but she wasn't going to let their prejudice ruin her fun.

Ewan's shadow loomed on the path as he closed the space between them. He brushed his hand past her waist as he walked in front of her, stopping at the wall of thick timber that lay before them.

There was no transition between high meadow and this massive wall of trees. The trunks of the red giants were like giant pillars, each requiring the width of half a dozen men to match their thickness. A gnarled root curved along their path. Was this root the threshold no one wanted to step over?

Ewan's white robes lay flat at his sides. No wind traveled through the trees. The sounds here, too, were different. The tree branches were gnarled, none the same, while each of the fat tree trunks appeared similar. No, she couldn't read trees like a woodland nymph could, but even a sea nymph could read that these trees all had a personality of their own.

Ewan held his hands together at his chest, his shoulders rising and falling as he inhaled and exhaled.

Amy felt each man hold his breath as he stepped over the root and into the forest. The men each took turns doing exactly what Ewan had done. After they clasped their hands together in prayer and dipped their heads, they stepped over the root and entered the frozen heart of Winter Forest.

Ewan did not wait for Amy, neither did any of his men. What had they said when they stepped over the root?

She stopped in front of the threshold root and clasped her hands in front of her. The second she stepped over the root, her ears filled with the rumbling echo of thunder. She hurried down the path, hoping to catch up with the others. Blue sky shone above the treetops. What was the source of the thunder?

It didn't take long for her question to be answered. The path dipped down, and the scent of fresh water filled her nose. A bustling river appeared behind the overgrowth.

She approached, stopping at Ewan's side to observe what they had stopped to marvel at. They weren't the only ones preparing to cross the river. There must have been a hundred elk funneling their way across. The reddish-brown beasts with white rumps clustered together. The elk in the river lacked antlers and had long slender necks and legs. Their ears were almost as large as their heads, flipping back and forth as they navigated across the water.

Her shoulders tensed. Great. A dangerous bustling river was the first obstacle between her and the frozen heart of Winter Forest.

She dug her heels into the riverbed. The water was too deep for her to cross without the risk of being swept away. The log bridge the men were inspecting looked like it had seen better days.

Ewan crouched, dipping his water gourd into the river. "This is the last fresh water we will have access to for a while. We will be required to melt ice and snow by the fire to make our drinking water."

Amy mimicked him, doing the same. They both stood, tucking their gourds beneath their clothing.

"One man at a time," Fergus said, and the others formed in a line behind the bridge. Water splashed upon the logs, turning the surface icy.

One of the huntsmen leapt onto the bridge and took off in a jog. The two logs bounced and creaked and groaned, but he made it across.

Ewan held out his hand. "Stay behind me."

Amy tucked herself under his arms as one of the massive stags came charging out into the open. He stood at the edge of the bank, stomping his front foot, nostrils flaring. The muscles in his neck tensed, his shoulders bulging.

"He's defiantly trying to impress the ladies," Amy said, watching the stag swing his head from side-to-side, massive crown of antlers making a *swooooping* sound in the air as the females hurried across the water.

Ewan chuckled. "He's nothing. Wait until you see Errindoor."

The stag stood watching Ewan and his men closely, making sure none of them threatened his females as they crossed the water.

Amy knew the men would hunt red deer and an occasional Irish Elk, but how did they know which ones were fae and which ones weren't? Fauna fae were so well camouflaged with other species, they were often mistaken for normal flora and fauna. She didn't have the trained eye the huntsmen had, nor did she have the stamina to watch them.

"How do you know which one is a member of Errindoor's herd?" Amy asked.

Ewan's eyes dipped to the doe standing with their heads dipped to the river. "None of the white herd will drink from this water source."

Ah, that made sense to her. The white herd saved their thirst for the top of the mountain, where the water was the purest. None of these elk seemed to be fae after all, as every one of the does dipped their faces to the rushing river water and took in heavy gulps.

Splash!

After the last man darted across the bridge, the log went tumbling into the freezing river.

Her stomach pitted. How were they going to get across?

Ewan removed his boots, and slung them over his shoulder. He bent down and began untying the laces around his legs.

"What are you doing?" Amy asked.

"I'm not getting my boots wet in this mess."

Amy stepped back as the river water splashed toward her. So much for her chance at getting across without getting wet.

When the final doe crossed, the stag swung his head in her direction. He stomped his foot.

"What's he waiting for?" Amy asked.

Ewan stood, slinging his boots over his shoulder. "He's waiting for the last female to cross."

In one fell swoop, Ewan scooped Amy up and slung her atop the giant beast's back. She trembled as a ton of wild animal separated her from the ground.

"Easy," Ewan said, stroking the stag's thick neck. "He's not afraid of me, but he is of you."

Amy's boots shook against his sides. "Why is he afraid of me?"

"The kings of this forest listen to their queens before they make any movement."

"Is he a fae elk, or a normal one?" Amy asked, feeling the stag's ribs expand as he sucked in a breath.

"Don't know. If he isn't fae, he'll probably sense your fear and send you into the river."

"Don't joke!"

Ewan chuckled again. "Relax. Fae or not, he is still a king of this forest. If he is wise, he will respect your wishes. Now, feel him beneath you. Feel his strength. His power. He is waiting for you to guide him out into the water."

Amy set her hands forward, struggling with what she should grab onto. She could play with salt extracts all day, but this? This magic between beast and man, whatever it was, she had *no* control.

She placed her hands on his withers, threading her fingers through his thick hair. The texture was strangely similar to Ewan's chestnut locks.

"To the water," she whispered. In a surprisingly smooth motion, the fur and muscle beneath her moved forward.

The sharp sound of hooves against river rock shifted beneath her as the stag walked into the river. Ewan walked next to them, using the stag's body to shield him from the powerful current.

"Oh, that's cold," Ewan said as the water came up to his waist. "There is a reason we wear kilts in these parts. Easier to hike up."

The stag's ears swiveled toward her as they approached deeper water. Was he expecting her to tell him what to do next?

A log was flowing fast toward them. While the stag's body could handle the current, his bulk was no match for the chunk of wood barreling toward them.

Amy closed her eyes, focusing on the sound the log made as it traveled through the water. She sucked in a breath as the sharp, angular heads of ice crystals flooded her vision. She exhaled, releasing the crystals upstream, ripping apart the water as the vein of ice manifested.

She opened her eyes just as the ice splintered the log in half. She held on for dear life as the stag spooked, his body lunging for the other side of the river.

The moment his hooves jostled over dry stone, Amy let out a sigh. She clung to the beast like he was her savior. She was so grateful for his strength and endurance against the frigid water.

The stag's ears swiveled back and forth, and he, too, let out a sigh.

Ewan's arm came to her waist. Amy looped her arm around his neck as he helped her down. She much preferred his strength over the ton of wild stag between her legs.

He held her, refusing to lower her to the ground, his green eyes leveling with hers. His cheeks dimpled as a smug grin spread across his face. "If I didn't know any better, I'd say you enjoyed that."

"Maybe a bit," she stammered as he lowered her to the ground.

"Did you get wet?" he asked.

"Maybe," she said, flushing. Parts of her were wet that *shouldn't* be. Why was it in these dangerous moments between man and the wild that Ewan always found a way to arouse her?

39

MASIKA'S TIDAL CAVERN

Selia

Selia followed Alex outside the lighthouse. The swarm of salt flies had disappeared, for now. Alex made it clear they would be back if she didn't begin using her salt trancing talents.

Alex kept walking, not slowing for Selia at all. The snow was thick and unforgiving, making it nearly impossible for her to see her surroundings. They dipped down the hill, heading for the North Sea. Alex seemed so naked walking in front of her. Someone was missing from her side, a very giant someone who accompanied her the last time they met.

Where was Balfour?

As the ground leveled, Alex stopped, turning to face Selia. "To practice your summoning technique, I'm bringing you to the tidal cavern where Amy and Masika summoned Celaeno's storm dragon over three thousand years ago. Within the cavern, you will find an item that will help protect you and your loved ones from the salt flies."

Fear pitted in Selia's stomach. Alex was taking her to meet with the sea nymph she'd been communicating with behind the journal. How could Naunet, who she remembered as such a kind, loving individual, have a sister who was so resentful?

"How do you know I won't end up doing what I did to you in the Temple of Isis?"

The scar on Alex's upper lip twitched. "I don't. But I would like to use the cavern to judge where we left off, and see what we need to do to move forward. In order for Celaeno's storm dragon to bond with you, your talents with pulse will need to be honed."

Selia swallowed. What if everything blew up in her face?

Alex leveled her gaze with her. "A word of caution, the salt venom has likely told her that we will be heading her way. She will be waiting for us."

Fear rippled up Selia's spine. "You make it sound as though this salt venom is alive."

"The venom speaks through Masika. It *possesses* her." She dipped her chin, wind whipping the blond spikes of her short hair across her face. "The venom has changed her over time. Don't allow her lack of a body fool you. Her spirit is very powerful, especially when it comes to her ability to manipulate water vapor."

Alex held out her hand, her palm facing up.

Selia blinked as snow flurries whipped between them. She grabbed Alex's hand. Shimmering white light wrapped around them.

Alex closed her eyes. Her eyelashes changed from black to white. When she reopened her eyes, light erupted from them.

Selia fell backward as the light exploded from Alex's body. The backdrop of the sea fell away. The light pulsed and expanded around her, ebbing and flowing like water. When the force was too much for her to bear, she released Alex's hand, falling backward.

She landed with a heavy thud on a cold, damp surface. The sound of crashing waves hovered in the air. Her hands slipped over the surface of a rock face.

The surf ripped over the dark, jagged rocks, threatening to tug her out to sea. Water surrounded her on all sides. Wherever Alex had taken her, they were definitely not landlocked. No landmass was visible behind the low hanging clouds.

Alex was already descending the jagged rocks toward the mouth of a cavern.

Selia staggered to her feet. Why did the rocky outcropping feel so familiar? She crouched to the rock, trying to find footholds that weren't too slippery. It was nearly impossible not to slip with the rock being so covered in algae. Sea spray blew through her hair and clothing.

She made her way down to the mouth of a cavern where Alex stood. Alex held her hand out at her side, palm facing up. An orb of light hovered between her fingers, illuminating the mouth of the cavern. "Welcome to Masika's tidal cavern."

Selia stopped at Alex's side, gazing into the dark mouth of the cavern. Sea water was swallowed by the opening in great heaving sweeps before it was tugged back out by the current.

Alex dipped into the cavern first. Selia followed. With every step she took, memories from her past began to emerge from her subconscious. As the surf surged around her, the past and present crashed into one another, nearly sweeping Selia off her feet. She'd been on this rock before. This was the same location Amy had brought her to bond with Celaeno's storm dragon.

The air was pregnant with moisture. The surf surged into the opening, then flooded back out to sea. Watching the violent movement of the water was enough to make Selia nauseous.

Alex stopped near a rocky overlook where the surf was calmer. The rocks appeared jagged and oblong. Dagger-like, the rocks glistened like dozens of tiny sharp teeth.

"Do you see the salt venom crystals?" Alex asked, her voice muffled by the crashing surf.

"Is that what they are?"

Alex's eyes darkened. "Wherever you see them, Masika isn't far behind." She held her gaze with the waves below. "When she emerges, I will work to distract her while you practice salt trancing with your pulse." She made a motion with her hand. "I will signal when it's time for you to dip into a trance, all right?"

"What am I actually summoning?" Selia asked, slightly terrified at what might emerge from the cavern. Her memories of practicing in the Temple of Isis were also partially fragmented. What exactly should she be practicing with her pulse?

A pod of seals was swimming about, jumping and playing in the surf. One of the seals wasn't like the others.

A woman emerged from the tidal pool, her long dark hair streaking over her back and shoulders. She stroked one of the seals on the head before it turned and dove back into the sea.

She tilted her head back, her angular face catching the pale moonlight filtering into the cavern.

"She's spotted us," Alex said, her voice a shiver.

With one swift movement, Masika dove back into the water.

The cavern quaked as though a thunderous voice was trying to speak. The wall to Selia's side shimmered as the rocky surface changed. Tendrils of water vapor emerged from the wall as the sharp, jutting edges of the crystals poked through. A face emerged. Staring at them was the selkie the locals of Montrose knew.

"Alexandra," Masika said. Her voice was as deep and liquid as the saltwater filling the cavern. A sharpness hovered in the air that echoed off the crystals.

When her eyes met Selia's an uncontrollable ripple shivered up Selia's spine. "And my dear Selia."

Selia's salt nodes burned with heat. Masika's voice had so much power behind it. She sounded so much louder, surrounded by her natural elements compared to the interactions she'd had with her from the journal. Something lingered behind her voice that was as alive as the waves surging inside the cavern.

Her skin had the same dark color and texture as the crystals emerging from the wall behind her. She wore a simple black dress. No shoes. Long strands of curling black hair tapered down her shoulders. Her eyes were not normal. Where there should be white, there was black. And her irises were a startling white. Even the aroma in the cavern changed at her appearance. The air smelled of damp earth mixed with the tang of iron.

This was the cursed selkie behind the journal she'd been speaking with.

"Why have you two come here?" Masika asked, stopping before them, holding her hands out to her sides. She curled her fingers, flexing her wrists as her eyes moved slowly between them. For not having a body, she sure could fool someone. The mist coiling around her created the illusion that she was one with the cavern.

Alex made a motion with her hand toward the water. "There have been some new developments with the fae queen."

The mist coiling around Masika's face thickened. "Are you referring to the fae queen who cursed me?"

Selia caught Alex's cue. She closed her eyes, trying to block out their conversation as she practiced her summoning technique. Something silver shimmered in her periphery.

A deep liquid *hiiiiisssssssss* filled the cavern as Masika's voice echoed around her. "Selia and I have spent the past few days discussing her ancestry."

Selia opened her eyes, breaking her concentration with her trance. The crystals on the wall behind Masika shimmered dangerously. Masika's eyes drifted over Alex's shoulder, locking with her. Her gaze was nothing like Selia remembered of her loving older sister. Her look was primal one. Something else lived inside of her that wasn't good.

"How did you find me after I opened the vault?" Selia asked.

Masika unfolded her fingers, revealing a small black fleck in the center of her palm. "The salt flies told me where you were as soon as the vault was opened. I was the one who placed the incantation on it, stating that only the Blind Moon could open it."

"What do you want with me?" Selia asked, anger rising in her chest.

Masika closed her fingers over the salt fly. "I would rather have the venom share the details with you about the darkness from your past."

Selia balled her hands into fists. Masika was avoiding her question, trying to manipulate her. "I'll have you know that I only opened the vault because I believed what was inside would help me learn how to practice the art of salt trance. I was not aware that Amy was using the queen to try and save you from the curse salt venom has placed on you."

The mist shuddered as Masika scowled. "*Save* me? Why would Amy attempt such a ridiculous feat? Besides, what body do I have to return to, when my spirit is free to live with the venom and do as it pleases?" She held her hand out at her side, tendrils of mist caressing her wrists and fingers. "I don't believe Alexandra has shared any of the history Amy and I have behind my sister's research around blue minca, has she?"

Selia broke her gaze. She took a step back, finding that there was no place to go. The sharp, jagged salt crystals on the wall had spread up the path, locking her and Alex in place.

Masika's eyelashes fluttered, salt crystals forming on the tips. "There is something I do not understand. If Selia opened the vault, why is the fae queen not with her?"

The lines around Alex's mouth twitched. "Amy made off with the queen before I could stop her."

The mist thickened, spreading out like tendrils of smoke from a fire. "My salt flies have found a victim of the fae queen—I can taste the salt from his blood on one of you who care about him." Masika tilted her head to the side, her angular cheekbones softening in the dim moonlight. "Tell me, who has she infected?"

Anger flared through Selia. She bit her lip so hard, it started to bleed. She wouldn't allow Masika's taunting to get the better of her emotions.

Masika's expression hardened as did the crystals behind her. "There is no cure for it. All one can do is hope the victim's heart can endure it."

Selia held her ground as Masika drifted past Alex. The scent of iron-rich soil saturated her nose as Masika's vaporous face came too close for comfort.

"Amy has taken the fae queen to the past to meet with an ancestor save your spirit from the salt venom," Alex said.

"Whose ancestor is this?"

"Damien Malloch's ancestor, Ewan."

Masika's pupils became vertical slits. "I see." Her vaporous form coiled around Alex. "Ewan, son of Atlantean kings?"

Selia blinked.

The silver tendrils of water vapor coiled around Alex's body like a silver serpent.

The crystals on the wall behind her began to shake. One jutted up from the ground, nearly impaling Alex.

A hand broke form the mist, gripping around Alex's neck.

"How dare you allow Amy to make such a ridiculous attempt to save me! The Order should have intervened!" Masika cried, her voice breaking into a shriek. Her grip tightened on Alex's throat. Her fingers turned dagger-like. "I may be cursed by the venom, but I know there are curses far worse than what I have suffered. The Order allowed my sister to be punished for something she had no warning for."

"Masika, wait..." Alex sputtered, the mist coiling around her throat.

"Stop!" Selia cried. She reached for Masika's arm, but another large salt crystal came jutting up from the ground.

"The Order should have left the business with the Codex to the midwife of the sea," Masika hissed as her fingers dug into Alex's neck.

Alex's eyes rolled into the back of her head.

Selia's pulse thundered in her chest. She threw her arms out to the crystal, a force inside of her surging forth as the cavern rumbled with a terrible shudder. "I said stop!"

40

CRYSTALS

Amy

Amy found herself falling behind the huntsmen. Staying this far behind worked to her advantage. They made quick work of the snowy trail, carving grooves that made her trek less exhausting. Preserving her strength was proving difficult.

Where Amy saw nothing but dense forest and snowcapped trees, the huntsmen were able to navigate this wilderness of opportunity. Game trails created by smaller animals wove between the trees. There were many species of fauna fae living in Winter Forest that Amy did not know. Rabbit and squirrel footprints were the only tracks Amy was familiar with.

Occasionally, Ewan would disappear off the main trail, likely picking up on some movement of the fae beast he was tracking. She had a whole lot of frozen terrain to trek through before reaching her goal. But that didn't mean she couldn't start developing a weapon of her own.

She would need something strong enough to pierce through Errindoor's tough hide once they reached the summit of the sacred mountain. Something told her the small flint Ewan gave her wouldn't be strong enough to achieve her goal. Stealing a larger weapon from Ewan's men didn't seem like a wise thing to do. The moment one of their flints disappeared, they were sure to suspect her.

Before she could assemble a weapon, she first needed to gather a very personal belonging of hers.

The trail took a turn for the worse. An incline of jumbled icy rocks and tree roots lined the path. One wrong step, and this part of the trail would surely snap someone's neck.

Amy swiveled in her spot. She really didn't want to hike up this death trap of root, rock, and ice. She knew the caverns were close to this area. There was something inside the caverns she needed if she was to slay the mighty Errindoor. All she needed to do was trust her pulse.

She slowed her pace, focusing on the crunching snow beneath her boots.

Breath. Memory. Salt.

She cycled the three principles in her mind, focusing not only on her pulse, but the pulse of Winter Forest.

An ice vein branched out from her feet. As the vein turned the snow into ice crystals, it tapered to a point, then slithered down the hill.

Amy dipped off the trail, following the ice vein as it branched down a snowy slope. Drifts made the trek difficult, and she struggled to keep up. As the forest thinned and a rocky outcropping appeared, a musty scent filled her nose. A familiar scent that made her salt nodes swell with heat.

Her boots transitioned from snowy ground to damp earth. The air coming from the cavern was warmer, breathing out in spontaneous humid bursts. The chattering voices inside the cave were either welcoming their friend home, or announcing Amy's arrival.

She stopped in the mouth of the cave and gazed up at the ceiling where the voices chirped and chattered. A cave full of fae bats. There were *dozens* of underground places where the fae bats lived. Masika knew all of the entrances to the caverns and the mineral springs that often bubbled up from them.

Amy's breathing became shallow as time stood still. Memories from her past manifested as a shadow before her.

Masika's hands came to hers, her fingers soft and warm. "Close your eyes, and salt trance with me."

Amy closed her eyes as Masika's lips came to hers.

Amy opened her eyes. Masika was gone. Only the taste of her kiss lingered.

Amy bit her bottom lip. Their first kiss was preserved here, along with what remained of her.

The far wall of the cave guarded the item she'd come for. She walked to the wall and crouched, finding the spot to dig. Beneath the earth was one of the many canopic jars she and Masika had brought from Egypt. This jar, however, was very specific.

She dug her hands down into the earth, finding the jar was still there. She tilted the lid open revealing the contents. Black powder sat inside, along with a single salt crystal. Amy had taken the crystal with her from Egypt after Masika had discovered Selia sleeping in Naunet's dwelling. It was the only physical item left of Masika she had in her possession.

The crystal was a piece of Masika's skin the salt venom had crystalized.

Her stomach turned over. Seeing the small remains of her friend, a single black salt crystal, was too much.

She turned away from the jar, her stomach preparing to become violently ill.

A shadow dipped over the water, traveling up the damp wall of the cave. The silhouette of a man appeared at the cavern's entrance.

"I was wondering where you ran off to," Ewan said, making Amy jump.

While Amy couldn't make out his expression, his tone rang with annoyance. She replaced the lid on the jar and tucked it into a pocket beneath her robe.

As Ewan hopped from one mossy rock to the next, Amy stood and turned to face him.

He stopped in front of her, folding his massive arms across his chest. "It is unwise for a woman to go exploring on her own. There are fae beasts in these woods who will eat you. If the beasts don't kill you, other things will. There are things that grow in these caves that have been known to put a man into a sleep he will not wake from." His gaze dropped to her lips. "Things that make poison."

Amy gripped the jar holding Masika's crystal remains. Poison and venom were two vastly different things. Keeping Ewan in the dark was all part of her plan. She needed him for one thing—to bring her to the top of the mountain to find Errindoor.

She had the remains of her friend. All she needed now was a means to spill the blood of the fae king. "How did you find me?"

"I followed that," he said, pointing to the ice vein melting at the cavern's entrance. "What is it called?"

"An ice vein."

Ewan chuckled. "I've always loved my women icy on the surface." He took a step toward her. "You used it to discover which of my men attempted to poison you. Then, you used it again in the river to split a log."

Amy's storm bond was *crystal*. Her bond allowed her to manipulate the crystal lattice structures of both salt and water, forming salt extracts in little to no time at all. Most of her Ocean Apothecary was composed of her crystal experiments she had performed with the maternal salts.

She locked her eyes with Ewan's hazel ones. "Ice has a magical way of making truth crystal clear. While the mouth may lie, the heart always beats true to its source."

"My men are fearful of your icy magic for good reason." He set his hand on the boulder next to Amy, which he dwarfed. He leaned against the boulder, closing the space between them. His shadow consumed Amy, and she was reminded how small she was beneath him. She didn't like feeling so short, even though she wasn't the tallest to begin with.

Amy's foot brushed past a root that climbed up the side of the boulder Ewan was leaning on. She stepped backward and propped herself up onto the root. Had she not, her face wouldn't have reached his chin. Standing near eye-level with this giant man made her feel like his equal.

"How does your magic work?" he asked, a cocky grin spreading across his face.

Amy propped herself onto her toes to reclaim her space. "I ask the water to tell me the truth, and it obeys me."

Ewan set his other hand on the boulder, locking Amy between his arms. His hazel eyes became a dangerous green. "What would your magic say about me?"

Amy's toes buckled. He wanted her to flatter him. "That you have the heart of a king."

His cheeks dimpled as her compliment sank into him. His forearms bulged against the rock, his veins thickening. "A king is nothing without his queen."

Ewan dropped his hands to her hips, preventing her from moving. His lips crashed against hers.

Ewan's lips were not tender like Masika's. They were chapped with cold. His facial hair was rough, and his lips tasted of fire and smoke.

Amy broke their kiss, jolting away from his mouth. "Ewan," she whispered. His kiss stole her breath.

The desire in his eyes wasn't only lust. He wanted more than her body. Ewan's desire was to repair the kin he had lost.

His hand came to hers, tender and warm. He grabbed her around the waist, forcing her against the cavern wall. Lifting her up, he thrust his hips forward, propping her onto the stone ledge. "While you are in my forest, I am going to worship you as a goddess."

She leaned back, propping her elbows onto the ledge as Ewan's wide hands reached under her robe. Cupping her butt with both hands, he pulled her toward him, forcing his face between her legs.

A moan escaped her lips as Ewan feasted upon her. With every suck and flick of his tongue against her clit, her body surrendered more to the generous huntsman.

Her fingers scraped against the cold stone as he pleased her. Her body trembled as heat branched from her breasts to her fingers. Her back arched as the peak of her pleasure rippled through her body. The dark cave burst into light as her orgasm released.

But Ewan wasn't done. He was already feasting on her again, this time digging his finger into her opening.

Amy grabbed his hair, "Once is enough," she whispered.

He kissed her legs as he withdrew his face. He grabbed her around the waist, lowering her to the ground.

Amy grabbed his arm, steadying herself.

Ewan's arms looped through hers as he positioned her away from him. She faced the wall as Ewan's body pressed against her back. In the thick haze of Masika's kiss and Ewan's pleasure, she had forgotten where she was.

He lowered his face to her neck, brushing his facial hair past her salt node. His hand moved up her cloak. "Set your hands on the wall."

Amy held her hands out to the damp stone wall, preventing him from flattening her.

"I want my goddess to bare me a son," he growled into her ear.

What words might make a woman weak in the knees made Amy tighten.

As he nuzzled her cheek and his hands wandered down her back and to her front, Amy's mind drifted to Masika. As his body hardened, Amy's thoughts traveled deeper into the cavern. The jar full of Masika's crystal remains felt cold against her side.

Ewan set his hands atop hers on the wall, dwarfing hers. He always enjoyed the mating ritual from behind.

She grabbed his thumb, squeezing it tight. "Ewan, wait."

If she didn't stop him now, he would slip inside of her and that would be the end of it.

He softened his grip on her hand. "Why are you resisting me?"

"You've made me quite sore. Can you spare a selkie her softness, until we reach the sacred meadow?"

He pulled his face away from her neck, his grip on her softening. "Why are you sore?"

"The other night," she breathed, "you don't remember how you ravished me?"

"Refresh my memory," he growled, his cock pressing against her leg.

Amy released her grip on his thumb and turned to face him. She looked up into his face, hazel eyes a dangerous green. His green was so different from the sea. His eyes housed the soul of an Atlantean king. "We have a long journey ahead of us, and I don't think my body can handle the generosity of your lovemaking right now."

His cock twitched against her thigh. "Are you saying you will reward me when we get to the meadow?"

"I am," she said, fighting the flush creeping up her neck.

"You sure know how to make a man work for his prize."

Crack!

A branch shifted in the forest. A pair of golden eyes peered into the cave, eyes that had the wild spirit of Winter Forest.

41
SALT RUSH

Selia

The cavern shook as waves crashed inside.

Masika's hand—a vice of blackened crystal fingers—began to retract.

Alex fell to the ground, her body lifeless.

Selia doubled over, gripping her knees with her hands. Panting, she sucked in sharp, forceful breaths. What pulsed through her? What was the force that had exploded like a thousand sharp daggers, demanding she surrender to it?

She staggered over to Alex, who lay on her back. Her arms and legs were mangled, her neck cocked at an awkward angle. She reached for Alex's shoulder.

"Leave her," Masika hissed, taking on her water vapor form again. She coiled around Selia's face as her tendrils of mist thickened. "I wouldn't have killed her so easily, not when the salt venom listened to you so willingly."

Selia threw her hand out. "Stay away from me," she spat, dropping to Alex's side. She grabbed her shoulder and tugged her aside. "I don't want to have anything to do with the substance that has possessed you."

Her stomach hollowed. Half of Alex's face had been crystallized.

Selia pulled away. "What did you do to her?"

"I didn't do anything," Masika hissed, a smile curling on her lips. "You did."

Selia backed away. Had she harmed Alex like she had done in the Temple of Isis? Was history repeating itself?

The cavern shook again, this time causing the salt crystals on the walls to shatter. The surf surged inside, quaking the cave with a violent thrash. Whatever she'd summoned was welling inside of her.

The cavern filled with torrents of water, the waves surging upward and consuming her.

"Stop this!" Selia cried as the waves crashed over her.

Masika's hand came to hers. "Embrace the sea and surrender to the salt venom with me."

Selia sucked in a breath as the water crashed over her and Masika. Alex was swept away from the wave, her body tumbling into darkness.

Selia couldn't see. Even if she did cry out, her voice would be drowned by the vertical walls of water now surging upward.

Masika manifested before her, arms outstretched and her eyes a luminous ebony. "Steady yourself," she said, her voice more powerful than the wall of rushing water surging around them both.

"What's happening to me?" Selia asked, her voice breaking with the waves that tumbled over her.

"You are experiencing a salt rush. All you can do is surrender to the sea and hope that the salt returns you to the surface. I can help you, but only if you give me what I want. The sensation you've experienced of stepping out of your skin, I can teach you how to master it. It is the state of existence my spirit lives in."

Selia threw her arms out, unable to scream. She didn't have Alex's guidance. All she had was Masika's venomous gaze threatening to rip her open if she didn't obey her. "What do you want with me?"

"Tell me what you remember last of Amy from Egypt," Masika's voice cloaked around her. "You took something with you from the Temple of Isis. All sea nymphs at your age did."

As Masika's voice swathed around her, so did the grip the salt crystals had on her. She couldn't tell if it was Masika still talking with her, or if it was instead, the venom.

Selia's vision blurred, blending in and out as the sharp angular heads of the salt crystals crowded around her. Some were silky smooth and white, while others were jagged and black. Images reflected inside the salt crystals. The salt was trying to share something about her past that she couldn't remember.

"Share with me the day you were practicing your salt summoning," Masika hissed, her voice filling Selia's head.

As Masika's words wrapped around her, Selia's vision blurred.

Darkness enveloped her, setting her back to that place in time. The Temple of Isis manifested before her. Golden rays of daylight filtered in from the window, dancing over the granite face of Isis.

Alex stood to her right. Amy stood behind her. Both their faces were concealed behind a shimmering blanket of dark salt crystals.

Alex held her hand out, preparing to teach their salt summoning lesson. "Begin."

Selia tried to close her eyes and partake in the trance, but her eyelids were frozen. She tried to walk, but something invisible grabbed onto her feet, holding her in place.

The golden rays of daylight were soon dulled, replaced with a dark, cavernous opening similar to the mouth of the tidal cavern.

Something was moving near the moth nest. There was no comforting lazy hum created by their wings. Something was there, but it was darker. A single moth emerged. Its eyes were full of sharp black crystals.

It took off in flight, darting past Alex, aiming for Selia instead.

Selia ducked as it aimed its razor-sharp wings for her face.

The moth dove into the shadows, circling back toward her. This time, it wasn't one, but many. A shadow of a thousand shimmering black wings came tunneling for her.

"Help me!" Selia cried as the salt flies tangled in her hair, ripping out strands as she covered her face with her hands.

Thousands of salt flies hovered around her. Their swarm was so thick, breathing became impossible. The taste of salt welled up on Selia's tongue, parching her mouth and closing her throat.

Masika came rushing toward her as her tendrils of water vapor closed in. Crystals jutted up from the ground, creating a barrier between her and the swarming shadow.

Selia was knocked backward. She landed in a puddle of water with a splash. Down she went, sinking into the inky blackness as Masika's silver tendrils coiled around her.

Her throat burned as she tried to swallow. The opening had sealed shut.

"Breathe with me," Masika whispered, her voice liquid and sharp.

The Temple of Isis faded, and the tidal cavern returned.

Selia fell forward, her palms scraping against hard, jagged stone. She coughed, spitting up salt water as the tidal cavern returned to focus. Her throat reopened.

Masika stood before her, those penetrating white eyes staring into her soul. Her lips turned up into a smile.

"What did I just see?" Selia asked, shuddering.

"During a salt rush, salt venom manipulates one's memories."

Selia shivered. "Why are you showing this nightmare to me?"

"You walked away from the temple with something the Order didn't want you to know existed—something I want."

The wall behind Masika shimmered with crystals that weren't quite solid. They were dripping.

Selia clutched her throat. The vapor in the air was so sharp, the edges threatened to rip through her throat. "I can't breathe..."

Masika's hand coiled around Selia's neck, morphing between her dagger crystal fingers and vaporous smoke. "I'll be waiting. All you must do is tell the venom that you are ready to surrender to it."

Selia choked as Masika's liquid voice filled her salt nodes.

42
WOLVES

Amy

A pair of golden eyes locked with Amy's, paralyzing her. She remembered seeing golds like this in Egypt. The only creature she'd seen with that look belonged to a lioness. While the pupils of a lioness and a wolf were vastly different, the golds swirling around the dark centers held the same protective instincts.

The instinct was not for herself, but for another smaller, less powerful creature. Instinct only a mother held inside of her—a look to kill. The maternal instinct was the most powerful force in nature. This mother wolf was about to prove it.

Ewan's body tensed. He grabbed Amy's hand and led her out of the cavern.

The wolf snarled, shifting its body to face them as they maneuvered into the forest.

"Get behind me," Ewan whispered, keeping his voice low.

Amy fell behind Ewan's crouched body, realizing one very troubling thing. As large as Ewan was, he had no weapon. They were both facing a beast with fangs and claws that could rip them to shreds in an instant.

Ewan postured himself low to the ground. He held his arms out, shaking his head as though cowering.

"We've trespassed into her home. We need to leave, now," Ewan whispered, taking slow steps back into the thick timbers.

Amy tried to mimic Ewan's body language as she had no idea how to communicate with a wild mother in the forest.

Her shoulder jerked to the side. Her cloak had gotten caught on a low-hanging branch.

Fangs snapped under a crinkled muzzle as the wolf took a step down from her den. One wrong bit of body language could make this angry mother charge.

She grabbed her cloak, tugging it away from the branch, sending a blanket of snow cascading over her.

Ewan grabbed Amy around the waist, tugging her out of the snowy disaster she would soon be stuck in. In her stupor to free herself, she'd startled the wolf.

A whirlwind of fur and snow lunged toward her.

Snap, growl, snap!

Ewan lunged, breaking the branch Amy had been tangled in. He held the branch in front of his body, blocking the impact of another wolf that lunged for him.

The wolf tumbled in the snow, staggering back to his feet and facing Ewan. This wolf was nearly twice the size of the female and a different color. Not white, but a startlingly beautiful black. Hairs on its spine rose. Its nostrils flared as ears pinned back.

This was the alpha male, who set his sights on Ewan.

While Ewan had the male preoccupied, the ground vibrated as footsteps hurried up the snowy hill.

Ewan's men darted up behind them, each with their bows strung.

Amy clutched her side. She was missing something. She'd dropped the jar full of Masika's crystal remains.

She backtracked her steps, crouching into the snow. The jar had to be somewhere. Where had it gone?

Movement caught her eye. She realized what the male wolf was protecting. The mother wolf whipped back to her den, where she began nudging a ball of dark fur.

One of her wolf pups had discovered the jar.

Panic struck Amy's body. She gathered her cloak and staggered to her feet. She needed to get to the jar without the mother thinking she would harm her offspring.

She began walking toward the wolf pup, a crazy force gripping her. Her approach only angered the mother. She pinned her ears, rounding and snapping.

Movement summited the hill as Ewan's huntsmen arrived.

"Men, freeze!" Ewan bellowed, crouching down to the ground again. The alpha male's shoulders arched, rippling with hair that stood on end.

The alpha male wolf lunged, snarling and snapping in the air as he dove for one of the men. Before he could draw his dagger, the wolf had snatched his leg.

The wolf whipped his head from side-to-side, ripping open his flesh and tossing him to the side.

"Help me!" the man cried.

One of Ewan's men notched his arrow, tugging the feathers to his cheek.

The alpha male released the huntsman, turning his sights on Ewan. The wolf lunged again, this time for Ewan's head.

Twang!

The arrow flew, cutting the air and striking the alpha male's side. But not before he'd taken Ewan's forearm into his mouth.

Blood sprayed, crystallizing as it hit the freezing air. The alpha male fell with a heavy *thud* onto the ground.

Ewan was knocked from his feet, landing next to the wolf.

"No..." Ewan growled, staggering to his knees.

The alpha male lay stiff in the snow next to him. His mouth lay open, tongue lashing out with his dying breath. The snow quickly turned red from the blood pooling beneath his chest.

The mother wolf grabbed her pup in her mouth and retreated into the den.

Amy grabbed the jar and scrambled over to Ewan, finding the blood wasn't only from the alpha male. Ewan's forearm had a deep bloody gash in it from the wolf's fangs.

Amy reached for Ewan's arm, but he jerked away.

He hiked is head back and bellowed, "Ancestors, forgive me!"

The confrontation with the wolf pack left Amy with more respect for the beasts who lived in the forest. In the moments it took for her and Ewan to leave the others, they'd crossed a boundary neither of them should have. One step out of that boundary had cost the life of a family meant for this wilderness.

Before Ewan tended to his own wounds, he tended to those of his men. Two of them had sustained injuries in the fight Amy was still blaming herself for. If she hadn't gotten caught in the branch, maybe the mother wolf wouldn't have charged, sending Ewan into a fight his body wasn't meant for.

Ewan had fared better, even after taking the brunt force of the wolf. The leg of one of his men had almost been ripped through.

As the sun dipped below the tree line, group's mood changed. Their first day out on the trail to track Errindoor's herd had left them drained. The men busied themselves setting up shelters, while some got to work building a fire and butchering the wolf they'd killed.

Amy had never been a huge fan of meat other than fish. However, living out here in the middle of the forest, one needed to rely on the resources at their disposal. Somehow, she felt like she'd cursed the entire group. While these men were hunters in every right, she could tell they didn't take killing lightly. Something told her that killing an apex predator on their first day wasn't viewed as a good thing, even if the encounter wasn't intentional.

Ewan worked with his men to gather firewood. His posture was different. His shoulders were hunched, and he refused to look her in the eye. He knew he'd been a fool. Both of them had. Neither of them should have strayed from the group for the sake of having intimacy in the cavern.

As they dismembered the body of the wolf, each chanted a prayer. The legs, back and ribs were all placed over a roaring fire, where the meat sizzled and snapped as it cooked. The men dispersed the hide and some of the internal organs, packing them away for processing later. Nothing was wasted. .

The wolf's head was set on a stone overlooking the flames.

Ewan took no part in harvesting the wolf's body. He stood with his arms crossed beneath his bloody cloak.

Amy wondered if he was trying to pay respect to the life lost by refusing to show his injury. She knew it had to be causing him a great deal of pain, however, he refused to show any weakness. From the way the blood was pooling through the white hide of his cloak, she knew the bite was serious.

One of the men approached Ewan and handed him a leather pouch.

Ewan took the pouch and held it over the fire . "Blood was spilled without reason today. Let this be a lesson for us all. We must learn to show our respect while hunting in Winter Forest."

The men dipped their heads, all gazing down into the hearth.

Ewan withdrew the concealed item within the pouch.

Amy swallowed. Clutched in his fingers was the wolf's heart.

He turned to face Amy, holding the heart in his hand. Steam issued from the tissue as it was still warm.

Her breath caught. Was he offering it to her?

She looked into Ewan's deep hazel eyes, a plea for forgiveness in them. She could manipulate a man all she wanted. But taking from the wild?

Ewan vowed to give her the same thing the alpha male sacrificed for his mate.

Devotion. Protection. Family.

He would give up his life to protect not only her, but the future of their offspring.

She looked at the bloody mass of his heart in Ewan's hand. Her stomach wallowed with guilt. "I don't deserve this." She got up from the fire, grabbing her cloak and tugging it around her.

She turned and walked toward one of the dwellings at the edge of camp. She was so angry with herself.

"I told you she was an ungrateful witch," one of the men said.

Amy lifted the flap of the dwelling and ducked inside. Tears were now burning in her eyes. Even if she wanted, she couldn't give Ewan what he wanted.

She found the bed bundle in the corner and crawled between the animal hides. Her thoughts drifted to Masika. She clutched the jar of Masika's crystal remains to her chest. She was here for one thing only—to put the spirit of her friend to rest.

But was she willing to break the heart of a king in the process?

PART 6
VENOM & VAPOR

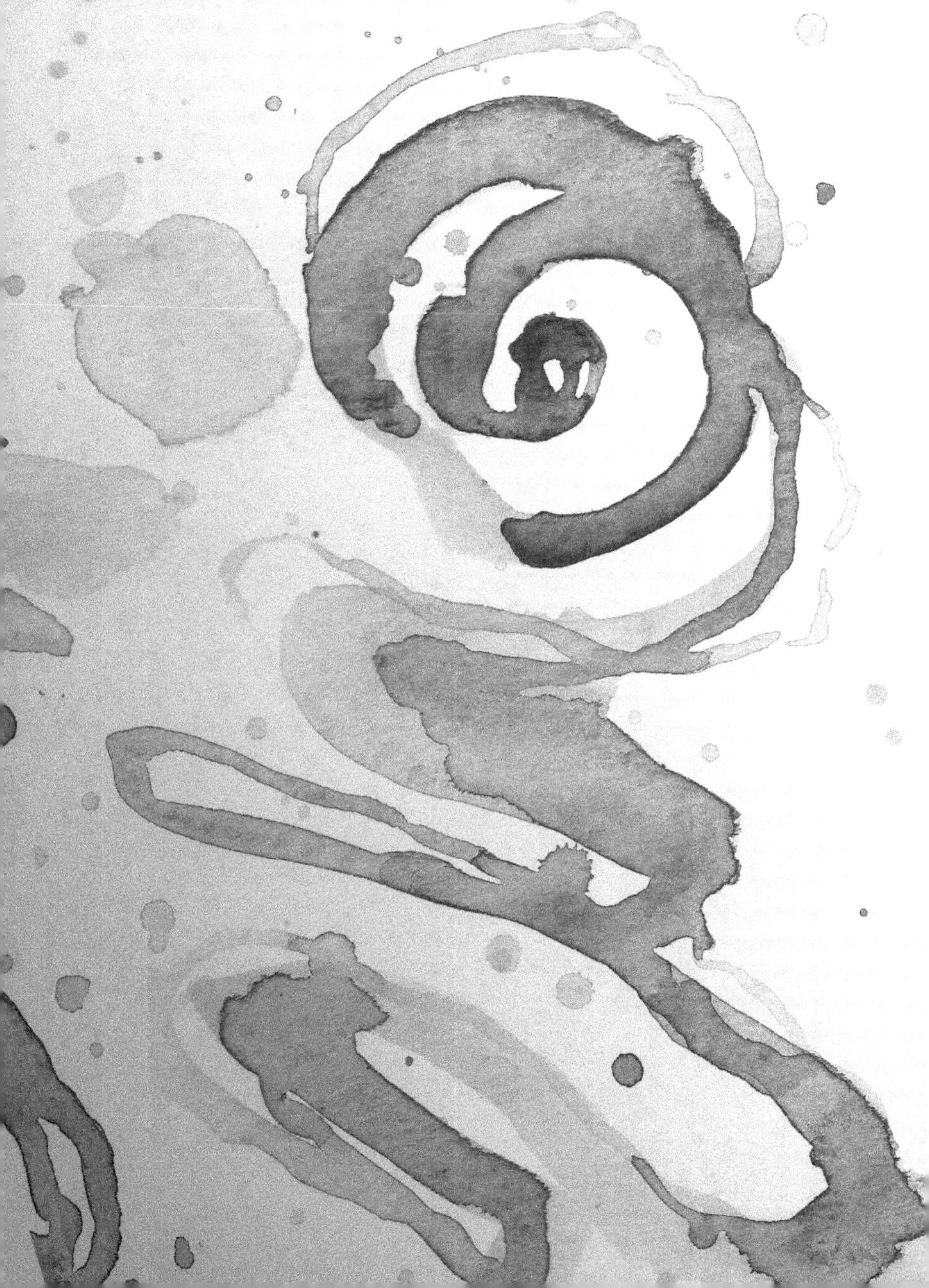

43

HALLUCINATIONS

Selia

Selia's body was shaking. Lights flooded into her periphery as Masika's tidal cavern was replaced with Gwen's frantic screaming.

"She's awake!" Gwen cried.

Selia squinted into the bright light streaming above her. It wasn't from her bedroom. The room reeked with the scent of disinfectant. She gripped the cold, starchy fabric from the bed sheet that lay atop her. "Where am I? Where is Damien?"

"Both of you are in the hospital," Gwen said as she walked up to her and sat on her bedside.

Selia's body cramped with adrenaline. Damien lay in the bed next to her. His face was turned away, his expression blocked by his elated sister.

Selia threw her legs out of her bed and jumped toward him.

"Oh, no you don't!" Gwen cried as she grabbed Selia's shoulders and forced her back onto the bed.

A nurse walked into the room, a clipboard in her hand. "Selia, you are extremely dehydrated. I believe you and your fiancé here had a little too much fun at the party."

"I'm not drinking!" Selia yelled. She flopped back onto her bed, panic surging through her. "Something stung him! Now the salt flies are draining his energy!"

"Salt flies?" The nurse asked.

Gwen shot Selia a confused look. "Delusional outburst, noted," the nurse said as she scribbled on the clipboard. "I'll be right back." She turned on her heel, leaving Selia alone with a very concerned-looking Gwen.

"How am I delusional?" Selia spat.

"Selia, they've done blood work on Damien. What are you talking about? Salt flies? Nothing stung him."

"Then why is he still sleeping?"

Gwen shook her head. "It's a classic case of too much alcohol. I promise, he'll be awake by tomorrow morning." She set her hand on her shoulder. "Is there something else going on that you haven't told Pixie and I?"

Panic surged through Selia. Had everything she heard in the tidal cavern between Alex and Masika been a hallucination?

Masika's crystalline voice wrapped around her. "*I'll be waiting. All you must do is tell the venom that you are ready to surrender to it.*"

Selia grabbed Gwen's arm. "Gwen, I took something your fireplace mantle. A bottle of salt venom that—"

"*Salt venom?* What's that?" Gwen gawked, cutting her off. "I can absolutely say for certain that I do not have any memory of having a bottle of something called salt venom."

Selia's stomach pitted. Was the venom erasing memories of its existence? If so, how long would it be before her own memories of it were destroyed?

Pixie walked into the room, her face flushing the moment she spotted Selia. "Oh, thank goodness! Gwen and I have been worried *sick* about you!" She darted over to the hospital bed and threw her arms around her.

"Pixie, do you remember the discussion?" Selia asked as Pixie released her. "We agreed that something either stung or bit Damien, remember? Gwen blamed Peppercorn for it!"

Pixie looked from Selia to Gwen, whose expression was just as alarmed.

Gwen folded her arms in front of her chest. "Sounds like a lovely thing for me to blame that little bat for, but I don't remember doing so. I swear, if I find out that my cousins spiked your drinks with something to mess with our memories, they will never hear the end of it."

Selia began to shake. Had the salt venom erased itself from the memories of those it had interacted with? Or was she really losing it?

Gwen grabbed Selia's hand. "I think you're having a nervous breakdown. With the engagement, the new home, the holidays, everything is happening so fast. It's normal for a woman to crumble under that amount of stress."

Selia locked her eyes with Gwen's hazel ones. "I'm not having a nervous breakdown! My fiancé has been cursed by a selkie!"

Gwen and Pixie exchanged glances. "Sika?" they both said at once.

"Yes, the selkie!" Selia gazed into the faces of her friends. One thing was for certain. Not even her memories were safe from this wickedly dangerous substance Masika called salt venom.

She jumped up from the bed and walked over to Damien. She tugged his shirt down from around his neck. The mark she could have sworn was there was gone.

All she could see was Masika's crystallized face glaring at her, the sinister look in her eyes demanding that she surrender to the venom.

"Selia, what's going on?" Gwen asked, walking to her side.

Selia stared into Damien's sleeping face. This *wasn't* alcohol. She knew Damien. He was a responsible, caring, and incredibly devoted father-to-be. During the gathering, he'd barely had anything to drink. All she remembered was Amy arriving, then bustling out into the stormy winter night.

Her last words blew through her, "*My window to the past has opened.*"

"She wants something from me," Selia whispered as she reached out and stroked Damien's face. She ran her finger over his jaw to his lips.

"Who wants something from you?" Pixie asked, walking up to Selia's side.

"The myth you shared with me around Sika at your house. That night is when this all started."

"Selia, do you believe you are interacting with Sika somehow?" Gwen asked, concern flashing in her eyes.

Selia had seen the tidal cavern *twice* now. Once, in a memory of her and Amy. Second, recently. One thing was for certain—something was haunting about that tidal cavern. She needed to feel the crystals under her fingers, to know if they were real, or a figment of her imagination.

Gwen's phone chimed. She retrieved it from her pocket. "Sean's coming by. It's Christmas Eve *Eve*, and I'm still not done with my Christmas shopping for the kids." She pocketed her phone. "Why don't you come with us?"

Selia shook her head. "No, I'm not leaving until he wakes up."

Worry flickered in Gwen's eyes. "I understand. Text or call me the moment he wakes up or if you need anything?"

Selia nodded. She couldn't convince words to escape her lips.

Pixie set her hand on Selia's shoulder. "My shop is right up the block. Come in and grab a bite, will you? Peter and I will be baking all day to restock for Christmas."

Gwen and Pixie left, leaving Selia alone with Damien.

She pulled a chair over to his hospital bed and sat down next to him. Exhaustion blew through her, zapping any energy she had to make sense of this strange situation. Masika's voice filled her head, pulsing through her again. "*You walked away from the temple with something the Order didn't want you to know existed—something I want.*"

Selia grabbed Damien's cold hand and set her head down on the pillow next to him as Masika's tidal cavern came flooding back into her memory.

317

44

HOT SPRINGS

Amy

Amy awoke to the sound of a man groaning. She sat up in her bed bundle, finding that Ewan wasn't the source of the painful grunts. The shelter was empty. There was no sign that he'd come to bed with her at all.

She fastened the jar full of Masika's remains to her side before tugging on her larger robe. She didn't want to make the same mistake again, having it almost fall into the jaws of a wolf pack. She stood and opened the hide flap of the dwelling, finding two other men huddled outside. No remains of the wolf lay around the stone fire pit. The head, too, had been removed. Frustration, and aching hunger, growled in her gut. She'd gone to sleep empty-stomached.

Ewan stood opposite the fire by the dwelling that sheltered the injured man. His back faced her, preventing her from studying his expression.

Amy gathered her robes around her and slipped her feet into her boots. She walked out of her shelter, scavenging for anything by the fire that might be a morsel of food.

Ewan didn't make any acknowledgement of her. He stood stiff-shouldered, gazing into the dwelling. The lines on his face were deeper, concern etched into each of them. His arm was concealed beneath his white robes. Blood pooling through the hide told Amy that the wolf bite wound was worsening.

Amy stopped at Ewan's side as the huntsman inside the dwelling whimpered in pain. She peered inside, finding him lying on the ground. His leg was torn open in multiple places. Muscle poked through his skin above his knee. White, shiny bone was visible. By the way he was perspiring, he also had a fever.

Ewan shook his head. "He will not survive the day if we don't find him medicine soon."

"I say we take him back to base camp. There is no way he can continue with the hunt in this condition," one of the huntsmen inside the dwelling said.

Ewan's eyes dipped to Amy. "Or, we turn to the medicine woman in our group."

Amy's heart jumped into her throat.

"Don't let her touch me!" the wounded man bellowed.

"Your wound needs to be cleaned," Amy said.

The man spit at her.

She ducked out of the way before his saliva found her face.

While Ewan stayed with his wounded huntsman, Amy used the excuse to go search for something that could help him. What was she kidding? Cleaning a wound that deep would require a large amount of water—something this frozen forest didn't seem to offer.

She walked a few paces from their camp, her boots crunching to a halt in the snow. She needed to wash the man's wound, and quickly. But where? The rivers were frozen, and her water gourd was nearly empty.

Her foot scraped against something in the snow. She crouched down, grabbing a leather parcel.

Amy's breathing seized. She'd found Ewan's medicine bundle.

She stood up, trying not to panic. What was inside of it that Ewan refused to share with her? He'd said specifically not to look inside, for the contents, if seen, could lose their medicine. If the men's prayers were to reach their ancestors, the items could only be revealed at the top of the sacred mountain in Errindoor's presence.

She fondled the leather bundle, feeling for the contents. A piece of twine was knotted around the opening, preventing her from peeking inside.

The crunch of footsteps sounded behind her.

Amy tucked the bundle into her robe and took off into the forest.

As she continued in her trek away from camp, the snow became a little less dense. A foul aroma drifted on the breeze as she dipped down a small hill. The aroma reminded her of rotten eggs.

She stepped on the rocks, eager to leave the snow. It would be more difficult for Ewan to track her movements. She could already hear his footsteps heavy behind her. He must have realized he'd misplaced his bundle.

Amy's heart was in her throat. What should she do? Abandon it? He would surely know that it was her who took off with it.

Unless, of course, she made it look like the forest was the thief.

A fox shifted between the trees, its snow-white fur camouflaging so well with the landscape, that only its golden eyes and black nose gave it away. The creature was probably looking for a morsel of food left over from the wolf that had been killed.

Amy tossed the bundle at the fox's feet. The fox sniffed the leather pouch, then dipped his muzzle into the snow. With a furious thrash of his tail, he took off with the medicine bundle. She bit her tongue as defeat set in.

A bubbling sound issued from behind a grove of red giants. The sound she had mistaken as someone following her was coming from around the trees.

Her boot caught the lip of a root and she collapsed to the ground. Her palms scraped against stone. She staggered to her feet. Steam coiled around her, snaking silver plumes up the wooden bodies of the red giants.

Her breath caught. The steam was coming from the pool of warm water glistening in the daylight.

She rushed back to camp, finding Ewan and his men staring at her. She'd been tricked by the fox, who had returned the medicine bundle to him.

It didn't take long for Ewan and his men to make the short trek up the hill, following the billowing puffs of steam. The air was thick with sulfur and other minerals bubbling up from a hot spring.

Ewan carried the wounded man up the hill, his injured leg strapped to a pole at his side. The fox followed them, keeping his distance while remaining curious about the strange huntsmen and a selkie traveling through his frozen home.

Or maybe, he too, wanted to know what Ewan kept in the medicine bundle.

As Ewan and his men dipped down the hill toward one of the bigger pools, Amy took the opportunity to scope out the steaming water that had appeared out of nowhere. Multiple steaming pools were scattered along the hill. She tugged off her boots and dipped her toes into the first pool. Much too warm. Maneuvering to the next, she tried again. Not enough zing.

"We hiked all the way up here, only to have a wolf turn on our group? The ancestors must hate us," the voice of a man sounded from over the hill.

"I'm surprised we made it this far," another said. "We were attacked because she is with us."

Amy crouched down. Hopefully the snowcapped trees and the steam would keep her concealed long enough to listen to their gossip.

She peered over the snowy bushes separating her from the men. They were submerged in the water, refilling their water gourds and guzzling down the fresh water from the pool.

Fergus's laughter ripped over the water. "Maybe if Ewan put something different in the medicine bundle like all of us do every year, we would have better luck tracking Errindoor."

"His father gave that to him, an item from Atlantis that is supposed to have some magical power tied to it."

"The guy puts way too much thought into his ancestors—they're dead!"

"We all know what Ewan puts in the pouch every year. It never changes. He might not carry a weapon with him, but what's inside of that medicine bundle is far more dangerous than any weapon any of us possess."

Amy strained her ears. A *weapon*?

"Is it a dagger?" one of the men asked.

"No, it's far sharper than any dagger." Fergus replied. "I've never seen the item, but I know it is something his father gave him. It can kill any beast, even a dragon."

Amy sank down. Whatever was inside of the bundle was exactly what she needed to draw Errindoor's blood. She hid behind the tree, her body trembling.

Snow fell from the tree behind her.

She ducked out of sight before the men could see her eavesdropping on them.

A pile of clothing lay on the rock. She recognized the bloodstain on his robes.

She dipped down to the pile of smelly kilts and robes and began sifting through Ewan's white furs.

Nothing. Where had he put the medicine bundle?

"Amy?"

Amy dropped the clothing. She spun around, finding a very naked and dripping Ewan standing behind her. The only thing covering his skin was a tattoo, one that branched out from the center of his chest. The tattoo had grown from the last time she remembered him. The head of a stag was centered upon his chest. Long gnarled antlers branched and knotted, weaving in and out with one another in a gorgeous knot pattern.

Her gaze dropped to his loins. The medicine bundle was tied to his waist. Of course that's where he kept it—dangling with his man parts.

"Why are you looking through my clothing?" he asked, amusement ringing in his tone.

She returned her gaze to his, realizing she'd been staring at his loins for far too long. "I—" her breath caught as a flush crept up her neck. "I was looking for your water gourd."

Ewan motioned his arm, shaking his dripping locks from side to side. "There is a better pool down this way. It's not as hot as the one they're drinking from."

She let out a sigh, relieved that he'd turned away from her. The muscles on his back and butt glistened as he descended down the stone path toward the other pools. The antlers from his tattoo wrapped around to his back, making the muscles on his shoulders that much more defined.

She followed Ewan down to the pool farthest away from the other men. She stopped next to him, where water pooled at his bare feet.

"Ladies first." Ewan said.

She took a step back, making a spinning motion with her hand. "Turn around."

"It's not like I haven't seen you—"

"—it doesn't matter what you have or haven't seen. I'm the queen here, and you are the huntsman."

An earthy chuckle escaped him as he clasped his hands behind his back and hung his head. "I'll do as my queen asks of me as long as I am out of the water."

Amy faced him as she worked her fingers through the cord that fastened her boots to her legs. The last thing she needed to see was his bare chest with that gorgeous tattoo of the fae king glistening with steam and sweat while she removed her clothing. Besides, she needed to keep the jar with Masika's crystal remains hidden.

Ewan's shoulders flexed as he kept his back to her. Water dripped from his hair, tracing the contours of his back and shoulders. The sheer size and bulk of him explained how he could saunter around soaking wet and not break out into gooseflesh.

With her boots finally removed, she turned her attention to her cloak. The furs fell in a heap at her bare feet. She removed the other garments from her upper body and legs until she was as naked as the huntsman flexing his back and butt muscles for her. She tucked the jar beneath her robes, concealing it.

"I guess my queen takes forever to undress herself. Are you sure you don't need any help?"

"No," she stammered, her remaining garments falling in a heap at her feet. Her nipples pebbled as a chilly breeze swept over her.

She stepped down into the pool, which wasn't too deep. She sank into the water, moaning as she submerged her hips and torso. Every muscle, tendon, and ligament in her body thanked her as the hot water rose up to her shoulders.

Snowflakes fell through the canopy of red giants, catching in her hair. She shook her head, scattering them where they melted the moment they hit the water.

She glanced behind her. No naked huntsmen stood there.

Something shifted past her ankle.

Amy jumped, kicking her leg out and striking a solid surface.

Ewan's face appeared in front of her. He shook his head, sending water splashing everywhere.

"What on earth were you doing down there?" Amy snapped, pulling away from him.

"I dropped my flint," he replied, dipping down and disappearing beneath the water.

Amy kicked off the side of the pool, splashing herself in the process. She'd not wanted to get her hair wet, as her mass of rebellious red curls took eons to dry.

Ewan rose out of the pool, sending a wave of water out onto the rocks. The water level lowered, revealing Amy's upper half.

Amy crossed her arms in front of her chest. "This is not a peep show."

"I wasn't peeping. I was working on this." He grabbed a branch hanging over the pool and tilted it away. The wound on his forearm appeared. Twine crossed over the bite mark. Apparently, he'd stitched the skin closed.

"Do you like it?" he asked.

Amy tore her eyes away from his swollen skin and stitches, finding symbols carved into the woody tissue of the tree. Ewan had carved a knotted symbol of a stag similar to the tattoo on his chest. "What does the stag symbolize?"

"Mallocchhhh!" he said, rattling out a thick brogue. "It means blood of *roooooyalty*!"

"Why didn't you come to bed with me?" She blurted, unable to hide the emotion in her voice.

Ewan's bushy brows drew up. "You turned me down in front of all of my men. I thought you were mad at me."

"Why would you offer me the heart of that beast? I didn't deserve it."

Ewan crossed his massive arms on the boulder at the center of the pool, his gaze leveling with her. "Is it not apparent how I feel about you?"

Amy blinked. She couldn't look at him like this. Ewan had the heart of a king. It was always his generosity that made her heart beat faster than it should.

The steam rising from his shoulders created the illusion that someone was standing there.

"What's wrong?" Ewan asked.

"Nothing," Amy lied. She could have sworn she saw a woman gazing at her from the water vapor. "I thought I saw someone."

"A spirit?"

"Perhaps."

"You wouldn't be the only one. Every time I make this journey, I believe the spirits trying to tell me something."

"What do you believe they are trying to tell you this time?"

He flexed his forearm, making the stitches over his wound bulge. "They say dangerous times lay ahead of us."

Amy's body went cold.

Ewan shifted along the rocks, leveling his gaze with hers. "When you told me you wanted to go on one of my hunts, I couldn't believe it. For as long as I've known you, you have never wanted to share the life of a huntsman. This life is dangerous. A man risks his life daily so he can provide for his loved ones."

She looked away. "I wasn't mad at you over the wolf. But I did not deserve the heart of that wolf after the situation I put it in."

Ewan leaned against the rocks, making his hair stick up. Ice crystals started to form on his head and facial hair. "I'm the one who is to blame. I'm embarrassed not only with myself, but with the performance of my men today. The wolves showed me just how very afraid they are. Fear should never take the place of respect." He leaned back, exposing his chest in the water. Steam danced on his skin, making the antlers from his tattoo appear larger. "We need more women like you to center us."

Amy locked eyes with him. "Don't try and flatter me."

"You selkies have magic and medicine that my forefathers couldn't even touch—medicine for the spirit, not the body. That is the most difficult medicine to come by."

"Maybe you should tell your men not to follow in their forefather's footsteps."

Ewan hiked his head back, sending steam up into the air with his boisterous laugh. A few ice crystals shook loose from his beard, melting in the pool. "My men mock you, because they fear you. They cannot see that fearing the sea is what caused the great fall of our kingdom."

Amy dug her heels into the bottom of the pool. There was truth to Ewan's words. "Why do you trust me? Why aren't you like your men, fearful of who I am?"

Ewan rose up from the water, steam issuing up from his chest. He towered over her. "Fearing you would do nothing to bring me closer to my ancestors. Fear would only lead to regret."

He lowered himself back into the water, closing the space between them. His eyes hooded, then closed as he pressed his lips to hers. His kiss was slow and tender, damp with steam, then hot with passion. "Amphitrite, I will make a goddess out of you yet."

Amy arched her back as his hips bucked toward her. He cupped her butt with his hands, thrusting his hips forward to prop her on the stone ledge.

She propped her elbows onto the ledge, bracing herself as the ice crystals on his beard brushed between her legs.

328

45
PROTECTION

Selia

Selia reached for Damien's hand. Cold, starchy fabric met her fingers.

She jolted up. The bed was empty.

Bounding up from her chair, she grabbed her jacket and tugged it on. Before she could grab her purse, a nurse walked into the room and shut the door behind her.

"I don't think it's wise that you leave the hospital just yet," the nurse said with a low, raspy voice.

Selia shouldered her purse. "I'm fine. I only stayed the night because I wanted to make sure he would wake up."

The nurse turned her back to Selia, her attention dipping to her clipboard. She stood in the doorway, preventing Selia from leaving the room. "How long have you been experiencing these hallucinations?"

"For the past few days, why?"

"For as long as you've been pregnant?"

Selia stared at her. "I never mentioned that I was pregnant."

The nurse turned to face Selia. Her eyes were black where there should be white, and her irises were a startling white. The tangy scent of iron filled the room.

A small black fleck buzzed near Masika's face, disappearing as her eyes leveled with her. "I told you in the cave to surrender to it, didn't I?"

Selia backed away. "What do you want with me?"

"It's not what I want with you," Masika sneered. "It's what the venom wants with your memories. I told you that you stole something from our ancestors. Your memory is tied to minca's disappearance." The nurse evaporated, leaving a coiling tendril of smoke. "I won't leave until you share it with me."

Selia threw out her hands. "Get away from me!"

Masika coiled around her, snakelike. "Savor it. Surrender to it. All salt daughters of Celaeno will be tempted by it."

"I can't remember anything with you in my head!" Selia screamed. "What do you want from me!"

Ring!

Selia lifted her head from the pillow. Her phone was ringing. Whatever hallucination she'd experienced evaporated, leaving her alone in the hospital room.

Damien was no longer in his bed. This nightmare was quickly becoming a reality. She grabbed her purse and flew through the door, tearing down the hallway to the checkout counter. "Where is Damien Malloch?"

The nurse at the computer typed on the keyboard. "Damien checked out this morning."

Selia's heart ached. Had he gotten up and left without her? "When?"

"Just a few moments ago."

A small black fleck climbed over the computer monitor. The fleck blurred in her vision, buzzing and shaking, until it took off in the air. It hovered in her periphery, zipping past her face, then disappearing.

Selia tore down the hall. He wouldn't have just left without her, would he?

She rounded the corner, bumping into the body of someone wearing a long dark robe. She staggered backward as the individual with short blond hair and cold grey eyes turned to face her.

"This can't be happening," Selia stammered, backing into the wall. "Tell me this is just another hallucination. Tell me I'm not going mad."

Alex tugged the fabric around her neck down, revealing three long bruises that tapered across her skin. "You tell me."

Masika's long, crystal dagger fingers flashed in Selia's memory.

Another black fleck buzzed over Alex's shoulder.

Alex grabbed her arm. "Come with me, now. You are not safe here."

Selia followed Alex. "Do you know where Damien is?" she asked, struggling to keep up with Alex's furious pace.

"*Surrender to it…*"

Selia threw her hands over her ears. "I can hear her in my head."

Alex spun on her heel. "Follow me. I will help you get rid of her venomous thoughts."

Alex led Selia out of the hospital and onto the street. Icy cobblestones blurred before Selia as she followed her. The alleyway opened, and the familiar scent of coffee filled her nose.

Alex didn't turn toward Pixie's coffee shop. She steered her through the back alley toward the greenhouse.

Selia's vision began to blur as the swarming black cloud buzzed toward her. The salt flies were swarming with ferocious force around her face, landing near her mouth and nose.

They were trying to suffocate her.

Alex grabbed her hand. "Stay with me!"

Selia's knees buckled. She couldn't walk anymore. The swarm was descending upon her.

Alex threw out her hand, and a brilliant explosion of light erupted from her palm. "Salt flies, be gone!"

The swarming shadow burst open as Alex shuffled Selia inside the greenhouse.

Damp earth filled Selia's senses, blocking out the suffocating hum of the shadow. She fell to the ground. Solid, damp earth between her fingers never felt so welcoming.

Alex slammed the door closed behind her and closed her eyes. She chanted something under her breath, and the light inside the greenhouse dulled.

The swarm rattled against the greenhouse like a great, terrible wind. Thousands of the fae parasites hovered in a giant black cloud outside.

"What's happening to me?" Selia asked, clutching her throat.

"Salt flies feed on the electrolytes of their victims, specifically salt." Alex straightened herself. "Your hallucinations are a result of them draining your electrolytes."

Alex dug her hand into her robe, tugging out a small glowing vile. She tossed it on the ground, where it rolled to Selia's feet. "Now drink, or you'll be dead before the day is over."

Selia reached for the vile and unscrewed the top. She tipped the opening to her mouth. The taste of salt vanished as she swallowed. Alex's face steadied before her as she gulped down the liquid.

Her breathing steadied, as did her pulse. "Thank you."

Alex crouched, lowering herself to the ground. She sat next to Selia, tugging her robes around her. "What happened in the cavern? What did you experience?"

"I tried to stop Masika from harming you, then, I lost control. I fell into something Masika called a salt rush."

Alex's eyes darkened. "I knew Masika would try and tempt you to use the venom like she does."

"It felt like I had left my body, wherever I was."

"In essence, you were. A salt rush occurs when a sea nymphs salt aura becomes activated."

Selia held out her hands, half expecting her skin to start glowing. "I have a salt aura?"

"A sea nymph's salt aura develops as she matures. Practicing salt trancing allows it to develop properly. Since you were sleeping in the Abyss for so long, your salt aura will need to take some time to develop."

"Masika said she could help me master the sensation I had of stepping out of my skin. It's the most liberating and terrifying thing I have ever experienced."

"Don't give in to the temptation. Masika has no body to ground her. Salt trancing allows your salt aura to step outside not only the physical world, but in Masika's case, the boundaries of time. She will try and take advantage of you as she tries to tempt your salt aura to surrender to her salt venom."

"During the salt rush, she stated that she wants access to one of my memories. She stated that I stole something from our ancestors that is tied to minca's disappearance."

"You have a memory that stems back to ancient Egypt, a memory from the Temple of Isis, where Naunet used to work."

Selia blinked a few times, trying to process what Alex was saying to her. "How can I steal something from my ancestors if I have no memory of it?"

"Think about the bottle of salt venom you found on Gwen's mantelpiece. When you asked her about it earlier today, she remembered it. Between you asking her later, what changed?"

Selia's mind twisted with the events, trying to make sense of them. "The salt flies attacked me."

Alex nodded. "As the salt flies feed on the electrolytes of their host, the memories tied to the venom's existence disappear. The venom erases the memories of the individuals it has interacted with." Her eyes flashed. "The venom erases any memory of its own existence."

A violent wind rattled against the greenhouse, making Selia jump.

Alex held her gaze, unblinking. "Shadow fae species are responsible for spreading some of the most dangerous plagues in history. This is why not even the Egyptian Book of the Dead has a record of the plague's existence."

"I don't understand. What is in this memory of mine that Masika wants that's tied to minca?"

"Naunet's work—think. She used to stay late at the Temple of Isis inscribing."

"Storm scrolls," Selia said, thinking back to what the journal demanded that she find.

"Naunet had a theory that storm dragons and minca were somehow connected, but she could never prove it. The day you practiced salt summoning in the Temple of Isis, you helped to answer something Naunet had been hoping to answer—what caused minca's disappearance." Her gaze dropped to Selia's left hand. "The reason the salt flies didn't do more harm to you is probably due to the fact that you are wearing that ring."

Selia held up her hand, eyeing her ring. "How is my ring protecting me?"

"I recognize the shimmer on it. The gemstone isn't a stone. It's the same material as this." Alex dug her hand into her robe, tugging out an item. An oval-shaped pendant lay in her palm that was fastened to a metal chain. No bigger than an acorn, the pendant was cream colored and oblong. "You succeeded in summoning the protection you needed from the cavern. This will help to tame that rush if it does happen again."

"Is that a salt trancing talisman?" Selia asked.

"Close, but no. It belongs to an ancient beast who helps create them."

Selia's mouth dropped open. "Does this belong to a storm dragon?"

Alex held the pendant out for Selia to take. "This scale came from Poseidon. Poseidon is the deceased father of Celaeno's storm dragon. His scales are known for their protective powers, along with their ability to cleanse."

Selia took Poseidon's scale, which was surprisingly light. It had an identical shimmer to what she thought had been a gemstone on her ring. "Does this son of Poseidon actually have a name?"

"He has a name the Order gave him. But his true name is still a mystery."

"Can you tell me what his name is?"

Alex shook her head. "He forbids me to share his name with you."

"Are you in communication with the dragon?"

"Yes. I have been for quite some time."

Selia's mind returned to Damien sleeping on the hospital bed. "Does he have any idea where Damien might have gone?"

"Not that I am aware of, but I know Masika will be searching for him."

"What does she want with Damien?"

"Damien is the window to the past that Amy is using to mingle with his ancestors. If Amy succeeds in her goal, Masika will no longer be possessed by the salt venom. She's spent the past three thousand years allowing the salt venom to corrupt her into thinking she is in control of it."

"But she's not in control, is she?"

The glass surrounding the greenhouse rattled again as the salt flies continued to swarm.

Alex's eyes darted toward the shadow. "Do you really think anyone could control that?" She stood, wiping debris from the greenhouse off her cloak. "I promised Naunet that I would look after her moon daughter. It is my duty to preserve any of Naunet's work in the Codex the venom has not already corroded."

"Is Naunet still alive?"

Alex dipped her chin, her face falling into shadow. "I wish I could say. She went missing shortly after Masika became cursed by the salt venom." She straightened herself. "If you want to find Damien and stop Masika from corroding your memory, you and I need to find Celaeno's storm dragon. I have a few things that I must arrange before we meet with him." Her eyes dipped to the pendant. "Make sure you keep the dragon scale close to your heart at all times."

Selia nodded as she looped the chain over her head and tucked the pendant into her sweater.

"I will come find you when the time is right." She reached out, helping Selia to stand. "Keep this in mind—fae creatures who eat insects are your friends."

The greenhouse door opened, bringing in a blur of snow flurries and wind.

Selia blinked. Alex vanished.

Pixie bustled into the greenhouse, her face a twist of emotion. "Selia, I just heard that Damien is gone."

46

MEDICINE & STARS

Amy

Ewan's group left the mineral springs with their bodies warm and their water gourds full. Everyone seemed energized and refreshed from the water, which energized the dampened mood after the wolf attack. As for the man who had been wounded by the wolf, the group decided that once his wound was cleaned, his hunt would be done. Two of the other men volunteered to take him back to base camp.

It was upsetting that Fergus wasn't one of them. With three less men in their group, Amy felt his gaze upon her longer than before, like he was watching her every move, making sure she didn't cause another wolf to spring on them.

The only thing Amy's body hadn't recovered from was hunger. While her muscles were happy, her stomach was not. She'd not eaten anything since the day before. Her stomach was starting to spasm, sending hunger pains through her, which were only remedied by walking.

She kept the jar full of Masika's remains at her center, tucking her hand beneath her robe every few moments to make sure it was still there. Her mind buzzed with ideas on how she could steal the medicine bundle away from Ewan's loins without turning him on. Timing would be everything when it came time to wielding that secret weapon to draw Errindoor's blood.

With each step they took, the forest became more hushed, like the breath of someone in a deep sleep. The afternoon light peaked and waned as Amy strode through snowy meadows that broke the forest apart. Just when she thought the forest would swallow their group again, it would reopen, and another glistening silver meadow would appear. This stretch of the journey was by far the most demanding she'd endured.

She kept walking a steady pace ahead of Ewan, hoping to put some distance between them. Her foot dropped, jolting as her leg was swallowed by a massive hole in the snow. She staggered and caught herself before she fell. Both of her feet fit into a giant track not made by wolf or man. It was pointed at the tip, then bowed out at the sides.

The track was cloven as it had been made by a hoof.

Ewan walked over to Amy and crouched where she stood. He studied the track, his brow furrowing in concentration.

He stood, waving over to his men. "We have a sighting of the white herd."

Amy stepped out of the track as Ewan's men circled back to where they stood. The tracks made circles, then long sweeping lines. That pattern repeated itself over and over, disappearing into the forest.

"Something has spooked them," He said, his gaze sweeping over the movements of the fae beasts.

Amy couldn't read the tracks like the men could, but even she could tell from the scattered movements the beasts were stressed about something.

"We must go now, or we will lose the herd," one of the huntsman said as he turned on his heel and led the others down into the forest.

Amy made a motion to follow them. Ewan caught her around the waist.

"They will do the tracking," Ewan said as his head fell back, his gaze turning up. "Come and sit with me while the stars arrive."

Amy huffed. Why did the men get to run off and have all the fun?

Ewan sat down on a snow-covered log. Amy fell back onto the log as her boots slipped out in front of her.

Time crept by. As the first stars appeared, her stomach gave a grouchy rumble, yet Ewan seemed like he wasn't in a rush to go anywhere—or eat. A great calm seemed to settle over the forest, and between them. If only that calm would transfer to her gut.

"We are not far from our destination," Ewan said, his breath huffing like great white clouds in front of him. "Before we know it, the journey up here will be over."

"Why are you getting so sentimental?" she asked, shivering.

A chuckle escaped him. He set his hand atop hers, instantly dwarfing her palm. "Winter is a time of self-reflection—a time when one can journey atop this sacred mountain and share one's soul with the stars." His shoulders rose and fell as he took in a deep breath and exhaled. "It's times like this when I miss my father. He taught me everything about hunting, from using the bow, to tracking. All my life, all I have known is this land. I've learned to love the frozen heart of this forest."

Amy gazed up at the brightest star hovering over them. "The last time I saw my mother was in Atlantis. Everything I know about magic, I learned from her."

"You don't speak of your mother often. Is she still alive?"

"I don't know if she lived or not. She had forty-nine sisters, all of whom disappeared after the city of your forefathers fell."

Ewan tilted his head sideways, facing her. "I didn't know selkies had such large families. What was your mother's name?"

Amy's gaze dropped to her hands. "She named me after her, actually. I share my mother's name, Amphitrite."

Ewan's brows drew up. "You're Amphitrite the *second*?"

"Yes. That's why I prefer to go by Amy."

"I always wondered why you never preferred to be called by your full name. Why is that?"

Amy gazed up at the sky once again. She dipped her free hand beneath her robe, clutching the jar. "Because I have never felt like I've lived up to her magic, what she was known for in Atlantis. She could mend any illness with a simple salt crystal from her Ocean Apothecary." Emotion cracked in her voice. "The salt crystals she used, how I used to think they looked like stars."

Ewan tilted his head back, gazing up once again. "If she's up there, I'm sure she's looking down at you right now."

Amy's eyes burned with tears. How she wished she still had her mother's guidance. When her mother had gone missing after Atlantis sank, Amy found refuge like Naunet and Masika had in Egypt.

The stars were soon replaced with snow flurries as they whipped down the mountain. Wind ripped through Amy's cloak, stealing away her warmth. Snow shifted through the giant elk tracks, filling them in moments.

Ewan grabbed his satchel and stood. Together, they descended the hill where his men disappeared. Amy huddled next to Ewan's body as he guided her toward a massive tree.

"The trees will be our shelter tonight," he said, crouching down. He lowered himself through a layer of roots, dipping out of sight.

Amy peered over the massive root, finding a dark opening. She descended into the roots Ewan squeezed through. Snow and pine needles fell into her hair as she followed him down into the earth.

Her boots hit frozen earth. Root threads gripped her hair as she maneuvered toward the dark mass she hoped was Ewan. She searched the dark, fearful they might have stumbled into the den of a fae beast. What if a wolf, or, Gaia forbid, a *bear*, come lunging out of the dark.

The crisp sound of flint cracked, creating a spark. The dwelling came to light as flames sprang to life. Good thing she had a huntsman to provide for her, or she wouldn't have survived a day out here in the frozen land where a winter storm could manifest in a moment's notice.

They worked to gather wood scraps, and piled them together. Soon, their root-laden shelter was brimming with sweltering dry heat. The smoke rose through the roots, while the warmth grew inside.

Ewan unfastened his robe. The furs fell into a heap onto the ground, the soft side facing up. "It's a small dwelling, but it will do for the night." He unraveled the satchel. The scent of dried meat made Amy's stomach grumble.

He kept stripping, except, of course, for his kilt. She knew where the medicine bundle was on his body. How could she get to it without giving in to his wild side?

She couldn't escape the hunger in his eyes. He'd feasted on her already in the cave, and again at the hot spring. What would he expect of her tonight?

He set out his food rations and sat down on the furs. His knotted tattoo of a stag danced in the firelight, creating the illusion his antlers were alive.

She stepped onto the furs and removed her boots. Her foot cramped when she stepped down. The ground was still cold, even with the furs beneath them. She lowered herself onto his lap, grateful for the layer of fur between them. She turned away from him, facing the fire.

Ewan buried his face into her hair and inhaled. His hand rose to her chest.

She grabbed a piece of dried meat and brought it to her mouth before he fondled her breast.

He mimicked her, grabbing a handful of dried meat and tore off a chunk with his teeth. They ate in silence, listening to the wind howling above them. With every moment that ticked by, Ewan's lap hardened.

He returned his face to her hair, brushing his lips past the cusp of her ear. "Are you really going to have me wait until we reach the summit of the mountain?"

Amy shivered in the desire in his voice. She turned to face him, tracing the antlers on his chest that branched over his heart. Their eyes locked. Even in the dark, there was so much warmth in them.

"Didn't you say we weren't far away from the top?"

He buried his face into her chest, nipping at her breast.

She jerked backward.

"You didn't pull away from me in the water. What's different about tonight?" he growled, his breath hot on her throat.

Amy locked her eyes with the fire in his. Men responded to actions—not words—much better. To convince him that she wanted him, not the bundle, she would need to be more direct.

She folded the furs of his kilt up, finding the length of him pressed between his legs. She shifted to his side, lowering herself onto the cold ground. "Maybe I feel like being the one in control."

A grunt erupted from his chest as she traced her finger along the length of his cock.

"Amy..." he breathed, his hips bucking forward. She pulled her fingers away from the head and fondled the medicine bundle instead. She had what she wanted in her fingertips.

Ewan shifted, suddenly atop her. The antlers on his chest danced in the firelight.

"I can't tease you with this in the way," she whispered, keeping a firm grip on the bundle.

Ewan knelt in front of her. He grabbed his flint dagger and shoved the weapon beneath his kilt. He removed the bundle and tossed it aside, allowing his cock the space it needed to grow.

He buried his face in her neck. Fire burned in her blood as he explored her with every flick of his tongue. She stroked him slow, then fast, working to find a rhythm that made his hips buck toward her.

Amy arched her back as he grabbed her breast, stroking her nipple with an experienced thumb.

She pressed the ball of her palm to his cock, gripping tighter as she reached the spot where he experienced the most pleasure.

"Amy, if you keep this up," he breathed, his chest heaving.

He threw his head back, his body trembling with release. Watching him tremble—the sheer force of him—was enough to make Amy's body quiver.

He slouched forward, laying his head in her lap.

Amy ran her fingers through the thick locks of his hair as he buried his face between her legs.

Even with that aching between her legs, now wasn't the time to ask for another orgasm. She needed him to fall asleep so she could open the medicine bundle.

She traced her fingers along his back. "I'd rather wait for you to claim me as your queen atop that mountain."

Ewan nuzzled her. "Sleep with me."

Amy lay on the bundles of fur next to him. He looped his arm around her waist. Before long, he was fast asleep, his shoulders rising and falling.

His prized medicine bundle lay only inches away from her.

She unraveled herself from his arm and crawled over to the bundle. At last, it was hers to open, revealing what weapon had the power to draw blood from the mighty Errindoor.

She dressed herself, making sure not to wake Ewan from his satiated slumber. The canopic jar too, was fastened to her side. With the bundle in hand, she grabbed his flint dagger and began her ascent up into the forest. Her heart was pounding. When she finally opened the bundle, what would she find?

Staggering out of the dwelling, she collapsed into the snow. Dragging the dagger past the twine, she turned the bundle over.

47

PEPPERCORN'S SURPRISE

Selia

By the afternoon, word had spread all around Montrose that Damien was missing. Gwen had notified the local radio station to put out a distress call, and Sean's fishing fleet volunteered to search for him.

Pixie was also in a terrible mood. Not only was Damien missing, but Peppercorn was still gone.

Selia sat at the coffee bar inside the Bat Blitz Coffee Shop, clutching the dragon scale pendant under her sweater. It felt like a great void had been ripped into her life. Only a few days ago, Damien had come up behind her and embraced her in one of his hugs, then whisked her away to the lighthouse that was to be their forever home. It didn't feel right going home without him. Staying at Pixie's shop was far better than going back to the empty lighthouse.

"Can I get you anything to drink?" Pixie asked as she pulled a couple of espresso shots.

"No, I'm all right," Selia replied as she set her elbows on the bar and shrank in her seat. She grabbed her dragon scale pendant, hoping that the shadow looming in the darkness outside wasn't another swarm of angry salt flies. It had started to snow again.

"Is that new jewelry?" Pixie asked, eyeing the pendant.

"I've had it for a while," she lied.

"It's absolutely gorgeous. It even matches your ring!" Pixie said as she set a piping-hot decaf latte down in front of Selia.

Selia eyed the drink, but her stomach didn't respond. While she should be working on staying hydrated, her stomach was pitting with emotion. She gazed out the window, watching the fluffy white snowflakes fall from the sky. A horrible thought crossed her mind. What if she didn't get to spend her first Christmas with Damien?

What if he never came home?

Tears burned in her eyes, making her vision blurry. She had to focus on something other than her self-pity. She walked over to the wall where Damien's watercolor paintings were on display. How much color he'd put into each of them. Just looking at the images took her to a spot overlooking the sea, watching the weather roll in. His art had always been something she could find beauty in, even when circumstances were bleak.

She counted them out, naming them each after their stormy theme. *Rain. Wind. Fog. Ice. Snow. Lightning...*" She ran over them again. Something wasn't right. "I thought there were seven," she said aloud, suddenly feeling robbed.

"Seven what?" Pixie asked as she set a mug of hot tea down onto the bar.

"Seven paintings. One's missing..."

Selia sucked in a breath.

The seventh storm scroll Masika asked her to find had been missing.

Gwen came bustling into the coffee shop. Sean and the kids followed.

"Any leads?" Selia asked, turning to face them.

Gwen shook her head. "No. We're searching all over town. I've contacted every one of our relatives. Nobody's had any sight of him."

Selia's stomach pitted. With each passing moment, Damien's absence made her want to scream. Alex told her that she had some details to sort out before they returned to Masika's tidal cavern. The only way to keep the cursed selkie away from her memories was in fact to find Celaeno's storm dragon.

Gemma came bounding over to Selia. She was wearing a frilly blue dress, complete with a fairy wand dangling from her fingers. "We're going to find Uncle Damien before Santa arrives!"

Selia's heart ached. What if the venom made Damien do something stupid? Like jumping off the dock and into the sea? She had to force those horrible thoughts out of her head. If only she had the faith of Gwen's enthusiastic daughter.

"I'm heading to the fairy hut!" Gemma tapped her brother on the shoulder. "Tag, you're it!"

Gwen rolled her eyes. "Oh, my goodness. My daughter's imagination is relentless. Selia, if you want kids one day, I'm giving you a warning. Once you have them, there's no going back."

Bram darted after his sister. "No, I'm not!" He was dressed like a knight and swung a cardboard sword over his head.

Selia stepped out of the way as Gemma tore past her down the hall and toward the back door that led to the greenhouse. Alex had said the fae creatures that ate flies were her friend. A certain fuzzy headed, brown fluff ball of a bat came to mind. "Pixie, when was the last time you saw Peppercorn?"

Pixie set down a coffee mug on the bar and shook her head. "I haven't seen her since before the winter solstice gathering. I'm starting to get very worried about her."

Selia followed Gemma and Bram outside toward the greenhouse.

"Hey! Stop it!" Bram's voice sounded from inside the greenhouse. The door had been left wide open.

Selia walked up to the door with Gwen on her heels.

"That's it, kids. Both of you out here, right now!" Gwen cried.

Selia walked into the greenhouse, finding Gemma holding her fairy wand high over her head. Bram had thrown his sword to the ground and crossed his arms in front of his heaving chest.

"Stop making those squeaking noises! It's so annoying!" Bram yelled.

"I'm not squeaking, you are!" Gemma shot back.

Gwen bustled past Selia, rounding on her two kids. "Would you two stop arguing? Santa is going to leave coal in both of your stockings if you don't get along!"

Gemma waved her wand over a pot, giggling as she looped the star in circles. "Mom! I found a fairy!"

"Gemma, stop," Gwen corrected her daughter.

"Look! There's lots of them! And they're super brown and angry!"

"Let me see this fairy that—"

Shreeeeeek!

"Ahhhh!" Gwen cried as she fell back between her children, landing on the ground.

Pixie came bustling over, clapping both sides of her mouth. "Oh, my goodness! Look at how adorable they are!"

Selia peered over Pixie's shoulder, discovering one of the most adorable things in sight.

"They are so cute!" Pixie said, squealing in delight.

An explosion of little squeaks coming from the pot made Selia's heart ache.

"Now I know why she's been acting so shy. She was preparing to give birth to her pups!" Pixie exclaimed.

Peppercorn's tiny, fuzzy head swiveled towards Selia. She opened her mouth, displaying a large set of tiny, but needle-sharp, teeth. She lifted her wing, revealing three little lumps with barely any hair on their brown scalps. With shriveled ears and upturned noses, they looked like little raisins that had absorbed too much sun.

"Gross! She had babies?" Gwen exclaimed as she climbed to her feet. "Oh, great! Just what we need, a bat to give birth to a bunch of nasty little batlings!"

"With all these mouths to feed, she's going to be a busy new mom!" Pixie said as she inspected the little brown cluster of babies. "Oh my, there are one, three, *seven* of you?"

"Gross!" Gwen cried.

"Would you stop it already?" Pixie boasted. "Bats usually only have one, maybe two pups. But *seven*? She's going to have so many mouths to feed!"

"I think they are absolutely beautiful," Selia chimed in, supporting Pixie. Her heart fluttered at the adorableness of seven little snouts, wrinkly ears, and glistening, ink-drop eyes.

Peppercorn let out a shrill *schreeeeeek*, her mouth splaying open in an apparent display of pride. Something told Selia that seven hungry bat pups would soon be the protective answer she and Alex needed when it came to dealing with Masika's salt flies.

48

MASIKA'S SPIRIT

Amy

Amy held her breath as she tipped the medicine bundle toward the snow. Nothing fell out, so she shook it over and over. She ran her fingers over the pouch, finding the leather was slack. She had to be imagining things. She could have sworn the bundle was full when she climbed out of the root dwelling.

The scent of wood smoke drifted on the cold night air. Had the men returned from tracking Errindoor?

She walked toward the smoke, gazing up at the sky as she trudged through the snow. Trillions of stars branched overhead. When she'd discussed her mother—the true Amphitrite—with Ewan, she hadn't been lying. Her vast knowledge acquired in her Ocean Apothecary was nothing but a star now, glistening softly against the night.

She scanned the silhouettes of the trees against the starlit sky. What should be the jagged outlines of spruce and pine were soft, dreamlike.

A figure crouched before a small fire. The figure was too small to be one of the huntsmen. A hood concealed their face from view.

Amy slowed her steps, fearing she might startle the individual who was making a soft, whimpering kind of sound. The voice was higher than a man's. Was it a woman? If so, was she sobbing?

The whimpering stopped as her footsteps came to a crunching halt in the snow. Orange firelight illuminated an arm withdrawing into the robe. A musty scent filled the air that was not burning wood. The scent was rich with iron and stung Amy's nose.

"Savor it. Surrender to it. All salt daughters of Celaeno will be tempted by it," the figure hissed.

"Naunet?" Amy asked. How could Masika's sister be here in this forest?

The figure turned, their hood preventing their identity from showing. "My sister trusted you, and here you are, taking advantage of her life's work."

Black hair uncoiled along the figure's shoulders as a dark hand withdrew the hood. A pair of onyx eyes with white pupils swept up to meet her. "I learned that you ventured to the past to meet with a son of Atlantean kings. I had to see for myself if Alexandra was telling the truth."

Amy's breath caught. "Masika?"

Masika's eyes narrowed. "It's been much too long since you've seen me."

Amy stared into Masika's face, trying to understand what she was seeing. With three thousand years between them, the venom had done something horrible to her appearance. Her hair fell in thick dark mats over her shoulders. Her skin was as white as the snow glistening in the starlight. But her skin was not without imperfection. Black, splotchy marks covered her face and arms. The splotches were scaly, some oily in texture. Her eyes were dark enough that if Amy gazed into them for too long, surely she would fall into them. She'd fallen in love with that dark gaze so long ago. But something hollow lived there now, something Amy didn't remember.

Masika's dark beauty had changed into something dangerous.

"How are you here?" Amy asked.

"I exist with the venom now, a timeless existence. I can bleed through the boundaries of time, just as the fae queen has allowed you to do. Salt venom was born from her blood. You knew this when you gave her to me, didn't you?"

Amy's mouth had gone dry. She reached into her robe, clutching Masika's crystal remains. Had they somehow summoned her spirit?

Masika withdrew her hand from her robe, holding out an item. "So this is the medicine Ewan, son of Atlantean kings, is taking to the top of the mountain."

The item in Masika's hand glistened in the starlight. Its shimmer was icy and silver, frozen like the atmosphere.

Amy's breath caught. "A storm dragon scale?"

"Not just any storm dragon scale—the storm dragon who sank his city, Poseidon."

Amy stared at the glistening silver scale in Masika's dark palm, wondering why Ewan saw it as medicine. The edges were incredibly sharp. She could see how it could be used as a weapon.

Masika turned the scale over, making the silver surface shimmer in the starlight. "And you journey with him, why?"

Amy's gaze dropped to the weapon in Masika's palm. "Naunet told me the blood of a fae king will neutralize the salt venom that's cursed you. I've come to the past to slay Errindoor."

Masika's eyes flashed, hollowness inside of them. "You see what I have become. What is left of me to save?"

Amy withdrew the canopic jar and removed the lid. She tilted the jar forward. "I have your crystal remains. All I need is the blood of the fae king to release your spirit from the curse the salt venom has infected you with."

Masika's face twisted, mocking her. A laugh escaped her lips. "You've come all this way for nothing."

Amy's vision blurred. Why did Masika sound almost elated? "You don't understand. I've come back for you. I never forgot you, or what the venom did to you," Amy whispered, her breath failing her. "You were never *nothing* to me."

Masika gripped the dragon scale in her fingers. "You act as though the venom should be feared. I can say with certainty that my relationship with the venom is a pleasant one."

Amy shivered. How could anyone with her appearance have formed a relationship with the venom and called it pleasant?

A hiss escaped Masika's curling lips. "Why have you come all this way for me?"

"Because I love you," Amy said, her words stolen by the silence of the night.

Masika stood, gathering her arms beneath her robe. Embers from the fire crackled around her, jumping across the snow.

Amy's chest stung. Had Masika not heard what she said?

"Do you remember the day we summoned Celaeno's storm dragon into the tidal cavern? Do you not remember what else the tide brought in?"

Amy shook her head. That memory was so long ago. She couldn't remember.

"For you to come all this way to the past, you must remember our secret. You must remember what grew on the tails of storm dragons the fae queen needed."

Amy stared into Masika's face. She couldn't remember what she and Masika had discovered. All she could feel was the twinge of jealousy that knotted in her stomach as Masika lusted after the sea. "I can't remember."

"You lie," Masika spat. "I think you knew what the fae queen would do to me when you gifted her to me." She took a step toward her, the flames behind her whipping out in the wind. "I think you wanted to take credit for what my sister discovered shortly before you left with Selia to bond her with Celaeno's storm dragon."

"How do you know what Naunet discovered?"

Masika dipped her chin, her black locks of hair falling into her face. "The venom shares truths with me your heart never could."

Amy tried to breathe, but her lungs refused. Masika was *furious* with her. "I didn't know Naunet made a discovery. If what she discovered was so important, then why didn't she share it with me before I took Selia to bond with the storm dragon?"

"Why would she tell you when you wanted to take credit for the discovery yourself?"

"How can I take credit for a discovery I don't remember?" Amy protested, her voice rising.

Masika's face hardened. "You were always jealous of my love for the sea. Your mother had knowledge about the kelp that disappeared after Atlantis sank. I think you wanted to keep it for yourself."

"Is this about minca?" Amy asked.

The whites of Masika's eyes turned black. "It's always been about minca's disappearance." Tears dripped from the corners of her eyes, streaking along her cheeks.

She withdrew her hand from beneath her robe and coiled her fingers around the dragon scale. Her fingers shredded around it, her blood steaming in the cold night air.

"Stop," Amy said, sickened by the sight.

Masika continued to mutilate her hand as she squeezed the scale harder.

Amy lunged for her. "Stop hurting yourself!"

Masika threw her arm out, sending her blood spraying into the air.

Her blood lashed out like a serpent, striking the canopic jar.

The jar shattered, Masika's crystal remains exploding into a burst of fire.

Amy fell back into the snow, withering in pain.

Flames erupted around Masika, licking the bleeding corners of her eyes. "My sister is *dead* because of you. I would rather live with the venom in my heart forever than have you put my spirit to rest."

Amy scrambled backward, kicking through the snow to escape the flames exploding from the fire.

A sickening cry erupted from the flames as a serpent's tail coiled around Masika. Masika's face twisted as her upper lip folded back. Her lips moved, but no words came out. A hollow, sickening sound, like someone expelling their last breath, filled the forest.

Amy tried to stand, but a flaming serpent erupted from the fire, arching over her. Its black scales glistened, catching the wind as it ripped through the forest. The scales turned dagger-like, jutting out from the serpent's coiling body. Salt crystals tore through the serpent's flesh, ripping through the scales.

Masika grabbed one of the salt crystals and broke it away from the serpent's body. She gripped the crystal, holding it up. Venom dripped from the end, glistening with starlight.

Swinging her arm, she drove the crystal into the dragon scale.

The scale exploded, sending shards of white-hot energy into the air.

Amy threw her hands in front of her face as the shards pelted against her. Like needles, the shards dove into her flesh.

Masika opened her mouth as a horrible, wail filled the forest.

Amy clasped her hands over her ears as Masika's voice ripped around her.

"Stop it!" Amy cried, but wind and rain and fire enveloped her. Masika's inferno was too powerful. Pain ripped up her leg as her skin caught fire.

49
SEVEN

Selia

As evening approached, Selia helped Pixie bundle up Peppercorn and her seven new bat pups for the night. They placed them in a pot Pixie had stuffed full of mulch and an old scarf. One of the pups hadn't removed itself from beneath the protective wing of her mother.

"She's definitely the runt of the litter," Pixie said, concern rising in her voice.

"Why don't I take them home with me?" Selia asked, feeling hopeful. She really didn't want to go back to the lighthouse alone to spend the night. Having the dragon scale Alex had her, along with a fae mother bat and her pups seemed a good idea in case those horrible salt flies decided to show again.

"That sounds like a marvelous idea," Pixie agreed. "I don't think the greenhouse is going to be warm enough tonight. The temperature is going to dip well below freezing."

Selia loaded into Pixie's car, propping the pot full of bats into her lap as she took her place in the passenger seat.

Pixie turned on the engine and steered the car onto the street. The local radio station blared through the speakers as she maneuvered the car onto the road. *"Local resident Damien Malloch has gone missing. Meanwhile, locals have begun reporting new sightings of Sika the selkie."*

Selia's stomach hollowed. "I feel helpless. I can't stand sitting here, not knowing what I can do to find him."

"There is nothing you *can* do. You, or Gwen. But it tears me up seeing the both of you go through this."

Selia shuffled her hands through her sweater. Her eyes began to burn as the streets blurred outside.

Pixie grabbed her hand. "I can't imagine how scared you must feel."

"Scared can't begin to describe it. I'm absolutely terrified thinking of not having Damien at my side. What will I do if—"

Tires scraped against pavement.

Selia gripped the pot of bats for dear life as the car slammed to a halt.

"Did you see that?" Pixie exclaimed.

"See what?"

Pixie's knuckles went white on the steering wheel. "A *massive* deer went sprinting across the road."

Selia blinked a few times as Peppercorn's pups all chittered in her lap.

Pixie drove the car up the street and parked outside the lighthouse. She grabbed the pot from Selia's lap and jumped out of the car. "There, there, little momma bat. Selia will take good care of you! She's gonna be a momma soon, too!"

"Are you staying?" Selia asked.

"Of course. I don't want you to be alone on Christmas Eve."

"It's Christmas Eve *eve*."

Pixie shrugged. "Same difference."

Selia sighed a breath of relief, grateful for Pixie's friendship.

Once inside the lighthouse, Pixie set the pot down next to the box of screaming ornaments, which the pups instantly got lost in. Soon, the room was full of the wild chatter of Peppercorn's offspring. Peppercorn's fuzzy little face swiveled back and forth as her pups all fought to nurse.

Selia couldn't imagine. *Seven* mouths to feed? Here she was, nervous about taking care of only one!

After a few moments, she reached her hand down into the box, gently coaxing the hungry pups away from their mother's chest. "You look like you need a break."

Peppercorn reached her little wing forward, gladly taking a hold of Selia's thumb and climbing out of the squeaking box of her hungry babies. The runt pup clung to her mother's belly, refusing to let go as she climbed onto Selia's hand. Once atop her shoulder, she swiveled her face to Selia's ear, where she voiced a loud *screeeeeeech*!

"What is it?" Selia asked.

Alex manifested in the kitchen as Pixie was walking into the living room.

"Selia," Pixie started. "Look at—"

Fwip!

Pixie's eyes hooded. She fell in a slump onto the sofa.

Alex closed the space between her and Selia. "She will be out for a few hours." Her gaze dropped to the box full of squeaking ornaments on the kitchen counter. "When did she give birth?"

"Just today," Selia said. "We discovered seven of them in the greenhouse. Is it normal for a fae bat to have *seven* pups?"

"Seven is a magical number when it comes to the fae. Their litters often reflect the sacred number of Gaia."

"What makes a creature a fae and not just normal?"

"Intelligence, paired with pure instinct. Their personalities are also far more direct than any normal creature. One of the biggest giveaways a creature is fae is finding seven born at a time."

"What other instances of seven can you think of?"

"Seven maternal salt pods. Seven storm dragons who guard them. Seven ancestral salt mothers the Abyss originates from." She shrugged. "Not to mention there are also seven total storm bonds."

"Okay, it sounds like seven does have a presence. I've been noticing a pattern regarding the number seven."

One of Alex's eyebrows arched. "How so?"

"When Masika was speaking to me through the journal, she specifically asked me to find the seventh storm scroll, which was missing. Then, at the coffee shop today, Damien's seventh painting was missing."

"I took the storm scroll, as well as the painting."

"Why?"

"The scroll has imagery on it that could give away to Masika what your storm bond will be. As for the painting, your fiancé's artwork has caught the eye of our storm dragon." She reached into her robe and tugged out a roll of watercolor parchment. "He requested that I bring this image to him as it has helped to inspire him when it comes time to forming your bond."

Selia's stomach hollowed. "Does the dragon know where Damien is?"

"He has alluded to his whereabouts."

Selia grabbed her coat. "What are we waiting for? We have to go find him!"

Alex tucked the watercolor parchment back into her robe. "We cannot go running blindly into the dark. Masika could have set a trap. We must focus on the task before us."

Selia's body heated to the point she felt like she might explode. "What task is more important than finding Damien?"

"Masika wants access to your memory because her sister Naunet inscribed storm scrolls in the Temple of Isis. She has been harassing you because she wants to know the name of the seventh storm bond. We must focus on protecting the memory of yours she wants."

"Does nobody know the name of the seventh storm bond?"

"Only Celaeno's storm dragon does. The name of the seventh bond has been corroded from the Codex by salt venom."

"You haven't actually told me what this Codex is, and I have no memory of it from my childhood. Is it some kind of document?"

"Gaia's Codex is the document the Order is responsible for protecting and preserving. Iridescents like me have a duty to a specific record of the Codex certain nymphs are in charge of inscribing. While in Egypt, I was assigned oversight of Naunet's work with the Codex. Inscribing storm scrolls with the bonds between sea nymphs and storm dragons was only a small portion of her work, which I was in charge of monitoring."

"How would discovering the name of the seventh bond help Masika?"

Alex touched her throat with her hand. "Masika had been researching minca's disappearance with Amy before she was infected by the fae queen. Both Masika and Naunet had hypothesized that minca's disappearance had something to do with storm dragons. If Masika discovers the name of the seventh storm bond, she can attempt to destroy it before you and Celaeno's storm dragon form it together."

"In other words, the salt venom is attempting to destroy its own cure?"

Alex withdrew her hand from her throat. "You've seen how salt venom has erased the memories of its existence from your friends' memory. Who is to say that it can't also destroy the means of neutralizing it?"

Selia didn't like entertaining the thought that salt venom was alive. But considering both Gwen and Pixie had forgotten events that involved it? "Let me guess, the seventh mystery bond is the one Celaeno's storm dragon wants to form with *me*?"

Alex's eyes flashed. "Exactly. The last time the seventh bond was formed, it was between Isis and Poseidon. Its formation resulted in sinking the city of Atlantis."

Selia shook her head. "I still don't understand. What connects minca with these storm dragons?"

Peppercorn let out a frivolous *shreeeeeek*, causing both Selia and Alex to jump.

Alex reached her hand out to touch Peppercorn. The mother bat didn't budge when Alex attempted to lift her protective wing and check on her pup. She gripped Alex's thumb, allowing her to cradle her in her hand.

Alex continued to inspect the pup. Her eyes weren't open like the others, and her ears were flat against her tiny body. "The runt is not eating—not a good sign. It will be at least a day before we can rely on them to help us."

"How do you know she isn't eating?" Selia asked.

"Her mother just told me."

"Can you communicate with her?"

"Somewhat. I wouldn't say I'm the most well versed in fae bat. But she's definitely concerned about this little one."

Selia eyed the small pup tucked under Peppercorn's wing. "Will the pup die?"

"It could, if we don't find a remedy, and quickly. Peppercorn said the salt flies are too toxic to feed to her offspring just yet. The maternal instinct is by far the most powerful force in nature, especially when it comes to fae and their offspring."

Selia's stomach turned over. "We need to help her. I can't just sit and watch one of her babies suffer."

Peppercorn continued making the high-pitched chirps, filling the room with an excited trill of anxious chatter.

Alex's brow furrowed. "Wow, that's an interesting detail. She said, *medicine found near tritons.*" She set Peppercorn back into the box, where she was quickly swarmed by her other pups.

"What are tritons?" Selia asked.

Alex's eyes darkened. "Juvenile storm dragons."

362

PART 7
ALT, STORMS & STARLIGHT

50
THE WHITE DOE

Amy

Hot, shooting pain rippled through Amy's body. A blanket of stars shimmered overhead, their pale light existing with no purpose other than to create silence. She lay on the frozen ground, snow-capped trees framing the starlit sky above. Paralyzed, Amy couldn't break away from the quiet of winter's night.

The burning sensation working its way down from her chest wasn't from fire, but from the cold. One of her hands lay on her chest where her cloak had been ripped from her body. Only a tremble of her pulse lingered beneath her skin, still fighting, even though the flaming inferno of Masika's rage was gone.

Masika had destroyed her own crystal remains along with Poseidon's scale.

Tears streaked down her cheeks, catching and reflecting the starlight as the salt froze against her skin. The moon's absence made the stars so much brighter. Masika had always disliked the moon, because she felt moonlight stole the beauty of the sea's darkness.

Amy found herself wondering if the dark ocean of light above was where sea nymphs went when they died. Masika *hated* her. She didn't want her in her life.

Amy forced herself to look away from the stars, finding the pointed canopy of the red giants returning her to the forest. She staggered to her feet and stood, her surroundings not registering. Disorientation worked around her. Winter Forest was a frozen cage, and she was suddenly trapped behind thousands of years of ancient wilderness.

Her ankle buckled, forcing her backward. She backed against a tree, her body trembling. She sank down to the ground. Her fingers grazed past the spilled contents of the medicine bundle.

As she worked to gather the items and return them into the leather pouch, snow crunched behind her.

"Amy?"

Amy lifted her head, unable to register the warm male voice.

"What are you doing out here?" he asked, dropping to the ground in front of her. "Did that fox come back?" the man asked, dipping down to retrieve the medicine bundle.

Amy didn't register who the voice belonged to. Masika had destroyed Poseidon's scale. Not only had she destroyed the medicine Ewan hoped to offer to his ancestors, she'd also stolen any hope Amy had of saving her spirit.

A familiar scent of earth and pine enveloped her. The layers of greens in Ewan's eyes flickered in the low light provided by the stars above.

Amy couldn't look Ewan in the eye. All she could see was Masika's bottomless gaze—the Abyss living inside of her soul. The storms were full of anger there, demanding that she leave her alone.

No matter how hard Amy tried, she couldn't remember what it was that she and Masika had discovered. Masika's spirit would forever remain angry with her. She viewed her lack of memory about a discovery Naunet also made about minca as a betrayal.

Ewan's hand came to hers. "What are these markings from?"

"It's nothing," Amy replied as she tugged her cloak over the bruises on her arm.

"Did one of my men harm you?" Ewan grunted.

"No man did this to me," Amy said, her voice trembling.

Ewan's brow furrowed, starlight catching the whites in his eyes. His hand came to her chin, tilting her face back to meet his protective gaze. "Then who did?"

The trees began to whip above her head, and the stars disappeared again. Another winter storm was blowing in.

Ewan looped his arms under her and stood. Carrying her, he took off into the forest.

Tears blurred in Amy's eyes as snow crunched under Ewan's feet. She buried her face into his neck, wishing she had a better answer. All she could see were Masika's eyes boring into her, liquid fire full of anger glinting in them. *I would rather live with the venom in my heart forever than have you put my spirit to rest.*

"Let me down," Amy demanded, beating her fist against Ewan's shoulder.

"You are not well."

Anger ripped through her. She grabbed a tree branch and kicked away from his body.

Tumbling down the snowy hill she went. No blunt stone against her hip or ribs could compare to the pain she was feeling. As trees and sky and snow blurred into a spinning spiral, she landed in a heap of fresh powder, bringing her to a slow.

"Amy!" Ewan called, but the wind stole his voice.

She huddled against the base of the gnarled tree. She wanted to sink down into the snow and forget she'd ever come here. If Masika hated her, how could she continue in her quest to save her?

She collapsed into the snow. She'd come all the way to this magical forest, hoping that her friend would welcome her when she found her. Instead, Masika met her with rage. She *hated* that she'd come here.

The cold wind penetrated her cloak. A white silhouette shifted beside her, blocking the icy wind. The creature was white like the snow sticking to its fur. Its head was too angular and ears too large for it to be a wolf. It had a wet, black nose with nostrils that flared with every step it took.

The beast walked toward her with silent grace. It stopped, bowing its head down to Amy's level. Dark sapphire eyes glistened like crystals against the violent winter storm.

Amy gasped. This was one of the fae elk from the white herd! By the lack of antlers, this elk was a female. Her fur was pure white. Had she not been so close, Amy could have mistaken her for starlight.

The doe towered over her, dipping her face down. Her knees buckled as she lay down in the snow. Amy huddled against her side, sheltering herself form the storm.

A blue fleck shimmered on her coat—the blue salt scale from a minca moth. Had the fae queen found her?

Finding the queen would mean escaping from the frozen past of Winter Forest.

Amy placed her hands on either side of the doe's furry face. "Can you take me to her, please?"

The doe nudged Amy with her nose. Amy grabbed a fistful of her thick white fur on her shoulders and draped her leg over her back.

The doe stood, bringing Amy with her. She pinned herself against the doe's back as the storm swirled around them. Off they went into the white-out blizzard of the mountain, leaving Ewan and his men behind.

51
TRITONS

Selia

Alex scanned the kitchen, her grey eyes sweeping the corner of the room. She walked to the cupboard and pulled out the brass device Damien had discovered a few days ago. Returning to the kitchen table, she set the device in front of Selia.

"Why do I get the feeling that you are going to use it?" Selia asked.

"Oh, I've already used it. How do you think I brought you to Masika's tidal cavern?"

Selia's breath caught. "Is it a teleportation device?"

Alex smiled. "Paired with an Iridescent's ability to manipulate light? Yes." She grabbed the device and began walking toward the hall.

Selia followed Alex down the hall and up the spiral staircase that led to the lantern room. "What is it called?"

"The Order has used beaconing devices for thousands of years. The technology predates Atlantis. Many beaconing devices still hold residual electricity inside of them. This power was generated by ancient storm dragons."

Together, they summited the spiral staircase. Selia walked into the lantern room the caught the remaining light of the evening sun. The North Sea changed from orange and yellow to blue and purple as the last rays of sunlight dipped below the horizon.

Alex set the beaconing device in the center of the room. She snapped her fingers, and a tiny glowing orb appeared at the center. She grabbed one of the golden spheres and gave it a spin. One, then three, then five spiraled faster, until all seven of the spheres spiraled around one another, creating a low, reverberating *hum*. She held her hand out in front of her, gathering the pulsing light between her fingers.

Selia stood back as the tower filled with pulsing yellow light.

Alex closed her eyes as an electrical hum filled the tower. "Storm dragon of Celaeno, may the light of Gaia show us your soul. With your power, we wish to find the tritons from which you grow."

Lightning zapped through the air from the beaconing device, tunneling like a brilliant pillar of light.

Alex opened her eyes and held out her hand. "Let's go find some tritons."

The moment Selia grabbed Alex's hand, her body was thrust forward. Gravity fell away as the pillar of light spiraled around her.

Alex released Selia's hand, and the light fell away.

Selia fell forward, landing on the ground with a muffled *thud*. Her palms didn't scrape against jagged black stones. The surf didn't crash about. The cold, damp scent of earth filled her nose.

The cavern they had arrived in was different from Masika's tidal cavern. The walls shimmered with ice, not water. Every few moments, it gave a heavy *crack*.

Alex manifested beside her, dull yellow light glowing around her robes. She tilted her face back, her high cheek bones catching the blue light reflecting off the cavern walls.

"Where are we?" Selia asked, climbing to her feet.

Alex folded her arms in front of her. "We are in a triton den."

"Is this den a cave?"

"Sort of," Alex replied, her breath huffing out in white clouds. "We're in a shelf of ice that's drifted south from the recent arctic front."

One of Selia's feet slipped out in front of her. "Are we in a glacier?"

"I believe we are," Alex said as she turned on her heel and motioned for her to follow. "This way."

Selia followed Alex through a corridor of glittery blue ice. The icy corridor opened, revealing a room that had been carved out by the sea. The walls were long, sweeping layers of ice that were so smooth, Selia's reflection shone back at her from the ice. A glacial pool sat beneath them.

Alex began her descent to the water. Selia followed, crouching as to not allow her boots to slip out from beneath her.

Ripples formed in the water.

Something dark darted out from beneath one of the ice shelves.

"Looks like this is the perfect spot," Alex said.

Selia's breath caught. "Look at them!"

The pool shimmered with the coiling tails of what appeared to be a dozen small tritons. They were no larger than Selia's palm. Each resembled seahorses, however, they were three times as long. Two pectoral fins jutted from their sides. Their eyes were ink black. A long, tube-like snout framed the center of their faces. Their blackish-blue scales shone with purple iridescence as they swam about the pool. Their swift movements were powered by the long, sweeping, sideways movements of their tails.

Selia pulled away as one of the tritons thrashed its tail, sending the icy glacier water splashing toward her. Electricity zapped through the air, making her hair stand on end.

"Careful," Alex said as she scooted back from the water. "They're still getting used to their electrical power when they're young. They generate electrical currents by thrashing their tails like that."

"Where do they come from? How are they born?" Selia asked as she stared transfixed at the pool.

"Tritons are born in one of two ways. They emerge from sea ice, or they rain down from the sky when it thunderstorms."

"Do they have parents?"

"There are only male storm dragons. How they actually spawn their offspring is a mystery. Just like there are no male sea nymphs, there are no female storm dragons."

Selia took a step back as the excited tail thrashing continued, sending an electrical *zap* through the air.

"This is a lively bunch," Alex said as she smoothed the tips of her frizzled hair. "Tritons born from glaciers often have little to no control over the electrical currents they generate. They are far icier, but not any less electric in their personalities."

"Do they ever develop wings?"

"Not all dragons have wings. A storm dragon's tail houses his power. They are the beasts who control the water cycle on the planet. A mature storm dragon has seven tails, one for each of the storm bonds he can form with a sea nymph. It is his tail that he presents to a sea nymph when he forms the bond."

Selia gazed at the tritons swimming in the pool. None of them had more than one tail sprouting from its body. "How do we learn about this medicine Peppercorn needs for her pup?"

Alex crouched next to her and set her hand in the water. "We ask them."

Selia's stomach hollowed. "You want me to stick my hand into a pool of water with these electrical creatures?"

"It's the only way to communicate with storm dragons, even the young ones. They are very quiet creatures, until they get excited about one of their storms."

Selia set her hand into the water, bracing herself for a shock. The tritons swam toward Alex's hand, then darted over to Selia. Their tails wrapped around her fingers as they swam past, each oddly smooth. She expected a rougher texture by the look of their scales.

A synchronized *hum* filled her salt nodes, one that sent a brilliant display of light into her periphery. Flashes of images paired with the gentle hum of electricity filled her mind.

"*Miiinnnnnccccaaaaa.*"

Selia jumped as a voice jolted through her. "Alex, I can hear their voices. They're trying to tell me something."

"Tritons communicate through electrical pulses of waves and light. What are they saying?" Alex asked.

Selia closed her eyes, focusing on the humming voices that trilled through her. "I think they're saying minca. Why would they say that?"

"Minca means *mother* in the language of your ancestors."

Selia focused on the pulsing voices as the word *minca* became louder and louder. The electrical current coiled like a serpent around her. "Now they're showing me something. It's a dark tunnel, one that's flooding toward me."

Another flash of light broke before her, followed by a shape drifting in the tunnel.

A face of a woman appeared.

Selia swallowed. Who were they trying to show her?

The woman's eyes were closed. Her face was tipped down, her eyelashes frozen over. A dusting of freckles scattered over her nose and cheeks, freckles that were shaped like stars.

Selia's heart stopped. "Amy!"

Amy didn't respond. She was frozen in suspended space, her body encased in ice. Her hair coiled out from her. Hands and arms were held out at her side. Her fingers were splayed out, frozen in place. A crystal cocoon of ice encased her.

"Amy, where are you?" Selia yelled into the void.

"Do not wake her," another voice rang through the glacier, one Selia didn't recognize. A thunderous male voice came surging up from the depths of the dark tunnel. *"If you wake her, she will be locked in the past forever."*

The electrical voices of the tritons fled as the bigger, thunderous male voice filled the cavern. The dragon scale pendant on Selia's neck burned as his presence dominated the electrical pulses of communication.

Blinding light pulsed around her, sending gooseflesh rippling up her arms. Where was this energy coming from?

The voice had absorbed the light in the cave. She stared out into inky darkness. She clutched the dragon pendant on her chest. Was the voice coming from it?

"Daughter of Celaeno, you should not be here."

"Alex, where are you?" Selia said, throwing her hands out in front of her.

"Alex cannot hear me. Shame on her for bringing you here before I am ready."

The ground beneath Selia's feet began to tremble. "Who are you? What have you done with Amy? Where is Damien?"

"Amy is sleeping. Damien is safe."

"I don't believe you," Selia yelled back at the large, echoing voice. She took a step forward, her foot slipping. She landed on her butt and began sliding.

Her feet hit something solid, stopping her from falling into the pool. The solidness moved beneath her, coiling and snaking its way in the dark.

"I have taken Damien far away from here. I can't tell you where he is, because the venom will tell Masika. Right now, you must focus on our bond, or Masika will kill Amy. If Amy dies, you will lose all that remains of your memory."

"No, I won't leave until you've told me where you've taken Damien!"

A grumbling huff blew past her face. "*Stubborn, as always.*" Lightning flashed, blurring as thunder echoed around her. "*I'm sending you back to the lighthouse.*"

"No!"

The pulses of energy from the dominant male voice were too powerful. His voice consumed her like a great terrible wind tunneling over open water.

"Damien…" Selia whispered. All she could see was him lying on the hospital bed, his face turned away from her.

The electric *hum* created by the tritons filled Selia's salt nodes. A pair of electric eyes flashed in the dark. Her eyes hooded as his voice filled the cavern. A long, shimmering blue tail flashed as an electrical pulse surged through her.

52

TEMPLE OF SALT, STORMS, & STARLIGHT

Amy

Amy tilted her hood up, protecting the back of her head from the blasts of arctic air tunneling down from the sacred meadow. She dug her fingers back into the doe's warm fur, grabbing what she could to stop her skin from freezing.

The doe kept her head down, ears pinned as the snow whipped around her. She walked at a steady pace, not making any sudden movements that might cause Amy to fall from her back.

Amy couldn't make sense of the light pulsing through the storm. The doe followed the light, which began pulsing faster. An outline of a stone structure blurred in the distance. Was it a building?

The doe walked toward the structure, sheltering herself and Amy from the wind. The closer she came to the structure, the less violent the storm became. She stopped by the wall of windows and dipped her head, signaling for Amy to dismount.

Amy slid off the doe's back, dropping next to her slender legs in the snow. The elk brought her head down to Amy's level, her shiny black nose bumping into Amy's shoulder.

"What is it?" she asked.

The doe flicked her giant ears forward. Eagerness shone in her deep blue eyes, which shimmered with the starlight above.

Amy gasped, looking up. *Starlight*? Were they really that high atop the mountain that they had ascended through the storm? The wind dispersed, allowing a cold calm to replace the violent breath of the blizzard. Clouds drifted over the mountaintop, kissing the land before blowing back out into the night.

Blurring outlines of additional doe appeared on the horizon. The doe who'd brought Amy to this spot stomped her front hoof, perhaps out of excitement to meet with the others who were making quick work of the mountain. Smaller white figures darted in and out of the doe as the group made their silent ascent.

Amy's heart jumped. These does had fawns! They frolicked and played with the others, sending snow flying from their tiny hooves as they raced in front of their mothers.

Her doe walked forward, snorting a quick burst into the cold night air. Was she calling to someone?

Amy walked up to the doe's side as the others circled around them. She was soon surrounded by six giant mothers and their fawns. The fawn's eyes were twice as big and their ears equally as heavy, flicking in eager curiosity toward their fellow doe who had a selkie in her company.

A loud burst broke through the night air. The sound wasn't the wind or the blizzard starting up again. The jagged outline of something large began to ascend the mountain.

A crown? What was coming up the hill now?

Amy's breath caught. Another shape morphed against the starlit sky. The torso of a man sat atop the back of a massive bull elk.

It couldn't be. Ewan was riding the fae king Errindoor, the great guardian of the sacred mountain.

Errindoor's ascent up the mountain took half the time it took for the doe and their fawns. His stride was full of power and purpose. Muscles rippled in his neck and shoulders as he walked in silent grace toward them. His coat was darker than the doe's. Browns and tans mixed with the thicker hair along his neck and shoulders. Crowned atop his head were his two massive antlers—each the length of a grown man.

Amy's chest ached. How could she slay such a beautiful giant?

As Errindoor closed the space between them, a burst of air billowed from his nostrils. He stopped a few paces away, towering over Amy. He was so large that Amy could feel the heat coming from his body. The king was much larger in bulk and height than his harem of does.

Ewan's gaze leveled with her. Hurt and questions shone in his eyes.

"How did you find me?" Amy asked.

"Only the king knows where his queen will go," he said, patting the great king's muscular shoulder. Ewan tossed his leg over the beast's side, sliding down from Errindoor's back. He landed with a soft *thud*. "Errindoor has come searching for his matriarch."

Amy marveled at the fae king, who, as soon as Ewan dismounted, set his eyes on the doe that had carried Amy up the mountain. Errindoor's nostrils flared, and his shoulders stiffened.

The matriarch swiveled her ears, flicking them back and forth. She stomped her hoof, flicked her tail, then took off in a trot up the mountain.

Errindoor swung his mighty head quicker than should be possible for such a giant beast. His antlers made a swift *whooshing* sound that nearly swept Amy off her feet.

Amy backed away as the fae king dipped his head toward her.

Ewan tossed his hand toward Errindoor. "You've helped me find my doe; go find your own."

Errindoor's head rose. With his nostrils flared, he opened his mouth and bellowed a sound so primal, it ripped through Amy's heart like an arrow.

The fawns took off first, then their mothers as they chased after the matriarch. Higher they went, up the slope and into the meadow, until their white bodies could be mistaken for nothing other than the starlight.

Ewan shook his head. "Kings will be kings, I guess."

Amy shivered, Errindoor's bugle still piercing her. The sound was so hauntingly powerful, it seemed to penetrate her heart.

Ewan didn't take a step forward to close the space like he had so many times before. He dropped his hands to his sides, turning his palms up.

Amy couldn't look him in the eye, fearing she would find anger there. "I didn't expect you to follow me."

Ewan dipped his chin, starlight casting shadows that made his deep-set eyes darker. "You can run away from me as long as you want, but I won't stop chasing you until you answer me one thing." He closed the space between them, grazing her cheek with the back of his hand. "Who did this to you?"

Amy winced as his knuckles rubbed against the wound created from Masika's violent outburst. The flames made of wind and rain had burned her skin in that nightmare, a firestorm that had consumed the entire forest.

Masika had so much anger. Why couldn't her friend see all the trouble she had gone through to save her?

He withdrew his hand and dropped his arm at his side. "I know you are a woman of the water, and I am a man of this forest. I know you will always desire to return back to whoever has held your heart captive at sea." He dipped down on his knee, leveling his gaze with her. "But I do expect that you respect my duty to protect you, at least while you are visiting this frozen land I call home."

Amy gazed up at his face, which was etched in silver starlight. The blur of Ewan's hand rose to her cheek. She grabbed his callused palm in both her hands before he could touch the wound again. Tears blurred his face, making his features appear like they were under water. The stars shimmered behind him, dancing like they were part of an ocean.

"I've lied to you," she bit out, her dry words burning her throat. "I came on this journey for a friend lost. A friend I loved."

His brow furrowed. "All of us make this journey to the sacred meadow to remember those we love."

"No, you don't understand."

Wind whipped between them, stirring the snow into wisps of shimmering white ribbons.

Amy let go of his hand. She turned away from him, wrapping her arms around herself. She looked up at the stars, wishing they had answers. Masika's spirit wasn't only angry with her, she *hated* her. "Your men were right about fearing me. The hateful words they've said all along, are true."

"How?"

"I am no medicine woman. In fact, I caused the death of my friend."

"Who was this friend?"

"Masika wasn't only a friend, she was my lover." She dipped her chin, her tears burning as they froze to her cheeks. "I can never forgive myself for what I did to her."

Her knees buckled. It took all of her strength not to collapse.

Ewan's knee shifted in the snow, creating a soft crunching sound. "This is the first time I have ever heard of Masika. Why have you not shared her with me before?"

"She never wanted to associate with the Sgàthan clan. Like your men believe me to be cursed, she had the same beliefs about humans."

"Was Masika a selkie, too?"

"Yes, a very opinionated, passionate one. She and I were working together to restore the magic our ancestors practiced while in Atlantis." She swallowed. "And I took that magic for granted."

Ewan's gaze leveled with hers. "Why did you keep all of this a secret from me?"

She tugged at her cloak, further distancing herself from him. "Her memory was too painful for me to discuss."

Ewan set his hand under her chin, tilting her face up to meet his gaze. "Amy, I never would have turned you away about losing someone you loved."

Tears burned, blurring Ewan's hard features. She'd gone numb. The only thing she could feel was the warmth of his hand now grazing past her cheek.

"How did she die?"

"She became ill with something a fae creature created long ago. Her spirit has been trapped, unable to move on. A little while ago, her spirit visited me."

"Is this mark from Masika's spirit?"

Amy nodded. "What hurts the most, is that I wasn't there for her when she died." She swallowed down the cold lump of dryness wedged in her throat. "I will always blame myself for the fact that she was alone."

"If there is one thing you will learn from the spirits who guard this frozen mountain, you are *never* alone." He set his hand on her shoulder. "While you are on this starlit mountain, our ancestors have the ability to speak with you. In some rare cases, their words can even harm." He removed his hand from her shoulder, grabbing her hand instead. "I will not let this spirit of your friend harm you again, do you understand me?"

Amy nodded, more from the fact that she was now freezing. She didn't know if she should feel grateful or relieved.

Ewan stood, taking her hand with his as he towered over her. As he did, Errindoor's crown of antlers became visible in the distance. "It's time you come and learn the story about how Errindoor got his name. I think it might help you with your grief."

Amy forced the memory of Masika's eyes away, replacing it with Ewan's warmth.

The two walked hand-in-hand toward the fae king, who seemed to know they were following him. As soon as Ewan's boots crunched in the snow, the stag sent a billowing snort into the air and took off up the mountain.

"He's such a feisty old man," Ewan huffed. "Look at him, all hoof and buck and show. Every time we get up here, he thinks he can prance off and I won't know where he's going."

"How many winters have you followed his ascent up here?" Amy asked.

"Far too many without good company," Ewan replied, squeezing Amy's hand.

The starlit sky above them soon transitioned into a rocky outcropping. Giant rectangular shapes lay scattered on the ground beneath at least a foot of freshly fallen powder. Were they ruins of some kind? Amy didn't know. All she knew was that nature hadn't formed them.

They followed Errindoor's tracks in the snow, approaching a wall of stone. Lights pulsed across Ewan's face again.

"Who created this structure?" Amy asked, stopping next to Ewan as he crouched down next to the wall.

He released her hand and set his palm on the stone. Lights branched out from his fingers, illuminating a spiral that appeared above his hand. "The Temple of Salt, Storms, and Starlight is much older than the great city of Atlantis."

The lights pulsed, then faded, returning Ewan's face to the shadows. "Long ago, my forefathers formed the new kingdom of Atlantis. These kings were men. They emerged after the old kingdom, a sea kingdom ruled by storm dragons." Ewan shifted his hand over the wall, and the lights began to pulse. "The Atlantean kings soon learned the source of the storm dragon's power over the weather—their bond with the daughters of the sea. These bonds fueled the storm dragon's power, the salty winds and storms that blocked out the starlight my kings used to navigate the seas."

The wall became a dazzling show of spiraling light that coiled and jumped as Ewan became quiet. "The daughters of the sea, your kind, had a very unique talent. They could summon the dragons with their hearts."

Amy's heartbeat jumped into her throat as the lights pulsed.

"Then, tragedy struck. When the great storm dragon Poseidon died, my city fell. We lost everything to the storm that swallowed my kingdom."

"I can imagine you would be angry with Poseidon."

"Angry at him? No. If I am angry at anyone, it is my forefathers."

"I don't understand."

"The kings of Atlantis *abused* Poseidon's power. We brought upon the sinking ourselves because, like Poseidon, we became obsessed with the power of storms. We forgot to practice Errindoor."

"Errindoor?"

"Errindoor is the name I gave the fae king. His name is Atlantean for fallen, or *crownless* king." He turned away, his hand dropping to his side. "I follow his footsteps to this sacred spot every winter, because he reminds me what a king must do if he is to remain powerful. A king must remove his crown and *sacrifice* his power. If he does not, he becomes a storm of anger and destruction, destroying the path for those who follow him."

A star fell from the sky, its light fading as it fell over the mountain.

Ewan's gaze dropped, following the star until his gaze leveled with her. "If there is anything I have learned from watching Errindoor make his journey to the sacred mountain every year, it is this." He took her hand again. "Kingdoms are lost in the past, however, they are rebuilt in the present."

Another bugle erupted in the air, sending Amy's heart with it. The piercing sound made Ewan's words sink deep inside of her, unraveling the emotions knotted in her stomach.

Ewan stood from his crouched position, not letting go of her hand. "Let's follow him."

They walked toward Errindoor's shrill bugle piercing the air. Soon, they were dipping past more ruins, entering some kind of chamber. They walked on the uneven surface of the snowcapped stones.

Light reflected on the stones that reminded Amy of water. They rounded the corner, finding the source of the light. A pool full of glowing blue water appeared.

The color of the water was so pure, it didn't really have a color at all. Amy imagined it was the kind of blue minca would create when it was bathing in moonlight.

"Is that the sacred pool?" Amy asked.

Ewan nudged her with his hand. "Look into the water and see for yourself."

Amy squinted into the water, finding the pool so bright, it was difficult to gaze into. She wondered if the pool was in fact absorbing starlight.

The source of the light wasn't from the sky, but from a collection of oblong shapes of at least a dozen dragon scales, all shimmering bright.

"How long were you and Masika in love?" Ewan asked, brushing up next to her.

"I loved her for many years, why?"

"These sacred waters want to know how long you cherished her before she became an ancestor."

Amy stared into the water, her emotions bringing tears to her eyes again. "I'd say that I was in love with her for at least a hundred years."

Ewan knelt down next to her, propping his arms upon his knee. "Feels like almost as long as I've been pursuing you."

The matriarch emerged to their right, walking up to the pool. She dipped her head down, flicking her ears forward.

Errindoor approached to their left. Two giant fae beasts, both gazing into each other's eyes—the only thing separating them was a giant pool of starlight.

The matriarch stomped her hoof again, but Errindoor did nothing.

"Gah," Ewan huffed. "He's being stubborn. He's trying to impress the matriarch by looking all majestic."

"How can you understand what they are saying to each other?"

"Fae beasts are all about body language. Right now, she's saying, *you are a big show off.*"

Errindoor strutted back and forth across the pond.

Ewan tugged Amy's hand, pulling her away from the pool. "He's getting a bit rowdy. It's best we give them some privacy."

They withdrew behind one of the stone walls with a window just low enough for Amy to peer through.

Ewan set his back against the wall, gazing up at the night sky. He dipped his hand beneath his robe, withdrawing the medicine bundle. "He won't drink from it until the stars above are just right."

Amy's body went cold. The medicine bundle no longer contained Poseidon's scale.

Would Ewan's prayers be offered up to his ancestors if his offering wasn't present?

She squeezed his hand. "Ewan, I need to tell you something, I—"

"—Shhh," he whispered as he dipped down to peer through the window. "Something is happening I've never seen before."

"Is he drinking?"

"I can't tell." Ewan removed himself from the window. "See for yourself."

Amy squinted through the starlit window. Her view of the pool became blocked as Errindoor swung his mighty head right in front of her. "He's blocking us."

Ewan returned the bundle beneath his robes, dipping down. "I'll prop you up."

Amy stepped forward as Ewan ducked his head. He grabbed her legs and hoisted her up onto his shoulders.

He shifted closer to the wall. "Can you see yet?"

"I can. He's bowing. His antlers, what's happening to them?"

Errindoor's crown was no longer dull, but, instead, glowing. The sharp points blurred, evaporating as mist into the night.

The matriarch entered the pool first.

Errindoor mirrored her movements, following.

They met at the center, where he lowered his mighty head first. His throat swelled and shrank with each gulp he took.

As he drank in the water, his antlers began to glow even brighter. They were no longer a giant crown of bone, but a glowing display of light.

The water lit up, reflecting a light that warmed her through. Maybe it was the light of the stars, a gift from her and Ewan's ancestors, who knew?

Errindoor lifted his glowing crown from the pool.

The matriarch flicked her ears toward him, then dipped her head and drank, too. As she drank, the water in the pool began to thicken with light. Both the fae king and his queen disappeared, leaving Amy to gaze into the pool of starlight.

"I think it's over," Amy whispered as the cold night air settled over the pool.

Ewan lowered her down to the ground. He walked out to the pool, where Errindoor's bony antlers had been left behind. He gathered the antlers, hoisting them both onto his back, motioning for Amy to follow him.

53
DRAGON SCALES
Selia

An endless sea of stars branched above Selia as she walked along the beach. Damien walked next to her, his hand clutched into her own. Was this real, or was she dreaming?

There was an extra spring in Damien's step. She knew he had something exciting to share with her. Something about the beach seemed so real, familiar even. She'd been to a place just like it before, walking in a blue memory so blue, she was in danger of becoming lost in it.

Damien slowed his pace, and Selia fell back into stride next to him. He took her hands in his and said, "The tide is coming in soon." The greens in his eyes seemed so bright against the grey backdrop of the sky and sea. "My ancestor has something to share with you."

The first rays of sunlight branched over the horizon. Damien's face was silhouetted by golden light before he vanished with the stars.

"Daughter of Celaeno, wake up."

Selia jumped as a low, male voice filled her head. No, the voice must have been a hallucination. It had all been a dream. She blinked into bright golden light that was streaming through the windows.

"Yes, I'm here. And no, nothing of what you saw in the cave was a dream. I told you that I would bring you back to the lighthouse."

Selia whipped her head around, searching for the storm dragon. She was sitting on the sofa in the living room. "Where are you?"

"*I'm swimming, currently.*"

Selia set her hands on her ears. That would explain the explosive waves crashing in her head. "I don't like this. It sounds like you are yelling."

"*Then maybe you should get closer to the water.*"

Selia got up from the sofa and walked to the windows. There was barely a cloud in the sky. Sunlight reflected off the surface of the North Sea, creating a gorgeous backdrop of color. "Is this any better?" Selia winced, bracing herself for his thunderous male voice from penetrating her mind.

"*I can barely hear you. Speak with your heart, not your lips.*"

"My *what?*"

Another gravely grumble followed. "*Has Alex taught you nothing about salt trancing with your pulse?*"

"Do you know the name of the seventh storm bond?"

"*I do, but stating it would steal its thunder,*" he grumbled, his own voice echoing after his reply. "*If I speak to loudly, Masika will hear me, and our bond will not form properly.*"

Selia thought back to the pair of eyes she'd seen in the triton den. They had such familiarity swimming in them. "I'm tired of calling you Celaeno's storm dragon. What is your real name?"

"*For now, call me by the name the Order gave to me, Balfour.*"

Selia froze as the name Balfour jumbled through her brain. Why did she envision the big burly man who'd punched Damien a few months ago at the Rusty Selkie?

Selia's breath caught. *Balfour was Celaeno's storm dragon?*

"*Yes,* and *Alex's henchman,*" his voice thundered. "*Let me tell you, had it not been for the tiny fae hermit crab helping you track down the vault, you never would have gotten as far as you did. Alex and I severely underestimated her.*"

"*How?*" was the only word Selia could think.

"It's been an ongoing bet Alex and I have had, wondering how long it would take for you to recognize me. My human form is much grizzlier than I'm sure you remember of me."

"Who won the bet?"

"I did. I said you wouldn't be able to figure out who I was without me telling you."

Selia didn't know if she should laugh or remain silent.

"Know this," Balfour huffed. *"Alex and I have both devoted ourselves to protecting you. Alex cares about you. She had a very big role in how you ended up at the Louvre."*

Pixie appeared in the kitchen, her face as red as a cherry tart. "You're awake!"

Selia stood up from the sofa as Pixie came bustling over and wrapped her arms around her.

"I thought I would let you sleep in since you've been so stressed with Damien missing," Pixie said.

"Why are you so cheerful?" Selia asked, the reality of Damien's disappearance suddenly slamming her in the gut again.

"Gwen called me this morning. Multiple people have said they've seen him around town."

Selia's heart felt like it could leap from her chest. "Damien? *Where?*"

"That's it! You are speaking with your pulse! I can hear you much better now!"

Pixie's cheeks burned red. "Not only that, but the lighthouse apparently lit up last night. Did you have something to do with that?"

"Oh, great. It turns out Alex wasn't very shy with her beaconing."

Selia shook her head no. Her body was trembling. She clapped her hands to her ears, hoping to muffle Balfour's powerful voice.

Pixie's brow furrowed. "Selia? Are you all right?"

"Yeah," she shook her head, hoping Balfour's voice would stay out of her head. "I had a very strange dream. Please, tell me about Damien."

Pixie walked over to the kitchen, motioning toward a platter of meat pies and pastries. "Here, eat something, and I'll share all the details with you."

A grumbling chuff filled Selia's head as Pixie swept into the room. "*You need to eat. You will need your strength for later.*"

Selia grabbed one of the blueberry scones Pixie had set out on the kitchen counter.

"*Trust me. Pulse speaking is as easy and as silent as breathing. Now, try actually talking to me.*"

Selia stared at Pixie as she also filled a plate.

"*She can't hear us, I promise.*"

Selia wanted to tell him. With Pixie in the room, now would be the time to give this telepathy known as *pulse speaking* a try.

She sucked in a breath, focusing on how her pulse slowed when she exhaled as she thought up a question. "*Where is Alex?*"

"*She's waiting for you to become acclimated to talking with me. I can hear you. Keep practicing.*"

Pixie's phone began ringing. She answered, but before she could speak, Gwen's voice bellowed through the speaker.

"Where the heck are you? Bring Selia down to the dock at once!"

"Okay, we'll be right there!" Pixie ended the call. "Gwen wants me to bring you down to the boatyard. Sounds like they have something new on Damien."

Shreeek!

Selia jumped as Peppercorn's voice cried up from the box of screaming ornaments. "I almost forgot about her."

"*Before you go, give the item in your pocket to the bat mother. She will thank you later.*"

Selia reached into her pocket. A small dry bundle of something brushed past her fingers. It had a similar coloration to the dragon scale pendant, yet it was slightly wider.

"*What is this?*"

"*It's a gift from my tail.*"

Selia held the item up to the light. "*Why would you give a fae bat pup something from your tail?*"

"*Just do it,*" he huffed, his voice gravely and dry. A hint of sarcasm rang in his tone.

"What's that?" Pixie asked, eyeing the strange item.

"Something from the greenhouse," Selia lied as she set it down into the box next to Peppercorn. She searched the box of screaming ornaments. "Where are her other pups?"

"I have no idea. I think they've actually fledged." Pixie grabbed her coat. "Come on. Gwen's waiting with news about Damien."

Selia's heart and head were so cloudy with adrenaline and Balfour's thunderous voice, she felt like she might never hear silence again. It took only a few minutes before Pixie pulled her car up to the boatyard.

A news crew was reporting on the dock.

"*What is going on down here?*" Selia asked as she and Pixie unloaded from the car.

"*I told you I was preparing something,*" Balfour grumbled.

"I see Gwen!" Pixie piped as she waved at the woman standing past the news crew on the dock. Sean's boat, the *Mad Malloch*, bobbed behind her.

"*What did you do to attract so much attention?*" Selia asked as she followed Pixie onto the dock and walked past the reporter.

"*Quiet down. I can hear you much better close to the water.*"

Selia's heart leapt when she stopped in front of Gwen. "What news do you have on Damien?"

Gwen's eyes landed on the pendant on Selia's chest. "Sean, she has one, too!"

Sean poked his head out of the boat's window, his expression worn. "Bring it here."

Selia walked over to the window and held up the dragon scale.

"Yep, that's definitely one of them," Sean said.

"You have dragon scales?" Selia asked.

"What?" Gwen stammered.

Sean shook his head. "Dragon scales or not, whatever this rubbish is, it's short-circuiting my engine."

Selia shivered. She had felt an energy pulsing from her hand through the scale.

Bvvvvrrrrimmmmmm!

A string of curse words slung through the air as Sean dipped back inside. "It's smoking again!"

Gwen jumped off the dock and disappeared into the boat after her husband.

Selia and Pixie followed Gwen into the inner quarters of the boat. The room smelled of burning rubber. The metallic lurch of gears and a high-pitched whine trilled through the air as smoke plumed up in giant black clouds from the floorboards.

"He's been at this all morning," Gwen growled, slamming her fist into the dash.

Sean pulled a lever, and the net worked its way up the pulley. "Have a look at what the arctic storm brought in."

The four of them walked onto the boat deck as the net worked its way out of the sea. Water poured out of the net as it rose above them.

Selia stood back as the net dripped overhead. It wasn't bulging with fish, but with something that resembled their scaly texture. A shimmering mass of hundreds of oval-shaped items ripped in the net, some falling through the openings. The ones that did escape didn't fall with a loud crash, but seemed to defy gravity. Like feathers, they floated down to the dock, barely making a sound where they landed.

"Are they fish scales?" Pixie asked as a few of the items fell onto the deck.

"No, they are much too light to belong to a fish. I agree with Selia—I think they very well could belong to a dragon," Gwen protested.

Pixie snorted.

Sean rolled his eyes.

"That's right," the reporter said as she clutched her microphone in hand and walked over to the *Mad Malloch*. "The entire bay area is filled with this mysterious blue substance locals have identified as dragon scales."

"*Why are there so many?*" Selia asked.

"*My tail scales have long been sought after for their healing properties by your ancestors. Exfoliating them has required lots of ice and snow.*"

"So you are the one responsible for the crazy cold weather?" Selia asked.

A grumbling chuff followed. "*They call us storm dragons for a reason, dear.*"

"*Seeing all of these scales, it makes me wonder. Are you the only storm dragon, or are there others?*"

"*There are many others, who are my brothers.*" Balfour grumbled, annoyance ringing in his dark tone. "*But they are sleeping.*"

"*Where are your brothers sleeping?*"

"*In the Abyss.*"

"Were they sleeping while I was sleeping?"

"Yes. And they refuse to wake up. The Abyss is where storm dragon territories are located. She is also where we sleep, sometimes for thousands of years."

"Ah, so the Abyss is like some kind of ancestral storm dragon lair?"

"Partially. It's been so long since I've experienced slumber, that I can hardly think straight."

"Why did you remain awake?"

"To protect you from Masika. Both Alex and I have worked together to try and keep your whereabouts a secret."

"As for Damien," Gwen said as she retrieved an item from her coat. "Look at what I found!"

Selia's stomach hollowed. "His watercolor set?"

"He's been here. Not only that, he's been painting. Sean and I found *dozens* of his works on the dock this morning."

Gwen set Damien's watercolors down. She grabbed a stack of watercolor parchment and handed it to Selia.

Selia began thumbing through the images. Damien must have spent all day and night studying the winter waterscapes. The paint had incredible textures like nothing Selia had seen before. Painting in the frozen elements had made the pigment do all kinds of spectacular things.

"Where is the one with the moon on it?" Balfour asked.

Selia kept thumbing through the paintings. *"There's nothing with a moon, only storms."*

"I specifically told Alex to return it to you. I feel it has a very important message for the family on it."

Gwen ducked as a small brown dart went flitting past her head. Then there were two. Soon, the boat dock was swarming with six small bat pups.

"Oh, my word! The little devils are flying!" Gwen screamed, backing into Sean's arms.

One of the bats dipped over to the net, where a crumpled piece of paper stuck out of the side.

"Look, one of them has found something!" Pixie said as she tugged the parchment out of the net.

"Let me see that," Gwen said, snatching the paper from Pixie. "I absolutely recognize my brother's handwriting."

Gwen flipped the painting of a moon rising over the sea over. Damien's writing was there, a simple title for the seventh painting Alex had stolen from Pixie's shop.

For Selia and Our Daughter

Gwen's mouth opened and closed as she glanced up from Damien's painting with a trembling hand. "Selia? You're *pregnant?*"

54

THE SACRED MOUNTAIN

Amy

Snow crunched under Ewan's boots as he led the way down the hill away from the pool. "Only, a few, more, steps," he huffed, sending out plumes of condensation with each of his labored breaths. Even for a giant like him, Errindoor's antlers were proving a hassle to carry.

"What do you do with his crown?" Amy asked, eager to see what was so important for him to carry such a heavy burden.

"You'll see."

They descended deeper into the snowy ruins, following a path of what could have been stairs at one time. Amy struggled to keep her footing as many of the icy stones were uneven.

"Ah, here we are," Ewan huffed as they entered an opening. He stopped. Tilting his body sideways, he set down both of Errindoor's massive antlers. They fell with a bone-rattling clatter onto the ground next to a few others.

Amy counted at least a dozen pair of giant antlers, each prior sheds of the mighty Errindoor. "You weren't lying when you said you've made this trek many times before." She surveyed the area, finding a structure created apart from the circle of sheds. A simple hut had been created from the antlers, with an opening that faced the circular structure.

"I figured I should make something out of his crown to commemorate my ancestors, right?" Ewan shifted Errindoor's freshly shed antlers next to another pair, closing in the circle. He reached into his robe, tugging out a flint. He struck it, sending a spark near the center. Soon, the antler hearth was pulsing with a brilliant orange fire.

"Don't ask me how the fire works without wood," Ewan said, walking up to the flames and setting his hands over the hearth. "I imagine it has to do with magic in Errindoor's crown. He is a fae king, after all."

Amy walked next to Ewan, stopping at his side. The fire didn't even feel like a normal fire—it warmed her from the inside out. All it took was a few moments for her feet, face, and hands to warm.

"Imagine what this temple must have been like years ago. Imagine what we could have seen up here atop this mountain," Ewan said, swinging his head to the left. "Toward the land, there would be forests full of every beast imaginable." He swung his head to the right. "And toward the sea? There would be guests journeying from every kingdom, which we would greet!" He hopped forward, sprawling his arms out wide. "Right here by the hearth, we would have a great hall fit for a king!" he boasted, his voice booming out, echoing into the night.

"And a queen!" Amy called, her voice echoing after his.

"It is too bad our ancestors could not see that vision in the beginning."

Amy's body felt cold again. "My mother was friends with Poseidon, the storm dragon who sank your great city."

Ewan's eyes met hers. He took her hand into his. "If only we'd learned to respect the powers of your kind from the beginning."

Amy's foot slipped out beneath her.

Ewan grabbed her around the waist.

"Put me down!" she cried, laughter returning to her voice.

Ewan slipped, his body tumbling forward. He landed on the ground with a *thud*, breaking Amy's fall as she landed on top of him.

"Ouch!" she cried out as her hand became caught between hers and his chest.

"Amy, I'm sorry." He grabbed her wrist, which had twisted as she'd dismounted him.

Ewan sat up, patting the ground.

Amy flopped down next to him.

"Are you sure I haven't hurt you?" he asked.

"I'm positive."

"I'm such a fool. Sometimes I don't recognize my size."

The medicine bundle lay on the ground between them.

Ewan grabbed it, holding the leather pouch in his palm. "I've made this journey so many winters that I've lost count. Every year, I put the same item into the bundle, and every year, nothing changes. But this year, something did change."

"What's that?"

"Having you at my side over the past few days has taught me more about medicine than I have ever known."

"What have you learned?"

"Medicine comes in many forms. It is always changing and never the same." He tossed the bundle into the flames. "We are never guaranteed answers to our prayers, no matter how much we ask guidance from our ancestors. What matters is that we spend the time we are given with those we love."

Amy's shoulders relaxed as the bundle caught fire. Ewan would never know that his offering had been destroyed by Masika. With Poseidon's scale destroyed, she could finally put Masika's memory to rest.

Ewan gazed up at the sky. "Pretty magical, isn't it?"

Amy gazed up into the night. "How come your men haven't come after you?"

"I told them not to, because I wanted to spend this night with you."

Amy bunched her robe in her hands. Everything about her goal had changed. She gazed past the fire, searching for any sign of the matriarch and the king. "Where did Errindoor and the matriarch go?"

Ewan shrugged. "Probably off to make baby Errindoors."

Amy tugged her robe around her.

The fire crackled, filling the silence. Errindoor's giant antlers danced as shadows jumped between them, each reflecting back the fire's warmth.

"Do you feel any better about Masika?" Ewan asked.

"I don't know quite how I feel." She sucked in a break, exhaling. "Overall, I'm starting to realize I've been numb about her for so long, that I've forgotten *how* to feel."

Ewan shifted beside her. "When Errindoor drank from the pool, I said a prayer for the both of you."

A star fell from the sky, darting in a straight line across the inky blackness. The darkness out here was so full and warm, compared to Masika's anger that left her feeling empty.

Ewan shifted beside her. "At first daylight, I promise to return you to the forest." The fire cracked, setting his handsome features aglow. "Know that I am happy with bringing you up here, even if it was only for a night to visit with both of our ancestors."

Another star fell from the sky. This one was much slower. A trail of blue light drifted behind the star, one she knew was really a fae creature.

The magical night of Yule was fading. Amy was running out of time visiting the past. As soon as the sun rose, this blue memory of Damien's would evaporate, and Ewan's spirit would return to the frozen heart of this beautiful ancient forest.

Somehow, she didn't want to leave this mountaintop, nor the heart of this huntsman who'd lived out his years alone. She and Ewan had separated in the past, long before he'd ever made his true feelings for her known.

In visiting him, she had learned more about his beliefs and the weight he bore about his fallen kingdom. She was so grateful for his protection and willingness to share this magical moment he viewed as an opportunity to reconnect with his ancestors.

Amy set her hand on Ewan's gripping his thumb. "Ewan, promises are made in the past, but they are kept in the present."

Ewan raised a brow at her.

Amy faced him. "Earlier, when Errindoor and the matriarch were trying to communicate with each other? I don't think he was picking up on something that she was trying to tell him."

Ewan turned his head, brows lowered over his green eyes dancing with oranges. "What are you saying?"

"Look—any guy can charge head-first into battle, wanting to impress a woman. He can make the biggest promises in the world to her. But sometimes, the size of those promises are what intimidate her."

His brow continued to furrow. "I'm not understanding."

Amy sighed. "Look, sometimes a guy is a lot *bigger* than you. And sometimes, you don't know if or how you can handle all he has to offer." She looked up into his handsome face. "Sometimes it's best if *she* makes the promise first, and he follows, does that make any sense?"

Ewan's eyes lit up. "Are you saying that you want to take control during our lovemaking?"

Amy squeezed his hand as the ache between her legs pulsed. "Yes, that is what I am saying." She leaned into him, pressing her lips to his.

A hard, passionate kiss followed. He kissed her lips, her neck, trailing his lips and tongue down her chest.

Amy lowered herself onto his lap, wrapping her arms around his neck. Nothing about Ewan was small. From the way his hands gripped her sides, to the enlarging bulge now pressing against her. His size had always been the one thing she struggled with.

Ewan was a master of foreplay, and he would gladly spend days attempting to arouse her. This lovemaking attempt would not be like what had resulted in the cavern. Right now, she wanted to return what he'd so generously given to her.

The ache between her legs was there. She was already dripping wet. The entire journey to the top of this mountain had been nothing but foreplay. She squeezed her thighs together, hoping to dull the pulsing sensation that begged for her to spread them.

He looked up at her with his hazel eyes so full of green and fire. "Show me how you want this."

Amy gazed around the hearth. All that surrounded them was snowy ruins, Errindoor's antlers ablaze with fire, and stars. Where should they attempt this mating ritual? The fire was blazing hot, warm enough she could shed her robe right here in the open.

She unraveled her arms from his neck and stood next to him, taking his hand with her. "Undress me."

Ewan reached beneath her robe, tugging at the fur that clung to her back. In one swift movement, her cloak fell to her feet, exposing her under garments.

He peeled away the hide and furs that kept her legs and torso warm. "Are selkies always so beautiful when they shed their skin?"

Amy flushed. "We are only as beautiful as the skin we feel comfortable in."

Ewan gathered her clothing and set it next to him on the ground.

She walked behind him, grabbing his cloak and pulling it away from his shoulders. She straddled his center. In one swift movement, he grabbed her, fell back to the ground, and pulled her down to his face.

She gazed up into the sky as his tongue dove deep inside of her. Every flick of his tongue intensified the swelling heat that threatened to burst between her legs.

"I want to taste you at the peak of your pleasure," he growled against her quivering thigh.

She grabbed a fistful of his hair before she cried out. "Wait," she panted as she crawled off him. "Stand with me."

He sat up and crawled to his feet. This was always the fun part—un-kilting the ancient Scotsman. The furs around his waist fell to the ground, exposing every inch of his body. That aching spot pulsed just at the sight of him.

Everything about him became visible in the orange light of the fire. His muscular chest and torso—his cock bouncing as it came out into the open. He could break her if he wanted to. Somehow, the idea of that happening aroused her even more.

She might as well try and enjoy herself, right?

She set her hand on his torso. "It might be best if we change the dynamics of this." She pushed him, and Ewan stepped backward, until he was standing next to one Errindoor's giant antlers.

He lowered himself to the ground, kneeling before her. "Anything for my queen."

"Sit down," Amy whispered.

Ewan did so, reaching forward and taking hold of her hands.

Amy stood directly over his lap. This time, she didn't allow him to pull her on top of him. She teased him with her hand, forcing his cock between her legs. She lowered herself, teasing her entry with his wide head. She winced as he slipped through the tightness of her opening.

She gasped as he thrust deeper, rooting himself in. The pressure was too much. What if she passed out?

She rolled her hips as he bounced her. Her pussy relaxed as he went deeper. He remained focused on her. His face and neck shimmered in sweat as he continued with the slow, undulating motions. He wasn't going to rush this, and neither was she.

His eyes met hers, greens and oranges mixing as she found a rhythm that pleased her. "Set your hands on me," he growled.

She gripped his wide hands, spreading her fingers through his. She relaxed, absorbing every glorious inch of him.

He gyrated against her, matching the rhythm she had created. "I'll make a queen out of you before morning."

He bucked his hips, bringing her closer to release. She focused on the stars, watching them blur as his thrusting became faster. By the way his chest heaved and his stomach tightened, she could tell he was getting close, too. She squeezed her legs, closing any remaining distance between them. Her neck snapped back as her body flooded with heat. If the sky was an ocean, she would fall into it, drowning in ecstasy as Ewan, son of Atlantean kings, filled her with pleasure.

55
CHRISTMAS SPIRITS
Selia

By the time the afternoon arrived on Christmas Eve, Balfour's insistent rumbles had gone quiet. Even if Selia tried to speak with him with her pulse, no reply came through. She, Gwen, Pixie, Sean, and Gwen's children left the boatyard to regroup on their next plan for finding Damien.

Selia sat between Gwen's two kids in the back seat of the truck, both eagerly awaiting to see their uncle's paintings as she flipped through them. A hollow sensation swelled in her gut as she drove with the group back to the lighthouse. Damien's artwork always made her feel warm and happy. For the first time in her life, having a stack of his paintings in her trembling hands made her feel empty.

Why hadn't he come home?

"I know what Uncle Damien is doing. He must be painting all of us Christmas presents!" Gemma exclaimed from Selia's right.

"I can't wait to see what he paints me!" Bram said from Selia's left.

Crack!

Rubber screeched against icy pavement, and Sean swerved the truck. The kids both let out a scream.

"What was that?" Gwen stammered from the front passenger seat.

The scent of burning pavement stung Selia's nose. "Was that lightning?"

"Sure was," Sean grumbled. "We almost got struck!"

Sean continued to swerve on the road, jerking the car left and right to avoid the electrical jolts. He pressed his foot to the gas and took off in a race against the violent electrical attack.

Selia glanced behind them to see if Pixie's car was swerving as badly as them. Pixie's white knuckles clenched the steering wheel as she followed.

The lighthouse appeared around the bend as Sean picked up speed.

"It looks like the bolt just hit the tower!" Gwen cried.

Yellow-white electricity turned bright neon blue as it spiraled up the lighthouse.

"*What are you doing*?" Selia asked Balfour.

Another bolt of lightning jolted down from the sky, narrowly missing Sean's truck.

"*Hey, stop it!*" Selia chided.

Only thunder rumbled in reply.

Had she lost her ability to communicate with Balfour? Or was he trying to tell her something?

"Is it done?" Gwen asked as lightning crackled in the sky.

"I sure hope so," Sean replied. He parked the truck. Pixie parked next to him. As the rain poured, the four adults and two children darted inside the lighthouse.

Selia's foot jostled against something as she walked into the foyer. She bent down, grabbing a piece of paper with vibrant blue paint on it. Her stomach hollowed. "Damien has been home."

Gwen's mouth dropped open. "Everyone, spread out and find him!"

"Uncle Damien!" Gemma yelled as she sprinted down the hall. Bram went darting after her.

Selia dropped the stack of Damien's paintings in the foyer and took off down the hall. She searched the bedroom, the restroom.

Nothing.

She ran to the door to the lantern tower and tore up the spiral staircase. "Damien, please be here," she huffed, her pulse quaking in her chest.

She ascended the stairs. Nobody was inside the lantern room. Only the beaconing device lay at the center. A soft, electrical hum filled her salt nodes, but no thundering voice of Balfour came.

A small, weak voice that filled her ears.

"Salt, storms, and starlight, of which we sing. Your light we find in the crown of a king."

The voice left as quickly as it entered her head, fading as the light in the beaconing device faded. Snow began to fall, cloaking the North Sea once again in a soft white blanket.

Selia descended from the tower, finding the others had returned to the living room empty handed.

"Nothing," Pixie said, shaking her head.

Selia's heart sank. "Okay. That's two places we've seen his artwork now."

Gwen propped her hands on her hips. "Look, I know my brother is an introvert, but this isn't like him. He wouldn't just sneak around and not show himself for days on end, especially around the holidays." Gwen's eyes landed heavily on Selia. "Can I see the image you found in the net?"

Selia retrieved the painting from the stack in the foyer and handed it to Gwen.

"Why would he paint a moon?" Gwen asked.

"The moon symbolizes my name," Selia showed Gwen and Pixie the portrait he made of her. "He gifted a painting similar to me the night we became, well, a real couple." She set her hands on her stomach.

The welcoming chatter of the pups quickly stole the attention of Gwen's children.

Gwen eyed the kids as they busied themselves with Peppercorn's pups in the box full of screaming ornaments. "I think I know how that evening played out." Distance rang in Gwen's voice. Since she'd learned that Selia was expecting, her demeanor toward her had changed. Like Selia, she was terrified. What if Damien didn't come home to her and the baby?

"*Can't you tell me anything about where he is?*" Selia asked Balfour. Nothing but an echo of thunder rumbled outside.

"Look at them!" Gemma cried.

"They're getting so big!" Bram said as he ran up to his sister's side.

Peppercorn lifted her wing, revealing her seventh pup.

"The runt still hasn't fledged," Selia said, but she noticed her eyes had opened, and she had a lot more energy about her compared to her siblings.

"I'm naming this one Stormy," Gemma said, pointing to one of the pups.

"How about Rain for this one?" Bram mimicked his sister.

"All right, kids, we're not going to spend Christmas Eve arguing over what the bat pups' names are going to be. Now, let's get to wrapping presents." Gwen's voice cracked with emotion.

Gemma brought over a bag, from which she withdrew a wooden box. "Mom, I wanted this to be a Christmas present."

"I forgot all about that thing," Gwen said. "Bring it over."

Selia blinked. It was the box that housed the storm scrolls.

Masika's voice crept into her mind, uncoiling like a serpent in her head. "*I know where Damien is. The storm dragon lies. He will not survive...*"

Selia clapped her hands over her ears. She wouldn't allow Masika's venomous vapor to plague her mind again.

"*Surrender to the venom, salt moon daughter of Celaeno, or it will erase all that you know after meeting Celaeno's storm dragon.*"

Selia choked. Could the venom erase her memories up to this point? What if she forgot the family she had made? It already threatened to erase her memories before.

Gwen sat on the sofa, tugging out a small book from the box she had read before. "I like this ending verse the most. With salt, storms, and starlight, of which we sing. Your light we find in the crown of a king." She said. "I love how that sounds. Clan Malloch, we are of royalty. We put our family before anything else."

"For Damien!" Sean said.

"May he come home on Christmas!" Pixie chimed.

Gwen avoided Selia's gaze as everyone shared heartfelt glances with one another. "His *real* family is waiting for him."

Selia didn't know why, but Gwen's words stung. The fire in her tone cut through the air like a knife. The room went quiet.

"I wish he was here," Selia said, her voice sounding louder than it should. "I can't imagine not having my first Christmas in our home without him."

"Well, maybe there are other reasons for him not being with his family on Christmas Eve," Gwen said, her voice trembling. "Why are you still wearing his ring, anyway?"

"Gwen," Sean started.

"No," Gwen said, holding up her hand. "Sometimes things in life prevent you from being with your family. But I believe Damien not being here isn't a situation—it's a choice."

Selia suddenly wished she had Balfour's deep, thunderous voice filling the silence in her head. Everyone in the room was staring at her—Gwen, the fiercest.

Gwen's hazel eyes locked with hers with the same emotional intensity of her brother. "He's lost a family before. He doesn't need to put himself through that kind of horrible pain again."

Selia clenched her fists. "You think this is my fault? That him not coming home is because of *me*?"

Gwen's nostrils flared. "I do. And the fact that you're both expecting a child together, and you're not out there searching for him?" She stood as well, her fists clenching. "What's wrong with you?"

Selia took a step back. "Fine. You're right. I shouldn't be here. I don't deserve to be part of this family, anyway."

"Selia, wait!" Pixie yelled.

"Let her go," Gwen said.

Selia went running out of the front door and into the snow. Gwen was right. She didn't deserve to be here. She never had.

Damien not coming home to be with her was proof of that.

The second she left the warmth of her home, Masika's crystalline voice coiled around her. "*This is not your family. You are Celaeno's moon daughter.*"

Selia tore down the hill, blinded with confusion. "Stay away from me!"

"*Without Alex or the dragon to protect you, you have no past or future to run to.*"

Selia's lungs burned as she continued in her sprint toward the sea. If only she could get closer to the water, maybe Balfour would hear her.

Fog manifested around her, rolling in like a foreboding mist. Selia slowed her pace as she could barely see. The crunch of gravel beneath her boots transitioned to gentler thuds, telling her she'd made it to the beach.

She stopped, rooting her feet into the sand as the surf crashed before her. "Masika, I'm not afraid of you. I demand that you leave me and my family alone!"

The mist coiled around her, sending the icy touch of crystals around Selia's neck. "*I will not rest until your memory is mine.*"

The pendant burned Selia's skin. She grabbed the dragon scale and tore it away from her neck, snapping the chain it was attached to.

She threw the pendant into the mist. It landed with a thud in the sand far away.

"Damien! Where are you?!" Selia yelled, her voice snatched by the cold wind blowing in from the sea. Tears burned in the corners of her eyes as she began to run again.

Her ankle buckled, and she fell forward. Cold, hard sand met her palms as she landed on the beach. Her foot fell into a hole in the sand. The hole was split, splaying out at the front. Was it a hoofprint?

Light pulsed through the fog. The beacon in the lighthouse lit up, illuminating the night.

She stared into the mist. Something large was walking toward her. A snort erupted in the air, scattering the mist.

Masika's venomous vapor evaporated, leaving Selia to stare into the mist as it parted. The surf crashing behind her had quieted.

A giant man appeared in the fog. Thick chestnut-colored locks of hair tapered down to his broad shoulders. He wore long brown and tan robes made of animal hide. A white fur robe covered his shoulders and arms.

Standing next to him was a massive white doe. Her fur was so white, she appeared to glow. Two giant ears swiveled forward, flicking in unison with her tail that swung behind her.

The man motioned to the doe with his wide hand.

Her knees buckled as she folded her slender white legs beneath her. Starlight caught in her eyes as she flicked her ears forward.

The man knelt on the ground, reaching his hand toward her. "Selia? Why are you here?"

Selia's throat had closed. It couldn't be. This giant man, why was he so similar to Damien? His eyes were so familiar, so warm. The wild of the forest was swimming inside of them.

This man wasn't Damien. It was his giant huntsman ancestor, *Ewan*.

Selia staggered backward. "How is this happening?"

"Are you hurt?" Ewan asked, his voice low and comforting. "Why are you here? How are you a woman now, no longer a child?"

Selia blinked. Had she somehow slipped through the boundary of time? Was she no longer in the present?

"What do you remember last when you saw me?" Selia asked.

"Amy told me that you left to bond with the storm dragon."

"Did she say anything about Masika?"

"I know that Masika was Amy's friend that she lost to an illness she had no cure for."

"She didn't say anything about releasing her from a curse?"

Ewan's brow furrowed. "I know she loved Masika, but I didn't know she was cursed. Amy asked to go to the sacred meadow with me to offer a prayer to Errindoor for her."

"Who is Errindoor?"

"Do you not remember? He is the fae king who migrates atop the sacred mountain every winter. When he drinks from the sacred pool, he offers our prayers to our ancestors."

Selia's mind filled with the words she'd heard in the lighthouse. "*Your light we find in the crown of a king.*"

Ewan's shoulders tensed. Dark red freckles dusting his nose and cheeks darkened, making the greens in his eyes stand out as his gaze dropped to the sand. "Do these dragon scales belong to you?"

"*No. They belong to the storm dragon who sank your kingdom,*" a thunderous male voice saturated the air.

Selia turned, finding another man standing in the mist. He was shirtless, with long streaking back lines that tapered down his chest and arms. The lower half of his body was concealed by the thickening mist. Long black mats of hair draped down his shoulders.

His eyes had storms swimming inside of them.

"*Selia, it is time,*" Balfour said, his low, powerful voice filling her head. Only he wasn't the grizzly-looking Balfour she remembered. She remembered his sickly face by the firelight when Amy had first brought her to meet him.

Then, he had avoided her, never saying a word.

Now, his thunderous voice filled her head, demanding that she go with him.

"*We must finish what we started,*" he pressed. His voice echoed in the clouds, branching and breaking like the surf behind him. "*If we do not, Masika will destroy what remains of your past, and you will not have the life you deserve to live in the present.*"

A brown dart went flitting past Ewan's face. One of Peppercorn's pups had dropped something in the sand before him.

Ewan's hand dropped to the sand where Peppercorn's pup had dropped an item. He picked up the dragon pendant Selia had torn from her chest.

"My father gave me Poseidon's scale after our city fell," he breathed, his voice heavy with emotion. "Why is it here, and not in my medicine bundle?"

Selia stared at Ewan. Did the dragon scale pendant Alex gave her belong to Damien's ancestor?

56

BETRAYAL

Amy

Daylight branched over the ring of antlers scattered around Amy. No snow, or blanket of stars glistened above. Golden rays of sun illuminated the landscape as daybreak crept across the sacred mountain.

She sat up from the furs she and Ewan had slept on, watching the clouds drift overhead. She grabbed the fur throw and tugged it up to her chest. Peering over the wall of antlers, she wondered if the white herd had migrated back down to tree line. Maybe they disappeared once daylight came, retreating into the shelter of the red giants.

Amy had slept better than she had in days. Ewan's lovemaking was a gift her body had finally accepted. She found warmth in him, protection she'd not felt in thousands of years. While burying herself in the past had been for Masika, she'd found refuge in Ewan's spirit.

Movement caught her eye through the opening in Errindoor's antlers. Ewan's outline blurred against the tree line behind him, the canopies of the red giants giving him away as he moved toward her.

Amy gathered her robe and dressed herself as his footsteps pattered against the icy stairs.

He stopped by the giant antler that arched overhead. His complexion was lighter, his eyes glassy. Even his freckles seemed to disappear into his face. His shoulders rounded. "I've seen something that I cannot unsee," he said, his gaze drifting past her.

Amy walked toward him. She stopped, sensing a thickness around him. She didn't like his tone, or how he refused to look at her. "What did you see?"

Ewan dipped his chin and spun on his heel. "Come with me."

Amy followed him up the stone path that was much easier to see in the light of day. "What's wrong?" she asked, stopping before the sacred pool. Her words escaped her lips too soon.

A dark film coated what was left of the water.

Ewan approached the pool, dipping down to the basin that was more empty than full. Sunlight didn't reflect off the surface.

Ewan reached out, grazing his fingers across the surface. "I checked the pool this morning. After Errindoor sheds his antlers, an ancestral spirit will visit and offer guidance for the prayers I have offered." He stroked the water. "I was visited by a spirit I did not expect to see."

"Who was this spirit?" Amy asked, lowering her voice.

Ewan continued to stroke the water. "Another selkie."

Amy's stomach turned over. Had Masika visited him?

"At first, this spirit confused me. She was not a spirit from the past, but from the *future*." Ewan looked up at her. "This selkie was a grown woman. I could see the passage of time in her eyes. I could feel the distance between this mountain and the future that would one day level it with the sea."

Amy stared at the scale resting in Ewan's massive palm. The water pooling at the center had the same oily substance she had seen in Naunet's canopic jars. "Who was this selkie from the future who visited you?"

"You tell me," Ewan replied, his voice low and hard. "What other selkie have you visited Winter Forest with who wasn't Masika?"

Amy's breath caught. It *couldn't* be. No possible way could he have interacted with Selia.

His jaw clenched. He reached into his robe, tugging out an item covered with ash and char.

Amy swallowed. It was the burned remains of the medicine bundle.

With a flick of his wrist, he tossed the medicine bundle onto the ground. "Tell me. Is this medicine, or poison?"

Amy froze. "I don't know what you are talking about."

He motioned toward the bundle. "Go on. Open it."

Amy grabbed the blackened bundle. She worked her fingers over the charred bits of leather, finding the opening. She tipped the bundle over, spilling the smoldered contents onto the ground. Pieces of wood, feathers, and bones fell out.

"Poseidon's scale," he growled. "Where is it?"

"I didn't steal it—Masika did when her spirit attacked me."

"Are you trying to blame your theft on a cursed spirit?" Ewan asked, his tone dangerously quiet. "By doing so, you bring nothing but her curse to our ancestors."

Amy bit her tongue. All she remembered was crawling out of her and Ewan's root dwelling with the medicine bundle and finding Masika. She had the dragon scale in her palm, before she erupted into a raging storm of venom, anger, and fire.

Ewan dipped his hand into the water, "Dragon scales have the ability to purify water. I offer it every year, to ensure the water is clean for Errindoor to drink." He withdrew his hand, his fingers dripping with the dark film. "You weren't trying to poison Errindoor, were you?"

Amy bit her lip. While Ewan struggled to make sense of the situation, his superstitions weren't far off. While she hadn't intended on poisoning Errindoor, explaining to him that she had intended to spill his blood wouldn't do her any favors, even if she had changed her mind. "No. I was not trying to poison him."

"I think you are lying," Ewan said. He reached into his robes, tugging out an item. The dragon scale lay at the center of his palm. "Selia returned the scale to me."

Amy's stomach hollowed. This didn't make any sense. The scale in his palm had to be another. Poseidon shed many of his scales before he'd sank the great city. "How could Selia possibly give you the scale when Masika destroyed it?"

"Regardless of how she obtained it, seeing the contents of a medicine bundle before they reach the ancestors removes their medicine." His eyes darkened. "Do you know how Poseidon died?"

"He became too powerful."

"Exactly," Ewan growled. "He lost his ability to control the storms he created. He became blinded by his own power. His storms became so violent, they ripped his tail from his body. His power became his own destruction."

Ewan grabbed one of Errindoor's antlers and slung it over his head. With a swing of his arms, he threw the antler across the pool.

With an explosive clatter, the antler shattered, sending bone shards flying.

Amy ducked as one of the spikes from the antler flew over her head. "Ewan, I—"

"Leave me."

"Wait, please listen to me."

Ewan rounded on her, towering over her like the giant wall of muscle he was. "Not only have you disgraced our ancestors, you've disgraced this forest." His gaze fell on her, anger flickering in his eyes.

He threw his hand out, grabbing Amy's robe.

"Let me go!" Amy said, but Ewan had already bound her arms behind her back.

A cloth came to her eyes, blocking out the light.

"No, let me expl—" Amy stammered, her head jerking back as a wad of fabric tugged against her mouth.

Ewan's lips grazed past the cusp of her ear. "Winter is not kind to those who betray the frozen heart of this forest."

PART 8
THE ABYSS

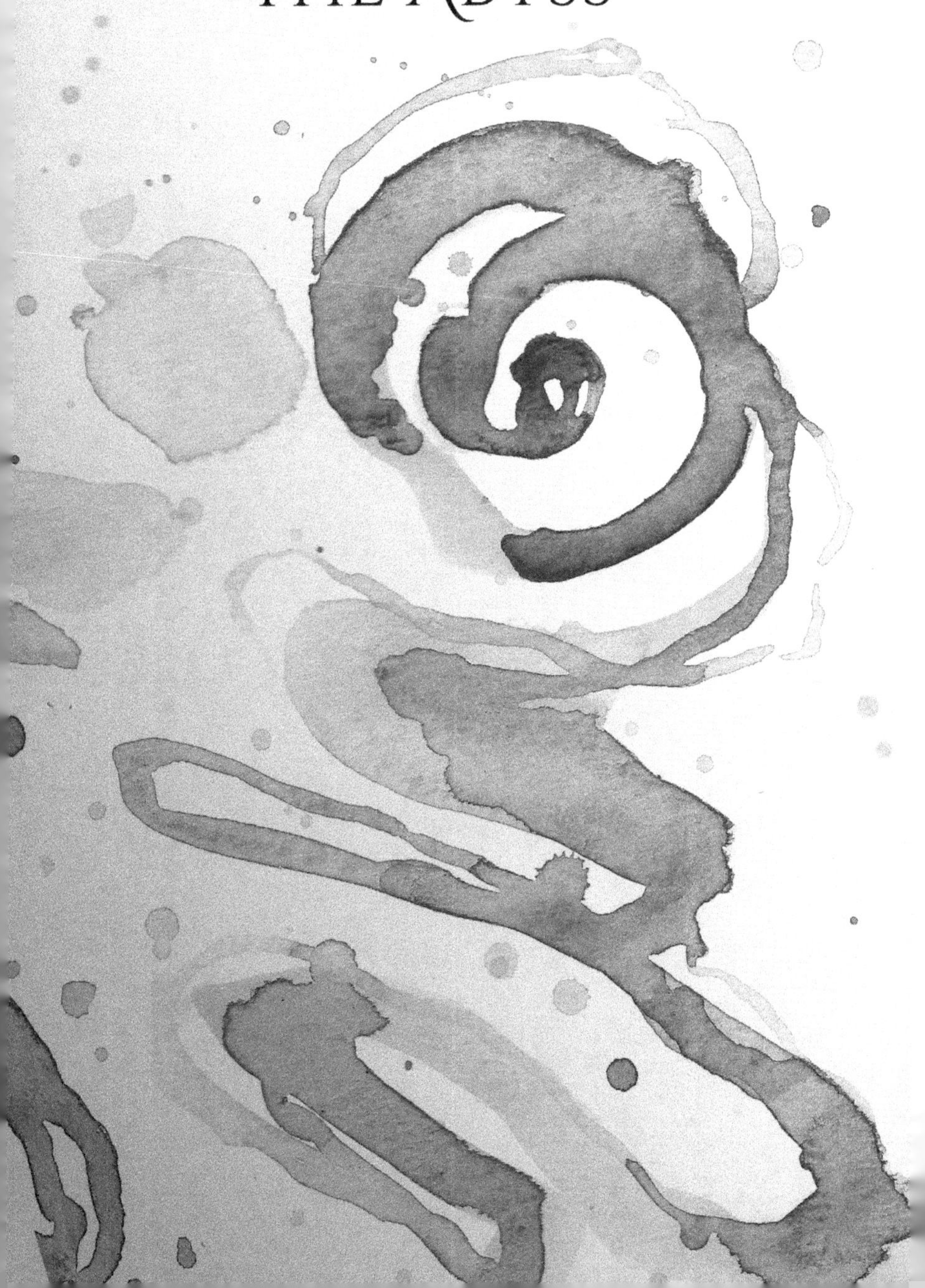

57
STORMS

Selia

Pulsing yellow light beamed from the lighthouse where Ewan had been. Like a ghost from Christmas past, the giant huntsman had vanished into the mist.

Selia gagged. As soon as Ewan vanished, her throat began to close.

"Selia, you must listen to me. Do not close your eyes. Whatever you do, don't stop breathing," Balfour's thick, thunderous voice echoed in her head.

Buzzing filled her salt nodes, replacing Balfour's voice with heat and irritation.

She dropped to her hands and knees, digging her fingers into the frozen sand. She'd been so stupid to tear the dragon scale pendant away from her neck and throw it at Masika's venomous mist.

Ewan had taken it.

"Selia!" Pixie's voice called from somewhere. Time and direction seemed to dance with one another, fighting as to which was better.

Selia's vision blurred as the high-pitched buzz of a thousand wings cut through the air. The salt flies were coming. She could feel them hovering around her, their angry wings buzzing, filling her ears as the light of the lighthouse faded in the distance.

Her skin began to itch as one of the black flecks separated itself from the swarm and landed on her wrist. Its feet scratched across her skin, irritating her. A dry, parched sensation rippled up her throat. Just a single salt fly could suffocate her.

It circled on her wrist, turning and buzzing, until it finally stopped to gaze up at her. Intelligence was present inside of the fae parasite. Its eyes were like deep voids that tunneled into her, hungry for any electrolytes it could feast upon. The parasite crawled over her wrist, scratching her skin with its needle-like legs.

A brown dart went flying past Selia's face, snatching the salt fly from her wrist. One by one, the salt flies were bombarded by Peppercorn's hungry pups.

Peppercorn dove through the air, her pups dipping and diving after her.

"*Blind Moon, hold on...*" Balfour's voice echoed around her.

Blue lights flashed in Selia's periphery as Peppercorn and her pups fought to save her from the salt flies draining her energy.

Balfour's booming voice was soon replaced with a vision. She could feel Damien's strength and protection. Wherever he was, she could feel his warming presence.

A memory drifted before her. The crisp scent of leaves filled the air. Flashes of red, orange, and yellow from a giant oak tree where he sat painting on a bench, overlooking the North Sea.

Selia stood behind him, setting her hands on his broad shoulders as he added the details onto one of his stormy paintings. "Why seven?"

Damien glanced up, his hazel eyes finding her. "Seven months is as long as you and I have been together."

The glint of silver flashed before her as Damien slipped his engagement ring onto her finger.

She lowered her hand, finding the nursery bedroom in the lighthouse.

The painting Damien had started for their daughter—it was moving. A giant silver moon hovered over the water, its reflection dancing over the North Sea. The reflection coiled back and forth, forming a long flowing tail. Seven sea serpents danced beneath the water as they fought to swim to the surface.

"*Alex, I have her,*" Balfour's voice broke out from the sea serpents that coiled into one.

The low, rumbling force of his voice began to thrash upward, a tail uncoiling into a thunderstorm.

"*What are you waiting for?*" Alex's voice answered. "*Her ancestors are waiting. Bring her, now.*"

Lightning broke across the painting, ripping and cracking into the sky. A great terrible wind blew past Selia's legs, lifting her from the ground.

"*Where are you taking me?*" Selia asked.

"*To finish what we started over three thousand years ago.*"

Coiling black clouds descended from the sky, blocking out the light. He grabbed Selia's hand, holding it tight. "*Stay with me.*"

The earth fell away as Balfour's body erupted into a shimmering blue mist, rising up into the sky. Sinuous membranes of fins and tail thrashed beneath her as his powerful movements rippled like a serpent unfolding into the night.

58

TRAPPED

Amy

Amy's situation was less than desirable, having spent the past few moments slung over Ewan's shoulder with her face beating against his back. He wasn't going to treat her with tenderness and care like he had the night before—not after he'd discovered her intentions with the mighty Errindoor.

Not being able to see or scream made her fight to escape impossible. She struggled not to let her imagination take the better of her as Ewan carried her either higher into the mountains, or back down into the forest.

The scent of pine flooded her nose. An occasional snap of a branch made her think he was taking her back to the forest. The wind whipped around her ankles in a way it should not. Every once in a while, she heard a wooden *crack*!

"Lef meh goooh!" she yelled, the gag in her mouth muffling her words.

Ewan said nothing. His silence was all she needed to know she'd pissed him off beyond reason.

The crunching sound of snow stopped. Ewan's body made a new motion, one that wasn't walking. His shoulder and back muscles tensed beneath her as his arms lifted up. Hoisting her off his back, he set her down. He bound her hands in front of her, then tugged the gag away from her mouth.

"Ewan, please! Let me explain," Amy spat, wishing she could see him.

"I trusted you." His voice broke. His stubble brushed past her cheek, his lips past her ear. "I am letting the ancestors decide what to do with you."

Amy tossed her hands up in the air, forgetting they were bound together. Her knuckles brushed against Ewan's chest.

He grabbed her hands, where his lips grazed the top of her fingers. He mumbled something about *angry spirits*, then released them.

Amy wiggled, trying to free herself, but she'd been bound to something, holding her in place.

"Ewan!" she cried, her voice oddly echoing.

Nothing. Only the sound of wind whipping overhead answered.

She shook her head, convincing the blindfold to fall away. Her stomach hollowed. Dozens of treetops surrounded her, each with their pine needles showing.

Ewan had placed her up in the crown of one of the red giants. She must be at least a hundred feet up in the air, exposed to the elements that left the treetops free of snow. She swayed in the breeze, which was starting to pick up again.

At least he'd removed the gag from her mouth to let her breathe. Heights had never been her thing. She wished that she had left the blindfold on.

The cord binding Amy's wrists together cut into her skin as the treetop she was tethered to swayed. As moments slipped by, her plan to escape seemed less feasible. Nightfall would be on her again soon. Stars were already beginning to shimmer on the horizon.

She didn't want to slay Errindoor. She simply wanted to leave the frozen past of Winter Forest.

Her mouth was parched, and her fingers and toes were frozen. Water—her soul needed it. As the parched taste filled her mouth, Amy's consciousness began to waver. It wouldn't be long before she would start to hallucinate. In fact, she *was* hallucinating. The snow-capped branches had liquid ice on them. Ice wasn't supposed to be liquid, nor was it meant to be so blue. There was not a shimmering blue light drifting down from the branches above.

No, there couldn't be a blurring blue snowflake that resembled the shape of a minca moth. A fluttering blue light descended from the sky, landing on her shoulder.

"Oh, thank goodness…" Amy whispered, the wind stealing her breath.

From the look of the queen's wings, they were running out of light. She only had so much time left to reach the sacred meadow, before this blue memory evaporated into Yule's night.

Amy wriggled her arms against the tree. "Help me out of this."

The queen's legs made quick work of her shoulder, working down the cord until she was tickling her wrists.

Snap!

Amy fell forward, catching herself on a branch before tumbling out of the tree. She steadied herself as the queen hovered next to her, a shimmering crystal next to the stars. She began her descent down the tree, preparing herself for what she hoped was her final journey through Winter Forest.

59
MOTHER MINCA

Selia

A great thundering echo filled Selia's ears as Balfour's dragon form coiled out into the night. As he descended, his tail thrashed and rippled into a shimmering mist, the sinuous membranes of his giant fins folding around her.

Selia's feet hit solid ground. Her strength returned with the salt flies gone. Cold night air never felt so good in her lungs.

Balfour's shimmering mist evaporated, revealing her surroundings. While the crashing surf surged in the distance, the sound was oddly calm. No other landscapes were visible.

She turned to the dark outline of a man manifesting beside her. *"For a dragon without wings, you sure know how to fly."*

"Who told you that us storm dragons don't have wings?" he grumbled.

"Alex did."

Balfour chuckled darkly as he resumed his human form. *"Alex has shared so little with you about my kind."* His arms and torso were covered in the blackened bands that seemed so much bluer out here beneath the stars. The lower half of him manifested, darkened like the salt crusted stones surrounding them.

"Where are we?" Selia asked, speaking aloud. She was so close to Balfour, she didn't feel the need for telepathy. While the crashing surf answered part of her question, the landscape still felt foreign.

"A temple that used to be atop a great mountain." He dipped his chin, his broad cheekbones catching the greyish-blue light from the sky. *"The storms of my kind are what shaped the ocean, long before sea nymphs began their ancestry."*

"But I thought we were planning to return to the tidal cavern to save Amy."

"Before we can wake her, we must speak with the ancestral mother of the sea."

"The Abyss?"

"Yes."

"Then why have you brought me out here in the middle of nowhere?"

As Balfour's head tipped back, Selia followed his gaze. Her breath caught at the sight. The sky was a vibrant blanket of stars above her, each like a diamond glistening in an inky blanket.

"The Abyss is best seen at night."

Alex manifested beside them, her robes falling to the ground as the wind created by Balfour's tail settled. "Sounds like you're feeling a bit nostalgic," Alex said, her breath huffing out in cold white puffs.

Despite the cold, Selia felt oddly warm as Balfour and Alex's banter heated the frigid night air. She observed the Iridescent and the storm dragon she'd met, so she thought, only a few months ago. Both admitted to being part of her past, and she had experienced memories of them. She realized Alex and Balfour were old friends she didn't know she had, all this time, with three thousand years between them.

"You've both been with me much longer than I have remembered," Selia said, emotion rising in her voice.

"Longer than you know," Balfour said, his voice returning to the lowness she was beginning to find comfort in. He towered over Alex, his shadow looming like a stormy cloud.

Gwen's words rang in Selia's ears before she'd stormed out into the night. *"Sometimes things in life prevent you from being with your family. But I believe Damien not being here isn't a situation—it's a choice."*

"It's not a choice, is it? Damien not being with me?" Selia asked.

Balfour dipped his chin, making his face look wide and powerful. *"No. Like I told you, Damien is safe. But in order to keep him as such, I cannot tell you where he is located."*

Selia searched his eyes. She couldn't find any lies swimming in their darkness, just more liquid layers to add to his mysteriousness. "How did I see Ewan? How did I interact with him like that?"

"Winter is a time when the fae share their magic with those who see and speak with their hearts," Balfour replied.

"Fae creatures like the minca moth?" Selia asked.

"Yes. There are many secrets to the salt trancing art gifted by them. One of their gifts is the ability to speak with one's ancestors."

Ewan's eyes had been so bright and green, wilderness flickering in them. Even with three thousand years between his time and now, all she could see in him was Damien.

"Why did Ewan take the dragon scale pendant?" Selia asked.

"The dragon pendant belonged to him. Ewan is a son of Atlantean kings. It was a dragon scale that belonged to the storm dragon who sank the city of Atlantis."

"If his spirit lives in the past, how did I return something that was his?"

"Does he not live on in the man you love?"

"And here I was thinking I was the sentimental one," Alex huffed, folding her arms beneath her robes. The white scar on her upper lip curled in the starlight. She took a step forward, her figure darkening as she stepped fully into Balfour's shadow. "Is she ready for the bond?"

Balfour's gaze dropped toward his left. *"It depends on what the Abyss has to say."*

Selia squinted in the direction Balfour was looking. A ring of giant stones lit up by stars lay before her. "Where did these stones come from? They don't appear natural."

"These stones are a result of your salt stash. What you brought to me from Egypt three thousand years ago formed them. All storm bonds are created through the Abyss as the bond's purpose is to serve her."

"What must I do?" Selia asked, settling next to Balfour.

"Step forward. If you listen closely, your ancestors will share their names with you."

"Your ancestors are named after the stars, seven in particular. Each of them represents one of the seven maternal salt pods, from which the maternal salts originate," Alex said as she stepped toward the stones. "Humans call the constellation the Pleiades."

"Stop giving her hints," Balfour grumbled.

Alex rolled her eyes. "She needs to remember them sooner or later."

Selia followed Alex as she stopped close to the first megalith. A pool sat between the stones, starlight rippling off the surface. Something shimmered in the water that looked identical to what Sean had pulled out of his fishing net.

"Is the pool full of your scales?"

"Yes. I needed to shed them so the Abyss can share a memory with you."

A gentle hum reverberated through the stones as the wind whipped through the circle.

"I can hear them," Selia whispered as the name *Alcyone* rang through her ears. As she circled around the megaliths, she set her hand on each stone. With each stone she touched, another name came through. Next came *Merope* and *Electra*. Then came a trilling *Maia* and *Asterope* and *Taygete*.

Celaeeeeennnnoooooo followed, ringing the loudest.

Balfour stepped into the stone circle, his body almost as wide and tall as one of the megaliths. "*Celaeno means the dark one. She is your ancestral salt mother.*"

"But I thought Naunet was my mother."

"*No. Selia, you are a moon child. You were born of the womb of the sea, not the womb of a sea nymph.*" He set his hand on Celaeno's stone. "*Naunet discovered you in the Nile. She fostered you as her own, raising you in Egypt.*"

Selia's chest stung with emotion. What little memories she had of Naunet were so warm, so caring. But here Balfour was telling her that the sea nymph she had memories of was not her real mother?

"*The memories you have of Naunet are very important. You helped her to make the discovery that Masika is currently trying to rob of you. Step forward and allow the Abyss to share a memory of your Egyptian mother with you.*"

The stars shimmered above, reflecting in the pool.

Selia walked up to the first of the seven giant megaliths that represented the Abyss. Both Alex and Balfour took steps back, settling outside of the circle.

Her salt nodes swelled with heat as the pool began to illuminate.

A bright flash of light filled the stones, and Selia was encased in it. The word *minca* saturated the air as the stones fell away, and she was thrust into a memory.

The gentle rush of water rippled in the distance. Warm sand crept through Selia's toes as she walked along the riverbank. The sweet scent of earth and spice drifted on the air as she surveyed the water.

She knew this place. She was walking along the Nile.

"Selia?"

Naunet's warm voice echoed behind her.

Selia turned, finding the midwife of the sea descending the bank, her long black hair falling over her shoulders.

Naunet stopped a few paces from Selia. Her honey-brown skin beaded with perspiration. The flowing river and waving groves of papyrus reflected in her dark eyes. "What are you doing down here? Why are you not salt trancing in the Temple of Isis?"

Selia's hands clutched around an item. "Alexandra said that I am forbidden to practice with my pulse."

Naunet's eyes widened. "Why is this?"

Selia held out her hand. "Because whenever I salt trance, I find this." She held an item up to the light. "They shimmer like starlight."

The scene changed again, morphing as mist filled Selia's periphery. A new scene manifested, one inside of a mud brick dwelling.

Selia ducked behind the half wall located in Naunet's home. Alexandra was walking up the bank, her expression riddled with frustration. Fear pitted in her stomach. She was in so much trouble. Today, she'd brought Amy to the Temple of Isis to observe her salt trancing lesson of salt summoning.

She had done as Amy asked—she'd salt tranced using her pulse.

Alexandra walked inside, stopping close to where Naunet sat. Storm scrolls were scattered across her table, surrounded by a few candles.

"What happened to your lip?" Naunet asked as she looked up from one of her scrolls. Amusement danced in her voice as she twirled her stylus.

"Your moon daughter," Alex replied, her tone ringing with annoyance. The cut on her upper lip was still fresh from the minca moth swarm Selia had summoned with her pulse.

Naunet set her stylus down. "Selia told me this morning that you are forbidding her to practice salt trancing with her pulse in the temple? Why is this?"

"That's precisely what I am here to discuss. It has to deal with your research on the disappearance of blue minca." Alex reached into her robe, pulling out a small linen bag. "When Selia salt trances with her pulse, the entire Nile feels it. She summons something from the very heart of the Abyss, specifically Celaeno's maternal salts."

Alex set the item down next to the item Selia had discovered that morning in the Nile. "You've studied the maternal salts long enough to know that they have a connection with storm dragons."

Naunet eyed the item. "A storm dragon scale. A scale from his *tail*."

Alex grabbed one of Naunet's storm scrolls. Her chart documenting the cycling of the maternal salt pods unraveled on the table. "You know the male minca moths migrate in from the maternal salt pods in hopes of mating with the queen. They also build their nests out of storm dragon scales." Her grey eyes flashed. "What if their nests have been holding secrets? Perhaps these scales could answer how blue minca is seeded?"

Naunet grabbed the storm dragon scale Alex provided and held it up to the candlelight.

The flames reflected on the damp fronds of something blue sprouting from the scale's underside.

A gasp escaped Naunet's lips. "Blue minca grows on the tails of storm dragons?"

Silence cut through the room.

Alex stared at the dragon scale with minca sprouting out of it. An oily substance coated the surface that made Naunet's pupils dilate.

Naunet dropped the scale, pulling away as the salt venom attempted to seduce her. The scale spun on the table, jostling against the wood, spreading the oily venom dripping from the now blackening minca.

Her elbow bumped into a candle, knocking it over. Flame caught the oily surface on the table, igniting it. "No wonder minca disappeared when Poseidon's sons retreated into the Abyss. If minca grows on their tails, they took minca *with* them. But *why* did they retreat? Why dive into the depths of the Abyss and sleep?"

Alex folded her arms in front of her chest, flames flickering in her eyes. "They were retreating from what was sure to make them sick. Salt venom corrodes minca, just like it corrodes the flesh. Not only does salt venom originate from the blood of the fae queen, it is also present within the sea. The Abyss has sent her sea nymph daughters a warning of what is to come."

Naunet's fingers trembled. "This isn't a warning, this is an alarm." She grabbed another scroll and unraveled it. Horror spread across her face as the flames burned across her table, catching the storm scroll on fire.

Alex dipped her chin as the flames consuming the scroll died. "What darkness you have foreseen is coming sooner than you predicted. There is no stopping it. A plague born of Celaeno's maternal salt pod will soon sweep Egypt."

"All salt daughters of Celaeno will be the victims of this plague."

"All sea nymphs with maternal salts originating from Celaeno will be the salt venom's target, including you and Selia."

Naunet's eyes dilated, fierceness flickering inside them. "You don't understand. Selia is my *moon* daughter. She is immune to salt venom. It cannot harm her."

"She might be immune to salt venom, but she is not immune to the shadow fae creatures who feed on it."

Naunet's gaze dropped to the table. A salt fly fumbled over to the scale and began to feed on what salt venom the flames hadn't burned away.

"The plague of salt venom will come within days," Alex whispered, her voice lowering.

Naunet's brow furrowed. She stood from her table, knocking her storm scrolls onto the ground.

Alex reached out, touching Naunet's arm. "You and Selia must leave Egypt at once."

Naunet pulled away. "No. I refuse to leave the mothers and daughters I devote myself to." Her eyes lifted, tears forming in them. "But there is hope. Amy has already agreed to take her on her salt stash in attempt to bond her with Celaeno's storm dragon." Her hands balled into fists. "Amy will bond her with the dragon. She will fix this."

"Amy will try, and she will fail," Alex said, her gaze dropping to the withering black minca unfolding from the base of the storm dragon scale. "You have seen his scales. Celaeno's storm dragon is far too ill to bond."

Naunet turned away from Alex.

"You named her Selia for a reason—you knew she would be blind to her mother in the sea."

"But not blind to *me*," Naunet said, emotion quaking in her voice.

"Is it not a mother's duty to protect her daughter, even if she is not her own? Sending her away will ensure that she is safe from Celaeno's darkness." Alex's profile softened. "Time is the only way to ensure that Celaeno's storm dragon will one day bond with her. The Order has already spoken with him. Time must pass for him to heal from the darkness Celaeno's fae queen introduced to the ocean."

Naunet locked her gaze with Alex, her mouth quivering. "How much time do I have left with her?"

"Days. When Amy returns, Selia must leave Egypt forever." She set her hand on Naunet's shoulder.

Naunet's shoulders rose and fell. "When the bond fails, what will happen to my daughter?"

"Celaeno's storm dragon has agreed to take her to the Abyss. She will sleep there until he has recovered. I promise you that when she wakes, the Order will be there to take care of her."

Naunet raised her tear-stricken face. "The day I found her in the river was the day I became a mother. And now, you're asking me to let her go?"

"The Abyss has always been her true mother, Naunet. You've known this since you discovered her."

Naunet's sobs filled the room as the memory evaporated, leaving Selia staring into the starry sky above.

60

ESCAPING WINTER FOREST

Amy

Frozen twigs snapped in Amy's hair as she descended from the tree. She dropped from the last branch, her boots landing in a deep drift of snow. The fae queen had left a trail of shimmering blue salt scales from her wings as she disappeared among the stars.

Amy's heartbeat thundered. She sucked in a breath, exhaling a burst of condensation into the cold evening air. She needed to get back up to tree line, or risk losing her window escaping the past that was created by Yule's magic.

Ewan's footsteps appeared in the snow. They traveled in the opposite direction from which the fae queen had taken off. As the last rays of daylight dipped beneath the trees, disorientation settled upon her. If she was to escape the frozen past, she needed to find the fae queen before Yule's magic evaporated.

She gathered her cloak and took off in the opposite direction of Ewan's footsteps. From here on out, their journeys would be separate. What coldness she felt in her toes soon crept into her bones. Every step she took became slower. Disorientation settled upon her. She didn't have the tracking skills Ewan had, nor the brute strength needed to clear a proper trail in the thick, unforgiving snow.

A flickering orange light caught her attention, forcing her to slow.

"*Oi*, we found prints," a male voice said.

Amy backed into a tree before the light of the man's torch came any closer.

"Do they belong to Ewan?"

"They belong to him and his slut," another man replied. "From the looks of their path, it appears they spent the night together in the temple."

Amy pressed her back against a tree, praying she wouldn't loosen the snow gripping the pine needles over her head. The group of huntsmen came into view as they maneuvered through the trees.

Fergus stopped a few paces away from her. "That bitch will have cursed all of us before the night is over."

"What do you suggest we do?" another asked, repositioning his bow on his back.

Fergus turned, eying the snowy path. "I say we follow him up to the pass and cut him off. The sooner we ambush him, the sooner we can be done with this hunt."

Amy held her breath. Had she heard them right? Were Ewan's men turning on him?

One of the huntsmen walked past her, dagger in hand. The flint glinted in the orange torchlight.

Movement shifted behind Amy. She turned, finding a pair of fuzzy white ears swiveling toward her.

"Am I glad to see you!" Amy squealed under her breath. The matriarch walked forward, her dark hooves slicing silently through the snow drift.

Orange torchlight flickered in the matriarch's eyes. A snort erupted from her nose. Her ears pinned as she charged the man holding the torch.

A sling of curses flew from his mouth as he fell backward, toppling into a heap of snow.

The matriarch circled back, prancing up to Amy's side, where she bowed down next to her.

"Nice work!" Amy said, grabbing fistfuls of her silky white fur. She jumped onto her back and squeezed her sides with her legs.

The matriarch stood, and as stealthy as the starlight above, she slipped back into the snowy trails of the forest.

"Where are you taking me?" Amy asked, leaning forward and whispering into the matriarch's fuzzy white ears that kept swiveling back and forth. The matriarch didn't slow or make any hesitation in her movement through the trees. Instead of moving up to the tree line where Amy wanted to go, she chose a path that brought her deeper into the thickening forest. She kept a steady pace, making quick work of the snow drifts and occasionally jumping over a fallen log.

Amy didn't know how to communicate with this fae beast. She could sync her pulse with minca moths and other aquatic forms of life, but not this snow-white doe who seemed to know exactly where she wanted to take her. As their trek down the hill leveled, a clearing in the trees emerged. The flicking white tails of the other does were all illuminated by the starlight.

The matriarch stopped before her herd, dipping her head low. The other elk greeted her in a similar way, some stomping their slender legs down into the drifts of snow.

The matriarch lifted her head. Her ears pinned and a snort erupted from her nose.

Two of the other does flew past her, taking off into the forest.

Amy turned, soon realizing what had caused them to spook.

A burst of condensation erupted from another beast's nose.

Errindoor emerged from the trees, his starlit crown of antlers glistening white. A familiar huntsman sat atop his back.

Ewan's gaze dropped to Amy, anger flooding his eyes.

The matriarch held her ground.

Errindoor dipped his great head, his attention landing on the matriarch Amy was astride. He snorted, a signal for her attention.

The matriarch dug her slender legs into the snow and stood her ground. She flicked her ears back and forth at the king, signaling him to stop.

"Amphitrite," Ewan said, his gaze hardening.

"Stay away from me," Amy said, wishing she could take the same annoyed stance as the matriarch. "You would have left me in that tree to *rot*. Why would I trust you?"

"I wouldn't have let you die. I needed to make sure that Errindoor was still alive."

"And if you discovered that he was dead, you would kill me instead?"

"As you can see, that is not the case."

"Okay, you'd let me *freeze*." She dug her heel into the matriarch's side, making her turn to face the king and his mounted huntsman. Amy smirked. Where the matriarch would go, the king would follow—even if Ewan didn't like it.

The matriarch reared back, kicking her legs forward. She was up for the chase this king of the white herd wanted.

While the matriarch was small, she was slender with speed. The king had brute strength and power, but he was slow. It would take him a long time to catch up with them.

Trees and hills blurred beside her as she tore up the hill. Amy couldn't tell if she was preparing to launch herself deeper into the forest, or evade Errindoor by throwing him off with her sporadic movements.

Something darted across her face, forcing her head to the side. A bat. This one was much smaller than the other ones.

Masika's dark eyes flashed before her, fiery anger swimming in them. *"I would rather live with the venom in my heart forever than have you put my spirit to rest."*

Fwam!

In the split second she allowed Masika's hateful words rip through her, Amy was knocked backward.

She landed on the ground, her fall softened by the blanket of snow. The taste of iron filled her mouth.

A hand came to her robe, and she was tugged upward.

"I got the witch," Fergus said, his tone darkening. "Why don't we see how well you hold up to the real kings of this mountain?"

61

MASIKA'S ANGER

Selia

Naunet's mud brick dwelling evaporated, leaving Selia's eyes burning with salty tears. The weeping sound of a mourning mother filled her salt nodes as the memory of Egypt vanished.

Her knees buckled. She fell forward, landing on the cold damp stone surrounded by Balfour's scales. They shimmered with silver starlight, blurring from her tears. "Blue minca grows on the tails of storm dragons?"

Alex moved into the stone circle, Balfour's large outline offsetting her from the starlight above. "I wish I could forget that day." Emotion pitted her voice. "With your help, Naunet was able not only to answer where minca had disappeared, but where it grew. But her discovery also meant you were in harms way. I had to find means to send you away. Separating you from the midwife of the sea was one of the most difficult decisions I ever had to make."

Selia looked up at the giant megalithic stone, wondering how she could forget such a caring, loving person. Time seemed to stand still out here under the stars as her emotions blurred. "Is Naunet still alive? Or is this memory all that's left of her?"

Alex dipped her chin. "I wish I could say. She remained in Egypt, devoted to her duties to the Nile. The salt venom corroded any record of Naunet after the plague."

Selia swallowed, but the lump in her throat refused to move. She gazed up at the stars.

Balfour's strong hand came to her quivering shoulder. "*Alex had come to me, telling me what Naunet had foreseen coming to Egypt. I am Celaeno's storm dragon. I agreed to protect you by bringing you to the Abyss.*"

"I kept my promise to Naunet," Alex said. "I promised her that once Celaeno's storm dragon informed me that he was ready to bond, I would retrieve you from the Abyss."

"What happened to Amy after that day? Did she also go into the Abyss?"

"No. Amy stayed awake. But as time passed, the salt venom slowly began to corrode her memory. She could barely remember how to practice the art of salt trance, let alone create salt extracts for her Ocean Apothecary." Alex looked up at the stars. "Then, one day, one of Amy's salt trancing talismans whispered to her your name. She soon learned where you worked, and that the Order would stop her from finding the fae queen. I knew a terrible thing would happen. She had salt extract samples in her Ocean Apothecary from Naunet."

"Samples of the selkie salt skin?"

"Exactly. When I discovered Amy had found you and started to teach you about the art, I knew it wouldn't be long before her selkie salt skin would be in your hands again. So I wrote you the letter, threatening you not to practice the art, as you would be haunted by the salt venom to find the fae queen who created it."

Selia glanced up at Alex's blurring face. "Why was the discovery of minca growing on the tails of storm dragons kept a secret? Why was this knowledge not shared?"

"*The last time minca's location of growth was shared with humanity, the bonds between sea nymphs and storm dragons were abused,*" Balfour interjected with his answer. "*Poseidon became too powerful, eventually sinking the great city Ewan's forefathers called their kingdom—Atlantis.*"

Alex set her hand on Selia's shoulder. "You understand why Naunet did what she did. To save you from the plague, she had to let you go. She had to give you back to your true mother within the Abyss, your ancestral salt mother, Celaeno."

"Alex and Balfour are still keeping you in the dark," a low, liquid voice echoed between the megaliths.

Selia turned, finding Masika's coiling tendrils of vapor spiraling up the megaliths.

"It's funny to see what the venom corrodes and what the salt preserves of our memory." Masika hissed. "I would say that, like the Order, it has an obsession with rewriting history."

Balfour stepped forward. Shadows of his long, membranous tail thrashed away from his body. "*If you touch her, you die, you venomous nymph.*"

"You're not the only individual who can manipulate water, storm dragon," Masika chided. "Besides, death is not a luxury salt venom has graced me with."

Alex positioned herself between Selia and Masika's venomous vapor as it thickened over the pool.

"Tonight, I will take back what Selia stole from my sister."

"*You won't without a fight,*" Balfour said, his voice booming like thunder off the megaliths.

Masika's face and body manifested at the center of the pool. Tangled black hair folded over her shoulders as her white pupils locked on Selia. "You might be immune to salt venom, however, the Blind Moon cannot run from the horror that went flooding into Egypt."

Alex jumped between Selia and the pool, shielding her with her body. "Get back!"

Masika clapped her hands together.

With a sickening *crack*, the pool shattered. Alex disappeared as the megalithic stones toppled over.

Selia fell backward, dipping into the darkness below. *"Balfour!"* she cried.

No answer.

She tumbled into the hole that had opened between the megaliths, their broken stone bodies crumbling over her.

She landed with a heavy *splash*. Her lungs seized as she was submerged in the freezing water. The sea siphoned around her, threatening to take her under.

"Welcome back to the Abyss," Masika's voice sank into the water with her.

Selia kicked with her feet, finding solid stone. She forced her legs out, kicking off the earth and pushed herself to the surface.

She gasped for air. She threw her hands out, feeling for any rocks she might be able to climb onto as water poured inside.

"Alex isn't far from you. I will find you both. Keep moving." Balfour's voice echoed in her head.

"I can't see."

"You don't need to. I've been preparing you for this. You should be able to feel your surroundings with your pulse."

Selia's body trembled with adrenaline. All she could feel was freezing cold water mixing with the hot vapor of Masika's venomous breath. Not only that, but the angry buzz of the salt flies was upon her again.

She crawled onto a rocky ledge, pulling herself out of the freezing water. She paused, panting on her hands and knees as something sharp brushed past her fingers.

Salt crystals were jutting up from the ground.

"Feel the salt's energy pulsing through you. The crystals will communicate with you."

Selia forced herself to trust Balfour's voice and began shuffling elbow over knee into the dark. With each movement of her arm, the crystals grew up through the ground. The cavern was filling with them faster than the water flooding in.

She grabbed her throat. Her lungs were paralyzed. Hot liquid vapor began to saturate the air as Masika's venomous vapor continued to pollute the cavern. Flashes of memories from Egypt came through again.

Something darted past Selia's cheek that was much larger than a salt fly.

Peppercorn was in the cave, flitting past her. Her wings brushed past her as she snatched the salt flies away from her face.

Masika manifested before her again. Her pale, splotchy skin glistened with something other than water. An oily film coated her body.

Masika waved her hand, forcing her venomous vapor around Selia's face. The salt flies dipped past her, and another memory of Egypt manifested.

The Temple of Isis appeared. Naunet stood near the altar, her body enveloped in Isis's shadow.

A group of men stormed inside, each carrying weapons at their sides.

"Where is she? Where is the moon child?" one of them asked as he approached Naunet from behind.

Naunet's brow furrowed as she turned to face him. "You will find no moon child here."

"We know you have kept her a secret from the Pharaoh," he spat, grabbing her arm. "We know a plague is upon us."

The men searched the temple, tearing open her scrolls and shattering vases.

One grabbed her hair, while another ripped her robe.

"You have foreseen it—the plague that will sweep Egypt, you venomous snake," he yelled, throwing her down to the ground.

"*Stop!*" Balfour's voice boomed overhead, breaking the memory.

"Selia needs to see the truth," Masika whispered, blocking him. "It is time she sees what the curse is I have lived with for the past three thousand years. Embrace the venom with me."

As Masika's voice coiled around her, the water she stood in thickened to the consistency of tar, restricting her from moving.

A salt fly hovered in her periphery.

Panic surged through her as the Nile appeared.

Women were lying along the salt bank, their bodies mangled and lifeless. Their salt nodes appeared like great gaping wounds.

They were dead, all of them. Their arms and legs mangled, like they'd tried to run from whatever had come out of the river.

Selia's breathing stopped.

Cradled in one of the sea nymph's arms was a bundle of cloth. The cloth drifted in the wind, revealing the face of...

"No!" Selia screamed as the bloody face of a child appeared. Her eyes were gaping holes, and there were swollen red scabs where her salt nodes should be. The Nile was full of blood, coated with an oily substance that drifted as far as the eye could see.

The salt flies evaporated, taking with them the memory of Egypt.

Selia doubled over as the memory evaporated, leaving her crippled.

A sea nymph lay on the bank of the Nile.

Cradled in her arms was a dead sea nymph child.

Masika's face danced in front of her, the whites of her pupils flashing in the starlight. "Do you want to know what those men did to my sister?" she asked as she slid her fingers down her throat. "Men who worship the sun are not kind to women of the water. When they found Naunet without you, they tortured her. Nobody came for her when she screamed out Isis's name. Only when the Nile ran red with her blood, did they cease in her mutilation."

Selia continued to pant, unable to move. Her hands and arms were scraped and bloody from climbing over the jagged salt crystals.

Masika's vapor coiled around her. "While you and Amy were safe and oblivious to the horrors going on in Egypt, my sister remained loyal to her kin. After that day, the fertility of the Nile would never return, not after what the pharaoh and his men did to her. The memory of my sister's death is my curse."

"I can't imagine living with this memory like you have for the past three thousand years."

"The venom corrodes the boundaries of time, allowing one to live forever with distant memory. Do you know what it's like to live with the dying breath of a loved one rattling through you? To be bound to that moment as her spirit begged to be released from her body?"

"You don't know if Naunet is dead!" Alex yelled, her voice echoing beside them.

Masika's eyes became bloodshot, black tears streaming from them. "The venom has shared nothing of her with me after that moment. Reliving it has cursed me to the point I will never forgive for it."

A wave crashed inside of the cavern, shaking loose the salt crystals framing Masika's trembling face.

Masika rose into the air, the crystal shards rising with her. "My sister sacrificed her life for a daughter who wasn't even her own. I will summon the Abyss, and take back what rightfully belonged to my sister."

Selia staggered to her feet, heat rising in her gut.

Damien's painting of the moon flashed before her, followed by the words he'd written. *Selia and our daughter.*

Selia threw her hands out, whisking Masika's burning vapor away. "Naunet might have sacrificed herself for me, but no matter how bitter you are about my past, I'm not letting you steal *my* daughter away from me."

The water thickened, unfolding into the coiling bodies of black serpents as Masika's crystal fingers emerged from the vapor. "Not if I kill you first."

62

CROWNLESS KING

Amy

The tang of iron filled Amy's mouth. She doubled over, coughing out the hot liquid gagging her. The snow was stained red with her own blood.

"Bind her," Fergus barked.

Amy was tugged up, hands gripping her cloak and hair. Her arms were tethered in twine once again.

Five of Ewan's men circled around her. The whites of their eyes glinted with torchlight, anger flashing in them.

"Let me go!" Amy spat.

Fergus approached her. A lustful look spread across his wind-burned face.

Amy was thrown backward, her back hitting the body of another huntsman.

Hands came to her waist, sliding up through her cloak.

"No," the man fondling her hips said behind her. "I think you are going to take each one of us, nice and slow."

Amy was thrown forward, her face landing hard in the snow. She sucked in a breath, her bloody hair choking her as she tried to prop herself up on her bound wrists.

Hands gripped her hair, tearing her sideways. The starlight sky and treetop canopies clustered around her.

The men laughed, spitting on her.

"Masika…" she breathed.

The blood in her mouth was no longer warm. It was cool. Was the frozen world of Winter Forest claiming her?

Fergus lowered himself onto her.

One-by-one, the furry bats dive-bombed the huntsmen, sending them away.

The fae bats were attacking them! What a blessing in disguise. She flipped over, rolling down the hill to evade the men as the bats worked their magic.

She tumbled and rolled, tumbled and rolled, until her body met the soft surface of something warm.

"Amphitrite…" a quivering male voice whispered. Ewan's body lay mangled in the snow. His white robes shone red with his blood.

An arrow jutted from his chest.

"What have they done to you?" she asked, her voice breaking. She dropped to his side, her hands shaking as they fell upon his bloody robes.

"I've failed you," he stammered, the greens in his eyes, even in the starlight, were gone.

"Did your men do this?" Amy asked, anger rising in her tone. The arrow quivered with each of Ewan's labored breaths.

"They ambushed me," he coughed. "You must go on without me. You must follow the light Errindoor has shown you."

"How? I don't understand what you are saying."

"Ride him north. He knows the way. He will take you to the temple of my forefathers and help you leave this frozen place."

"I can't leave you, not like this, not…" her voice broke again.

His bloody hand came to hers. "I knew from the moment you asked me about the sacred mountain that this journey wasn't about me. It was about someone you would die for. Someone you loved, named Masika."

Amy's breath caught. She grabbed his hand, threading her fingers through his bloody ones.

"I told you I offered a prayer for you and Masika. I asked them to show you the light." His eyes gazed up. "Right now, that light is Errindoor. Follow the king. He will guide you through this winter night."

She looked into his eyes, the light in them fading. "I won't let you die."

"It's too late for me," he said, blood spewing from his mouth.

She pressed her lips to his, the hotness of her blood mixing with his. "I won't forget you, son of Atlantean kings." Hot tears streamed down her cheeks as Errindoor's high-pitched bugle pierced the air.

He was calling for her.

Ewan stroked her cheek with the back of his cold hand. "I won't forget you, my queen," he whispered back. "Go now. You only have so much time."

"We found her!" one of the men called.

Amy squinted through her hair curling in front of her face. Ewan's men descended the hill, their bows and flints drawn.

"Lookie here, the two lovers have reunited."

Amy was tugged upright, her hair gripped back as the hands of his men assaulted her again. "I think you *knew* she would betray us."

Amy ducked as another swarm of brown bats swarmed above.

The man holding her hair released her as they dove into his face. She staggered away from Ewan and his men, following Errindoor's piercing bugle. The sound had preserved the moments on this mountain shared with Ewan more than Masika.

Flashes of their journey through Winter Forest flooded through her. Moments from the smoke rising from the fire at base camp, to the cavern. To the wolves he'd protected her from, to the moment she saw him riding atop the great fae king who guarded the mountain.

"Errindoor!" she cried, hoping he would hear her. If only he would come find her.

Light burst through the trees, catching branches and splintering out like fingers.

Errindoor was not standing like she expected. He lay on the ground, his legs tethered to one another. His massive hooves thrashed in the air. One wrong move, and he could decapitate her.

A dagger lay in the snow, reflecting the blinding light as Errindoor's crown darkened. She grabbed the dagger and walking toward the fae beast. His crown was fading fast, the light darkening.

With each step she took, she released her own fears to the mountain. She was *part* of this ancient forest. She had traveled through her frozen heart, which had helped her to feel things she had spent the past three thousand years numb to.

She was not afraid of fae beasts. She was not afraid of man.

She was afraid of leaving this frozen world without the love of her friend.

Amy dove as Errindoor's massive leg kicked out over her head. She tumbled, rolling through the snow as she ducked beneath his flailing body.

She tore the dagger across the rope that bound his legs.

He fumbled to his side, staggering as his hooves met the snow. Billowing clouds of white condensation issued from his nostrils as he steadied himself. He held his head low, his face cluttered with debris pine needles from his recent tumble.

She crawled toward him. Errindoor's dark eyes caught the flint as she tossed it into the snow.

She gazed into his eyes, finding the same fear she felt reflecting in them. Fear she would no longer be numb to. With his light, she would face it. "Crownless king, show me your light," she said as she climbed to her feet.

63
POWER OF THE TIDES

Selia

"Selia! Don't listen to he—"

Masika snapped her fingers, drowning out Balfour's voice with the steady drone of rain.

Selia backed away as the cavern walls began to quake. The wall of crystals began to steam. The air became nearly impossible to breathe.

As the venomous vapor filled the cavern, Masika held her arms out to her sides, folding her wrists as her oily black salt crystals jutted from her fingertips. Her hair coiled out from her shoulders, reflecting as serpents in the whirlpool the Abyss was preparing to emerge from.

"Salt venom is much more fun when you add a little flame to the water," Masika hissed. "Like oil, it burns its victims until all that is left of them is their spirit."

Masika clapped her hands together, sending a terrible shudder through the water. The crystals on the wall shattered, spewing more of the steaming vapor into the air.

With a burning *snap*, the pool ignited. Spiraling orange and red flame licked up the megaliths, burning up into the night.

Flames spiraled into the air, sending burning embers and steam into the cavern.

Selia coughed as the hot, venomous vapor ignited around her. Her foot caught against a sharp stone, forcing her to level her gaze with the cursed selkie whose eyes had become devious orange pits of flame.

"Celaeno, I'm sending your moon daughter back to the Abyss!" Masika cried as the violent flames licked up her body. The whirlpool became a spiraling firestorm as salt venom dripped from Masika's fingers into the liquid inferno.

Selia choked, staggering away from the vapor.

"Don't allow her to intimidate you," Balfour's voice thundered in her head.

"Is she telling the truth?"

"Yes. The maternal instinct is the most powerful instinct in the ocean. The moment the Abyss is summoned, all seven of the maternal salt mothers who embody her will attempt to reclaim you as their own. You must not allow them to take you under."

Selia's stomach hollowed. She had to fight to not go back to where she had been for the past three thousand years. *"How?"*

"I'm here to help you. Lower your body to the ground and touch the salt crystals."

She did so, finding the crystals were too sharp to touch.

While Selia tried to find crystals that didn't threaten to slice her fingers, Masika's summoning ritual echoed in the cavern. "I call upon the Abyss, great womb of the sea. With the power of salt, storms, and starlight, I summon thee!"

A wave erupted from the pool, sending sea spray into the air. Folding and thrashing, the fins of sea creatures began to uncoil into the cavern.

Selia held her arms up, shielding herself as the tentacles of an octopus thrashed over her head. *"Balfour, hurry!"*

"Be patient. Timing is everything."

A giant green fin thrashed in the water, sending another wave toward the rock she was trapped on. The pool began to churn as the Abyss manifested herself.

The ancestral salt mothers who emerged were half sea nymph, half embodiment of the sea. Their long slender arms reached up from the pool, followed by their dripping faces. Some had crowns of coral perched atop their heads, while others had their hair tangled across their necks and shoulders. Their eyes were similar to Balfour's, swimming with the churning motion of the sea. Only there were no storms glinting inside of them—only a powerful, beckoning motion that wanted to swallow her.

Masika threw her arms back, sending out another wave of venomous vapor into the air. "Maia, Electra, Sterope, Celaeno, Alcyone, Taygete, and Merope! I summon the seven salt mothers of the Abyss!"

One of the salt mothers stood out from the others, her legs and arms crab-like. Her mouth was deep and cavernous, stretching and twisting as the waves thrashed around her wide angular face.

"*Ceeeelaaaaaaeeeeeeennnnnnooooooooooo...*" she bellowed.

With an earth-shattering force, Celaeno's aquatic bellow shattered the rock Selia was sitting on.

Selia fell into the water and was quickly sucked into the whirlpool.

Masika's hand came to Selia's throat, tearing her away from the whirlpool. She forced her to the wall, the dark pools of her eyes boring into her. "Any last words before you rejoin your ancestral mother?"

Selia stared into Masika's eyes, forcing herself to look past the dark holes full of hate and vengeance. Like giant black mirrors, they reflected memories back at her—memories of her and Amy together.

Beneath all the hate, there was still a memory of love there. Two young sea nymphs stood facing each other, hands together.

Selia grabbed Masika's crystal hand and tugged it away from her throat. "I'm turning the tides in my favor, you bitch!"

Water thrashed up from the pool, knocking Masika away.

She fell to the ground, catching herself as the whirlpool spiraled upward again. She dove out of the way as the flames licked her face.

The seven maternal salt mothers withdrew into the whirlpool before the fire could touch them. Celaeno, remained, her giant gaping mouth swallowing the flames as Masika fed them to her.

Selia ducked as Celaeno's face enlarged with each flame she devoured, soon taking over the space where the six others had been. A crown of jagged coral sprouted from her head, the gnarled points all funneling the liquid flames.

"Celaeno, take back your moon daughter!" Masika cried, her voice rising into a fit of high-pitched laughter.

Selia grabbed a rocky ledge and climbed out of the water. She backed away from the whirlpool as Celaeno's liquid gaze found her.

"*Balfour, where are you?*"

She had to escape. The air was becoming too hot for her to breathe. She had to hold her breath, fearing that inhaling could scorch her lungs.

The water thrashed, scattering the salt mothers. Something else was emerging from the whirlpool.

Balfour's long membranous tail unfolded from the water. His scales were elongated and wide, much larger than anything Selia had seen on him before. Tapering from the ends of each scale were long blue ribbons.

"Nice try, storm dragon," Masika hissed. "By the end of this, I will have shredded and burned everything you have regrown."

Salt crystals shattered above Selia's head, raining down on Balfour's uncoiling tail.

Selia ducked as they shattered against Balfour's giant trembling scales. A wave caught her around the center, forcing her back. His tail was too powerful. The waves were exploding now, the tide rising as his dragon form dominated the water.

"*Hold on to me,*" he said, his voice breaking like thunder into the air.

Selia grabbed one of the blue ribbons of minca, and an electrical pulse surged through her.

The cave went silent.

There were no waves. There was no storm.

All that existed was the ebb and flow that Balfour was channeling through her.

With each thrash of his tail, another wave came surging through her. Silent and electric, the power pulsed.

Her periphery was flooded with silver strands of moonlight.

The energy flowed in and out. Side to side.

The power rippling through her was as endless as it was wide.

An open ocean lay before her. No boundaries, no time.

Balfour's tail thrashed silently in the whirlpool, breaking the Abyss open.

The cries of an infant filled Selia's salt nodes.

Naunet's tear-stricken face flashed before her.

"*The day I found her in the river, I became a mother. And now, you are asking me to let her go?*"

Alex's hand came to her shoulder. "*The Abyss has always been her true mother. One day, the tides will turn in her favor, and she will remember you. I promise.*"

Selia's grip on the minca was torn as a salt crystal ripped through the air, breaking Naunet's memory away.

"At last, the bond is mine!" Masika cried. "A *tidal* bond!"

Selia shook, her eyes burning with tears as Naunet's words vanished. "*We have a tidal bond?*"

"*Yes, now hurry and grab the minca!*"

Selia dove for Balfour's tail, but a wave knocked her back onto the rocks. She fell, rolling into the sharp salt crystals that sliced through her arms.

No.

The energy pulsing between her and Balfour was fading.

A terrible growl erupted, a growl of pain.

Balfour's tail was on fire, the blades of healthy blue minca devoured by the flames.

Selia was jerked back as hands came to her shoulders. Alex's face appeared before her. "You must not give up!"

Alex was knocked aside as a wave thrashed up from Balfour's tail.

"Alex!" Selia cried, staggering to her feet.

Alex stood, her robes whipping out into the wind as Balfour's cry of agony filled the cavern.

Masika's vapor tendriled around Alex. Sharp jagged crystals sprang up from the ground, pinning Alex against the inferno.

Masika's hand thrust forward, gripping Alex by the neck. "It is not wise to come between a mother and her daughter," she hissed.

"I promised your sister I would protect Selia. I devoted myself to her work in the Codex. I will die for it."

Masika's crystal fingers dug into Alex's throat. "Then die, Alexandra. I hope the Order burns just like you let my sister."

Alex's robes ignited as her body was engulfed by the flames. "May the light of Gaia one day return to your soul."

"No!" Selia cried as Alex fell into the inferno.

Masika rounded on Selia, insanity burning in her eyes.

A sickening *crack* ripped through the water, shattering the walls of the cavern.

Selia was too late. The tide came flooding in. She dove, grabbing a handful of Balfour's rippling blue tail before the tide took her under.

64

ANCESTRAL SALT MOTHERS

Amy

Errindoor tipped his head up, nostrils flaring. With a mighty bugle, his crown burst into light.

Amy grabbed the glowing crown of the fae king. The light was cool to the touch—silver and rippling. With a swing of his massive head, the great Errindoor slung Amy onto his back.

"Stop her!" Fergus cried.

Arrows snapped above Amy, splintering in Errindoor's glowing crown. She gripped his thick white fur as he took off into the forest.

She couldn't look back. Tears burned in her eyes. Why did Ewan have to be such a fool? Why had he come after her?

To *protect* her, as he'd always done. Even when he didn't understand what he was protecting, he'd done so out of love for his ancestors.

Son of Atlantean kings, he was. A greater king he would have been one day.

No.

"I can't do this," she whispered, but Errindoor kept charging ahead. Thousands of pounds of muscle thundered beneath her as he charged through the forest.

"Go back," she said, her hair snagging on the branch of a tree.

Errindoor kept thundering up the hill, his footsteps bringing her closer to the thinning line of trees.

"I said go back!" Amy screamed, digging her heels into his sides.

Errindoor reared. Tree, rock, and soil whipped around Amy's head as she fell from his back.

She landed in a heap of pine branches and snow. She'd fallen near the threshold between the forest and the sacred meadow.

She staggered to her feet. "Ewan!" she cried, her voice stolen by the night. Her words became nothing but silvery condensation drifting out from her lips.

She collapsed into the snow, balling her hands into fists as defeat took over. She couldn't save anyone here in the past. Not Ewan. Not Masika. She'd come all this way, only to have her goal ripped away from her by the frozen heart of this ancient forest.

"I've failed you," she whispered, tears burning her eyes. Nobody could hear her up here, not even the stars.

A soft blue light drifted down from the sky. The fae queen hovered in front of her, a trail of glowing blue salt scales trailing in her wake.

"Leave me," Amy said, succumbing to the cold.

The queen drifted past her face, her wintry magic of Yule nearly over.

Amy wiped her hair out of her eyes, blinking tears away. Defeated by the cold breath of the past, the elements of Winter Forest would claim her.

Movement caught her eye. The figure was too small to be Errindoor or the Matriarch. It walked on two legs, not four. A man was walking along the rocky path out in the open meadow.

He spun and turned, spun and turned, kicking up his heels in dance. "Heel for heel and toe for toe! Arm and arm and off we go, all for Selia's wedding."

Amy stood. Who was singing about Selia's wedding?

"*Oi*, Amy!" He walked over, stopping a few paces in front of her.

"Damien?" Amy said. She blinked. Was it really Damien she was seeing? "Why are you out here?"

"I came outside to get away from the gathering. I'm pretty sure I had some bad whiskey. I had a heck of a time trying to make sense out of what I've been seeing." He spun around, hands held out wide. "I saw these *massive* deer. The buck, he had this crown that looked like it was something right out of a fairy tale."

Amy eyed Damien, wondering if she had lost her sanity. Was time standing still? Had the salt trance she'd put him in somehow allowed his spirit to bleed into the past with her?

Damien's gaze dipped to Amy's cloak. "You are dressed differently than I remember. Were you about to change up your wardrobe?"

"Where is Selia?" Amy asked, trying to ground herself in Damien's understanding. It seemed that his memory of the party was still fresh inside his mind.

"She's inside trying to figure out if she's going to tell anyone about our..." he set his hands on his stomach. "Did she tell you yet? We're expecting."

Amy's mouth dropped open.

Selia was *pregnant*?

"That's absolutely lovely. I did not know that you were going to be a—" she caught herself before saying *father*. "I'm so happy for the both of you."

A proud look swept over Damien's face. Damien's eyes had so much depth to them, so much hidden emotion. Even beneath the stars, the greens looked so much like his ancestor. He spun on his heels, stringing his fingers through his thick unruly hair. "I think I need to sober up. How did we get up on this mountain, anyway?"

"We need to leave," Amy whispered, forcing herself not to think of Ewan's mangled body.

"Why?" Damien asked, cheer ringing in his voice. "The party has just started!" He propped his hands on his hips. "Oh, I get it. You were waiting for the others to show up. You couldn't put on your full show without them!"

"What do you mean, the *others*?"

"There were seven other women walking up that way," he said, hiking his thumb over his shoulder. "Follow me."

Amy and Damien followed the footprints of the elk in the snow. They soon tucked behind the Temple of Salt, Storms, and Starlight.

"There," Damien said, pointing down the hall she remembered her and Ewan walking through. "Do you hear that?"

Amy nodded as she dipped down the stairs. The temple resonated with light and a single, undulating sound. The walls seemed to echo with female voices, each cutting through the cold night air with a rich liquidness that didn't seem like it should exist up here by the clouds.

The voices were not joyous. They were sad, their pitch dipping lower and lower with each step she took. Even the starlight above seemed to fade as she descended into the temple.

Her footsteps slowed as she rounded the corner. Her breath caught. Damien wasn't lying. There were seven women all right, and every single one of them was absolutely *gorgeous*.

They appeared as marble sculptures, their skin and dress an identical silver. Each had long locks of silver hair that tapered down their backs and shoulders. Their faces dipped down, their mouths moving as they chanted their song. *Minca*, they were chanting.

"The Abyss," Amy said, turning to where Damien had been.

He was gone.

Amy walked toward the maternal salt mothers as their mournful chanting continued. She stepped between two of them, discovering how large each of them was.

She stopped. A smaller woman lay on an alter before her ancestors.

Amy's breath caught. "Masika?"

Masika's hands were clasped on her chest. Her long dark hair curled out on either side of her face. Her eyes were deep voids, staring out into the night.

"Masika, can you see me?" Amy whispered.

Masika's head jerked to the side. "Amphitrite?"

"Masika, I'm here," Amy said, dropping to her side.

The fae queen landed on Masika's hand. She lifted her hand up, bringing the queen to her face. "I remember you. You are the one who cursed me."

Amy swallowed. "Please don't be angry with me. I only gave her to you because I thought she would help you to explain why minca was disappearing."

Masika tilted her wrist, turning the fae queen so that her wings shimmered with the starlight above. "She's so *healthy*. I don't understand how such a beautiful creature could..." her voice broke. "I'm lost without knowing what will happen to minca. What will the queen do if she has no home at sea to return to?"

The fae queen flapped her wings, then took off into the night.

Masika's glassy eyes returned to the sky. "Can you hear them? Our ancestors are here, singing. I think that is why the Abyss has gathered around me. She is grieving."

Amy looked up into the solemn faces of the seven maternal salt mothers. Their song about minca continued, their voices resonating off one another. Each of them embodied the mournful song of a grieving mother.

The Abyss had manifested around their dying salt daughter.

Amy looked up at the ancestral mother of Masika. "Celaeno, I love your salt daughter. Long ago, I betrayed her trust." She bit back the urge to sob with the others. "I was scared that I couldn't give Masika what I wanted, an explanation for the disappearance of blue minca."

Celaeno's mourning stopped. She closed her eyes, and her face and body evaporated.

Another woman appeared, one with long red hair and emerald green eyes.

Amy looked into the sea nymph's face. Seven freckles the shape of starfish dusted her cheeks and nose.

Amy's heart stopped. "*Mother*?"

EPILOGUE

Damien

"Selia!" Damien yelled for what felt like the thousandth time. His feet wobbled beneath him as he stood, gazing out at the empty water. Still, no reply. He was surrounded by cold night air and starlight.

He didn't know how long he'd been in this small wooden boat, rocking on the open sea. Maybe his cousins had slipped something into his drink other than whiskey. Other than the stars, the moon was the only thing keeping him company. It seemed like he'd battled the waves for hours with no luck of convincing his boat to go anywhere. If only he could turn the tides in his favor.

He slouched back down, landing with a *thud* on the wooden seat. He could have sworn he'd heard a female voice on the water, drifting in and out as though a dream. The voice was singing *minca*, chanting the word over and over.

He exhaled another frustrated *huff* as he hung his head and rolled his shoulders. He looked up as a blue light fell from the sky, shattering into a thousand small reflections as they sank into the freezing water. He'd seen another fallen star dying in the night. They were everywhere. Yet Selia was nowhere. Damien remembered seeing the lights for the first time on her at the Celtic Sea, then at the Louvre when he'd asked her to critique his watercolor paintings.

The blue lights were really fae beings that followed her everywhere. Maybe if he followed them, he could find her.

Looking up at the moon, all he could think of was Selia. His heart ached for her. Selia was the moon, the light of his life, pregnant and glowing like a goddess. Selia brought light back into his life, when all he could see was darkness.

He knew that sailors used stars to navigate the sea. Perhaps he could learn how to use them combined with the dying ones falling from the sky to get him off this boat.

Light blinked in the distance, pulsing past his face. The light beamed over his head, spiraling back to him again. The beacon from the lighthouse was signaling him home.

Damien jostled up, nearly falling out of the boat. Water lapped against the side. Finally, the tide was taking him somewhere!

He stood up in the boat. "Hey!" he yelled, waving. Maybe someone would hear him and bring him in sooner.

The grinding sound of wood on sand was music to his ears. Finally, solid ground.

He launched from the boat, landing on the cold damp sand. How amazing it felt to be standing on land again.

His painting set lay open on the ground, the pigments frozen and the brushes tossed about the beach. That's what he'd been doing—he'd been painting before the waves snatched him out to sea.

His artistry utensils were all there, sitting where he'd left them. As long as a feisty little hermit crab didn't dart in and steal them.

One of his paintings lay on the ground not far from his painting set. He crouched, grabbing the paper and flipping it over.

A lump moved in his throat.

He'd painted this image before. A painting for his first daughter, Sophie.

"Damien?"

Damien glanced up, finding a woman standing before him.

He blinked as his throat closed. "Maria?"

Maria walked toward him, a smile on her face. "I have something to tell you. Walk with me?"

Damien forced himself to stand. His feet were rooted in the sand. Somehow, he convinced them to move, following Maria as she walked along the beach.

Her brown hair swayed in the wind just as she remembered it. No, this had to be a dream. Maria was dead, a decade between them. Yet here on this beach, there seemed to be no distance that separated them.

"She wants to speak with you," Maria said.

"Who wants to speak with me?"

Maria stopped to face him. The North Sea lit up behind her as the moonlight reflected off the water. "The moon goddess you've spent the past ten years painting."

Maria vanished, leaving Damien staring out at the moonlight reflecting off the North Sea. An image appeared, rippling as the silver strands of moonlight unfolded into a river that originated from the ocean. Its long, snaking body wove back and forth, uncoiling toward him.

ACKNOWLEDGEMENTS

Writing is not only a self journey. The written word is a work of art that pieces together thousands of little interactions, combining layers of self-doubt and dreaming. My hope is that the result is something my readers will enjoy and connect with.

I could not have created this book without the help of many others. I wanted to acknowledge a few prominent influences in my life that continue to encourage me on this writing journey.

My mom and brother who have always supported my random creative endeavors, whether it be panting, drawing, or writing.

My father who is no longer with us, but still encourages me to write in spirit.

My husband Bill, for supporting me on this journey and for making me laugh with your feedback on my first drafts.

My critique group, who has put up with my stories for the past seven years. Carly, Debbie, and Ed, you've helped me to craft my character's voices as well as find my own author voice.

My readers, because you are what brings the written word to life.

My taiko group, Sun Mountain Taiko, for drumming with me and driving the rhythm behind my stories.

My local library, where I work in the family and children's department. To my fellow library staff who provide energy and enthusiasm for reading, art, and the community. Your energy is contagious!

The park where I work, providing me with the opportunity to connect others with nature. I'm so blessed to have the Colorado outdoors in my backyard.

UPCOMING RELEASE

Ocean Origins, book three of the Ocean Apothecary Series, will release in 2025.

Visit Amanda's website at www.amandacaseybooks.com to follow along with her writing adventures.